# Unlawful

## The Comp

### By M.S. Parker

ISBN-13: 978-1523605088

ISBN-10: 1523605081

# Table of Contents

# Unlawful Attraction Vol. 1

## Chapter 1

*Dena*

The woman in the mirror looked back at me with pale gray eyes that matched the suit. It was a good suit, one I wore when I needed to look at least close to my twenty-six years, or when I wanted to look my best. Since today was my last day at Webster & Steinberg, it was my only choice.

I couldn't believe it was finally here. I'd gone through the follow-ups with my biggest clients and handled the ones who needed to be gently handed off to the woman who'd fill my shoes. They'd all been sorry to see me go, but not as sorry as my boss. I'd be the fourth lawyer she lost in a little over a year. The other three had been friends of mine, and their absence here made leaving a bit easier.

I thoroughly expected to get through the day without anyone really noticing and I'd managed it up until a few minutes ago when my co-workers had sprung a surprise going-away party for me. Surprise because I wasn't really that close with any of them. Without Leslie, Carrie and Krissy here, I'd mostly kept to myself. I wasn't shy or a snob, but I liked to focus on my work, and they'd been the only ones who'd ever really managed to keep me from being a total workaholic.

The bathroom door swung open and I leaned forward to finish checking my make-up. I hadn't cried because I didn't do that, but I had gotten a bit teary and I wanted to make sure nothing had run.

Emma smiled at me as she came in. "Don't think for one moment we're going to let you hide in here."

I gave her a small smile. "I thought for once you guys wouldn't make a big deal of things."

"You're such a sweet kid, believing in fairy tales." She winked at me before disappearing into one of the stalls.

I laughed and affably called her a bitch before stepping back from the counter. With my white blonde hair chopped into a short pixie-cut and my petite frame, I looked years younger than I was, which meant I spent plenty of time being referred to as a 'kid.' Instead of

2

letting it bother me, I usually took advantage of people underestimating me.

"By the way, Dena, one of the partners came down to tell you good-bye. Better get out there," she added.

Sighing, I pushed away from the sink. "Why would they want to do that?" I'd already said good-bye to my boss, Mimi. She wasn't a named partner, but rumor had it she would be by the end of the year.

Emma answered my question, "Probably because you know exactly when to go for the balls and exactly how hard to squeeze. You'll be missed. For your ability to squeeze balls if nothing else."

I rolled my eyes as I turned toward the door.

Another hour and I'd be done. I both dreaded and anticipated the moment. I'd miss the stability, the familiarity of Webster & Steinberg, but at the same time, I'd been preparing for the step I was about to take for what felt like my entire life.

As soon as I stepped out of the bathroom, scents of food assailed me from the break room. My belly started to rumble almost immediately. They'd kept me running all day, so when I hadn't been finishing up with my clients, I'd been handling busy work or running errands, even making calls that generally the interns would've handled. I hadn't thought anything of it since I'd known I couldn't take on anything new.

Now I saw they'd kept me busy so I wouldn't figure out what they were up to. It also meant I hadn't had a chance to eat lunch. Most people thought that since I was barely five feet and maybe a hundred pounds that I didn't

3

eat much. That wasn't the case, and I was seriously hungry.

As I stepped into the break room, the decorations hit me all over again. The entire room was done up in streamers, and on the far wall there was a sign with bars that read *Put 'em away, Dena!* Behind the bars, it showed the scruffy, tired face of a man glaring sullenly at the camera.

Two weeks ago, I'd accepted a position as an assistant district attorney. I wouldn't be arguing the big cases or anything. Not for a while yet, but at least I had the ever important foot in the door. Once I'd proven myself, I'd get to start on the big stuff.

"Are you excited?"

At the question, I looked over at Lori Martin, the attorney the firm had hired to take my clients. Since Leslie had left a couple months back, I carried too heavy a load to just shunt my cases off onto others in the firm. The divorce business was booming.

Smiling at Lori, I nodded. "I am."

For as long as I could remember, this was all I ever wanted to do. Some little girls grew up dreaming about being a nurse, a doctor, a teacher. Not me.

A friend of mine from high school had majored in archaeology. That had been her dream ever since she'd been a kid. Working in the garden with her mom one year, she'd found a bone and in her child's mind, it had been a bone from some rare, undiscovered dinosaur. In reality, it'd been a dog's hind leg, but that hadn't mattered in the long run. It sparked her interest and she'd gone for

4

it.

I'd always wanted to be a lawyer. A prosecutor, to be specific. Working at Webster & Steinberg had only been a stepping stone.

Unfortunately, I didn't have some fun little story about why I'd decided I wanted to put bad guys away. My desire had come from tragedy.

Late one night, more than twenty years ago, sirens had woken me. I'd crawled into bed with my parents and gone back to sleep. As a child, that wailing sound had been common enough in my neighborhood.

The next morning, both of my parents had been unusually quiet. My father had gone to work like usual, but Mom stayed home with me. When I asked her why my sitter hadn't come yet, she told me my sitter had gone away. I persisted, but all she'd say was that Miss Jenny was gone and I'd understand when I was older.

The problem was, I'd always been a precocious child, too nosy for my own good, and I discovered the truth myself a couple of days later when I'd seen a newspaper with a picture of Jenny.

Mom had come in when I'd been sounding out the headline.

She'd tried to take the paper away, but I'd already figured out enough of the words to ask the question.

*What's dead, Mama?*

My mother had softened the blow as much as she could, but how could anything about murder be soft to a four year-old? I'd understood sick and old, but I'd known Miss Jenny hadn't been either one of those.

Mom told me that the man who'd killed Miss Jenny had been a different kind of sick and that he hadn't meant it. My childish mind had accepted that, but I'd come back to her explanation years later when the older sister of a boy in my class had been murdered. At twelve, I'd been old enough to read the stories in the newspapers and online. And I'd been old enough to research when I recognized the name of the man's previous victim.

Jennifer Kyle.

That's when I'd found out that Jenny's killer had been an ex who'd beaten her before. That he'd been arrested with her blood still on him, but a defense attorney had found a loophole that had let the murderer go free. Free to kill my classmate's sister.

That was when I'd decided what I wanted to do with my life. I wanted to be the one who made the bad guys go to jail.

Soon, I'd be doing it. Very soon.

Looking over at Lori, I nodded again. "Yes. I'm very excited."

My excitement must've been showing on my face when I walked into Club Privé that night. My friends were already waiting for me at our regular table, Carrie's and Krissy's men at their sides. Carrie and her extremely rich and hot fiancé, Gavin Manning, ran the club together and they were almost sickeningly in love. Not that Krissy and her equally gorgeous and wealthy man, DeVon, were any better. They both lived on the West Coast, but DeVon was rich enough that he and Krissy came to visit as often as possible.

I hugged Leslie first as she stood to push out my chair. Krissy was next, and then I was in Carrie's arms for a quick, but heartfelt embrace.

I didn't have a chance for anything more than that, though.

Carrie's eyes narrowed as she released me. "You're up to something. It's written all over your face, Dena. Tell us. What is it? Tell us."

Krissy leaned forward a little bit, her expression speculative.

Shit. I'd forgotten how intuitive the two of them could be. Even Leslie was looking at me with suspicion, and she usually let me alone.

"You're right, Carrie," Krissy agreed, nodding sagely. "You're up to something, Dena. I know that smirk. What's going on?"

I reached for the glass of water in front of me and took a sip, trying to buy time. I didn't want to just blurt it out. These three women were my best friends, the closest things I'd ever had to sisters. They would understand why this was so important to me.

In those brief seconds, Krissy took over, falling easily into her usual role within the group. Her dark eyes glinted as she propped her elbow on the table. Chin in hand, she asked, "Did you meet a guy? Say you met a guy. Tall and blond, or dark and mysterious?"

"Both?" Leslie wiggled her eyebrows suggestively. At least with her there, I wasn't the only single one.

With a snort, I glanced over as a woman stopped by to check on our drinks. I put my order in before answering, "No. I didn't meet a guy." Mentally, I added, *I wish.*

I'd hooked up with a couple men off and on over the past year, but none of them had been worth more than one night. A part of me wanted what Krissy and Carrie had, but it wasn't as easy for me as it was for them.

I wasn't exactly blaming myself for my single state, but I had certain...quirks that made it hard for anything long-term. Club Privé, ideally, should've made it easier, but in reality, it hadn't.

There were plenty of good-looking guys – and hell, I wasn't so shallow that the man had to be a ten. Other things mattered besides washboard abs and a face that looked like he'd been carved by the very hands of Michelangelo. I *did* want somebody I was physically attracted to, but somebody who made me laugh and somebody who *got* me did a hell of a lot more than a pretty face.

And that was where everything got fucked up.

Club Privé was a sex club, and one that catered to the bdsm lifestyle. Except most of the guys who came here already had it in their head what they wanted from a sub, and I didn't fit that role. Oh, I might've looked the part, but there weren't a lot of men who had what it took to dominate a switch. And that's what I was.

8

Some of the time, I loved being in control in the bedroom, but there a lot of times I needed something else. It freed something inside me, gave me a place where I could just let go and know that I'd be taken care of. But it'd been way too long since I'd had that.

The men who saw that I could also dominate took it as a challenge, something to work out of me, especially the men who got off on humiliation as a way to top their partner. I didn't judge the ones who were into that, but it wasn't my kink. Sub or Dom, I enjoyed the control part of things. A little rough play wasn't bad, but the whole punishment / humiliation part of things wasn't what I wanted.

So, more often than not, I ended up on top. And while that did speak to my control-freak side, it didn't do that much for the part of me who wanted to be taken care of.

Feeling the watchful eyes of my friends, I glanced up and smiled a little ruefully. "No. No guy. I wish that was my surprise." I gave a lusty sigh. "Man, do I ever wish."

"But there is a surprise?" Leslie asked.

"Well..." I drew the word out, not bothering to fight my grin. "Yes. Usually, you two are the ones with all the good news and stuff, but it's my turn."

Across the glossy surface of the big, round table, Krissy and DeVon shared a secretive little smile. Or at least, Krissy had a secretive smile on her face when she looked over at him. He smiled back at her, but he just looked laid back and relaxed as he traced his fingers over the skin of her arm.

Reaching for my wineglass, I asked, "All right, you two. What's going on?"

"No, no, no. You have news. I want to hear your news." Krissy shook her head emphatically, her eyes sparkling.

I glanced at DeVon. Maybe he wasn't grinning the way she was, but his dark brown eyes had a glint to them, and there was definitely something different in the looks he was giving her. I was used to him looking at her like he couldn't wait to find somewhere private he could do some seriously naughty things to her, but these looks were different. Gentle, awed.

I glanced over at Carrie and she shrugged. "Beats me. She's been all giggly ever since she got here, and she won't say anything. Now spill your news before I have to beat it out of you."

Gavin nuzzled Carrie's neck. "Can we watch?" He winked at me, a playful gesture that had absolutely no heat to it.

Carrie elbowed him sharply and he kissed her cheek. I would've suggested they get a room, but they probably would've done exactly that and disappeared for the rest of the night.

I rolled my eyes. "Okay, I'll spill." I may have sounded like they were twisting my arm, but I knew my friends didn't believe it for a minute. I allowed myself another dramatic pause. "As of today, I'm unemployed."

All five of them exchanged glances that ranged from worried to confused.

Unsurprisingly, it was Krissy who spoke first.

10

"Okay. I don't get it. You look happy. Having a job is a good thing, right?"

"It is." I smiled and continued, "Technically, I guess you could say I'm only temporarily unemployed. First thing Monday, I'm starting my new job as an assistant district attorney."

They stared at me for a moment as they processed the news, and then the women erupted. Krissy practically climbed over DeVon to get out of the booth while Carrie wrapped me up in a tight hug. Leslie was next, her squeal loud enough to make the nearest table stare at us. I didn't care though. As Krissy joined in the group hug, I closed my eyes and sighed.

I might not have had a fantastic guy, but I was getting ready to start my dream job and I had great friends. Life was good.

"I think her bladder has shrunk down to the size of a peanut," Carrie said as she scrolled through her iPad, showing me pictures of some of the places she and Gavin were planning on going for their honeymoon.

Krissy had been looking at pictures with the rest of us, but now she was in the bathroom for the third time.

I studied the serene, blue-green waters on the screen before glancing up at Carrie. "I'm dying of envy, you know."

"Take a vacation and go. You don't need a guy to go on vacation," Carrie said.

"But they do make some things more fun," Leslie put in with a wicked grin. "You could pick one up over there in a heartbeat. Get your brains fucked out. You probably need it." She nudged me with her elbow, green eyes shining.

Rolling my eyes, I shook my head. "It'll be a little bit before I get a decent vacation. Starting a new job, remember?"

"Doesn't mean you can't pick up a hottie to have some fun with right here," Leslie said. She tossed her red curls over her shoulder and surveyed the prospects again.

Across from us, DeVon caught my attention by getting to his feet. Even if that hadn't been a clue, I would've known by the way his face softened that Krissy was coming back from the bathroom.

As she took her seat next to him, I glanced at her. "That's like your third trip to powder your nose, honey."

"A girl must always look her best," she said primly. She gestured to the tablet. "Carrie still teasing us with her honeymoon plans?"

"It's not teasing," Carrie huffed. "It's *sharing*."

"Teasing, sharing. It's all the same thing," Krissy made a dismissive gesture with her hand.

"If you want to go on a fantastic trip with your man, nobody's stopping you." Carrie waved loftily in DeVon's direction.

"No, travel is something we won't be doing for a while." Krissy looked up at the man sitting next to her and stroked her hand across his arm. He gave her a slight nod. "As a matter of fact, in a few months we won't even be able to travel out here much."

DeVon slid his arm around her shoulders and leaned over to kiss the top of her head.

I frowned as I looked at Leslie and Carrie who looked as lost as I was. "Is everything okay?" I asked.

It seemed like a stupid question. Krissy looked fine. She was smiling, her face glowing. And it wasn't like she was drunk or anything. I glanced at her glass. All Krissy had sipped on all night was water...

"Son of a bitch. You're pregnant." The words popped out without me realizing that I was planning on saying them.

"Seriously?" Leslie asked with a raised eyebrow.

"Take a look." I pointed at Krissy's glass. "No alcohol. Three bathroom trips in just a couple hours. Travel restrictions. And the two of them have been practically purring over something all night."

Carrie, Gavin and Leslie looked at Krissy and DeVon. The matching smiles on their faces confirmed everything I was saying. Leslie squealed again as we all moved to hug our friends.

Babies and marriages and new jobs. It seemed like my little group of friends and I were all moving toward new chapters in our lives, and I was more than ready to see what the future held.

# Chapter 2

## *Dena*

Krissy and DeVon had left nearly half an hour ago. They were leaving in the morning so they could stop over in Chicago to tell Krissy's family the good news. Leslie had been on the prowl for a while, but seemed to be setting her sights on one dark-haired man who seemed to be thoroughly enjoying her attention. Carrie and Gavin were dancing somewhere, although he did occasionally have to stop to deal with business. She didn't seem to mind though. She seemed more at home here than she ever had at Webster & Steinberg.

Swaying on the dance floor, I contemplated my own prospects for the night. I hadn't spent time and money on the sexy little black number I was currently wearing just to hang out and watch my friends. With my petite build, I had to be careful I didn't pick things that made me look twelve, and I'd chosen this dress specifically because it didn't. Matched with a pair of four inch heels, I knew I looked good. Now I just had to find someone worth the effort that had gone into looking like this.

I'd already declined several offers when a sleek, chiseled guy approached me, his hands coming out to grasp my hips sure and confident. The way he moved would've given me high hopes if I hadn't already done this song and dance a hundred times before. At least it felt that way.

Lazily, I spun around on the floor, putting my back to his chest, enjoying the feel of his body moving against mine. It was a trick of mine, a way to gauge if I wanted to do anything more than share a dance with him. If he got all grabby then and there, then it would end here. There was a fine line between sensual and out-and-out groping.

He dipped his head and skimmed his lips along my bare shoulder.

I felt disconnected.

That didn't bode well.

His palm stroked up my side and I caught his wrist. Too bad.

"A little shy?" he murmured in my ear, just loud enough to be heard over the music.

"I prefer to think of myself as selective."

He chuckled, and I felt a warm puff of air against my ear. It didn't feel erotic. The gut instinct I relied on as both an attorney and a New Yorker told me this wasn't the right guy.

Still, I kept my movements easy as I swiveled around to look at him. I needed to see how he'd take me not melting in his arms.

He gave me a slow, sage nod as if his approval was somehow necessary. "I like that. Picky. You just need the

16

right man to take you. Make you obedient. Break you until you're the perfect little submissive slave."

Was he serious? Any lust I'd been feeling vanished. Lip curling, I came to a stop in the middle of the dance floor.

"Break me?" I said. At that exact moment, the music fell into one of those odd lulls – the DJ switching to a different song, or an electrical issue – and those two words hung in the air.

I didn't normally care to be the center of attention unless I was addressing the court, but at that moment, I was too pissed off to care. As he took a step toward me, still smiling that smug smile, I let my disdain show through. The music started again, but the attention was still on me.

"*Break* me?" I said again. I hated men like this, the ones who gave the entire lifestyle a bad name. "Is that what you think this is about? Either you're new, or you never had a decent teacher, so let me give you some advice. Being a Dom has nothing to do with *breaking* anybody. Submission is all about willingly giving up control to someone you trust. Not someone who *broke* you."

His face bled to an ugly shade of red and he took another step toward me.

Suddenly, a large body stepped between me and the idiot. A glance up told me that it was one of the regulars, a Dom who was easily six and a half feet tall and built like a brick wall.

"I think you need to leave the lady alone," he said,

towering over the much smaller man.

The wannabe Dom gave me a scathing look around the man between us before storming off. For a few seconds, the tension held, but then it was gone and everyone went back to what they'd been doing.

I thanked the man who helped me and smiled as I watched him walk away. A tall, muscular man was waiting and the two shared a sweet embrace that made something in my chest ache. It seemed like everyone but me could find what they needed.

Twenty minutes and a glass and a half of wine later, Gavin found me brooding at the bar. "I showed that asshole to the door."

"Ugh," I groaned. "You didn't need to kick him out for me." Picking up my glass of wine, I swirled it around before meeting his gaze.

"It wasn't just for you. It was for everyone here. And for me."

Gavin leaned back against the bar, resting on his elbows. Not for the first time, I thought of how lucky Carrie was to have found him.

He continued, "Apparently, he was here on a guest VIP pass, trying the package out. After you shut him down, he came stomping up to me and got in my face, wanting to know why the subs weren't better trained."

Amusement danced in his deep blue eyes. "Dena, why aren't you better trained?"

I chuckled, and then asked, "Was Carrie around when he asked that?"

"Yeah, she was." He grinned at me.

I burst out laughing, my melancholy mood gone. He leaned over and kissed my cheek. "I thought that would make you smile."

Someone called his name and he headed off, but I wasn't left alone long. When somebody settled down next to me, I glanced over, a dismissal already forming on my lips. I'd already decided I wasn't up to messing around tonight.

But then I met a pair of soft blue eyes and something stayed my tongue.

"Hello."

The man's gaze fell away for a brief moment, and then he looked at me and smiled.

"I enjoyed your show on the dance floor."

"That wasn't meant to be a show." I gave him a wry smile before taking another sip of wine.

"I figured as much." He quickly brushed his fingers across the back of my hand before pulling away, his eyes dropping for another moment. "Are you looking for company tonight?"

I took my time deliberating the question. This guy wasn't exactly what I'd been planning on, but no one had been lately. Besides, he looked like he might be fun.

Private rooms at Club Privé were nothing short of amazing to begin with. As a VIP member and one of Carrie's best friends, I had access to the best of the best.

In this case, it involved a room where I could stretch myself out on a king-size bed, while the sub who'd approached me knelt between my thighs and went to work on me like there was nothing else he would rather do than lick me straight into orgasm.

And he was damn *good* at it too.

After he'd brought me to a second climax, he paused, his cheek on my thigh as his breath came in rough, ragged gasps. I propped myself up on my elbows and looked down my body to meet Jack's blue eyes.

"Would you like another?" He licked his lips, clearly having enjoyed himself as much as I had.

I did, actually, because the first two had been wonderful, but what I really wanted was his cock. Absently, I tried to remember the last time I'd been the one on my knees, a man's hands fisted tightly in my hair while he thrust his cock past my lips, deep into my mouth until I couldn't take him deeper – and then he had me take just a little more.

I could've gone down on Jack, felt the weight of him on my tongue, but it wouldn't have been the same. There was a term, 'topping from the bottom' that could've worked, where I was technically still dominating the sub, but performing various things that one would normally consider to be the function of a sub.

It wasn't the actions I wanted though. I wanted the loss of control. But since I couldn't have that, I'd have him.

Sitting up, I fisted a hand in Jack's dark hair. He made a small sound in the back of his throat.

"I think what I want right now is for you to get on the bench over there."

"What do you plan to do to me?" Jack asked, voice ragged.

The excitement in his voice was palpable, and something monstrously close to envy burned inside me. Pushing my initial plan aside, I didn't answer him. "I changed my mind. Kneel down in front of the bench. Facing it."

His long, lean body flushed as he moved to do as I said. His cock was hard and he hadn't even touched it. I knew he was waiting for me to tell him it was okay, but we weren't there yet. Since I'd brought him up here, I'd agreed, even if it had been silently, to take care of his needs. That's what a good Dom did, made sure their sub was taken care of.

As he knelt down in front of the bench, I moved to the wall with its display of various tools and toys. Upon using one, it would be added to my account and I could either take it home, or they'd keep it for me for the next time. I took my time and found a crop that was both functional and elegant.

What could I say? I was a girl who liked having

pretty toys.

Testing it against my hand, I glanced over to find him staring at me in the mirror.

The naked heat and raw desire in his eyes fired that part of me that did enjoy the domination side of things, and I turned, walking lazily over to him. Pressing the end of the crop to his neck, I nudged him forward.

"Bend over."

After he complied, I took a moment to admire the designs tattooed across his skin. I traced them with the tip of the crop and watched goosebumps break out across his skin. When he was practically shivering in anticipation, I lifted the crop then brought it down across his muscled ass. He tensed, a harsh noise escaping him.

I knew that sound. It wasn't one of pain, but rather the sound that someone made when pain had been relieved. My gut clenched and I pushed aside my own desire for that same relief.

I brought the crop down again, this time on his right flank.

Another tight sound escaped him followed by a shudder.

I settled into a pattern that alternated from side to side, working up and down from his buttocks to a few inches above his knees, staying away from the joints where it could cause damage.

He was moaning and writhing, demanding sounds falling harshly from his lips. He was panting, begging, swearing...but never once did he say the safe word we'd agreed on.

Finally, I brought the crop to my side and moved forward, straddling the bench. "Sit up," I ordered.

He did, swaying a bit, his eyes glazed with the headspace that came with someone thoroughly into what we were doing. I waited until he was steady, watching to make sure I didn't need to help him maintain his balance. When I was sure he was okay, I reached for him.

Fisting a hand in his hair, I brought his head to my breast. "Suck on me. Hard."

He immediately took my left nipple into his mouth, using his tongue to work the tip into a taut point. He seemed to know instinctively how much pressure to use, and when he scraped his teeth over me, it brought a ragged cry to my lips.

He paused, eyes flicking up to my face.

I brought the crop down on his ass, hard enough to sting, but not to hurt. "I didn't tell you to stop."

He went back to the task at hand with as much enthusiasm as before, this time alternating between my breasts. After a few minutes, his talented mouth had me aching and ready.

"Sit down." I gestured to the space in front of me.

He moved with easy fluidity and I took another moment to admire him before I grabbed the condom I'd gotten ready earlier. Tearing it open, I leaned forward and slowly rolled it over his thick shaft. My knuckles brushed against his stomach, the tense muscles twitching under my touch.

"Are you enjoying yourself?" I asked softly.

"Yes." His voice was a low, husky rasp and the

gleam of satisfaction in his eyes made me smile.

"Good." I trailed my fingers down his thigh. "That's good, Jack. Now you get to show me how much you appreciated it."

I moved to straddle his lap, but didn't sink down on him. Not yet. He was strung far too tight. No matter how much control he had, I doubted he'd be able to overcome his body's natural needs if I slid down on him right now. I pushed my hands through his hair, making slow, even strokes across his scalp until I felt the tension in his body start to ease.

"Now, Jack, are you ready to show me how much you appreciated it?"

"Hell, yes," Jack said and the words were ragged, underscored with an unspoken demand. He didn't say it, but I knew he was almost dying for release.

I was, too.

Smiling at him, I finally lowered myself enough for contact, brushing the tip of him against me. His latex-sheathed dick felt good, and I shivered in appreciation. He was hot. His cock was average size, but he was thicker than normal, and I knew he would feel amazing stretching me.

Taking his hands, I guided them to my hips. I was the one calling the shots, so I was at least going to get at least one thing I wanted.

Oblivion.

"I want you to fuck me now, Jack. Hard."

I put my hands on his shoulders as I dropped a bit lower. We both moaned. My hands flexed on his shoulders, nails digging into his flesh.

"I want to feel it in the morning. Got it?"

His eyes widened slightly, pupils spiking. Something flashed across his face and then a slow smile curled his lips. "Yes, ma'am."

"Any rules?"

"Yes. You don't stop, and you don't get to come until I do."

He nodded and his grip on my hips tightened. He raised his hips even as he pulled me down, driving himself deep and hard. My head fell back and Jack began to prove that he was a man of many talents.

As he dressed, Jack asked if he could see me again. I gave him a noncommittal shrug. I wasn't totally opposed to the idea. I had to admit, he was the best partner I'd had in a good long while. He was definitely the best sub I'd ever topped. And he was an all-around good guy from what I saw.

On my way to the front of the club, my body ached in all the best ways and I knew that I'd be able to sleep better than I had in a while. He'd done exactly as I'd asked, fucked me good and hard, and all the stress that had been caged inside me had drifted away with each climax.

He hadn't just held back until I came. He'd held back

until I came *twice*.

Jack wasn't a novice, or somebody looking to hold his hand, either. He was doing the same thing I was, looking for a partner. Someone who got everything he needed. If he'd been a switch, the two of us would've been perfect for each other.

But he was a sub through and through, and in the end, I needed more.

Still, I wasn't against the idea of us hooking up again in the future, and that had been what I told him. He'd taken my lack of commitment with good-natured humor and kissed me gently. Proving again what a great guy he was.

And then, right before he'd left, he said, "It can't be easy."

I'd looked at him in confusion and he just shrugged.

"It can be a bitch sometimes, finding a decent partner. I'm sure you've heard it. I'm not a submissive guy outside of here, but when it comes to sex...well, all I want is to please the woman I'm with, and I enjoy submitting. Finding a partner who gets that can be complicated. I've been with more than a couple of female Doms who deal with the same sort of crap, just the opposite side of the coin. The guy is supposed to be on top and the woman is supposed to submit. All that shit. I figured you probably got it too, except from both ends."

"How'd you know?" I'd asked, curious. Nobody ever figured out that I was a switch, unless I told them. And I didn't make a practice of that. In the BDSM world, being a switch was almost like how some people looked at being bisexual. That you could only be one or the other. Both was somehow confused. Not everyone thought like that, not even the majority, I thought, but I still always kept it to myself.

"It wasn't hard, Dena." His eyes had roamed over me appreciatively and then he'd given me a smile before turning back to the door. "A good partner picks up on what the other one wants or needs. Same way you did with me." He'd opened the door then, and looked over his shoulder. "If you're ever in the mood, look me up."

# Chapter 3

## *Arik*

Music blasted around me as I stepped into the club, but it wasn't so loud that I couldn't hear myself think. I took that as a good sign. This was only my second visit to Club Privé since moving to New York. So far I hadn't decided on whether or not I wanted to join, but so far, things were looking good.

I was greeted by one of the hostesses, and she led me up to the VIP floor. She hadn't asked for my name, but she'd greeted me with it. I assumed that meant she remembered me from my initial visits here. That was service for you. But that was also why they had a VIP section, and why they charged buckets for it.

I'd been places where their VIP section was a joke, but here, it seemed to be worth it. I was moving through the scattering of bodies on the top floor when a good-looking couple approached. After a moment, I put a name to the man's face.

"Gavin, right?" I held out my hand. "The owner?"

"Yes. And you're Arik. Arik Porter, if I remember

correctly."

I nodded, not elaborating any further. It was a habit. I only gave the needed information, never anything more.

"What do you think of my club?"

I gave him a noncommittal smile and nodded to the woman with him, a gorgeous blonde who he clearly adored.

She held out her hand. "I'm Carrie. I hope you're enjoying yourself."

"Right now, I'm just looking to get a drink and sit down for a little while." I hadn't decided on anything beyond that, although I hoped to scout the group out and see if I couldn't find somebody to...keep me company.

Carrie smiled brightly. "Well, let's get that taken care of. Would you care to join us?"

It seemed like as good a plan as any to get the lay of the land, so I nodded. A few minutes later, I found myself sitting at a table with them, a drink in hand while Gavin, Carrie and I chatted easily.

"What brings you to New York?" Carrie asked, tossing her golden curls over her shoulder. "You mentioned that you were new to the city?"

I nodded. She wasn't a native either, judging by the slight Southern drawl. "I was offered a new job, and it was worth the move."

I didn't offer anything more, and Gavin moved the conversation in a different direction. He asked if I'd belonged to any clubs back home, mentioning that he had briefly thought of expanding into other cities. When I said I was from Chicago, Carrie immediately mentioned that her best friend was originally from the windy city, and the conversation meandered from there.

After nearly twenty minutes, Carrie excused herself to go talk to someone she knew, and a short while after that, somebody came to haul Gavin away on business relating to the club. He told me to enjoy myself and let him know if I needed anything. I assured him I would.

I had to admit that even though I enjoyed talking to them both, I wasn't sorry to see them go. I hadn't come to make conversation, and now that I'd had my drink, I was ready to find a distraction. That wasn't the sort of thing I wanted to do with an audience.

As I made my way to the stairs, a cute redhead bumped into me. She looked up at me from under her lashes, offering a giggling apology that suited her youthful appearance.

I smiled, but before I could brush around her, she moved closer and rested a hand against my chest. A bold move for someone I immediately marked as a submissive. Then again, she might've been the kind of sub who liked to flirt and push until she finally found someone to punish her.

"Are you...looking for anybody particular?" she asked, her gaze flicking to my mouth.

"I might be."

She bit her lower lip and slid the hand on my chest down. I caught it before it reached my belt, but I didn't move her away. I was curious to see what she'd do next. I wasn't opposed to delivering a little bit of punishment at the moment.

"I can be anybody. Somebody." She licked her lips again and moved in closer. "Nobody. Take your pick."

I let my eyes run down her body. She was about average height, slender, and wearing a few strips of silk and lace that barely covered her essentials. She was beautiful, and I had a feeling she'd do every single thing I told her.

Wrap those cherry-red lips around my cock and suck. Let me fuck her mouth.

Spank her ass until it was hot and pink, my hand stinging.

Use a flogger. A crop. Any one of the dozens of toys I was sure the club provided their VIP patrons.

Fuck her in every position possible. In her pussy. In her ass. As hard and as fast as I wanted.

Make her scream my name, and beg me to let her come.

I knew she would let me do all of that and more. All I had to do was say the word, and she'd be mine for however long it took for us both to be sated.

My gaze came back to her face. "So, anybody. Somebody. Nobody. Do you have an actual name I should call you?"

# Chapter 4

*Dena*

I'd expected to be nervous. After all, this was the job I'd been working toward my whole life, so it made sense that my stomach felt like it had butterflies as I walked into the Manhattan DA's office. The offices were huge and not a little intimidating, but I had my game face on and didn't let the nerves show.

Dressed in what I considered my best power suit, I crossed the black and white tiled floor with slow deliberation, my briefcase swinging from my hand and my head held high. I'd spent hours yesterday picking out exactly what I wanted to wear this morning.

The pinstripe two-piece suit fit me to perfection. The pencil skirt stopped at my knee and the fitted jacket stopped just a little below my waist. I wore a white camisole under it that displayed a hint of lace at vee of the double breasted bodice. It was feminine and flattering, but understated and more powerful for it.

My shoes, on the other hand, were anything but understated.

They were murder red Manolo Blahniks – my favorite shoes.

They matched the bag I carried and I know both the bag and the shoes made a statement, but it wasn't as much about the statement as it was about me personally. I liked how the entire outfit made me feel, and today, I needed that. I needed to feel like I was a woman to be taken seriously and not a child to be overlooked.

As planned, I arrived five minutes early and took a few moments to look around. Despite the power suit and kick-ass shoes, I felt out of place, and started to worry that I looked out of place too.

I mentally chided myself. I wouldn't be here if I didn't belong, if I couldn't do the job I was assigned to do. I belonged here just as much as anybody else and I knew that. At least most of me did.

"Well," a low voice said, drawing the word out. "Hello there."

Even before I turned around, I knew what I was going to find. Years of experience had already taught me this lesson. I deliberately waited a beat before turning to meet a set of turquoise eyes set in the face of a man who could only be described as pretty. And judging by the look on his face, he knew it too. Every inch of him said he spent more time in front of the mirror than I did.

His gaze slithered over me, and I set my face into an expression of cool disdain. He was smiling, although the smile wasn't directed at me. How could it be? He was too busy checking out my rack and my legs.

I cleared my throat and waited for his gaze to swing

upward. When it did, I gave an icy smile. A practiced mask settled on his face, one I recognized. I was supposed to be charmed or flattered by his clearly appreciative perusal.

I didn't blink, holding his gaze until he looked away first. Still, he didn't look the least bit embarrassed or ashamed. As he stepped forward, he held out a hand.

"I'm Pierce Lawton, the new ADA. Would you by chance be...ah, Dena, I believe? The other one?"

The other one. Nice. "Yes. Dena Monroe." I took his hand and gave him a short, quick shake, long enough for him to know he hadn't intimidated me, but too short for him to read into it.

"I don't know about you, but I'm looking forward to diving in. Getting my hands dirty." He gave me a quick wink that I was sure he thought was charming. "It's okay to be nervous, you know. Between the defense attorneys and the scum they represent, it's hard to know who's sleazier."

I had an answer to that question, but kept it to myself. A moment later, I was glad I had.

A woman strode in, pausing only briefly when she saw us. Sharp blue eyes moved from Pierce to me, and then she nodded. "Good," she said, her voice crisp. "You're both here. Follow me."

She didn't introduce herself, but I had to assume she was Bethany McDermott, the ADA I was told I'd be working with. She looked to be in her mid-forties, but with plenty of make-up and her honey-blonde curls professionally done, she might've been older. When she walked into an office, I saw her name on the door, confirming her identity.

She strode around the desk and only then turned to face us. Bracing her hands on the desk, she studied us for a moment. She wore her own version of a power suit. It was the same sapphire color as her eyes, and close-fitting, flattering her lush curves without being obvious.

She looked like the kind of woman who drank souls and had the hearts of her victims for breakfast.

"Okay, so this is how it's going to work. Due to our current situation, we aren't going to do our usual six-week training period. I don't have time to coddle or baby either of you. Figure out how to swim, or you're out. Be prepared to learn and learn fast. We hired you because we assumed you could do the job without us having to hold your hand along the way." She paused, her eyes sliding over to me. "Will that be a problem?"

My spine stiffened as her gaze locked with mine. It felt like I was getting singled out, and I didn't care for it. But I didn't let my reaction show. "Of course not."

She flicked a look at Pierce and arched one perfectly plucked eyebrow.

"That's how I work." He gave her the same slow, smug smile he'd given me earlier.

I resisted the urge to roll my eyes, but just barely. What a schmuck. But every office, firm, classroom, had a guy like him, if not two or three. I learned how to deal with them years ago, and generally it was best to ignore.

"Good." She pushed a button on her phone and when a voice came on, she said, "Darcy, I wanted those files now." She looked up at us again. "I've got a lot of cases on my desk, and basically, the two of you are going to do all of the scut work I don't trust to the paralegals. You won't say a word to a judge until I've determined you won't fuck up my cases." She gave me a condescending smile. "Is language an issue for either of you?"

I had a few choice words I wouldn't have minded sharing with her.

"Of course not." I smiled blandly.

"Excellent." She gave a short nod as the door swung open and a rather harried young woman stuck her head in. "Bring in the case files."

While Bethany addressed the person I assumed was Darcy, I mentally sighed over the fact that I was back to being the bottom rung on the totem pole. Part of me had anticipated it, but it was still grating. I might not have argued criminal cases before, but I'd been presenting to judges on my own for a couple of years.

As Darcy stepped out again, Bethany turned back to Pierce and me. "As you've probably figured out, I'm your direct supervisor, which means I'll be deciding if and when you're ready to take on cases of your own. You do a good job and I'll get you into the court room. Screw me over and you'll be lucky to argue shit in traffic court."

Darcy shuffled in with an overflowing file box, looking like she could barely hold on. I was petite, but this skinny wisp of a woman looked like she was about to fall over. Instinctively, I moved to help, taking it from her as I glanced toward Pierce, waiting for him to step in.

He didn't, solidifying my opinion of him as a total

asshole.

"Thanks for taking the initiative, Dena." Bethany gave me a cool smile. "There's a list in there that details everything I need. I also had Darcy send it to your email so there aren't any excuses. Pierce, you're with me."

The box gouged my hips with its sharp corners as Bethany strode out of the office, Pierce at her heels. Staring at their backs, I briefly imagined giving into the childish urge to stick my tongue out at them. I didn't, of course, but it would've been satisfying.

"You have an office." Darcy gave me a small, nervous smile when I looked at her.

"Excuse me?"

"You already have a space to work. I'm not sure I'd call it an office, but it's yours."

I nodded and grimly tightened my grip on the box. "Lead the way."

Some nine plus hours later, I collapsed face-down on the couch in my apartment, more thankful than ever that I didn't have a roommate. I had a sweet little place in Chelsea, and it was my pride and joy. Just then, though, I couldn't take the time to appreciate the restored brick walls or the view, or anything else for that matter.

All I wanted was peace and quiet, and maybe in a little while, a glass of wine.

Fuck that. I might just have the whole damn bottle.

My first day as an ADA hadn't exactly been what I could call glamorous. It hadn't been exciting. I couldn't really even say it had been fulfilling. I could have handled the lack of glamour and excitement. Those stars had been wiped from my eyes a long time ago. But it would have been nice if the day hadn't completely sucked.

Once Darcy had shown me into my office – it was hardly more than a closet – I had spent the first hour dealing with a computer that had come straight out of the Stone Age.

Then I'd spent several hours going blind on legal briefs. There were filings and reports, things that were generally handled by paralegals. Except Bethany didn't seem to have any paralegals around. I knew things were tight since they'd let Pierce and I slide on the usual training, but it still seemed excessive.

Then again, my boss seemed like that kind of person. Excessive. And not in a generous kind of way. When I'd been coming back from lunch, Bethany had found me and demanded to know how far I'd gotten.

"You're not done yet?" she'd snapped. Then with a shake of her head, she'd shoved a clipboard into my hands. "People up for parole. I argued the cases in court. Write the letters. You can pull up the details on your computer."

I'd seen the conference table through the glass behind her, and both she and Pierce had looked to be working on something else, something that apparently required them to have meals brought in. Rather than ask why he was working with her rather than me, I simply nodded end and retreated to my cell. My office.

And that was where I'd stayed until I'd realized it was after five. When I left, I saw Pierce coming out of an office a few doors down from Bethany's. I'd managed to catch a glimpse into the room before he shut the door completely.

"My new office." He'd given me a smug smile. "You like yours?"

"It suits me just fine," I'd lied.

I wasn't a superficial person, but I did believe in equality and fairness. Two people starting out the same should be treated the same. There was no reason for Pierce's office to be an actual office, with room for a real desk and some movement. But there it was.

Now, I was lying on my couch and trying not to brood too much. It didn't mean anything. Maybe he actually had more experience than I did. I was pretty sure he was nearly a decade older. Maybe he'd transferred from another DA's office, and he had more seniority. It didn't matter.

That was what I told myself. I didn't particularly believe it, though. The phone rang, but I ignored it. I didn't want to talk to anyone, didn't want to deal with anyone asking me how things had gone, didn't want to have to listen to anyone else talk about their problems. I just wanted to be left alone.

I ignored pretty much everything right up until my bladder forced me off the couch and into the bathroom. I could see the screen of my phone showing that I had messages, but I didn't answer any of them. I didn't even look at them.

What I did do was get myself something to drink.

After pouring myself a glass of wine, I retreated into my bathroom and settled down for a nice long soak.

"Tomorrow will be better," I said. Relaxing back into my lavender and vanilla bubbles, I sighed. "Tomorrow will be better."

What a line of bullshit.

The next day wasn't any better, nor were the days that followed. I felt like I was an associate all over again, and it annoyed the crap out of me.

It only got worse on Wednesday morning when I took some files to Bethany's office. I paused in the doorway, listening while Pierce explained a tact he would have tried if he was first chair on some case they were working on.

I stood there stiffly, my hands gripping the files I held, waiting for them to notice me. When they finished, Pierce glanced over at me and gave me a surprised look as if he'd just now realized I was there. Bethany, however, eyed me dismissively before going back to the notes she was working on.

"Did you need something?" Pierce asked.

"I just need to give Bethany the research notes she needed." Keeping my voice level, I walked across the floor and put everything down. As I was turning away, I heard papers rustling.

"Oh, great. I needed this for that filing I was doing for you, Bethany."

I stiffened even more, one hand curling into a fist. Unlike a lot of lawyers, I didn't thrive on conflict. In fact, I didn't even really like it. I liked making logical arguments, presenting clear and concise evidence.

But a girl could only take so much for so long, and I was heading down that path.

I was being jerked around and I knew it. I'd need to address it, but I wouldn't do it without thinking things through. This wasn't some asshole at a club. This was my job, the place that I'd always dreamed of being. I wasn't going to lose that in a moment of rash temper. No matter how justified.

But just as I reached the door, Bethany spoke, "Actually, Dena, it's a good thing you stopped by. It saves me from having to hunt you down later."

I turned toward her, letting her know I was listening.

"I've been given the okay to put the two of you up for the next case that comes across my desk. You'll be taking second chair, of course. I'll be arguing the case, but you'll be there to see how things work."

I blinked, almost certain I'd heard wrong. Pierce grinned as he shoved his hands into his pockets. Bethany ignored him, her pen scratching across the surface of her notepad.

"In the meantime, I'm presenting you two with a case. It's already been closed, but I want to hear strategies on how you would've handled it had you been trying it." Now she looked up, sliding her gaze from Pierce to me. "Consider this trial by fire. Don't fuck up."

Something hot and pleased settled inside me.

Pierce glanced at me, but I didn't waste my time looking at him now.

Trials by fire suited me just fine.

# Chapter 5

## *Arik*

"I have news for you." I looked up at the sound of my new boss coming from the doorway of my office.

While I wasn't a senior partner anymore, I had a big office, and once I did make it, I expected to move from this office to a corner one.

Charles Sheldon stood in the doorway, smoothing down his burgundy tie in a gesture I'd already come to recognize. "Do you mind?" he asked, gesturing to the door.

"Of course not." Giving him an easy grin, I added, "After all, you are the boss."

"For now." His eyebrow quirked, reminding me of the response I'd given him when I agreed to take the job his firm had offered me.

I'd been a senior partner at my old firm back in Chicago, well on my way to convincing them to make me a named partner. I hadn't been overly enthusiastic about the demotion to junior partner here, but the promise of practicing for one of the most prestigious defense firms in the country had been one hell of a lure.

I'd agreed to take the job, and then told them I planned to be a senior partner in a year. Sheldon had been the man to make the final call. He'd laughed, but he hired me.

"What can I help you with, Sheldon?"

"Got a case for you." He hitched up his pants and sat down in the chair across from me. "It seems like it's right up your alley. Regular clients of ours – well, I should amend that. Client. Anyway. We're on retainer. We just got a phone call. The man who retained us is now dead. You'll be defending his wife."

Holding up my hand, I cut him off before he could say anything else, "Don't give me any more information. Just tell me where she is and how I can contact her."

"She's at home." He gave me the address and rose. "And you might want to hurry. You might get there before the cops do."

For a split second, I gaped at him. Was he kidding me? He'd sat there, all casual, while our client was facing the possibility of having to talk to the cops without us. I didn't know what the circumstances were, but any woman whose husband just died shouldn't have to worry about saying something incriminating, even if it was something petty.

I jumped to my feet and grabbed my briefcase. As I hurried past Sheldon, he gave me a small smile, as if he'd done all of that on purpose. It was too bad, I thought as I stepped outside. I'd actually liked the guy. Now, not so much.

Then I pushed the thoughts aside. I had a job to do, a client to defend.

The address, thankfully, was close.

Sheldon, Simon and Sharpe chose to operate out of a converted house not too far from Central Park and the over-priced, and overdone, glamour of the Trump International Hotel. They weren't the biggest defense firm in the city, but they had one of the best reputations.

My client, one Leayna Mance, lived in a house just a couple blocks away. If I hadn't wanted to seem unprofessional, I would've walked rather than grabbing a cab, but something told me that this wasn't about some parking ticket or even a home invasion.

Now, standing at the door, I pounded on it after my polite knock didn't garner any response. The place was quiet, and that worried me. There weren't any police cars, no uniforms hanging around.

And still, no one answered the door.

If my gut hadn't been telling me something was off, I would've wondered if maybe this was some strange joke they played on the new guy.

I knocked again, pounding hard enough for it to make my hand hurt. "Ms. Mance? It's Arik Porter, from Sheldon, Simon and Sharpe." I paused and then added, "Charles Sheldon sent me. I understand you've got a problem."

I had a bad feeling that the problem was going to be a dead body. I'd stopped Sheldon from telling me too much because I didn't want to form an opinion before I met with my client, but I couldn't stop hearing his comment about Mrs. Mance's husband being dead.

From behind the door, I heard a slight noise. The door unlocked and through a crack, I saw a woman's face. She peered at me and through that narrow slit, I could see that she held a phone clutched to her chest. "I called the cops."

"Good. That's good. Why don't you let me in, Ms. Mance? They'll be here soon—"

Sirens sliced through the air and she jerked.

"Mrs. Mance, may I come in? I'm your attorney, ma'am. I think it's a good idea I come in before the police get here."

She hesitated, then nodded as she opened the door. I went inside, and even before I crossed the threshold, I smelled it.

Death.

The metallic, sickly sweet smell of blood. Something else underneath it. Something that made it clear that, here, blood meant death.

I breathed slowly and tried not to focus on the smell. I had a clearly freaked out client. "It would appear you have a problem, ma'am," I said calmly.

She started to cry as she nodded. "My husband's dead."

The next few hours were a rush of cops, questions and tears.

Leayna hadn't made the wisest decision in calling a lawyer first, not as far as the cops were concerned. And the fact that I'd gotten there before them just added to their annoyance.

I already knew the district attorney would find plenty of ways to spin that in a bad way if this went to trial, and it wasn't a far stretch to see things getting to a jury, even though I believed she was innocent.

Maybe her tears had gotten to me, or maybe it was easier to con me than I thought, but as Leayna sat there holding my hands and repeating the same statement over and over again, I believed her.

*I didn't do it. I know it looks bad, but I didn't.*

I hadn't asked her if she did it. Each defense attorney has their own way of handling client guilt, but personally, I didn't want to know. Even the guilty were entitled to a defense, but it was easier to move forward with the knowledge in my gut that the woman sitting next to me hadn't killed her husband. Plus, it kept me from knowingly supporting perjury if I had to put her under oath.

It had been cleverly arranged to make it look like she was guilty, but in my gut, when she said *I didn't do this...*my instinct was to believe her. And I'd spent most of my life trusting my gut.

"What am I going to do, Arik?" she whispered, her voice raw and broken.

Her grass green eyes were red rimmed and swollen,

not the sort of thing one would've expected from a trophy wife decades younger than her late husband. She sniffed, then blew her nose on the handkerchief I'd given her when we left for the police station.

She'd been officially arrested, though I would do my best to get that thrown out since they'd made the arrest without any clear evidence. They hadn't found her standing over the body, and there'd been no time to process any real forensics. Someone had gotten a little overzealous.

Leayna sent a furtive glance toward the door to the interrogation room. "Am I...do I have to stay in prison or do they let me out on bail or what?"

"There will be a hearing to determine whether or not you get out on bail. Then we'll look over every piece of evidence..." I trailed off. She wasn't fully taking this in.

She'd heard the words *whether or not.* "I might not get out on bail?" Her voice cracked and I wished I'd worded that differently. "But I didn't do anything!"

"Leayna," I said firmly, trying to ground her. She was slipping away, lost in a maze of fear and confusion. Squeezing her hands, I said her name again.

She patted down her short hair. It was a warm hazelnut color that I was pretty sure wasn't natural. She looked at me, her lashes sweeping down before slowly lifting back up.

"I won't get out on bail," she said, her lips stiff.

"We don't know that–"

There was a knock at the door, but before I had a chance to say anything, it swung open. Immediately, I stood up, a hand on Leayna's shoulder, placing my body partially between her and the door. She might've been close to my age, but I felt strangely protective of her.

"Excuse us, we're..." Shit. "Hello, Bethany."

Assistant district attorney Bethany McDermott stood in the doorway, her lips pursed as she looked from Leayna to me. "Oh, I'm sorry, Arik. I thought you were ready for me. Hello, Mrs. Mance." She glanced to her watch and then back at me with a lifted eyebrow. "Should I give you a few more minutes?"

"I'm not sure a few minutes will be enough."

"It's going to have to." She started to tap her foot. "We'll be seeing the judge shortly for a bail hearing. I thought you might want to confer for a few minutes before that happens."

"Bail hearing?"

Leayna flinched at the abrupt sound of my voice. I mentally kicked myself. Out of all the ADAs in the city, I had to get the only one I'd already met.

And loathed.

I gestured to the door. "Let's step outside."

"I do have other cases, Arik." She gave Leayna a look of mock sympathy. "Not everybody has a high priced defense attorney who can hang around all day. I need to prepare for an appearance before the judge shortly, and then several other things need my attention."

I wanted to roll my eyes at the obvious theatrics. "Fine. Now, outside for a few minutes."

She followed, so I counted that as a win. I closed the door behind me and took an extra few steps.

"What is this about the bail hearing? She was only processed thirty minutes ago. We've barely had time to talk."

"Bail hearing is at two." Bethany gave me a wide-eyed smile before reaching up to smooth down my tie. "Really, Arik. You should be more up on what is going on with your client."

"I'm trying to figure out why nobody bothered to tell me about my client's bail hearing." I brushed her hand aside and resisted the impulse to rub my hand on my pant leg.

"Well, I'm sure they tried to contact you." She gave me a sweet smile that I knew only went skin deep. "Now that we've settled that, shall we go back inside? I'm sure your client is just beside herself with...grief."

My mouth flattened into a line. "She is. She's also scared and confused."

"With the prospect of life behind bars, she *should* be scared." Bethany shrugged, absolutely no sympathy in her expression or voice.

"She didn't kill him," I snapped.

"Save it for court." Bethany rolled her eyes and took a step to go around me.

I barred her way. "You don't talk to my client without me being present." I scowled down at her. "I'm not in the room so you're not going in there."

"Then get in there." She scowled back, any pretense of politeness gone. "Or I'll make it clear you're getting in the way of me doing my job, and that won't do anybody any good. She's in enough trouble as it is, Porter. Your best bet is to get her to plead out. Either we talk now or you can make an appointment with my office, and we'll talk when I've got time in a few days."

"I don't much care for having you trying to steamroll me," I said softly. "I'm not one of your puppets, Bethany."

She gave me a little smirk. "Whatever do you mean by that, Arik?"

I didn't bother to respond. Turning around, I opened the door and shoved inside. Bethany followed me, but I ignored her, keeping my focus on Leayna. She was sitting in the chair, arms wrapped around herself and rocking as if she ached deep inside.

Her eyes, big and scared, met mine.

I went back to the seat I'd been using and took her hand. "Good news. We'll be having the bail hearing soon."

"That's good news?"

"Once you post bail—"

"We're going to ask that bail be denied," Bethany interrupted as she gave Leayna a smile that brimmed with mock sympathy. "Standard procedure in murder cases."

Leayna flinched and I almost wanted to put my arm around her.

"You don't have any proof," I said.

"I'm simply pointing out—"

I stood up and cut around the table, moving out into the hall again. Bethany was too much a bulldog with her cases to chance having this fucked up by her staying in the room alone with my client, so she followed, as I'd expected her to.

Once she did, I closed the door again, resisting the urge to slam it. Once it was shut, I pivoted on Bethany, eyes narrowed and voice cold. "Don't pull that shit again. I'm not some idealistic public defender fresh out of law school. I've been arguing cases almost as long as you, and I'm better."

Her eyes glittered bright and hot. I'd seen this side of her before, and it hadn't been pleasant then either. She opened her mouth.

I cut her off before she could speak. "I've had less than thirty minutes to discuss things with my client and she's been in shock the entire time, which means she isn't yet capable of assisting in her own defense. So, unless you want me to bring this up to a judge, you're going to back the hell off and do things the right way."

She sauntered closer, reaching up to stroke her fingers down my jawline. I jerked my head back out of her reach.

"You know, when we first met, I'd really hoped we could be...friendly," Bethany murmured.

I shook my head. "No offense, I'd rather be friendly with a snake."

She laughed, but it wasn't a nice sound. "Better prepare your client, and yourself. It doesn't look good for either of you."

I was starting to regret coming to New York after all.

# Chapter 6

## *Dena*

"Interesting." Bethany looked at me after I finished and gave a slow, thoughtful nod. Her eyes were hard to read.

My new boss might've looked like the meaner, harder version of Lawyer Barbie, but she had one hell of a game face. After a moment, she shifted her attention to the file I'd given her and tapped it with a French manicured nail.

"You present a good argument."

That sounded suspiciously like a compliment. I didn't say it out loud, though. I simply inclined my head and said, "Thank you."

She made a noncommittal sound under her breath and flipped through a few pages. "It wouldn't have convinced a jury, of course. But it's still a good argument." Now she did look back at me and gave me a patronizing smile. "I think you'll get there, Dena. It just takes a bit of time to make the switch from divorce and family law to criminal law."

Without waiting for a response from me, she looked

at Pierce and began to fire a barrage of questions at him.

I tried not to let any reaction show, returning to the chair a few feet away from the one where Pierce normally sat, sinking down into it. I wished I could've just walked out since it was clear that she wasn't going to treat me like she treated Pierce, but I wouldn't stoop to being petty. I was an adult.

No matter how much it sucked.

"Impressive." Bethany drew the word out long and slow and I continued to study the window so I didn't have to see the pompous prick preening.

Her phone buzzed on her desk and she picked it up, effectively letting us know that the rest of the discussion was over. That was fine with me.

Rising, I gathered up the information I'd brought in for my presentation, and began stuffing everything into my briefcase.

I was almost out the door when she called after Pierce and told him to wait a few more minutes. Obviously, he did so, relaxing back in the chair as I ducked outside, quick as I could. I was ready to get out of there.

It was finally Friday.

As I was making my way out along with the rest of the people who were done for the day, I heard snatches of conversations and greetings. Plans being made. People laughing.

Loneliness settled along with a knot of edginess that grew with every step I took.

*It's finally Friday...*

I hit the doors and decided I needed to go out.

Club Privé wasn't high on my list of places to go tonight.

I was feeling a little too rough to have the watchful eye of my best friend's husband on me. Not to mention the best friend herself. As much as I adored Carrie and Gavin, they'd taken it upon themselves to look out for me every time I came in, and I didn't need that. I could look out for myself.

What I needed was...

I sighed. What I needed was something I was beginning to think I could never have.

So I went to Leather and Laces. It wasn't quite as upscale as Club Privé, but they played excellent music and looked out for their guests as well as Gavin did. I knew the guys who handled the doors too, and when they saw me approaching, they automatically waved me in, much to the disgust of the people waiting in line. I ignored them. Once upon a time, I'd been the one waiting in line. It was my turn to move ahead now.

The dark silver mini dress I wore stopped a few inches below my butt and I'd paired it with boots that came up a few inches over my knees, leaving only a couple inches of thigh bare in between.

I'd chosen a pair of platform boots for tonight since I didn't know if I'd be staying here or going somewhere else, and I wasn't overly thrilled at the idea of walking a lot in heels. The platform boots were a lot more comfortable and solid, and they still gave me three more inches. That might not have sounded like a lot, but to someone who barely hit five feet, any extra height was nice.

Inside the club, low lights pulsed in time to the music, and I breathed in the familiar scents that came with any sort of place like this. Sweat, perfume, soap. Sex. Here, there was also just a hint of leather since at least half the crowd was wearing it.

I let the rush of energy wash over me as I moved deeper inside and looked around. I hadn't been to L&L in a few months, and while there were some familiar faces, more were unfamiliar. I wondered how many of the patrons had left for Club Privé when it'd reopened its doors.

Somebody bumped into me, and a hand followed to steady my hip. When the hand didn't immediately fall away, I shifted my gaze over and stared levelly at a short – at least relatively speaking – rail-thin man who wore a leather vest and equally tight pants to match. I continued to stare until his hand fell away and then I continued my trek toward the dance floor.

One of the men caught my eye and a slow smile spread across his face even as his gaze dropped so that he was looking at me through his lashes.

I smiled back. Leather and Laces had private rooms

58

in the back as well. They weren't as nice as the ones Gavin and Carrie had, but they were far better than some sleazy hotel.

I held out my hand and he came to me, his head bowed. He was average height, which meant I didn't have to strain to whisper in his ear.

"I'm Dena."

"Edward."

"Do you want to come with me?"

A shudder ran through him, and while that answered my question, I waited for him to nod before I turned and started for the back. He trailed after me, his fingers still twisted tightly in mine.

Sweat still dewed my flesh as I pushed my skirt back down and adjusted my underwear. I hadn't been able to climax, though not due to lack of trying on Edward's part.

I'd gotten him worked up first, trying to lose myself in his trust, in controlling his pleasure, but it hadn't worked. Well, it hadn't worked for me. He'd been practically shaking with need when I'd made him stretch out on the bed. I'd ridden his face, my desperation growing as his tongue and lips weren't able to get me off. When I'd finally rolled on the condom and lowered myself onto him, I'd resigned myself to leaving without being satisfied. I'd focused all of my attention then on making sure Edward found his release.

He moaned from beneath me, his eyes half-rolled back in his head. When I rose, he started to lift his hand. I caught it, squeezed, hoping he'd take the hint and not say anything. He smiled as he rolled onto his side. I brushed some of his dark hair back from his face, using the touch to make sure he was okay. Some subs needed extra aftercare, but we hadn't done anything particularly intense so I was thinking he'd be fine. When he nodded at me, I squeezed his hand again.

"I'll take care of the room. Thank you." I leaned down and kissed his cheek, leaving before he could ask me what was wrong.

I couldn't tell him that I was miserable because nothing made me happy lately. It wasn't his fault. I was pretty certain I'd given him what he needed, but it hadn't done anything for me, and it wasn't fair to him to make him think that any of this was his fault. Plenty of subs got pleasure from the actual submission and knowing it was arousing to their partner. Edward was one of those.

But I didn't want anybody submitting to me right now.

I was tired of being in the driver's seat. I just wanted an hour where I didn't have to think, didn't have to be in control. An hour where I could completely rely on someone else to take care of me.

When I stepped out of the hall, I was tempted to head for the door, go home and find my vibrator. If I closed my eyes and imagined really hard, I could make myself believe for a few minutes at least that somebody could give me what I needed.

Instead, I went to the dance floor.

I had to burn out this energy, and it looked like dancing was my only option. I threw myself into the music with sheer, reckless abandon, grateful to at least be able to shed the straight-laced image I wore most of the time.

A couple of hard-bodied, younger wannabes were there and they quickly surrounded me, keeping just enough space free that I didn't feel claustrophobic or threatened. I'd never be interested in joining any of them in a room, but for dancing? They looked like they could be a welcome distraction. When one of them came up behind me and lightly rested his hands on my hips, I let him.

If this was the only outlet I had, I was going to make the most of it.

# Chapter 7

*Arik*

"Is there anything else I can do for you, Mr. Porter?"

The soft, almost breathy voice coming from the doorway had me looking up from the reports and other files I had littering my desk. A few days ago, the glossy black surface had been clean, not even a paperclip out of place. Then Charles Sheldon had dropped by my office with his little bombshell, and my nice, neat organization had gone straight down the path of hell.

I didn't like that very much. I liked things to be exactly where I wanted them. I knew I had some control issues, but I also knew that was one of the things that made me good at my job. That and the fact that I was a bit of a workaholic.

The paralegal standing in the door smiled at me, her pretty face not showing any of the exhaustion I knew she must be feeling.

This case was a big one for the firm. Leayna was rich, well-known and her marriage had been almost as sensational as the death. All eyes were on us. I hoped I didn't fuck things up. I'd been told any extra hours I needed from my paralegal were fine, and when I mentioned it to her, she'd told me she didn't have any family or children, no boyfriend.

She'd hesitated on that last one, her voice trailing off.

At the time, I'd wondered if she had been trying to tell me something. Now I was sure of it.

She slid into the room, sauntering closer with a slow, deliberate walk. Ella Pott was a beautiful woman in her early twenties, and a sensual one at that. It was in the way she moved, the way she used her body. The way she watched people. I was usually a good judge of women, and I had a feeling she'd be a pleasure in bed. The way she was watching me now made me think she wouldn't be put off if I invited her back to my place. She'd probably beat me out of the door.

Chestnut brown hair. Big blue-green eyes. Nice curves. She had a full, pretty mouth that looked slightly puckered all the time, almost as if she was waiting for a kiss...or to kiss something. I tried to imagine her on her knees, wrapping those pouty lips around my cock.

I felt sluggish interest, but nothing strong enough to warrant acting on it.

That was good though. I didn't want to fool around with someone I worked with, let alone someone who was technically working under me.

"No. I think I've got everything under control," I told her, shaking my head. "I'll be wrapping up soon, Ella. Have a good weekend."

I hated that her shoulders sort of drooped when I said it. She was cute, but even if she hadn't been my paralegal,

I most likely wouldn't have gone after her anyway.

She wasn't exactly my...type.

Since I'd come to New York, when I wanted to go out, I usually went to Club Privé, but I wasn't in the mood for its sleek elegance tonight. I hit another place a friend from back home recommended. Leather and Laces was still a decent club, but the crowd was a little rougher than I usually went with. I was more into the control than some of the...other aspects of the lifestyle. Tonight, however, I was in the mood for something a little darker than normal.

A little less than a year before I'd moved, I'd had a somewhat regular thing going with a woman, and it had worked for us, but then she'd wanted something more like a relationship, and that wasn't something I wanted. I liked her well enough and the split had been amicable. I'd even been happy for her when I heard she'd found a serious boyfriend, but I never once regretted not ignoring my instincts and giving in. Relationships and I didn't work.

Since moving, I'd had a few encounters, but they had been brief and not particularly satisfying, nothing more than taking care of a physical need. The part of me that needed that extra...edge hadn't been sated.

Briefly, I thought about Ella, and knew she'd be willing, enthusiastic even. She might even be willing to learn about what I needed, but I wasn't in the mood to teach someone. Some men might've leapt at the chance to teach some wide-eyed newbie, but I wasn't one of them. I knew what I wanted, but I wasn't sure I'd ever find it.

Music pounded in the air, and I leaned against the bar, raising my voice to be heard so I could order a scotch. A brunette with a short cap of hair crossed my line of sight and paused, looking at me speculatively. A smile curled her lips, soft and hesitant, but the shyness was more for show than anything else. I could tell she was one of those people who came to a place like this looking for a thrill. She'd play a bit, then go back to whatever vanilla boyfriend or fiancé she had waiting for her.

I ordered another scotch before moving into the crowd. There was a stage to my left and people were setting up for some sort of show. I didn't need to know what was going on to know I'd be bored. None of the displays that happened in the BDSM clubs had ever appealed to me. There were plenty who enjoyed the spectator aspects of the lifestyle, but I wasn't one of them.

I preferred to be involved. Once, I'd told a sub that spectator sports were fine for something like football, but anything else, I wanted to be hands on. It was like how I wasn't really into the whole humiliation and pain aspect of it. I had no issues with anything that happened between consenting adults, but it just wasn't me. I mean, a little spanking and punishment were fine, but I didn't go for any of the harder stuff.

Strobe lights pulsed in time to the music as I cut around the edge of the dance floor. I glanced over almost reflexively, and that was when I saw her. For one moment, she was clearly illuminated in the light, and that moment was enough.

She was slender, delicate. Yet the way she moved on the floor exuded confidence and strength. Three men crowded around her, and one of them reached up, his hand moving to her throat in a clearly dominant gesture.

A smug smile curled her lips. I watched as she reached up and caught the man's shirt, hauled him toward her as though they might kiss. Their faces hovered no more than a few inches away, and when he moved to close the distance, she pushed him back and spun around. Now with her back to the man's chest, she caught his hands, guiding them to her hips.

A second man moved in. Her slim form was practically hidden by the two men for a moment, and then she slid out from between the two of them. When they tried to close her in again, she pressed her hands to their chests. There was something both playful and commanding about how she did it.

She was controlling every damn thing about the dance, and those two men – barely old enough to drink, I suspected – didn't even realize how completely she was doing it. They clearly thought themselves dominants, but they were clearly no match for this tiny little thing.

Intrigued, and more than a little curious, I finished my scotch and passed the glass off to a nearby server without taking my eyes off the woman. Her eyes flicked toward me, and then moved back to her partners. Then, slowly, she looked back at me again. Her chin angled up, head cocked slightly to the side, as if she was reading me.

The smile on her lips tugged up at the corners just a bit as I moved closer, arching an eyebrow. She responded in kind, and moved away from the men she'd been dancing with. When they made to follow, she shook her head, and then looked back at me.

She caught her lower lip between her teeth and then let it roll out. I imagined her doing the exact same thing before I kissed her. She had an absolutely perfect mouth.

I made up my mind then and there that I was going to taste that mouth tonight.

I reached out as soon as she was close enough and settled a hand on her waist, slowly drawing her toward me. She came easily, and when I set my other hand on her hip, she did the same thing to me she'd done earlier. She brought her hand up and curled her fist into the front of my shirt. She didn't pull me in or push me away, though.

She just kept her hand there as though she was still debating what to do with me.

Or maybe she was waiting for me.

The thought sent blood rushing south.

She'd been controlling those men, but the dominant in me had felt something else, and now I was thinking my instincts had been right.

Leaning down, I pressed my lips to her ear. "I'd tell you you're the hottest thing here, but I'm pretty sure you already know that."

When I straightened, I found myself looking into the most gorgeous pale gray eyes I'd ever seen. I brushed my thumb across the curve of that delicious mouth. She slid her tongue out, almost as if she was tasting the path my thumb had taken.

My gut clenched. Fuck me. I'd never had such an immediate, visceral reaction to anyone before.

Normally, I wouldn't kiss a woman within two minutes of seeing her.

But when she opened her mouth under mine, I knew it hadn't been a bad call.

# Chapter 8

## *Dena*

His mouth...

Oh, damn.

His mouth.

I'd wanted him as soon as I'd seen him, watching me with those eyes that I now knew were a rich emerald green. He was handsome in a rugged way, not the usual pretty-boy or classically handsome men I usually saw.

But that wasn't the only thing different about him.

The hand on my hip slid up over my ribcage, tangling in my short hair, tightening and tugging, a slow rhythmic sensation that drove me to distraction even as his tongue pushed demandingly past my lips.

He tasted me before pulling back to rake his teeth across my lower lip. It was all I could do not to moan right there. Starving for a deeper kiss, I flicked out my tongue and he nipped at it. I shuddered and he wrapped an arm around my waist, tugging me in close against his hard, muscular body.

One kiss turned into two, and I went from clutching at his shirt with one hand to hanging onto both of his shoulders. All the while, he moved us off the dance floor and into a darkened corner. My back was to the wall, as he wedged himself between my thighs. I could feel his cock, already hard against me.

He let go of my hair, and I might have been disappointed, because he stopped kissing me too, but he didn't pull away. His mouth moved down to my neck and I gasped as he raked the sensitive skin with his teeth.

He muttered something against my ear, but over the roaring of my own blood, the racing of my heart, I had no idea what it was. I wasn't even sure I cared.

The heel of his hand brushed against my breast. It was a light touch, not hesitant, but more like he was...feeling out the territory. I arched into his touch. He could feel out whatever in the hell he wanted.

My nipples tightened. Between my natural build and the style of the dress, I hadn't bothered to wear a bra. As his hand moved to cup my breast completely, I could feel the intense heat of him through the thin fabric.

I sucked in air, my eyelids fluttering, as his teeth teased the shell of my ear. The oxygen exploded out of me in the next second when he pinched my nipple between thumb and forefinger, twisting just a little before plucking gently. He repeated the move as he moved his mouth so he could speak.

"I want to push your dress up right now and sink my cock inside you."

I managed to swallow my moan, barely. "Is that a fact?"

"Yes." He lifted his head enough that we could see

each other's eyes.

Shit. I really didn't want to get my hopes up, but I was pretty sure I'd just found someone who could finally take care of me.

"We could be at a hotel in less than twenty minutes. In a room in under thirty."

I wasn't sure I could wait that long, but I'd do it if it meant I could finally have some relief.

Holding his gaze, I nodded.

He was right.

One of the beautiful things about New York City was that a hotel was within a stone's throw of just about everywhere. Especially in Manhattan.

He'd taken us to one of the boutique hotels, a glitzy little place that spoke of the glittering glamour of the 1920s. The black and white art deco was gorgeous, and I probably would have taken a lot more time to appreciate it if I hadn't been burning from the inside out.

I barely paid attention to anything as he checked us in, and even in the elevator, the only thing I really was aware of were the sliding doors before he turned and pulled me to him. One arm wrapped around my waist, settling his hand at the top of my ass.

His other hand came up and closed around my throat,

his thumb nudging my chin up. "Open."

I obeyed immediately, and a split second later, he was kissing me, filling me with a drugging, intoxicating sort of want. Not want. Need. Hunger.

Dazed, I thought *this*, this was what I'd been missing.

There was a muted beep as the doors slid open, and he pulled away. I barely had enough composure to walk alongside him as we found the room. I'd been kissed, fucked, manhandled, but I'd never had anyone affect me the way he had.

I managed to maintain that thin composure as he unlocked the door, and we moved inside. As he relocked the door, I looked around the room, checking it out. Nice, but not so opulent that it was disconcerting.

When he turned to me, I inhaled slowly. The blood rushing in a heated frenzy through my veins was making it hard to think, but thinking was still required. Things had to be said before this could go where I wanted it to go.

I took another breath and kicked off my shoes before moving over to the small bar service and taking a bottle of water.

"My name's Arik."

As I cracked the bottle open, I slid him a small smile. "Dena."

He took a step forward, and stroked a finger down my bare arm. I noticed earlier that his hands were callused, and now the roughened pads of his fingertip felt delicious against my skin.

I shivered, feeling that heated need swelling inside

74

me again. *Deal with the practicalities first, girl.* I had to admit, he was the first man who'd ever made me almost forget.

Taking a drink of water, I turned away and walked over to the bed, taking a seat on the edge before looking back at him. There was always a bit of nervousness with a new partner, adding an edge to the excitement that some people enjoyed. I actually didn't. I liked to be sure of things. I was a pretty good judge of character, but anyone who didn't have at least a bit of anxiety was either lying or an idiot.

"Are you going to go first?" I asked before I took another sip of water.

He gave me a crooked smile that made me like him even more. It was real, that smile. "My mother raised a gentleman. By all means, go ahead."

"I snapped a picture of you," I said without preamble, staring at him levelly. "It's on my phone. It's also on my cloud storage. If something happens to me, I have friends who know how to access my account."

I waited to see if he understood what I was getting at. After all, a girl couldn't be too safe, no matter what she was into.

A grin curled his lips and he nodded. "That's smart." His eyes narrowed slightly. "Although, just when were you able to get a picture of me?"

I touched my tongue to my lips. "I have my ways." With a shrug, I added, "Also, my phone has password protection. Don't try to get in it."

He continued to smile, but a look of appreciation

entered his eyes. "You really do have this all thought out." He paused for a moment, then spoke again. "Don't worry, I'm just looking for a sub for the night. I'm not some raving psycho, but I appreciate your candor. Once the night is over, can I assume you will delete the picture?"

More than once, I'd had men get pissed over my little speech. I only did it when I left a club with a stranger – and that didn't happen often – but if a guy didn't understand my need for caution, then he wasn't getting anything anyway.

"You can," I answered. I was careful not to say more than that. I would delete the picture as I said, but not right away. I'd just wait until I was secure in the knowledge that he wouldn't turn out to be a...well, a raving psycho. A friend of mine had gotten in trouble once because she'd gone to a hotel with a man she thought was nice. He stalked her for two months before the police were able to find something to arrest him for. That's why I was cautious.

"Noted." His eyes slid to the bed and back to me again. "Safety concerns? Limits?"

"You will wear a condom. For everything. If you try to do anything without one, this all stops."

"That's a rule of mine as well." Arik took another step toward me, absently raking a hand through carelessly tousled hair. The lighting in here was better than it had been in the club and I could see a that his hair was a rich, dark red.

Damn.

I wanted to tangle my hands in those dark, silken strands as he kissed me again.

I wanted his hands in *my* hair.

"I don't do humiliation." My voice was ragged, raspy now. I had to force myself to focus on the common sense things that had to come first. Ground rules. Had to set up the ground rules. "I enjoy submitting from time to time, but I'm not looking to be somebody's slave or toy. Not even for a night. I don't call *anybody* master."

His voice was low, sliding over my skin like silk.

"I think we're on the same page, Dena. Of course, I'm the one who's looking for your submission, not the other way around." His eyes narrowed thoughtfully and his tone changed. "From time to time?"

"From time to time." I didn't elaborate further, and I raised an eyebrow almost in challenge.

"Anything else?"

"No toys," I said, my brain struggling to recall the things I normally said. "I don't play with things I don't know."

That hot, sexy smile curled his lips once more, and he nodded as he came to me. For a moment, he simply stood, towering over me by more than a foot. Then, he slid his hands into my hair. That action alone fired a dozen fantasies, and as they came simmering to life, I had to fight to keep from trembling.

"What's your safe word?" He brushed his thumb over my mouth.

"Uncle." The word breathed out of me as my skin sang from his touch.

Arik's brow winged up. "Uncle?"

I gave him a sharp smile. "When I was first getting into the lifestyle, there was this guy. I was still fairly ignorant, and not all that good at picking my partners. He was one of the first. I hadn't yet figured out what I needed, and he was convinced he knew. Told me he'd have me crying uncle in no time flat." My smile flattened. "He was crying after I nearly ripped his balls off because he didn't stop."

Arik's eyes widened slightly, but he didn't move away from me.

"I picked *uncle* as my safe word after that to remind me." I bit off the rest of what I was going to say. That it was this word, no matter how caught up I got, that reminded me to always take measures to make sure I was safe.

Arik's fingertips brushed across my cheekbone, before trailing down my cheek. His voice was rough as he murmured, "I think it takes a certain kind of man to top a woman like you, Dena." His touch lingered for a moment, and then he straightened. "Fortunately, I think I'm up to the task."

I really hoped so.

He shrugged his jacket from his shoulders, then watched me as he moved on to his shirt, exposing a broad, muscled chest. When he was done, he pulled out his wallet and tucked it into his jacket, then gathered up the garments and carried them to the closet, hanging them inside. The open door obscured him for a brief moment and when he reappeared, he had removed his shoes.

Inside my boots, my toes curled. He shouldn't be allowed to be so fucking hot, standing there in only his well-tailored slacks.

He came back toward me, and I saw a flash of silver in his hand. Condoms. At least I didn't have to dig them out of my purse. He put them on the bed next to me and then turned away again. I didn't speak as he looked around the room. I had some idea of what he was doing, and when he disappeared into the bathroom for a moment, I wasn't surprised when he returned carrying a couple of long strips of cloth in his hand.

The belts from the hotel robes.

"Any problem with being bound?" He stood in front of me again, his voice dropping to that low, sexy sound that sent another blast of lust through me.

My pussy throbbed at the thought. Sometimes, bondage was about testing limits, stretching endurance, but for me, it was about everything I wanted out of tonight.

I shook my head as I peered up from under my lashes, knowing there was no way to hide the anticipation curling inside me. I was rarely one to be submissive enough to keep my eyes down, but something about Arik spoke to that primal part of me that few men had ever managed to reach.

"No problems with being bound."

"Good. Now, I'm going to have you suck my cock." Arik delivered this statement in a level voice, as though we were discussing the weather.

It made me shudder how matter-of-fact he said it. I

nodded, waiting for my next instruction.

"Open one of the condoms."

I did so, pleased to see I was able to keep my hands steady even though everything inside me was starting to quake. I knelt in front of him, taking a moment to look up at those gorgeous emerald-colored eyes again before dropping my gaze again. I couldn't stop the shiver though as he freed his belt and slowly dragged down his zipper. I was definitely getting a lesson in anticipation as he removed his pants and underwear, tossing them aside before straightening to reveal a thick, heavy shaft that made my mouth water just looking at it.

"Put it on." Still that calm, almost cool voice.

I wanted him to control me, but it would be nice to hear him struggling to control himself...because of me.

As I rolled the cool latex over him, he continued to speak.

"I don't think I'll have you take off that dress. Or those boots. I might even keep your panties on." His eyes gleamed. "What are you wearing under there? A thong? Boy shorts? A bikini?"

I swallowed hard. "Boy shorts."

"Would you like it that way, Dena?" He brushed his fingers across my hairline. "Would you like it if I fucked you while you were wearing your clothes? If I just pulled your panties aside and took you that way?"

A rush of heat and wetness escaped me, dampening the soft cotton of my panties as I made sure the condom was on snuggly, lingering a bit longer than I needed to. He just felt so good pulsing under my hand, long and hot.

I pressed my thumb against the vein on the underside. His harsh intake of breath was the only reaction he gave, but at least it was something.

He wasn't completely indifferent after all.

I closed my hand around the broad base of him and lifted my eyes to his. "Yes. I'd like that."

His eyes darkened. "Did I tell you that you could touch me yet?"

Shaking my head without looking away, I tightened my grip on his cock.

"Why are you doing it?" He sounded honestly curious.

I gave him the truth. "Maybe because I want to see what you do." Squeezing, I began to drag my hand up, then down, wishing I could feel skin instead.

"Dena." His voice was chastising, but that didn't stop me from leaning forward. Suddenly, he took a step back. "Stand up." The words were a growl.

My legs were shaky as I stood.

"Turn around."

I did it, anticipating his reaction.

Except Arik didn't do what I thought he would. Instead, he did something better. He used one of the belts to loop through my elbows, effectively restraining me. I could still move my hands to some extent, and if I tried, I could get free. I appreciated the thought behind it. I'd often done the same thing with the subs I met. It was a safety net of sorts. Security but also an escape if needed.

He turned me back around and took my shoulders, maneuvering me back until I was sitting on the bed again.

81

He studied my face and I watched as several different expressions crossed his eyes.

"You want to be punished," he said quietly.

I caught my breath. He did understand. For me, it was all about giving over that control, and that was a part of it.

He brushed a lock of hair back. "You'll get what you need later, but for now, you're going to suck my cock. And the better you do, the more inclined I will be to take good care of you."

The words sent a shiver of longing through me, and again I tightened my thighs against the ache pulsing in my cunt.

His hands threaded through my short hair.

Breath hitching in anticipation, I let him tug me forward, guiding me toward his cock. Although I knew it was necessary, a part of me resented the latex barrier between us, the taste of it against my lips as I slowly took him into my mouth. A wild part of me wished that, at some point, I'd be able to find out how he tasted for real.

I slid almost halfway and then pulled back up. He tried to nudge the head deeper, but for now, this was my show. I let it fall from between my lips before taking him in again, deeper this time.

After a few more teasing movements, a harsh growl escaped him and he widened his stance, hands tightening on my hair as he began to pump against the rhythm I'd established.

I had taken a little more than half of him now, lips stretched wide around his wide shaft, the tip butting up against the back of my throat. His hand slid around to the back of my head, gripping me firmly as the other went to his cock, marking my limit.

"How much can you take?" he asked, raising an eyebrow.

He pulled back enough for me to answer. I knew what my answer would mean, knew what he wanted. I wanted it too.

"I can take whatever you can give me."

I caught a flicker of something and then his fingers tightened in my hair.

"More," he growled, his hips surging and driving his cock in a fast pace that stole my breath.

I pushed against his hand, trying to slow things, control the pace. The need to touch him rode me hard, but when I tried to lift a hand, I couldn't. Groaning in frustration, I scraped my teeth across the sensitive underside.

He grunted, his hips jerking. "Suck me, Dena."

Instead, I tried to use my tongue to tease him.

He gripped my hair and pulled sharply. "Suck."

I did.

Hard.

He yanked me back, his eyes narrowing with a heated gaze.

"You told me to do a good job." I licked my lips and lowered my eyes to his cock. "Am I doing a good job?"

"Open that smart mouth, Dena, and I'll show you how to do a good job."

He guided it back to my mouth and slowly slid

inside. This time, the grip on my hair was so tight, I couldn't move at all. Then a hand moved down to grip my jaw in a way that took the last of my control. Need clamored inside as he began to slowly and thoroughly fuck my mouth. The first thrust took him to the back of my throat and he held there for a long second.

"Swallow me."

Fuck.

I nearly gagged before my throat relaxed enough to obey, but I didn't struggle. I knew I could take it. The hand in my hair tightened and I heard him mutter something in a harsh growl as he slipped down my throat. That calm composure was gone.

I intended to use the tricks I'd learned from some very experienced subs to make him completely lose it.

I swallowed, hummed, used everything I knew until I felt a shudder go through him.

At that moment, he seemed to grab some control back. Part of me hated to give it back, at least until he pulled away, caught me under the elbows, and pulled me to my feet. He bent his head and I thought he was going to kiss me. Instead, he pressed his lips underneath my ear, a soft gentle kiss that belied the urgency from just a few moments ago.

"I have a feeling you like to push your limits, don't you, Dena?" he asked.

"I push the limits other people set for me," I answered, surprised at how casual I sounded.

"Let's see if we can expand those limits a little."

Less than five minutes later, he'd come up with a

very inventive way to use the belts. I was bent facedown over the padded, plush ottoman, still completely clothed, but also completely helpless. The utter deliciousness of it left me feeling like I might explode at any minute. But explode in a good way.

For so many months, I'd felt like a caged animal, unable to escape the restlessness inside me. But now that I was now effectively restrained, I felt freer than I had in a very long time. It might not have made sense to a lot of people, but some of us were just wired that way.

And Arik understood that.

He knelt behind me, one hand fisted in the material of my panties and I shivered as he tugged, dragging the boy shorts upward. The garment rasped over my clitoris, rubbed against the slick folds of my pussy, and the cleft between the cheeks of my ass.

I moaned as he slid his free hand over my ass, the touch light and teasing. "I think it's time to punish you. How do you want it?"

I shivered, shaking my head. My entire body was quivering with need. It felt like everything I'd had building inside me for months was coming together all at once.

"Tell me, Dena. Tell me what you need."

I whimpered, lust clenching almost violently inside me as he spread his hand wide over my butt.

"Spank me," I said. I was half afraid he wouldn't do it. Half-afraid he would.

"Is that what you need?"

"Yes." It was halfway between a demand and a plea.

85

"If I spank you, will you be a good girl?" He kept his hand on my ass for a few more seconds.

I didn't even know how to respond to that question. Even though I had a deep need to have a man take control from time to time, I could never be a "good" submissive, a *good girl*. I sometimes fought the men who topped me, made them work for the submission they wanted. I never gave in completely, not the way most submissives did.

"You might be able to talk me into it," I finally said, need making my voice shake. "But I'm never very good at being good."

He chuckled, a dark sound that I liked...a lot.

"But I'm sure you're excellent at being bad, aren't you?"

Without waiting for an answer, he brought the flat of his hand down on the curve of my ass. It was a light blow, too light and I made a sound of sheer frustration. He repeated the gesture on the other side, equally as light. I moved as best as I could, trying to lift myself higher.

"Be still," he ordered. He shoved a hand into my hair. He pulled sharply, and hot little licks of fire radiated from my scalp. I whimpered in appreciation. I didn't get off on serious pain. But I did like that.

"Be still," he growled. "Or this stops, and you'll go back to sucking my cock until I come. I might even stand right over there where you can see me, get myself off until I come, and you'll just have to watch me."

The image of him masturbating while I watched was enough to make my heart skip a beat, but his next words did it for a different reason.

"Then, I'll order myself up a drink, and relax a bit while you stay here, and think about whether or not you're going to obey."

A harsh jolt went through my pussy at the thought, even as a snarl twisted my lips. I almost told him to try it.

But then he spanked me again. Harder.

Oh shit.

I didn't move. As much as I wanted to lift myself, arch my spine, do *something*, I fought the need and put everything I had into not moving. Into obeying.

Submitting.

Arik fell into a rhythm, each swat on my ass coming with a little more force. I began to cry out, need twisting through me as moisture gathered between my thighs.

He pulled on my panties again, the material tightening almost painfully against my clit.

There was a pause, and then he leaned over me, putting his lips against my ear.

"See...you can be good, Dena, can't you?"

The noise that came from my throat was low and wordless. But it was apparently close enough. The head of his cock prodded against me, rubbing me through the barrier of my panties. Then I felt his fingers, roughly pulling the panties to the side, exposing me. Arik's palm came down harder on my ass, more force than I was used to, right as he drove inside me, burying himself balls deep in that single thrust

It sent me screaming into the best orgasm I'd ever had.

But it wasn't over.

Even as I was still coming, he kept moving, driving straight toward another peak, riding me hard and rough, each thrust so forceful, we would've slid across the floor if he hadn't anchored me with one strong arm around my hips, the other fisted in my hair and arching my spine up.

"You're right," he spoke in my ear, his voice harsh. "You're not very good at being good, Dena. But damn if you aren't excellent at being bad."

I shuddered under the impact of his thrusts, squirming and trying to find...something. I didn't know if I was looking for a release, or a reprieve, from the inexorable, dominating possession.

"Come," he ordered. "Come for me, Dena. And maybe this time, I'll reward you for being *bad*. Would you like that?"

I groaned in response, every nerve in my body on fire.

"That's no answer."

"Ye–" I could barely speak. "Yes, dammit. Make me come, you son of a bitch."

He let go of my hair and worked a hand between me and the ottoman, unerringly seeking out my clitoris. Slow, deliberate strokes, and I was flying into another bone-melting orgasm.

I thought that first orgasm had been the best of my life. I was wrong.

# Chapter 9

## *Arik*

Dena wasn't what I would've called beautiful. She was delicate and elfin, almost cute, but I had a feeling she'd have words with any person who used that word to describe her. Or maybe cut their balls off.

She was also the most amazing woman I'd ever dominated. Drawing each small submission from her had been like winning a battle, and it had made everything that much more erotic.

She sighed into the pillow as I slid a hand down her back.

Her ass was still pink from the spanking I'd given her, drawing me. Sliding my way down her back, I pressed my lips to her skin as I went, feeling the warmth of it against my lips.

"Feeling okay?" I murmured. I was always careful with my subs, making sure they had what they needed, but this was the first time I wanted the answer not because I wanted to know if I could leave or to make sure I'd done a good job. I honestly wanted to make sure she was okay.

"Better than." She turned her head and cracked open one eye to look at me. The pale gray gleamed almost silver in the dim light.

Having her in bed next to me did something odd to me. I couldn't quite put my finger on it, but instead of climbing out of the bed the way I typically did after making sure my partner was fine, I was content to lie there and stroke my hand up and down her back. We were done. It was edging up on midnight. I should go. That was how this was supposed to work. Get what I need. Give what they need. Leave.

But I could see myself staying in bed beside her for another couple of hours. For the rest of the night. Waking up in the morning and rolling her onto her back. Sliding into that tight, wet, heat. A slow and lazy wake-up call. I'd like to hear those rough, raw moans again. Feel her hips lift to mine as we took our time.

But that wasn't how this worked. How *I* worked.

Rolling onto my back, I ran a hand through my hair, then scraped my nails down the shadow on my jaw. I was telling myself I needed to get my ass up and moving when the bed shifted. Slanting a look over at Dena, I saw her already easing out of bed, the elegant line of her back arching in a sleek curve as she stretched her arms over her head.

I watched as she got up, picked up her dress and panties, then headed into the bathroom. I wasn't entirely sure when I'd taken her clothes off of her. Probably some time after I untied her, but before I'd gone down on her.

Forcing her to stay still when every muscle had been quivering with pleasure had been extremely satisfying.

When she came back into the bedroom, she was dressed. She bent over to pick up her boots, and that was when it hit me.

She was leaving first.

I couldn't decide how I felt about that.

"Am I going to see you again?" I surprised myself by asking the question.

She slid a look at me over her shoulder as she tugged her boots on, then shrugged before answering, "I don't know. I don't usually go to Leather and Laces. Do you know Club Privé?"

"Yeah." I couldn't help but smile. I wasn't surprised. She seemed to fit there, all sleek and elegant. She'd stood out in Leather and Laces, a highly polished diamond in a box full of cubic zirconia. "That your normal spot?"

"More often than not."

"Maybe we'll see each other there, then." The idea of meeting with her again made my heart skip a beat.

She came to me then, bent over me, pressed her lips to mine in a brief, chaste kiss. "I can't say I'd mind."

Then she slid away, leaving without a sound.

Blowing out a breath, I flung my arm over my eyes. Somehow, I knew it would take awhile to get her out of my head.

# Chapter 10

*Dena*

Today was one of those perfect days.

I got in late – or early, depending on how I wanted to look at it – and took a long, hot shower, then collapsed into my bed and slept until noon.

When I woke up, I decided the best way to spend the day could only involve Chinese food delivery and wine, followed up by finishing a book while curled up in the window seat. When I finally closed the last page, I headed into the bathroom and sank into a long, hot soak where I allowed myself to enjoy a replay of the past night.

Arik.

His name was Arik, and whether or not I ever saw him again, I knew one thing for certain. It was entirely possible to find a guy who could give me what I needed.

Last night had been *amazing*.

Arik had made all the Doms I'd been with before pale in comparison, rank amateurs at knowing how to handle me. I knew I might feel discouraged and disappointed later on when others didn't measure up, but I'd never regret what had happened last night. Finally feeling that release...

My breath shuddered into my lungs, then out as the memories pulsed, then flashed through in hot, rhythmic pants, echoing in time with my heart.

It was everything I'd ever hoped for.

*He* was everything I'd ever hoped for.

What if I never found that again?

Groaning, I slid down into the water and soaked my hair. Honeysuckle-scented water caressed my skin, and I sighed. I felt better, more relaxed, than I had in months. Maybe even longer.

And who knew when I'd get to feel like this again.

I opened my eyes. I needed to stop thinking about whether or not I'd ever have another night like last night and focus on what I did know.

Bethany had said she'd give us her decision first thing. I had the chance of a lifetime in front of me. I would've liked to pretend that I could spend the rest of the weekend relaxing, but I knew better.

I was going to think through every line and detail of my presentation.

I'd done better than Pierce had.

I wasn't thinking that out of arrogance. I knew when I was being arrogant. My parents had called me on it enough growing up for me to recognize that line. I also knew when I was being realistic. The choice should be logical. I'd presented the better argument, regardless of Bethany's differing reactions.

I also knew I was the better lawyer. I was the one who'd do better for the DA's office. I'd actually done some research on Pierce since meeting him. He wasn't a bad lawyer, really, but he wasn't exceptional either. He took short cuts, made deals when he didn't need to, failed to push when he should have, compromised when it was simply convenient. Basically, he took the easiest route possible rather than fighting for the best outcome.

There was no question how this should go.

Operative word: should.

Fighting to keep my face expressionless, I stood in front of Bethany's desk and listened to her describe the process that had led to her decision. I nodded at the right times, made the appropriate noises and managed not to say something I'd regret.

According to her, Pierce and I had both made fantastic arguments, but Pierce seemed to have a little more experience when it came to trial law.

Experience.

Like hell he did.

His entire argument had been built on smoke and subterfuge, but since he'd argued something other than divorce and child custody cases, he was the one who'd be better in front of a judge and jury.

She hadn't said it flat-out like that, but I knew what she meant.

When she finished, she gave me a guileless stare. After a long moment, she rose and came around the desk, leaning against it as she held my eyes. "You're a good lawyer, Dena. I think after a while, you could be exceptional. You just need a little more...seasoning."

What was I, a turkey?

She continued, "Right now, I need all hands on deck. If you can help with the research and legwork, it'd do me a world of good, and it can get you that much needed experience. Are you onboard?"

"Of course." I gave her a polite smile, and then nodded at Pierce before cutting around them.

He'd been given second chair.

I was relegated to gopher and glorified donut fetcher.

They might not say as much, but that's what I was doing. That behind-the scenes-shit was just that – shit. I knew what they wanted. I'd be doing a bunch of grunt work, and I'd be lucky if I made it into the gallery for any of the actual trial.

*On this one.*

I tried to console myself by saying that it was only one case. I couldn't take it personally. I was just starting out, and I knew what that meant. Just because I'd paid my dues at Webster and Steinberg didn't mean I didn't have to pay them here.

Except I had a strange feeling about this.

No, it was more than that. It was a *bad* feeling. I'd been knocked down a hundred times since I'd gotten into law school, sometimes justifiably, sometimes not. I knew the difference.

Just as I went to push through the door, Pierce called my name. I braced my shoulders, prepared for whatever crap comment he had. But when I turned to look at him, he was holding out a fat manila folder.

"This is some of the information we need pulled. Can you get to work on it? As soon as possible, please." He gave me a wide smile. "Thanks."

"Of course." I gave him a stiff smile and took the file.

I could get through it, I told myself. I'd done it before. I could do it again. Just keep my eyes on the prize.

*As soon as possible…thanks.*

Pierce's words had been echoing in my head all week, driving me bat-shit crazy. I let myself out of my so-called office and turned toward the steps, intent on finding Bethany and Pierce. They'd be holed up together, I had no doubt of that, doing all of the trial work.

I had the utmost respect for the difficulty and importance of research, as well as for those whose job it was to do it.

I just didn't want it to be my job.

I'd already made up my mind. Once I turned over the information I'd dug up, I was going to do something I hadn't ever done.

I was going to play hooky. Well, not exactly, since it was technically the end of the work day. I just wasn't going to spend today like I had the rest of the week, working late on some of the pointless shit Pierce had thought up. I had everything they needed here, but I'd already learned that it didn't matter if I thought my work was done. They'd find something else for me to do so I wasn't included in their little two-person team.

I'd had it. I'd do my work and do it well, but I was through letting Pierce be an ass.

Resolved, I strode down the hall toward Bethany's office.

There were a few paralegals and associates still here, and I saw at least one other ADA's light on, but Bethany's door was shut and her blinds drawn.

Strange.

I knew Bethany and Pierce should be there. They'd told me they needed this information.

Knocking briskly on the door, I waited.

And waited.

And waited.

And acknowledged that I was waiting on people who had likely left already without bothering to tell me.

*Assholes*, I thought sourly.

Blowing out a breath, I tried to decide what to do. Bethany locked her office when she left. I could try it, but if they were inside and I opened the door, she'd probably be pissed. And if she was gone and the door was unlocked, she'd probably be just as pissed if I went into her office when she wasn't there. But I had to do something with the files.

I'd leave them on Pierce's desk, I decided. His office was near mine and we were on the same level, so it wouldn't be the same as going into a supervisor's office. Plus, I knew he left his office unlocked since I'd gone into it yesterday to get something for him.

I headed back down to where our offices were located, trying not to let my frustration get the best of me. As I neared the door to his office, however, I stopped suddenly.

Was that...

My skin prickled.

Heat rushed up to suffuse my face.

Oh, hell.

It was.

And before I could figure out what I should do, everything shifted.

Because the rough voice I'd just heard was most definitely Pierce's.

And he'd just grunted out, "Bethany…fuck. Yeah. Just like that."

Son of a bitch.

A rush of emotion welled inside me, stronger than anything I had felt in a very long time. I still held the information that Pierce had needed in my hands, my palms growing slick with sweat while my jaw locked to keep me from doing something stupid.

Anger, disgust, a seething sort of self-righteous fury that burned away the headache residing at the base of my skull – all of them thrummed within me in a cacophony that was almost loud enough to drown out the moans coming from Pierce's office.

I didn't know what to think in that moment. All I could do was stand there. Stand there and listen as Bethany urged Pierce to fuck her harder and faster.

She was his superior. Bethany was supposed to be his boss.

While there were a whole host of ethical issues brought up by what they were doing, it wasn't even those things that were causing the anger to bubble up inside me.

Bethany had shoved me aside and given second chair to Pierce because they were involved. That's all there was to it. I was smart enough to know that I should've been given second chair. I had a lot to learn, true, but I was a better fucking lawyer.

And now I knew the truth.

But they didn't need to know that yet. I waited a few more moments and pulled my emotions under control, closed my eyes and breathed deeply. I was going to take some time and think this through, calm down.

Anything I did right now would be driven by emotion, and that wasn't the way to handle things. This wasn't some asshole in a club. This was my job. One I'd been working my whole life toward. I needed to be smart.

As much fun as it might be to call them both on it, I knew I'd be better served by moving forward with calm deliberation and making sure I was reacting for the right reasons, rather than the petty ones.

I turned and headed back to my office. I'd wait until I heard Pierce's door close before I went to give him the files. Then I was getting the hell out of here.

By the time I finally got home, it was late and I was tired. More than that, though, I was still pissed.

Part of me was so tired, I wanted to just lay down and sleep, but at the same time, I knew there was no way I'd be sleeping any time soon. I ducked into the bathroom for a quick shower, then pulled on a pair of tight leather pants and a silk tank top.

Club Privé was a little farther from my place than I would've preferred to go considering how tired I was, but I desperately needed to blow off some steam, and part of me was hoping that I might find Arik there.

A little while with him and I'd be able to forget about the lousy day. Maybe it'd even clear my head enough that I could think through the problem with Pierce and Bethany.

And if not, well, hell, I'd still have had one more night with Arik.

When I strode through the doors, I met the eyes of the woman manning the door and nodded. Arlene was in her mid-thirties, a lesbian in a committed relationship, and one of my favorite people at the club. She was built like the side of a barn, and had a face that looked like somebody had smashed it with a hammer. She was also one of the sweetest people I'd ever met, and she could scare some of the toughest looking sons of bitches I'd ever met. She could also talk people down in a blink.

That was why she handled the door. She could have been a bailiff.

I doubted Carrie would be here tonight since she was busy with wedding preparations, but that was good. I didn't want to talk to a friend.

I wanted to fuck.

Hopefully Arik.

Bodies swayed and moved to the music. Skimming the crowd, I studied the dance floor for a long time before moving off to the staircase that led up to the VIP floor. I couldn't see him.

It should've bothered me that I knew I'd be able to spot him in a crowd, but it didn't. I just wanted him.

One familiar form did catch my eye, and I paused briefly when Jack caught my eye, but that wouldn't do it tonight. I gave him a smile and turned away. Settling at the bar, I ordered a drink.

Gavin found me before I was halfway through my glass.

"You look like you've had a hell of a day."

"It's been one hell of a week." I crooked a smile at him and shook my head. I considered elaborating and then decided not to. It wasn't going to help, wasn't going to make anything any better.

"Carrie is off looking at..." Gavin frowned, looking more perplexed than normal. "Table favors and hand fans."

I grinned at him, amused. Seeing Gavin confused and thrown off his stride was something I might've paid money for at one time. He was definitely one of those men who always seemed to know what to do in any situation. "What, Gavin, don't you know your way around a doily and a jar of mints? A personalized bottle opener?"

"It's not the favors." Gavin let it go at that.

There was a shiver of fear and awe in his eyes that left me amused.

Men and weddings.

I knew beyond a doubt that he loved Carrie more than anything, but he was still freaking out a bit. Maybe it was just the planning, but it was still amusing.

Rising, I moved to the railing that faced out over the dance floor on the lower level. As Gavin moved to join me, I gave him a smile. "It won't be long until you're well and truly chained for life."

"Yeah." He nodded slowly, a glint showing in his eyes. "I can't wait."

It was just the event itself. Good.

Envy curled inside me, but I didn't let it show as I leaned over and bumped his shoulder with mine. "You're such a sap."

He snorted, then said something else, but I didn't hear him.

A tall, lean figure moving out on the dance floor had caught my eyes. He'd emerged from the shadows and I hadn't seen him. My heart skipped a beat. I steadied my breathing and mentally prepared a little exit strategy.

Those few precious seconds saved me from doing something stupid.

Arik wasn't alone.

He had a woman with him.

One I knew.

She was a regular here at the club. She was pretty and funny and nice.

She was also a submissive. More of a traditional 'yes, Sir' one.

Not like me.

As Arik led her off to the area where some of the private rooms were, my throat went tight.

I closed my hand tighter around the stem of my wine glass, and told myself that it didn't matter. We hadn't made any promises to each other.

Then why the hell did my chest hurt so badly?

**Continues in Unlawful Attraction Vol. 2**

# Unlawful Attraction - Vol. 2

# Chapter 1

## *Dena*

The words kept blurring in front of my eyes, and when the words weren't outright blurring together, my thoughts were drifting away.

None of it was adding up to a productive morning. And it sure as hell hadn't been a productive weekend.

I never should have gone to Club Privé.

Every time I started to make a little bit of progress on the background report and various witness statements I was supposed to be working on, my mind would take a little sideways trip and there I was, standing up on the VIP level, Gavin talking about...whatever he'd been talking about while I watched Arik leading the Sub down the hall to the private rooms in the back.

Even though I hadn't actually seen him take her inside one of the rooms, I might as well have. My imagination took over from there, and I could see the two of them as he closed the door behind him, walked around her, pacing the perimeter of the room, considering what he wanted to do before turning to look at her.

He'd do the same thing he'd done with me, let her go first, establish the ground rules, smiling at that pretty young thing while watching her and planning just what he'd do to her. For her.

Something twisted inside me and it took me a moment to realize what it was.

Envy.

I had no reason to be jealous. He wasn't *mine*. We'd had sex. Once. That was it.

It had been amazing sex, and yeah, I'd loved to hook up with him again, but I had no reason to be sitting behind my desk feeling like I'd caught my boyfriend cheating on me. I had no reason to spend the weekend lounging on my couch, watching shows I wasn't really seeing.

There was no reason to feel hurt or disappointed...cheated.

But she couldn't give him what he needed.

Arik could give her what she needed.

For a night.

But I knew the woman I'd seen him with.

Her name was Sabrina, and as sweet as she was, she was a hardcore submissive and with her, it didn't stop at the bedroom door.

We only knew each other casually, but Sabrina was a submissive through and through. The man who'd been her Dom for over a year had just ended their relationship, and she was already trying to find somebody to replace him.

She was barely functional outside a serious

Dominant / Submissive relationship. Carrie knew her better than I did and had given me the story a few weeks ago. Sabrina had been involved with the kind of guy who'd given Doms a bad name. When it ended, she'd forgotten what it was like to make choices and decisions on her own. He hadn't protected and cared for her. He'd used and abused her, his needs always superseding her own. His sadism hadn't been to bring her pleasure, but to please him.

She'd needed a man who made her feel safe, and she'd given herself to the worst. Now, she needed someone to help her be her own person again, but while I felt sorry for her, part of me thought she'd do better if she'd get her ass into therapy instead of coming to the club, trying to find a replacement for a man who wasn't worth it.

Yeah, Arik could give her what she needed for a night, but he wouldn't want to master somebody outside the bedroom.

He clearly didn't want anything outside the bedroom, I thought as my heart twisted in my chest.

*It's not what he needs,* a small, petty voice in the back of my head whispered. He didn't want to lead somebody's life for them, didn't want to control them. He craved a woman's submission, the thrill of it, the rush that came from that kind of trust, the sheer eroticism of it. I understood that, better than any submissive could.

*I* could give him what he needed...and more.

A voice from the doorway, followed by a knock and my name had me jolting back to attention. I blinked, staring at the cop standing just inside my door.

Heat crawled up the back of my neck, but I battled down the discomfort. "Hello, Officer Dunne. Can I help you?"

The middle aged officer had already gone completely gray. He was a short, stout man, maybe five foot four and he was wide through the chest and arms. He reminded me of an old, stunted grizzly bear. We knew each other fairly well thanks to an...altercation that had happened in court a year ago. Dunne been passing by the doors just as my client's ex-husband decided he wasn't happy about the decision the judge had handed down.

He'd lost it, plain and simple, grabbing a cane from an older man who'd been walking by. The older man toppled with a frail cry while I pushed my client behind me, somehow thinking my tiny body was going to hide her five and half feet, big-boned frame.

The man had clearly been coming after both of us, swinging the cane wildly.

But he'd never made it.

The solid, sturdy form of Officer Dunne had rammed into him and my client's ex had gone flying like he'd been hit with a battering ram. After arresting the jerk, Dunne had come over and comforted my sobbing client. Ever since then, he and I had always made a point to greet each other whenever our paths happened to cross.

Now, after a brief pause to look around, the cop stepped inside, and gestured to the door. "I'd like to talk to you, if you got a minute, Ms. Monroe."

"By all means." I put my pen down and leaned back,

relieved at being able to take my attention from the papers covering my desk. Maybe what I needed was something else to distract me for a few minutes, and then I'd be able to focus better.

Dunne came inside and shut the door, pausing again just inside to look around the office before shaking his head. "This isn't an office, Ms. Monroe. They might as well have shoved you into a coffin and been done with it. How do you even breathe?"

I gave him a wry smile. "I try not to. I'm conserving oxygen so when they do decide to bury me, I have plenty of reserves."

He laughed humorlessly and shook his head. "I ain't never seen them stick *anybody* in this box." He waited another moment and then just shook his head.

"I manage." Without wanting to, I thought about Pierce, and how I was in here because it would have been too cramped for Pierce and Bethany to have sex in this tiny, cramped space. They needed his bigger office down the hall.

"I hear you've been assigned to work with McDermott on the Mance murder case." Dunne sat in the chair across from me. "Is that right?"

"Yes." I flipped through my notes, most of them made from the few facts that Bethany had given me. She hadn't given me much of anything official which was making it hard to do my job. She'd told me all the reports were still in the process of being finished. I wondered how much of that was because she'd been a little preoccupied lately.

I gave Dunne a narrow look. "Do you know much about the case, Dunne?"

He made a non-committal gesture. "A bit. I was the first officer on scene. The prime suspect, well..." He blew out a breath.

"It sounds like an open and shut case," I said, glancing at my notes.

He shot me a look, one that made my stomach drop.

"Is that what McDermott is telling you?"

I decided to hedge a bit. I didn't like Bethany, but she was my boss. "To be honest, I'm just going by the facts I have available." I paused a moment, then added, "And there aren't many. I need to get reports together, make sure I'm familiar with the case so I can write up anything Bethany needs."

He nodded slowly, a speculative expression on his face. "My shift is wrapping up soon. I got some time, if you'd rather talk to me than read a copy of my report. And, to be honest, I'd like a word with you."

"Well, okay." I stared down at the paperwork on my desk. I'd filed forms and organized stuff, but I hadn't really done any real work. Smiling a little, I gathered up my files and locked them in my desk. "Let me go talk to Bethany. You want to meet at the coffee shop on the corner when you're off the clock?"

"It's a deal."

We moved to leave and then stopped, laughing. There wasn't enough room for us both to stand side by side at the bottleneck created by the door and filing cabinet. Dunne stepped aside to let me pass, and once we were out, I locked the door. "See you soon."

It was almost lunchtime anyway, I reasoned as I made my way to Bethany's office. I was sure Bethany would prefer I wait for the reports, and I probably would have...if Dunne hadn't come to see me. Something was up there, and after being bored out of my mind doing all this scut work, I was itching to get some answers of my own.

The light in Bethany's office was on, and I could hear her through the door, but when I knocked, she didn't answer. Irritated, I checked my watch.

I knocked again and heard a muffled, "Come–"

"Hi, Bethany, sorry to bother you," I said, already talking before I opened the door.

I stopped there.

"Shut the door!" she shouted, her face flushed.

Slowly, I reached back and nudged it shut.

"I wanted..." her voice caught, and then she continued. "You on the other side."

"You didn't mention that." I kept my voice flat. "I knocked twice and heard you say come in."

Her cheeks went an even hotter shade of red. "That wasn't what I...yes, of course." A shudder went through her body. "Of course. My apologies."

Her eyes darted around, something akin to panic on her face.

I followed her gaze, cocking my head when I found myself staring at the briefcase sitting on the floor next to the desk. A suit jacket was hanging on the chair.

The briefcase was Pierce's.

I looked at it a moment longer, then looked at the

jacket. As I raised my eyes to her face, I struggled to keep my expression blank. Her body shuddered again and I almost asked her where Pierce was, what he was working on.

But I already knew the answer. He was up under her skirt, hidden by that desk, working on getting her off.

They were enjoying a little afternoon delight. I was all for some fun and games, but they were dumping buckets of work on me, not getting done the things she needed to do. I'd even overheard her this morning foisting a case off on another DA earlier, claiming her workload and training her new ADAs was just too much. Maybe she was training. Just not this ADA.

And I was pretty sure what she was training Pierce to do wasn't anything I wanted to learn.

I gestured back over my shoulder. "A friend of mine with NYPD is going to help me with something regarding the case. I just wanted to give you a heads-up. I'm heading out."

I turned to go.

"Dena."

I really didn't like her saying my name when Pierce was doing who knew what under there.

"I've got this," I said easily. "You go back to...whatever you were doing." I didn't look at her as I spoke. "Maybe I should lock this."

I glanced at her, catching a glimpse of her face growing even more red. She was speaking when I shut the now-locked door, but I tuned her out.

How did that woman get anything done if she was

112

that caught up in Pierce and getting laid?
  Oh, wait. That's why I was there.

# Chapter 2

## *Arik*

A headache pulsed behind my eyes and I hadn't slept worth shit.

If I didn't get some serious sleep, and soon, I wouldn't be worth much of anything for my clients, and it wasn't just Leayna I needed to worry about.

Granted, the petty thugs who had "requested" my services probably would've benefited from doing some time behind bars, and taking some of those anger management courses. The world wouldn't suffer if any of them were found guilty and served out the sentences they had rightfully earned.

I wouldn't let that happen, though. My job was to offer a defense, no matter who my client was. I wasn't at a place where I could be choosy about who I defended. So I had to get through the day.

I had to stop thinking about Dena every ten minutes.

I had to focus past the headache and finish the motions I was putting together for–

The door flung open.

Bethany McDermott stood there, cheeks flushed while her shoulders rose and fell in a ragged rhythm.

Well, now there was one less thing I didn't need to follow up on. Clearly, she'd been notified about my motion to have her removed from the case.

"Ms. McDermott, what a nice surprise. How are you doing today?" I didn't bother asking what she was doing in my office. Or if she'd forgotten how to knock. Bethany could bulldoze just about anybody, and I knew she got off doing it. I had a feeling one of the reasons she'd fixated on me had to do with the fact that I didn't get bulldozed. Not by her. Not by anyone.

I refused to think of the petite submissive who'd pretty much done just that.

"You son of a bitch," she said, her voice low. Striding forward, she stopped in front of my desk, shoulders rising and falling, breasts straining the decency of the lace camisole she wore. She hadn't buttoned her jacket up, and I had a feeling that was intentional.

Whether or not she was aware of the audience gathering behind her, I didn't know. If she was, she didn't let that stop her.

Slamming her hands down on my desk, she said it again. "You son of a bitch."

"I'll have you know, my mother is a very nice woman." I gave her a tight smile, knowing it'd just piss her off even more. I kept my voice even so that the people gathering would have no doubt who was losing control here. "I don't appreciate having you talk about her

115

like that."

"Do you know who I just heard from?" She practically spat out each word.

"I'm going to assume it wasn't my mother." I could see a darker flush creeping up her neck as I continued, "If you had, you would've realized I was right. She's a very pleasant lady."

Bethany slashed a hand through the air. "I don't give a damn about your mother, you bastard."

I couldn't resist. "My parents were married."

"Shut up!" she shrieked. Her eyes narrowed and she leaned on my desk, giving me an unwanted eyeful of her cleavage. "You arrogant ass! How in the hell did you possibly think the judge would take you seriously? Did you really think he was going to buy that I have some sort of personal vendetta against you? What were you thinking, trying to have me to knock this case, Arik?!"

From over her shoulder, I could tell that our audience had grown, and now they were edging closer to the door. I ignored them, keeping my focus on Bethany's face. Once I got statements from all of them, I'd present them to the judge as proof.

"I was thinking, Ms. McDermott, about the fact that even though you were only assigned the case a few days ago, you've already come perilously close to violating all sorts of ethical issues." Lifting a hand, I started to tick off my fingers. "You interfered while I was still conversing with my client."

She flicked a hand dismissively.

I ticked another finger. "You pushed two other cases

116

off the docket to get Ms. Mance before a judge for her bail hearing."

"Are you complaining about that? He actually gave her bail." She still looked pissed over that.

"Oh, no. I'm not complaining." As a matter of fact, I even chuckled a little, just remembering the look on her face when the judge had agreed Leayna Mance wasn't a flight risk. I ticked down another finger. "Then there's the fact that I hadn't been made aware of the schedule change until it was practically time."

"I was told you'd be contacted." She lifted a shoulder, studying her nails.

"Really? That's odd, because the clerks I talked to said that you'd assured them you already had plans to see me, said you'd told them you would advise me of the schedule change." I had signed statements from them, even though they'd taken a little finagling to get.

"What are you implying?" There was a snarl quivering on her lips.

As I rose, it fell away. Slowly, I leaned forward, hands braced on my desk. I smiled at her, and it wasn't a nice smile at all. "Ms. McDermott, I'm not implying anything. But you should know that I have a hard copy of the schedule change. I talked to those clerks and have their sworn statements. Now, if you were just trying to help us out, I appreciate that. Maybe it slipped your mind and you forgot to give me a call like you said you would. That's fine."

Eyelids flickered, but her face was otherwise impassive.

117

"But don't think I don't know how to play hardball." Lifting a shoulder in a shrug, I said, "Take a look at my track record. Just about all I play is hardball. I've had much bigger bullies than you try to push me around." I lowered my voice as if I was telling her a secret. "You don't scare me."

Something ugly moved through her eyes as she straightened and stepped away from the desk. It was gone by the time she smoothed her hand down her suit and leveled a calm smile in my direction. The coral material clung to her curves, outlining them in sleek perfection, making her look both elegant and efficient.

Her eyes, however, were empty. That expression would've been unnerving, if I hadn't known lawyers like her.

I'd done my homework on her after my first encounter, and it hadn't taken me long to figure her out. She didn't give a damn about the law or justice. She wasn't there to put away the guilty. She was just there because she cared about winning. Nothing else mattered. Not guilt or innocence. Just a win.

"You should know that your motion to have me removed from the case was dismissed." Her composure restored, she adjusted the gold pin on her lapel. She checked her cuffs and then smiled at me. "I'll be sure to pass along your *concerns* to my boss and let him know you are attempting to smear the office of the district attorney. That might not go over too well with your new boss."

I laughed. "If you're trying to intimidate me, you're

gonna have to do better than that. I don't give a damn what the office of the district attorney thinks. I'm not interested in playing politics. I only care about doing the best job I can for my client. As far as I'm concerned, having an incompetent lawyer handling the prosecution isn't the best thing for anybody."

Her nostrils flared, but she didn't say anything.

I dropped back down into my seat and gestured to the door. "I don't think any of the partners are free, but you're welcome to leave a message for them. They have pretty tight schedules, but they might be able to get in touch with you in the next couple of weeks." I paused, then added, "Feel free to mention how you offered to go a little easier on my client, Dukowsy, if I'd share a cock...tail or two with you." I made sure to phrase it just as she had, smiling as her face went red again. "You remember that?"

Behind her, out in the hallway, there was a series of low, heated whispers. Bethany's mouth tightened, and I knew she'd finally heard them.

I nodded at the door. "The partners get pretty busy, but I think one of the administrative assistants could take a message. Just pick one, but I wouldn't recommend offering any them that cocktail thing."

She stormed out and the audience scattered in front of her.

"I understand you had a run in with one of the DAs." Sheldon stood in the office doorway, smoothing down his tie, and not bothering to hide his smile. "My administrative assistant told me that she didn't think I had any time open this week, but I might be able to speak with her the middle of next week."

Leaning back in my chair, I studied the benign smile on his face. It was going to be interesting to see how this played out.

He arched an eyebrow and busied himself with a thorough study of his nails, the gesture so similar to Bethany's that I almost smiled.

"She also said that while I might enjoy the occasional scotch, I might wish to decline any invitation to a...cocktail."

I smothered a laugh behind a poorly disguised cough.

"Well, sir." I cleared my throat. "That would be up to you entirely. But it might be wise to decline."

"Yes, I believe it might." He pursed his lips and studied me. "While my wife might be a few years her senior, I suspect we'd be defending her if she ever got wind of any such an invite from Ms. McDermott."

I felt my lips twitch in a partial smile. "I take it that Ms. McDermott is known to like a...drink from time to time."

Sheldon gave me a cagey grin. "You didn't hear it from me." He rubbed at his chin and gave a thoughtful nod. "I'll have to be the one to talk to her, of course. She's...well, she likes to stir the pot, and I'm most suited to handling her. You did mention it might take a week for me to get back to her? Do you think I'll be free that soon?"

Recognizing the amusement in his eyes, I studied the calendar on my desk and then gave him a look. "Well, it seems to me you've got enough work to keep you busy until hell freezes over. But you know it's always a good idea to at least pretend to play nice with the DA's office."

Sheldon snorted.

"It may be. It may well be." He shook his head and then turned to go. "I'll probably try to work it in before the end of the week. Just to maintain my sanity. A phone call, that's about all I can manage. She's already left two messages for me and called my assistant twice."

Leaning back in my chair, I gave Sheldon a level look. "Do I owe you an apology?"

"Is she acting in a manner that seemed unethical to you?" He'd almost made it back to the door, but now he turned and studied me, eyes thoughtful. "Do you think you had justification in requesting to have her removed from the case?"

"Absolutely." Shrugging, I looked away from him to study the drab panoramic of the New York City skyline that had been used to decorate my office. "Can I handle it? Of course."

"Why don't you give me the run-down, and assume I'm smart enough to figure out the real answer?" Sheldon sighed.

Blowing out a breath, I nodded, and then gave him a quick, concise summary of everything that had taken place, not just about the Mance case, but between Bethany and me from the first time we met.

When I was done, the question Sheldon had for me caught me off-guard.

"Why did you go into defense instead of prosecution? It seems to me you're very much interested in having people adhere to the letter of the law."

"It's not just about the letter of the law. It's about the spirit of the law and doing what's right." I kept my fingers spread wide on the desk, even though in my mind, I was thinking about how often I'd been expected to compromise doing what was right. It'd been one of the reasons I decided to leave Chicago, truth be told. I'd never compromised the rules, but I'd been pushed. I wasn't going to do it here either.

"Well, that just makes your response to my question that much more important. You're not so naïve as to believe that all of the people we defend are innocent." Sheldon folded his arms around me and focused intense eyes on me. "So, why?"

"Because everybody is entitled to a defense." I lifted a shoulder in a shrug. "And I believe in the importance of a working system of checks and balances. There are layers to that answer, of course. Like, is a woman who's been abused her entire life until she snaps and kills her husband as guilty of murder as the man who walks into a convenience store and kills the cashier for whatever was in the register?" I paused a moment, eyeing Sheldon. He made a gesture for me to continue. "And the woman who kills the man who raped her child, doesn't she deserve more leniency, even perhaps a walk, when you compare her to the eighteen-year-old kid who decided he was going to bash in his girlfriend's skull because he found out she was cheating on him?"

A sad smile twisted Sheldon's face. "I had a feeling I was going to like you, Porter. We need balance in this practice. A couple of the partners are absolutely in it for the same reason you are. I'm one of them. A couple are very much focused on the bottom dollar. Some are in it because they believe in the letter of the law. It's good to have a balance."

He turned and took a step back into the office, his expression growing more serious than I'd seen it before.

"Now, about Ms. McDermott. I had a pro bono case where she was the prosecuting attorney. She was still new, hadn't quite had all the shine knocked off of her. But she was hungry, even then. My client wasn't guilty. Solid evidence proving his innocence came up during our investigation. Even the cops admitted that if they'd been aware, they would have focused much harder on somebody else. We eventually managed to have the guilty verdict reversed on appeal, but I'd known in my gut when I talked to him that he hadn't done anything. There are times when you just know, isn't that right, Porter?"

I just held his eyes. Waiting.

"But the key evidence that would have proved our case went missing the day before I would've presented my argument. He was found guilty. That case would've haunted me my entire life if we hadn't had a successful appeal. Even now, I think about him and the year he lost while we waited to go back to court. And then I think about the smug look she had on her face when that crucial bit of evidence was lost. Nobody can prove anything, but I still had that funny feeling."

Shit. I hadn't thought she'd go that far. There was a big difference between bending the rules a bit and breaking the damn things.

He stood and started for the door. "If she wants to talk to me or have her boss make a call, that's fine by me. But all she can do is blow hot air. I'm not worried about her. Your nose is clean, and so is your work. You don't need to worry about that, because I checked you out before I even extended you the job offer."

Before he left, he added one more thing.

"Watch your back with her, Arik. And take care of Ms. Mance. She's one of those who'll haunt you if she's found guilty. I can promise you that."

It was past eight by the time I let myself into my condo.

The place was small and sparse, nothing to make it home. Not now, and not six months from now. It had absolutely no personality at all, but it didn't bother me because I wasn't planning on staying here. Sooner or later, I'd find a place that appealed to me. The cold, icy condo with its professionally outfitted rooms had been available when I needed it, and that was why I'd taken it.

I didn't intend to buy anything permanent in a rush. When I did find a home in New York City, it would be a real home. Something I hadn't had since my dad passed five years back.

One thing this place did have going for it, however, was the balcony. After I poured myself a drink, I took that and the Chinese takeout I'd picked up, and headed outside.

I'd brought home notes and reports, but I didn't bring any of them onto the balcony with me. I needed a little bit of time away from my cases, away from the chaos and the rush.

I just needed to clear my head and relax.

I managed to clear my head...for all about five seconds, and then Dena was there.

Thoughts of her had been lurking ever since she'd walked out of that hotel room. Staring out over the multi-hued lights of the New York City skyline, I wondered if she was at Club Privé right now. I wondered if she was looking for me. If she'd make that same raw moan when another man made her come.

She hadn't been there when I'd gone the other night.

A sub had approached me, all cool elegance and demure sensuality, but the subtle sheen of confidence had faded once we'd gone inside one of the private rooms. I'd almost turned around and walked out. Unfortunately for me, I'd recognized the look in her eyes, in the way she'd bit her lip and hadn't been able to meet my eyes.

She reminded me of somebody who'd been kicked too many times, and one more blow would end her.

I wasn't into this lifestyle to be anybody's therapist, but that didn't mean I shouldn't have paid more attention.

We hadn't had sex.

I had bound her, making the restraints tighter than I usually did. I'd spanked her, taking her into the subspace, that blissful zone where she'd found something more than release.

When she'd come back down and I freed her, she'd crawled to me, rubbed her cheek against my thigh. I'd felt nothing.

She hadn't done anything wrong really, but there was just nothing there. I'd left her alone in the room after stroking her hair for a few minutes so she'd known I wasn't mad at her.

Dena hadn't been there when I left either, and I'd been glad for it.

I thought about going back to the club again, but if I didn't see her, I didn't know if I'd be stupid like I had been before, or smart enough to just have a drink and leave.

Brooding into my scotch, the takeout growing cold on the table next to me, I let my thoughts drift back to that one amazing night.

I should've gotten her phone number.

Screw the fact that it went against my rules.

I should have gotten her phone number.

I'd woken up thinking of her this morning, my hand wrapped around my cock while I'd driven my hips into the mattress.

I still had the taste of her on my lips even though it had been more than a week since I'd touched her, and now, all I could think about was having her under me again. Under me. On her knees in front of me. Bent over a table with her hands tied at the base of her spine.

Even just having her clutch at my shoulders as I pinned her up against a wall and shoved inside her hard and fast. Fuck the rest of it.

Yeah, I should have gotten her phone number, because if I didn't see her again soon, I was going to go insane.

# Chapter 3

## *Dena*

Talking with Officer Dunne was proving to be...well, enlightening.

The law was supposed to be blind and impartial, or so we're supposed to think, but sometimes, you just get a feeling about a person. Good cops, good lawyers, we were trained to listen to those gut feelings.

Dunne was a good cop, and I didn't like the way he was looking at me right now.

"I can't tell you much." Shaking my head, I spread my hands wide. "I'm sorry. I'm not even arguing the case. I'm...assisting."

The word left a bad taste in my mouth. I'd already known I'd be doing all the work and getting none of the credit. But it was worse than that.

They were letting me work blind, and that could be dangerous.

"They didn't tell you anything, did they?"

Glancing up at him over the rim of my coffee cup, I

held his eyes for a moment, and then shook my head. "No."

Shifting my attention back down to the police report, I tapped it with the tip of my left index finger. "What happened when you went to your superior and told him your report didn't match the reports filed by the detectives assigned to the case?"

Dunne looked away, his eyes grim.

"He's still 'looking into it.' My uncle and I..." Dunne shrugged. "We chewed the fat on it a while. He told me to give it time. I'm doing that. But it's rubbing me wrong."

"Your uncle? Oh, yeah. Never mind." I rolled my eyes.

Dunne's uncle was the former chief of police, now retired and enjoying his days sitting in front of the slots down in Atlantic City. Apparently, he was Midas when it came to the slot machines. He was sitting very pretty and according to Dunne, he was including three – and only three – entities in his will. Dunne, a pretty bartender by the name of Jolene, and Marlie McTierney.

I could see why he would choose Dunne to include. Dunne was a wonderful guy and if he hadn't been old enough to be my father, I just might have fallen a little in love with him.

Jolene...well, if the old guy wanted to give his heart to a cute bartender in his old age? Good for him.

Marlie, though...

The chief had been pushed into retirement some ten years ago. Dunne and I had talked about it one late night when I'd run into him at a coffee shop. I'd been dressed in a long coat that hid the leather I'd worn to Club Privé. Dunne had been dressed like a bum, apparently on stakeout. So I'd brought him a cup of coffee and sat at the bus stop a few feet away.

Dunne did some moonlighting as a private investigator. He'd entertained me more than once with some of his stories.

But the story between Marlie McTierney and his uncle wasn't a pretty one.

Her husband had been murdered by some dirty cops.

There was no other word for it.

He'd been driving home after a day of teaching. They'd lived outside the city and they'd liked to travel, so they'd dealt with the expense and hassle of having a car.

Marlie maintained that more than once, her husband had been stopped by the same two cops, several times while she'd been in the car. She'd even known who they were. One of them had a son who'd been doing just fine in school, according the cop and all his teachers. Save for one class.

The cop had insisted that Marlie's husband had tried to draw on them using an unregistered gun, and they'd ordered him out of the car, tried to disarm him. He'd gotten away and tried to run, reaching into the waistband of his pants for another gun.

Ironically, neither gun had ever been found. And every entry wound of the twelve that had gone into him, had been in his back.

Marlie had gone broke trying to find justice for him, but she'd gotten nothing. The chief of police had

131

suspended the officers. He'd believed her.

He'd also been quietly forced out within six months.

The officers hadn't even been charged, and the boy's grades had miraculously improved, so much so that he'd won a basketball scholarship somewhere down south. He'd killed himself a week after receiving the call.

A few months after that, Marlie had a son.

"Listen to your uncle," I said to Dunne, dragging my attention back to the matter at hand.

"Ms. Monroe–"

"Dena." I sipped at my steaming hot coffee and wished like hell it was something stronger, but I was stuck with coffee because my job was nowhere close to done.

"So what are you going to do, Dena?"

"Keep doing what I've been doing. Investigating and talking to witnesses. At least that witness pool has widened, right?"

But so had the list of other possible suspects.

I really wanted to know why Bethany hadn't seen fit to include in any of the reports that the defendant's former husband had ties to the mafia.

I had another long, restless night. This time, though, it wasn't dreams of Arik that haunted me. Nope, this time, I got to live-out some of the most horrific moments from documentaries I had seen about the Russian mafia. In Technicolor.

The *Russian* fucking mafia.

I was from New York. Born and bred. Stories of the mafia were almost like bedtime tales for people raised in the city, but this was something different altogether.

The various forms of mafia that had once ruled much of New York City weren't the same beasts they had once been. They were, however, far from gone, and a smart person steered clear of them. The Italians, the Irish...

The Russians...

Even thinking about them made my stomach clench uncomfortably. And now I was involved in a case that just might bring me into contact with them.

What. The. Hell.

"Cheer up," I muttered to myself. "It could be worse. You could be dealing with, I dunno, somebody from one of the Mexican cartels?" After a moment, I sighed. "Nope, can't be worse."

Somehow, less than a month into my new job, and without even arguing a single case, I'd gotten tangled up with the mob.

On my first case.

Except it wasn't even *my* case. It was Bethany's, and Pierce had second chair. I was just a gopher. Chances were, nobody would even know I existed.

That didn't help at all.

After brooding in bed for a few more minutes, I forced myself to open my eyes. I had to get out of bed.

Not because I wanted to, but because I had things to get done, and I planned to do them before I went into the office.

I didn't know if Bethany was doing something shady or she was just distracted by Pierce, but she couldn't present a case with holes big enough to drive a truck through. As much as I despised what was going on right now, I hated the idea of an innocent person in jail while the real murderer went free.

Somebody had to do their fucking job, and it might as well be me.

And I even had somebody concrete I needed to talk to.

Of course, up until yesterday when I'd talked to Dunne, I hadn't even been aware of an alternate theory to the crime. Odd that Bethany hadn't seen fit to tell me about it.

The report Dunne had filed said that the late Mr. Mance had been involved with someone who had known ties to Russian organized crime, both prior to the marriage as well as after the marriage. There was no clarification on just what that relationship had been, but I didn't think that was really necessary. A man married to a woman while involved in a homosexual relationship was less surprising to me than a lot of other options.

Of course they'd been fucking. Dunne had been doing follow-up since then and had found enough receipts to support the theory. Except he wasn't a detective, so he'd had to turn over that information to the pair who were working the case. And they didn't seem to care.

134

While it did offer an alternate suspect for the murder, it also gave a nice motive for the widow. Money was a good motive.

Sex was better.

Eyelids closing, I slid my hand down my belly until my fingers brushed through the thin layer of curls between my thighs. Last night had been the first time I hadn't dreamt about Arik since we first met. But it wasn't the relief I'd thought it would be. I would've rather had those dreams than the half-formed ones where I'd come home to find somebody I didn't know sitting at my kitchen table, waiting for me.

I needed to forget.

A hiss escaped my teeth as I found the wet heat. Just thinking about Arik had made me ready. But I didn't want to be ready for my fingers.

I wanted him.

Here.

Between my thighs.

Inside me.

Just those few thoughts managed to push back the anxiety I'd been feeling since I'd woken up. Circling my clit, I gave in to the tantalizing promise of his memory.

The climax was short and bittersweet, but when I climbed out of bed, my head was clearer.

I could work now.

Some people laughed about the idea of sex being restorative. Clearly, they'd never had really, really good sex.

Or at least the memory of it.

The strip joint wasn't disgusting.

It was actually about three steps below that.

How those girls shimmying and swaying around the miniscule stage could bear to take their clothes off in here...I hadn't even wanted to step inside. I was no prude, but all of this made my skin crawl.

None of the women paid me any attention, but that was fine. I didn't need to talk to them. They didn't need to pretend they hadn't seen me. We could all happily ignore each other, and I'd leave some money with the guy at the door for any inconvenience I caused them. He looked like the kind of guy who actually looked out for the girls. So they'd get an extra twenty a piece tonight...I hoped.

It made me feel a little better, but I wasn't going to feel really good until I stripped out of my clothes, burned them, and then scrubbed for about thirty minutes. Maybe with bleach. And perhaps some sulfuric acid.

At least one thing seemed to be going in my favor. The man I needed to find wasn't exactly hiding.

He sat, staring drunkenly up at a young blonde who was probably barely sixteen. A part of me wanted to go outside and call the cops, get this place shut down. But I knew she'd run. Her and any other girls here trying to hide. Which I assumed was most of them.

I mentally blew out a sigh and noted her face. I'd think about her later. Runaways were common in New York. It always bothered me, but it'd gotten worse since I started on my path to be a lawyer. I wanted to rescue them all.

Some of the lucky ones ended up stripping. That was a sad fact since the unlucky ones ended up turning tricks until the life killed them in one way or another.

When the guy I was eying reached out a hand toward the girl, I started forward, disgust and loathing boiling up my throat. Somebody else cut me off first though, and irritation had a cutting remark leaping to my lips.

I stopped, however, as the bouncer from the door caught the man's wrist and gave it a savage jerk that made me wince involuntarily.

"Duggar, you remember what I said I'd do if I caught you trying to paw one of my girls again?" The bouncer spoke in a calm, easy tone as he manhandled the skinnier man away from his spot.

"Hey, hey, hey!" Duggar yelped and swore, trying to wiggle his way free as the bouncer dragged him toward the door.

Shit.

This was going to hell in a hand-basket. I needed to talk to that guy, but if the bouncer threw him out, he could vanish before I could get to him. I tried to cut around the man in front of me, but it seemed he had the same plan in mind.

"Look, man, I didn't mean nothing! I didn't do nothing!" Duggar was flailing now, all arms and legs.

"Yeah, that's what they all say," I muttered, disgusted.

My human barrier stopped abruptly and I crashed into him.

Jerking away, I snapped, "Hey, watch it!"

He turned, and all the noise, the bouncer's voice...all of that faded as the tall, muscular man in front of me faced me.

"Son of a bitch," I breathed.

Arik stared at me.

The man on the floor shouted. Somebody else swore.

Under any other circumstances, I might've been curious as to what was going on, but in that moment, Arik's mouth caught mine, and everything else no longer mattered.

# Chapter 4

## *Dena*

His fingers raked through my hair.

The rocking, pulsing beat of the music. The strobe lights. The disturbance going on just a few feet away.

It was nothing more than background noise even as Arik raised his head. My eyes opened and I looked away, not wanting to see those emerald green eyes.

"Dena?" His breath was hot against my skin.

Backing away, I pressed a hand to his chest. "Not so fast."

"Fine." The smile that canted up one corner of his mouth was so devilish and hot, my knees practically turned to jelly. "We could go nice and slow. I can call the office. No one will think twice if I take some time off."

Rolling my eyes, I turned on my heel, but it was too late. The man I needed to talk to was gone. Shit. Now I had to track him down. The bouncer. He'd known the guy's name. He might know where to find him.

All the while, there was a voice in my head screaming at me to forget chasing after some maybe witness who might be able to give me something for Bethany's case. The hottest, sexiest man I'd ever met, the only man who'd ever been able to hit all those right notes...he was here. And he wanted me.

Yeah, and last week, he clearly wanted another woman.

Stiffening my spine, I reminded myself of the plain, simple facts. We hadn't made any commitment or promises between the two of us.

And he'd already been with another woman.

A series of flickers passed across Arik's face, as though finally realizing something wasn't quite right.

"How is Sabrina?"

Son of a bitch. Had I really just said that?

The words had come out before I could stop them. Blood rushed to my face as I realized how terrible it sounded.

Arik's eyes narrowed, and then slowly, the tension faded from his face and he smiled. It was a sad smile, though, tinged with a bit of ruefulness.

Damn. It was the exact opposite of the reaction I'd been expecting.

"I went there looking for you, you know." He dipped his head, and brushed his lips across my cheek. "I couldn't get you out of my head. I only went with her to stop thinking about you."

My heart lurched up into the general area of my throat.

His lips moved to my ear. "It didn't work."

Things twisted low inside me.

His hand came up and cupped the back of my neck, tugging me in closer. "Call me an ass if you want, but I haven't been able to stop thinking about you."

I wanted to be pissed at him, but what he said...Damn him.

"Dena?"

"You're an ass." I turned my face toward his as I made my decision. "Now shut up and kiss me."

For a Dom, he actually followed directions well.

Some twenty minutes later, my hands tucked inside the shallow pockets of my blazer jacket to hide their trembling, I gave Arik a cool smile.

"Think you can find it?"

I didn't have any doubt he *could* find the address I'd written down for him. But I wanted him to stop stroking his thumb over it and agree so we could get out of here. He might be willing to call off early, but the way my work had been going, I didn't have that luxury.

But I sure as hell planned to leave right on time today, just on the off chance that Arik was still interested in a couple hours.

"Out of curiosity, how many different clubs do you belong to?" he asked.

With a slow smile, I shrugged. I like keeping my options open. "That's a trade secret." I couldn't help but ask. "Will you be there or not?"

"It almost sounds like you're daring me not to come." Arik leaned in and pressed his lips to my temple. "As soon as I get there, I want you naked and waiting for me. It's all I'll be able to think about until I see you

141

again."

The luxurious old house was quite impressive, and the exclusive club it housed was even more so.

Though every member was screened with equal vigor, it catered to the dominant, with very few memberships being offered to those who weren't Doms. Everyone else who came through the door had to be with a member. I'd been here with a sub once or twice, and I doubted anyone – including the woman who'd sponsored my membership – knew that I played both sides of the coin.

I'd been met at the door and told them I was expecting a guest. I gave them his first name and a description so he could come in without me. As a member, I was allowed to bring anybody I wanted, but I had a feeling his appearance was going to cause a bit of a stir.

I hadn't brought a Dom here. Ever.

And I'd never submitted to any of the Doms here. While the members prided themselves on their discretion and acceptance, I knew that none of them would look at me the same way again.

I pushed the thought from my mind as I stepped into the bedroom I'd chosen for the evening. It'd been all I could think about at work, trying to decide if I wanted one of the dungeons or an actual bedroom. If so, which one. The club had a variety to choose from and I'd used several of them. This one seemed like a good choice.

It was luxurious but stark, no attempts to make it seem romantic or personal. The mattress was stripped down to only the fitted sheet. Granted, it was a nice ivory color and a decent thread-count, but it was still bare. There was a thick, warm quilt and pillows tucked into the chest that sat against the wall, but the bed wasn't meant for rest, as evidenced by the leather restraints on each of the corner posts. A nearby closet held hangers for clothes as well as a few...well, I couldn't exactly call them garments, but they were things to wear. Any member could take them and have it billed to them.

Once inside, I closed the door behind me and began to strip. Anxiety and anticipation twisted my stomach into knots until I couldn't tell where one ended and the other began. I wanted Arik to come, but a part of me was terrified of what would happen if he did. If I was having such a strong reaction to him now, how much worse would it be if we were together again?

He could be a drug. I saw that now. If he was truly able to give me what I needed, not just once, but over and over again, I wouldn't be able to walk away. I'd need him. Crave him.

And I wasn't sure I wanted that.

Then the door opened.

My friend Marcus stood behind Arik, but I didn't flinch or attempt to turn away. Marcus was in a very committed relationship with his Sub, Brendan, both in and out of the club. I didn't need to worry about him seeing me naked.

Marcus glanced at Arik as Arik stepped inside the room, and then looked back at me. Whatever he read on my face must've answered some question he'd had, because he nodded once and then shut the door behind Arik.

I straightened, my panties in hand, and met Arik's eyes. We held each other's gazes for a moment, and then I moved to put my panties in the closet with the rest of my clothes. As soon as I closed the closet door, Arik spoke.

"On the bed."

Turning, I moved toward the bed, feeling his eyes on me, a palpable caress that made me burn.

"What should I do to you?"

I knew it was a rhetorical question, but as I sat, I had to ask, "What do you want to do?"

"Everything."

His answer made my body go cold, then hot, every inch of me flushing, both with thoughts of the pleasure to come as well as pleasure at his desire for me. I wasn't a self-centered person, but I couldn't deny liking it when someone appreciated me.

He came toward me, stripping off his jacket and tossing it carelessly over a nearby chair. He unbuttoned the cuffs of his shirt as he walked...no, he wasn't walking. He was *stalking*, like some sort of predator.

And I was the prey.

"Just how much of *everything* are you willing to let me do, Dena?"

Mouth suddenly dry, I licked my lips. So many possibilities and I wanted him to do them all to me.

"We could..." I had to stop and clear my throat. "Start at the top and work our way to the bottom of the list."

He chuckled, a sound I could only describe as liquid sex. "Interesting you phrased it that way. Your bottom is what I was thinking about."

My heart lurched to a stop as he leaned over me, pushing his hands into my hair, twisting the strands around his fingers hard enough to hurt. Each little bite of pain made my skin burn hotter and, for the first time since I was ten, I considered growing my hair out, if only to see what he could do with it.

"My bottom." My heart thudded in my chest. I knew what he meant, or at least I thought I did. I just wanted to make sure. "You want to start at my...bottom."

"Your ass, sweetheart. From the moment I spanked you, watched your porcelain skin turn pink, I haven't been able to stop thinking about it. What else can I do that to that pretty ass? Can I fuck it? Paddle it?"

"Yes." That single word came out of me in a ragged moan, my pulse racing at the mere thought of him doing any of it. All of it.

He pushed a thumb into my mouth and I bit down, then sucked on it until he made a sound in the back of his throat.

Fuck that was hot.

145

"How rough do you want it?"

There was an edge to the question, and I knew it was more than him simply asking for my preference. He needed to know my limit. I'd asked the question before myself.

I let my eyes meet his. "Why don't you try whatever it is you want to try, and find out for yourself?"

"'Try and find out.'" He gave me a searching look as he backed away and gestured for me to stand. "You want me to push you, don't you?"

The question was musing, meant more for himself than me, but he was right. I needed him to prove that what happened before hadn't been a fluke. I needed to know that I could give him control and he would give me everything I'd been missing.

He gestured to his shirt, not taking his eyes off me. Following his direction, I went to work on unbuttoning the shirt and peeling it away, exposing his tanned skin and firm muscles.

With a flick of his eyes, he directed me to his belt. He remained quiet as I freed the button and zipper, but when I started to push down the slacks, he stopped me.

"On your knees, Dena. I've been dying to see how pretty you'd look kneeling in front of me and taking my cock."

I'd lost track of time. After kneeling and taking off his pants, Arik had instructed me to put a rubber on him. Fortunately, there'd been plenty to choose from.

Once that was done, he'd instructed me to perform oral sex – and that had been how he'd worded it, keeping his instructions almost clinical. Something about the way he'd spoken, paired with the burning heat in his eyes, had my pussy throbbing.

I'd done my job, sucking and licking until my mouth ached and the muscles in my neck screamed.

Finally, unable to take anymore, I pulled away.

Arik's fingers traced my bare shoulder. "What are you doing, Dena? Ready to cry uncle?"

I glared at him. My knees hurt and need turned me an itchy, twitchy mess. I couldn't move my hands. He'd tied them at the base of my spine not long after I'd sheathed him with a condom. I'd been working him with nothing but my mouth for who knew how long.

I gave him a defiant snarl. I'd be damned if a blow job made me use my safe word.

He ran his hand up the back of my neck and cupped the base of my skull. "Take my cock," he demanded.

Our eyes met as he dragged me back to him. His cock brushed against my lips and I knew he was waiting to see if I would say it. When I said nothing, he pushed into my mouth. Fast.

I half-gagged as he hit the back of my throat, then glared up at him. Eyes slitted, he stared down at me.

Waiting.

I didn't dare pull away, not if I wanted this to keep going. And I did want that.

He spread his legs wider and started to move, thrusting back and forth, controlling the motions of his hips while he used his thumbs and forefingers to provide support for my mouth and jaw.

I closed my eyes, let the sensations run over me. This was what I wanted, to surrender, give myself over to someone who knew how to take care of me. I shuddered, feeling my nipples grow tighter, pulsating in time with my clitoris.

A low noise came from above me and I opened my eyes, rolling them up so I could see.

His head had fallen back and his fingers flexed against my skin. His cock twitched against my tongue and his hips jerked. Then he was coming, filling the condom rather than spilling down my throat.

I resented that piece of latex, how it kept me from tasting him, and I sucked harder, barely aware of the hungry growl in my throat.

He pulled me away, and a second later, I was on my back and he was on top of me, his cock between us, sticky and wet, still in the rubber.

"You want my cum, don't you?" he asked, the words ragged as he panted against my ear. "Taste it. Swallow it."

"Yes. Damn you." My voice was hoarse, throat raw.

He laughed, kissing me thoroughly, but without the fierce need he'd had before.

I was the only one left with that.

Or so I thought.

His hands slid over my body, leaving me on fire every place he touched. My nipples were already hard when he cupped my breasts. When he leaned down, flicking his tongue across the tip of one nipple, I hissed. The hiss turned into a moan when his lips closed around it.

I writhed beneath him as he sucked. Hard. He worked my nipple as I'd worked his cock and when his hand moved down between my legs, I knew he'd find me practically dripping.

His teeth skimmed my nipple and my body jerked, only to do it again when his fingers skimmed my nearly bare pussy.

He raised his head and I almost whimpered at the loss. Only the smallest thread of steel kept me biting back the sound. He pushed himself up off of me, then grasped my hips and pulled me off the bed. He flipped me over, taking care to protect my face as my hands were still bound. He settled me on my knees, then pushed them apart even as he curled his body over my back.

"Are you empty?" Arik asked, his cock throbbing against my thigh. "Do you need something inside you? My cock?"

Somewhere in the closet, my phone rang.

Logically, I knew I needed to care about it. It was most likely Bethany, calling about something she needed me to do first thing in the morning. But I didn't care about any of that at the moment. I was off the clock.

The question Arik had just voiced summed up the

only thing I cared about right now.

"Yes," I said, panting.

I heard a ripping sound as he straightened. Then, even as I processed what he was doing, he buried himself inside me, my pussy stretching almost painfully around him. My entire body shook as muscles and nerves both protested and welcomed him at the same time, a conflict of sensation.

"Is this what you need?" he asked calmly after the sound of my wail faded.

My eyelids fluttered. "More."

I saw him reach for something on the bed. He'd put several items there at some point, whether to taunt me or promise me, I didn't know. What he picked up made my breath catch.

"What about...this?"

A moment later, something cool and wet dripped on my anus, quickly followed by the pressure of a finger. As he pushed it inside, Arik spoke again, "Is that what you want?"

My ass burned as he worked the lubricant deeper inside me.

"More," I gasped.

I could almost feel his smile as he pressed in a second finger. I gasped as he began to move, roughly working his fingers in and out of my ass as he hammered his cock into me. Every stroke stoked the fire inside me until I was burning, dying. I whimpered and arched, whimpered and moaned, a climax clamoring to be free.

And just when I was ready to explode...he stopped

moving.

I stiffened, jerking back against him, but it did no good. He pulled his fingers out of my ass and I swore, my body twitching. Then he caught my elbows and forced me up, pressing my back against his chest.

"Feel my cock?" He slid one arm around my waist to steady me, to hold me upright. "Feel how deep I am?"

"Yes..." It was a plaintive, ragged moan. There was enough of a height difference between us that I was essentially impaled on him, impossible to move.

"Now tell me you want me in your ass like that."

I shuddered, trying to twist around on his dick, but he held me tight. I wanted him, but to be honest, I wasn't sure I *could* take him like that. As it was, I felt stretched wide. Too wide.

"Dena..." he murmured my name.

Fuck. I needed him...all of him.

"Yes, please."

He didn't say anything, but I felt a slight shudder go through him.

He pressed his lips to my neck, then lowered me back down to the floor, all without pulling out of me. I shivered as I settled on my knees and his fingers slid between my ass cheeks again.

Fuck. He was adding more lubricant. This was really going to happen. I whimpered when he began to scissor his fingers, forcing me to open wider for him. I wasn't an anal virgin, but it had been a long time, so when he began to press against me, I instinctively tensed up.

The head of his dick popped past the tight ring of

151

muscle, and I took a deep breath, trying to relax even as my ass burned. I closed my eyes. Fuck.

Maybe this hadn't been the best idea.

"Push down, Dena." It was an order, not a suggestion.

I couldn't. I knew I needed to, but he was so big. Too big...

From the corner of my eye, I saw him reach for the other thing on the bed next to me. A small wooden paddle, about the size of a hairbrush and only lightly padded. Apparently, he hadn't been kidding when he said he'd been thinking about my ass for a while.

I tried to twist around as he picked it up. "Arik, wait...no. Stop!"

"That's not the magic word." His voice held a warning. "Let me in, Dena."

But I tensed up again, squeezing his cock hard enough to make him swear.

A moment later, I cried out as he brought the flat side of the paddle down on my ass. Hot pain bloomed, joining the pain already in my ass. Before it faded, he delivered another blow to the other cheek.

"Push down, sweetheart. Take my cock, or cry uncle and say you're done."

Except it wouldn't just be me who was done, I knew. *We'd* be done. He wouldn't be angry, but he'd never top me again.

Shuddering, I pressed my face to the soft cotton sheets, the breath exploding out of me as he spanked me again, alternating sides. Then he started to withdraw and I could feel his latex-sheathed cock rasping over swollen, sensitive tissues...

Another swat from the paddle.

He surged forward.

I pushed down and he went deeper.

The promise of pleasure bloomed side by side with the pain and I shuddered, fought against it, tried to accept it.

Again and again...every time I started to lock up, he used the paddle. He taunted me, teased me, until every cell in my body was screaming for release.

Then, just when I knew I couldn't take any more, that I'd have to make him stop, he grabbed my hair, and pulled me up again. It drove my weight completely down on his cock and I keened. Spots danced in front of my eyes as my body struggled to adjust.

"Do you have any idea how badly I wanted this?"

He slid one hand down my stomach until his fingers brushed my pubic bone. Against my back, his chest rose and fell in a rhythm nearly as ragged as mine.

"What?" I felt drugged, dazed, my brain struggling to process words along with everything else.

"You're so tight, sweetheart. Just like I imagined." His hands slid to my hips. "Now, watch this."

He lifted me up. Startled, I caught his hands. I had no idea when he'd freed my wrists, but I could suddenly move. And that's when I realized he'd shifted us until we were facing a mirror.

"Watch us."

He lifted me higher and my hands moved back to

lock behind his neck. I whimpered when the head stopped, caught in place by the muscles near my entrance. My feet found the floor, and then he was pulling me back down, our eyes meeting in our reflections.

"Watch," he said again.

And again.

With every thrust, he said it. And then I started to move with him, pushing down, pleasure beginning to blur the pain, the pain giving the pleasure an edge.

"That's it, sweetheart. Take me. Take it. Take it all."

Arik was muttering into my ear now, but I barely heard the words. I just felt him, like he'd told me to. Then I felt his fingers slide over to find my clit. I gasped, jerked. His fingers dropped lower, palm pressing against my clit even as his fingers pushed into my pussy.

And then I was coming.

Harder, faster than I'd ever come before.

The world went white, then black.

# Chapter 5

## *Arik*

It didn't seem right, feeling so mellow and relaxed, standing there at Leayna's door in the middle of the night. There was no getting around it though. I hadn't felt quite this good in a while. Not even after that first night with Dena. I'd been too confused then.

Now I knew we'd find each other at Club Privé soon, and all I could feel was anticipation.

I wasn't going to take another woman back to a private room again. Not after what Dena and I seemed to have going between us.

The sounds she made when she came...

Shit, I was getting hard just from the thought of it.

Yeah, we were going to hook up again. Soon.

A date, even. Yeah. I liked the idea of that, more than I probably should.

But I didn't need to be thinking about that right now. I had just managed to set my face in a somber yet comforting expression when the door opened.

It was a damn good thing, too. Leayna looked brittle. Fragile.

No, I realized suddenly. It was more than that. She looked broken.

Since her condo was a crime scene, she'd come back to the luxury high-rise where she'd lived before marrying her late husband. I'd told her it was for the best and she agreed. For a while, a friend had been subletting, but the friend had moved to France a few weeks before Mr. Mance's death, leaving Leayna a place to go. I'd hoped she'd be comfortable here, surrounded by happier memories. She needed support and comfort while all this was going on.

She was innocent. And while yes, sometimes the innocent were found guilty, more often than not, it was the guilty that went free.

There was a saying that it was better to let the guilty go free than to imprison the innocent. The system was set up to protect the innocent and punish the guilty.

It was an imperfect system, but I had to believe that it would work for her. Though that didn't exactly make things less stressful for her.

I was a damn good lawyer and Leayna was going to get my best. She believed that, or I assumed she had. Now, however, something was wrong.

Instinctively, I reached out and took one of the hands she wrapped around her middle. The part of me that craved control, that exerted control in every aspect of my life, was also driven by a need to care for people. That part of being a Dominant carried over, even when the situation wasn't sexual.

She used my hand to pull herself to me, immediately wrapping her arms around me and clinging tight. "Thank you for coming."

Shit. Taking care of people needed boundaries. Hugging was definitely crossing over the line.

"You said you needed to speak with me." I carefully disentangled myself and took a step back, keeping my hands wrapped around hers, both to keep control over her movements and to reassure her that I wasn't exactly pushing her away.

Leayna's gaze came back to mine. With a sharp, jerky nod, she confirmed what I said. Yes. She needed to speak with me, but she didn't say anything.

Okay. Mentally, I sighed, but I gave no outer reaction. I'd done this thing before. "Should we go inside?"

"No. This won't take long."

A feeling of foreboding fell over me as she squared her shoulders and took a deep breath.

In a soft, shaking voice, she said, "I've decided to plead guilty. Can you contact that woman you spoke to on Friday? She would know how to proceed, wouldn't she?"

For a split second, I was so caught off guard that she almost managed to shut the door in my face. I hadn't even realized she'd pulled away from my grasp.

Just before the door closed, I managed to slam my hand against it. Her eyes went wide. Well, wider. A good look at her face showed several things. There were dark circles under her eyes, which really wasn't surprising. She was pale, and her cheeks looked almost gaunt instead of fashionably thin.

Shit.

Her pulse slammed away in the hollow of her throat, and her pupils were so large, only the thinnest rim of grass green iris showed. Enlarged pupils, elevated heart rate. That brought several things to mind, but something told me she hadn't gotten high right after she called me and decided she'd just take the blame for whoever killed her husband.

So she was scared.

Hell, screw that.

She was *terrified*.

Keeping my voice gentle, I said, "Leayna, you're going to invite me in."

"Why?" She glared at me. She started to brush her hair back, and my gaze lingered on the trembling hand.

"Because I'm your lawyer. If you really want me to set up a guilty plea, fine. But I need to ask some questions, get some things down." With a gentle smile, I lied through my teeth. "It's just part of the job. I have to have things in order. You want me to do my job, right?"

She let me in.

That goal accomplished, I stood aside as Leayna fumbled her way through the series of locks on her door. One set was new. Brand new. As in I'd probably find the packaging in the trash. I wanted to take a step closer to study the security bolt, but I held still, watching as she checked all of the locks, and then went through the routine a second, then a third time.

Double shit.

Whatever was going on, it was serious.

Finally, she turned and faced me.

"Now, how about we go into the kitchen and make up some coffee?" I smiled in what I hoped was a reassuring way. "This could take a while."

"I don't want coffee," Leayna said, but she followed me down the hall to where I remembered the kitchen was.

Considering how she jumped at every shadow and gasped at every small noise, I wasn't actually surprised that she didn't want to be alone.

"Mind if I make some for myself?" I asked, still wearing the grin I used when I wanted a client to think I was sincere. "I think better if my hands are busy."

Actually, I didn't want her doing something stupid. That look in her eyes had me worried, and I'd had somebody do something stupid once before. The memory of a woman's blood on the floor still haunted me.

When Leayna didn't protest, I took that as a go-ahead and started for the cabinets. After nosing around a bit, however, I didn't find coffee. What I did find was tea. There was quite a bit of it and something told me that the now deceased Mr. Mance hadn't been the tea-drinker, so I pulled out enough for two cups. As Leayna fussed with the trim on her sweater, I set water to boil and looked for cups.

"Cabinet by the window," she said, her voice as distracted as the rest of her.

"Thank you."

While getting things ready, I kept up a steady stream of talk about the weather, the differences between New York and Chicago, how I was trying to decide if it was worth keeping my car. Anything to try to get her to relax.

It didn't work.

When she jumped at the shout of a dog barking somewhere outside her penthouse, I decided I needed to stop trying to get her to loosen up and just deal with the situation. I took our cups to the table and sat down across from her, grateful she'd at least stopped pacing.

"I know you didn't want coffee, but I imagine you like tea, or I wouldn't have found so much."

She managed a weak smile and accepted the cup, taking a small sip.

"I couldn't find any sugar," I said.

Leayna looked away, a distracted, distant fear returning to her eyes. "I detoxed from sugar a few months ago. It's all the rage, you know? Stop the sugar. You'll live longer, have more energy, look better, feel better..."

She laughed, the sound harsh and bitter enough to make me wince. Fortunately, she didn't seem to notice.

"So that's what I did. I detoxed from sugar. I missed my candy bars, but I thought maybe if I looked younger, felt better..." Her gaze came to mine. "I had a boob job and a tummy tuck. I fucking gave up chocolate, thinking it would make a difference! That he'd love me!"

Abruptly, she stood. It caught me off-guard but I jumped up, catching her arms before she could start pacing again.

160

"Calm down, Leayna. Just tell me what the problem is. I can help."

"Get me a damn candy bar!" she half-shouted, eyes glistening with tears. "I gave up *everything* for him and he was going to leave me! He didn't...he didn't want me. He didn't love me. And now he's gone and if I don't..."

Her voice broke and she started to cry. She sagged suddenly, and if I hadn't caught her, she would've ended up on the floor. I managed to get her back into her chair and crouched in front of her.

I let her cry for a few minutes, but when it became clear she was going to work herself into hysterics, I knew I needed to intervene.

"I understand the need for sugar, Leayna, but I can't believe you killed him over it," I said, trying to lighten the mood.

It worked.

She laughed. It was a watery, half-hysterical laugh, but still a laugh, so I was counting that as a win.

"If I'd...if I'd just let him go, maybe..." She sniffed and looked away. "Maybe he'd still be alive. I don't know. But I'd have sugar and chocolate and nobody would be threatening to kill me too."

The moment she said the words, she froze.

I kept my voice gentle. "It's okay, Leayna. I already figured that part out." I moved out of my crouch and back into my chair.

"You..." She blinked, lowered her eyes to her lap. "You did?"

"Yes." Taking a sip of the tea, I tried not to make a

161

face. I never understood why some people liked drinking tea that tasted like flowers. After I put the cup down, I continued, "Why don't we start over, from the beginning this time?"

"And that's it." With a tight smile, Leayna pushed around the pasta noodles on her plate.

We'd called for late night take out – or, I guess, technically it was early morning now – about an hour and a half ago. It'd arrived with surprising speed, half-way through her recount of the past few days.

I hadn't interrupted, instead taking the time to eat while I listened, but now that she was done, I put down my fork and leaned forward, waiting for her to look at me.

"Why didn't you call me from the beginning?" Despite how exhausted I was, I managed to keep from sounding annoyed.

"They..." Leayna cleared her throat and sniffled. "They said they're watching the doors, the exits. Everything. If I called and it wasn't because I was pleading guilty, they'd come and...and..."

Her breath started to come in hard, shallow pants, and her eyes took on a glazed look that I didn't like.

Shit. She was having a panic attack.

162

"Leayna!"

She didn't respond. I said her name again, harder, louder, calling on every ounce of authority I used in other aspects of my life.

She jerked her head around and stared at me, the whites of her eyes showing.

"They won't come after you."

She shook her head. "You can't know that."

"No," I agreed. "But we can see what we can do to protect you." Rising, I went over to the window and stared down over the city. "You didn't know anything about your husband's involvement? Nothing about the men he was involved with?"

And, apparently, *involvement* wasn't only limited to business. Hence the reason Leayna had been doubly upset. I wondered if she'd had her suspicions, about that part of her late husband's life anyway. I couldn't see how she hadn't known.

"Scum," she muttered. "That's what they are. All of them. And no, I didn't. Not until recently." She made a disgusted sound. "Not soon enough."

I nodded slowly, my sleep-deprived brain trying to put together a plan. "Okay. I need to make some calls. I want to see if I can get you some protection."

"Protection?" Her eyes came to mine as she processed the word. "What do you mean?"

"After what you've just told me, I think your husband's ties to organized crime are what got him killed, if they didn't kill him outright," I said bluntly. "Even if you hadn't been threatened, I'd still believe your life was

163

in danger." I reached out and put a hand over hers. "Let me protect you."

# Chapter 6

## *Dena*

"What's this?"

Bethany looked up from the report I handed her.

I'd given her Dunne's original report, or rather, a copy of it since the real one had apparently been mysteriously misplaced. Fortunately, Dunne made copies of everything, and he'd given me one early this morning. His superior was doing some digging of his own, now that several interested parties had expressed questions about how Dunne's filed report had sounded too much like the detectives' reports.

"It's the original report from the night Leayna Mance was arrested," I repeated what I'd already told Bethany. "From the first officer on scene. It doesn't match up with the report that was eventually filed. This one says that Mrs. Mance had called her defense attorney before the police arrived, but when Officer Dunne arrived, she willingly told him that she'd touched her husband's body to see if he was breathing. He also wrote that the blood on her clothes supported her statement. He said she was shaken and upset, appearing devastated by what happened."

Bethany sighed. "What's your point?"

I bit back the sharp retort I wanted to give her. "Every other report from that night states that Mrs. Mance's clothes were bloody and that she refused to give a statement. That she didn't appear to be in any distress and only wanted to know when she could go to sleep. And the clothes she was wearing that night aren't in evidence."

Bethany's eyes narrowed. "Listen to me, Ms. Monroe, you can't let this woman get to you. She's a manipulator of the highest order. A trophy wife who couldn't handle that she was about to be traded in for a newer model. I've dealt with her, and she thinks all she needs to do is spin a sad sob story and we'll all automatically believe her."

"Actually, I haven't spoken with her," I replied, careful to keep my tone even. "I've only spoken with Officer Dunne about how the official report we received doesn't contain a copy of his actual report. We're prosecuting a woman based, in part, off evidence and information gathered from the official report, but the information we had *isn't* completely accurate. It can't be because we've got two conflicting reports. Not to mention missing evidence."

Bethany tapped a finger on the file I'd given her. "This isn't the official report, Dena. And Officer Dunne is something of a loose cannon. Look..." She sighed and leaned in, as if she was confiding in me like we were friends or something. "You're new. I get that. You don't know how all of this works. But Dunne, he's had some problems, and with his uncle not here to clean up after him, they're getting worse. Why do you think he's still in uniform rather than behind a desk or working a shield? You can't rely on what he says without corroboration."

Bullshit.

I thought it, but knew better than to say it. Bethany could have a foul mouth sometimes, but I was trying very hard to be professional. I didn't want to give her anything she could try to use against me.

"I know Officer Dunne too." Giving her a tight smile, I put the report back into my briefcase. "I might be new to the DA's office, but I'm not new to New York, and I'm not new to law. I know plenty of cops, and I've had to have some on hand when I went to pick up a client. And sometimes I needed them when I had to bury a client because this office failed to keep an abuser behind bars."

Bethany's face went red. "Now you listen—"

"I'm afraid I can't," I said sweetly. "I have a job to do, remember? You wanted me to dig up skeletons on Mrs. Mance, anything we can use against her. Don't worry. I'll continue keeping an eye on things since you and Pierce seem so..." I raked her up and down. "*Busy.* I'll keep you posted."

Turning on my heel, I stormed out.

So much for hoping that Bethany wasn't deliberately obtuse.

Pierce was standing in the doorway of his office

when I passed.

Jerking up my chin, I glared at him. "You got something to say?"

His head jerked up, as if I'd startled him. He looked distracted, and, for the first time since I met him, he wasn't wearing that sleazy expression on his face. It almost looked like something was bothering him.

"Uh, no. No, I didn't have..." He glanced down the hall. "I have to go. I'll see you later."

I frowned as he went, but didn't bother trying to figure it out. He was probably trying to think of a new place for he and Bethany to fool around. You know, since they didn't really have anything else to do.

"It's bullshit!"

Leslie Calvin, one of my best friends, sat across from me and sipped from her water, green eyes dancing. "Come on, honey. Tell me how you really feel."

I threw my hands in the air. "The reports don't match, Leslie. At all. And then she acted like I was some..." I let my voice trail off.

What was the point in continuing to complain when it wasn't going to do any good? It was venting some of my anger, but the frustration knotting my stomach wasn't going anywhere.

When Leslie had asked if I wanted to meet for lunch, I'd told her no at first. Mostly because I was in a bitch of a mood and didn't want to take it out on her. When she pushed, I'd told her exactly that.

She'd just laughed and said, "All the more reason to meet me. You need to vent."

And had I ever. But now I was winding down, and I didn't know where to go from there. I was just glad she'd picked a place with an outdoor patio. I was way too keyed up to be inside.

Leslie's eyes narrowed and she leaned forward. "Listen to me, Dena. You're where you've always wanted to be. You aren't going to let some ignorant piece of work chase you out. If you can't make *her* listen, then you find somebody who will." Her red hair tumbled into her face as she tossed her head. Impatient, she pushed it back and fixed me with a determined look.

"But," I started to protest.

"No!" She held up a finger, the expression on her face forbidding. "Look, there's no denying why I went into law. I'm in it for the bucks." She shrugged, an unrepentant look on her face. Then she reached out and caught my hand. "And we both know why you're in it. You believe in justice, in all of it. So, here's what you're going to do. You're going to deal. You will not let her chase you off. You will not ignore this. If the reports aren't right, then somebody's fucking with things. They are messing with the justice system. You're too good a lawyer to ignore that, right?"

Huffing out a breath, I stared at her.

But the knot in my gut began to unravel, and I smiled.

"Yeah," I agreed.

"Yeah." She nodded at me, a firm smile curving her lips. "It's like you told her. You're not some novice. You know how the law works. We both do. If the police reports don't match, if evidence is missing, what does that tell you?"

Sighing, I reached for my glass of tea. "I know. I know."

"Good."

We lapsed into silence as the server brought out our food, and over our meal, we shifted to talking about small, inconsequential stuff while I mulled over the right direction to take with my work dilemma.

"So are you?"

Glancing up, I realized Leslie had asked me a question. "Am I what?"

"Seeing anybody?"

"Ah..." Arik's face leaped to mind.

Shit. Definitely didn't want to go there.

"Ohhhhh..." She beamed at me. "You are! Spill."

"There's...look." I shook my head. "I'm not dating him. It's a guy I hooked up with at the club. That's all."

I kept my voice as nonchalant as possible, but I couldn't control the hot flush creeping up my neck.

"But you're blushing over him." She sounded delighted. "You don't want that to be all there is, do you?"

"It's sex," I repeated. I took a sip of water to cool my

burning throat, trying to ignore my racing heart even as everything in me went hot and ready. All from thinking about him. "It's seriously amazing sex," I admitted. "Some of the best I've ever had, but it's still just sex."

Her eyes glittered. "Uh-huh."

# Chapter 7

## *Arik*

Grinding music, the pulse of lights as they danced over bodies moving to the rhythm...all of it wrapped around me.

And all of it blocked me from seeing the one person I'd come here hoping to find.

The first time I'd seen Dena at Club Privé had been on a Friday.

It was Friday.

Ergo, she should be here.

That was my mental reasoning, simple as it was.

Except she wasn't here.

After nearly thirty minutes of cruising around the dance floor and watching the bar on the lower level, I still hadn't seen her. Wondering if I was wasting my time, I started toward the stairwell, intending to go to the VIP section and see if that offered a different perspective.

On anything.

*Why didn't you get her phone number, genius?*

*A phone number smacks of commitment,* I told the idiot in my head. *An expectation that there was something more than the physical involved here.*

I was a lawyer. I knew how to make a logical argument, even with myself.

I hardly ever asked a woman for a number. If we bumped into each other, that was all well and good. Even the sub I'd had a semi-regular thing with back in Chicago hadn't been someone with whom I'd had phone conversations. We'd exchanged emails through private accounts, but outside of having to cancel previously-arranged engagements, we hadn't communicated. Certainly not about anything personal.

But as I worked my way through the crush of bodies, any number of men and women made their way off toward the private rooms, reminding me that I was still waiting. If I'd gotten Dena's number, the two of us could've already been in a room.

I hadn't done it though.

And I was beginning to feel like my commitment reasoning was more an excuse than a logical argument.

I wasn't commitment-phobic or anything like that. I didn't have some ugly past relationship that made me shy away from another woman. Actually, if it'd been that, it might've been better. Maybe then, at least, I could explain why I was so reluctant.

I just didn't want the commitment.

Except now, I wasn't so sure.

I wanted more with Dena, but I didn't know what that meant. Or how to handle it.

I sighed. Maybe the problem was that I didn't actually know what I wanted.

But I did know, I forced myself to admit, at least to an extent.

I wanted *her*.

I could see myself wanting to know more about her, and I already wanted more from her than I'd ever wanted from a Sub. Like a phone number. And...

Shit. I closed my eyes for a moment as the realization hit me. I didn't even know her last name.

I knew she smelled like sweetness and sin, and that she felt and tasted even better. I knew that her hair was silk under my hands, her skin satin. I knew that she liked to submit, but not all the time, and that she had a wicked, dry sense of humor.

I knew she could make me burn.

I knew she was both strong and soft.

But I didn't know her phone number or her last name.

All the things I did know were intimate details, the sort of things a lover should know, but none of it would help me find her.

I swore under my breath. I'd been convinced she'd be here, but it looked like I was wrong.

"You sound like some idiot kid with his first crush," I muttered to myself as I reached the VIP area.

I spied a relatively isolated spot and moved toward it, once more eying the crowd for Dena, looking for the one part of her petite body I thought would most likely stand out in a crowd. Her white-blonde hair.

The upper level gave me a better view, but it also made one thing clear.

Dena wasn't here.

"Back again, are you?"

At the voice, I looked up to see Gavin coming my way. He moved to join me at the railing, resting his elbows on it, his stance similar to mine.

"It would seem that way," I answered easily.

When one of the servers came by, I asked for some scotch. She named the brand I ordered last week and I nodded confirmation. As she walked away, I looked over at Gavin, curious.

"What do you do, provide them with ID cards for the VIP members along with our purchase history so they know what it is we like to drink? Flash cards, maybe?"

"I think it'd be a bad idea to give away trade secrets." He grinned.

*Trade secrets.* Dena had used the same phrase. I went back to studying the dance floor for her, as if she might've materialized in the last few seconds.

"Are you looking for somebody?" Gavin asked.

I almost shrugged the question off, but the man standing next to me was the owner. Who better to ask than him?

"Actually, yeah. I met up with a woman last week. First saw her down on the dance floor." I nodded toward it, my eyes still studying the throng of bodies. She wasn't there, but I couldn't seem to keep from searching for her.

176

"Petite, blonde hair."

"That could be any number of women. I assume she was a sub?"

From the corner of my eye, I could see him watching me, but I didn't turn toward him. Whether he could help me or not, I was going to find her. It was just a matter of when. A matter of time. A matter of patience. Normally patience wasn't much of an issue with me, but I had little when it came to Dena.

Why hadn't I gotten her phone number?

"A sub," I mused over how to answer his question.

With just about anybody else, the answer would have been simple. But *simple* described nothing about Dena. Nothing at all.

"The first time I saw her, she'd been dancing with a couple of...well, they weren't much more than boys. I imagine they thought she was a sub." I looked over at Gavin finally. "She's more complicated than that. Her name was Dena. She's about..."

I had been getting ready to give a physical description beyond petite and blonde when I saw something flicker across his eyes. It was brief, but enough. "You know her."

At that moment, the server arrived with our drinks and Gavin lapsed into silence as she delivered mine.

"Mr. Porter's is on the house tonight, Angel," he said.

"Of course." Her eyes slid to mine and she gave me a nod that was only polite. Employees were off-limits at Club Privé. Once we were alone again, Gavin tipped his glass in my direction.

"Yes," he said quietly. "I know Dena." He took a sip of his drink, seeming to mull over his words.

As the silence stretched out, a fiery, tight sensation settled in my belly. I wasn't sure I liked it.

It was jealousy. Didn't take an idiot to figure that out. Something about the way Gavin had said he knew Dena made me think he really *did* know her. And not just in passing like he knew me. He knew her for real.

And I didn't even have her damn phone number.

Gavin was stupid in love with his wife, but that wasn't particularly reassuring. In our world, it wasn't odd to be in love and still have an open relationship. For all I knew, Gavin and Carrie liked to share. The problem was, I couldn't wrap my head around it because the idea of sharing my woman with anybody else...

Shit.

My woman.

I actually thought those words. I thought them and they'd been accompanied by jealousy and possessiveness rather than panic and frustration.

Gavin's eyes narrowed and he took a step toward me.

"Dena's a close friend of mine, one of Carrie's best friends."

The knot in my stomach eased some. He hadn't said that she was part of something with him and Carrie. He'd said friend.

He continued, "I'm going to offer you some advice. Be careful with her." He paused, and then added, "I'm not going to say something stupid like keep your hands off of her. That'd be pointless considering where we are.

However, if you hurt her..."

He let the sentence trail off so I could imagine how he'd finish it. I was pretty sure I wouldn't like it no matter what.

He nodded at my drink. "Enjoy, but you're not going to find Dena here tonight. She already left."

Before he could walk away, I opened my mouth to...do what? Reply? Assure him I wasn't out to hurt anybody? I had no idea how I felt, and the words didn't want to come anyway.

Gavin cocked his eyebrow, waiting. "Is this when you tell me that she's a big girl and can take care of herself?"

I snorted. "I think you probably know that by now if you're friends with her."

We held each other's gazes for a few seconds longer, and then he turned to walk away.

I called out, "Hey, Gavin?"

He paused.

"She's a big girl. She can take care of herself."

His laugh was quick and sharp. "I think I could like you, Porter." He half-turned. "Tell you what, let me offer you some advice. You don't need to be careful with her because of me, even though I will beat your ass if you hurt her. She could cut your balls off, and you wouldn't even see the knife until you were on the floor. Dena...well, as you said. She's complicated."

I nodded at him, and he left without either of us saying another word. I didn't bother finishing my drink. She wasn't here, so there was no reason for me to be.

Next time, I told myself, I'd get her phone number.

# Chapter 8

## *Dena*

I picked up the book at the store two weeks ago, hoping I'd be able to read it soon. Now, it lay on the floor next to my chair while I stared up at the ceiling. I'd tried three times today to read it, and it hadn't been able to hold my interest for anything. I didn't think it was the book or the author, either.

My head wasn't exactly here.

My thoughts bounced back and forth from Arik to the case, making me feel like one of those little silver balls inside a pinball machine.

Arik.

The case.

Arik.

The case.

Arik.

My bitch of a boss.

Arik.

The reports, missing or hidden.

Arik.

The witness I still hadn't been able to find.

Arik.

Some sort of connection to organized crime.

Arik.

Arik.

Arik.

Swearing, I jack-knifed up into a sitting position and stared at the exposed brick on the far wall. This place was my haven, my home. I loved every square inch of it, but right now, it felt like the walls were closing in around me.

I didn't really *want* to go out, but if I didn't leave here, I was going to go insane.

The idea of hitting Club Privé seemed off-putting, yet if I was going to have a decent chance of finding Arik anywhere, it would be there. I'd gone in for about an hour last night, but hadn't had any success. A part of me couldn't help but wonder if he'd purposefully avoided the club so he didn't have to see me. I told myself that was silly, but I couldn't quite completely shut off that voice.

Rubbing my hands over my face, I tried once more to tell myself to just try to get into the book. Or maybe head up to Times Square, see what was playing in the theatre district. There were always shows. I could see a play. I hadn't been to one in forever.

That idea wasn't at all appealing.

I just continued to sit there, even though in the back of my mind, I knew what I would be doing soon.

I'd go to the club.

I'd go and try to find Arik.

It was, really, the only thing I could do. Unless I wanted to grab my vibrator and a bottle of wine and pretend. But I'd done that last night.

It hadn't helped.

"I have to ask, just who are you looking for?"

Carrie's insightful eyes cut into me and I winced, lowering my gin and tonic back to the table. "That obvious?"

"Well, gee. Let me think..." She leaned back in the booth, one arm draped along the back, her nails tapping against the cushions in time with the music coming from the dance floor. "You're wearing your best *come get me* clothes. You're wearing heels, and you hardly ever wear actual heels. It's usually those platform boots, which frankly, terrify me. You can't seem to look at me–"

"Oh, I'm looking at you, sweetie," I said with a sardonic lift of my eyebrow. "And, by the way, those boots are a lot easier to walk in than heels. You should try them. Great for cutting down the difficulties that come with height differences." I grinned at her.

Her eyes narrowed as she threw a chip at me.

"Don't waste good food." I wagged a finger at her.

"Why? You're not eating it." She countered as she gestured at the finger foods she ordered when I had

183

arrived.

Normally I ate like a horse, but I'd barely eaten anything, a combination of distraction and anxiety taking away most of my appetite.

Carrie poked a finger toward me, pulling my attention from the spread of food in front of me. "And that was going to be my next point. You're not eating."

"Maybe I'm just not hungry," I countered.

She lifted an eloquent eyebrow. "If you're not eating, you're either sick, dead or distracted. You don't look sick, and I don't think you're dead. Ergo, you're distracted."

I rolled my eyes. Sometimes being friends with lawyers sucked. "Oh, bite me."

"It's not me you want biting you. You've got a man on the brain." Carrie gave me a wicked grin. "What's his name?"

"Are you talking about another man, darling?" Gavin slid into the booth next to her, but before she could answer, he kissed her.

The kiss was passion and heat and love, and everything that made my heart ache with jealousy. I didn't have a thing for Gavin, but I did envy what they had. I wanted that. For myself.

I just hadn't realized how badly until now.

When he broke the kiss, she reached up and wiped at his mouth, sighing as she did so. "False advertisement strikes again. Is there really such a thing as smudge-proof lipstick?"

"Smudge-proof, yes," I said, smirking at them. "Eat-me-alive-proof? They haven't invented lipstick that can handle the way you two kiss each other."

Gavin grinned at me without the slightest bit of embarrassment on his face. "Hello, Dena. You're looking...delicious tonight."

"Hey!" Carrie smacked him on the arm without any real rancor. "Your appetite belongs over here."

"Oh, it is. I'm just stating a fact." He brushed another kiss across her mouth. "Eat you alive, indeed." His voice was low, intimate. Then he slanted a look back at me before things could get weird. "Were you meeting somebody?"

I didn't even have a chance to sidestep that. Carrie beat me to it. "I'm trying to drag that out of her. You interrupted. I'm betting on yes. She's dressed to kill, but I haven't gotten his name yet."

"I see." Gavin quirked a smile at me and nodded to the dance floor. "You'd probably have more luck if you got up and looked around. If who you're looking for is looking for you, they might not know to look up here. You're usually down there dancing."

"Trying to kick me out?" I sipped my drink even as I deliberated over what to do.

"Absolutely," he said without compunction. "I'm going to grope my wife under the table, and she'll be more willing to go along with it if you're not here."

"Gavin!" Carrie's face bloomed red.

"Enough said." Laughing, I got up. I wasn't sure if he was serious or not, but I did know that very little was out of the realm of possibilities.

I moved to the railing, leaving Carrie giggling behind me. I hadn't been there more than thirty seconds when a tall, muscular form caught my eye.

My heart skipped a beat as our eyes met. Caught in a criss-cross of the lights down below, he seemed to be waiting.

*He is.*

That small voice in the back of my mind settled every jumping, nervous thing inside me. *He is waiting...for me.*

I heard somebody say my name, but I didn't look back. I had only one thing on my mind.

Him.

Sliding my hand along the rail, I started down the steps. He moved toward me at the same time. A few bodies passed between us, but they didn't matter. Nothing mattered but getting to him.

I'm sure I blinked at some point between the top level and when he met me at the foot of the stairs, but I didn't remember it.

I didn't remember even walking down the stairs.

I just remembered seeing him.

And then I was kissing him.

Or he was kissing me.

His hand tangled in my hair, tugging my head back, even as his mouth came down over mine. His tongue slid across mine, learning the inside of my mouth all over again.

He didn't touch me anywhere else, and it was all I could do not to lean into him. My body was desperate for him, but I'd given up enough control simply by looking for him, coming to him. I needed to keep something for myself.

When he lifted his head, our eyes met, and all the tension inside me shifted rather than faded. Shifted into something...safe.

"I was here last night–"

"I'd hoped you'd–"

We both spoke at once, then stopped, chuckling, easing the intensity of what was between us.

"You first," Arik said as he took a couple steps to the side.

I followed automatically, moving with him into a more shadowed corner. "I came here hoping to see you last night," I said. I curled my hands into fists to keep myself from touching him.

He sighed. "I know. Gavin told me. You left just before I got here."

"Seriously? Why didn't you call?" I stopped, shaking my head. Of course. "Stupid question."

"I want your phone number." He stroked his thumb across my lower lip, leaving fire burning across my skin. "I usually don't do this, go with a sub enough times for it to matter. But I want your number."

Shit. I knew what he meant, knew that exchanging numbers meant something more was going on between us. More than either of us had ever expected.

Catching his wrist, I squeezed lightly. "That might be doable. But you do need to understand something. I'm not a *sub*." He had to get this if we were even going to attempt anything more than that one time, and I really wanted it. "I'm not expecting you to let me top you or anything, but I'm not always going to be in the mood to let you tie me up, spank me." I thought carefully about how to word the next thing I needed to say. "Sometimes you're going to just have to take me as I am or just..."

The words *find another woman* wouldn't come out. I couldn't say them.

His eyes narrowed, desire radiating off of him as he stepped into me, his body less than an inch away. "Dena, please. I'm already two steps from fucking you up against that wall. If you tell me that sometimes I'll just have to *take* you as you are, I just might look at it as a challenge."

The air rushed out of my lungs. The idea embarrassed me, but under the embarrassment was a strange, wicked delight. Nobody else would have even tempted me. I didn't do public sex.

At all.

Ever.

I wouldn't do it with Arik.

At all.

Ever.

But he tempted me all the same.

Still, I wasn't going to do it. Other things, however...

Curling my arms around his neck, I brushed my lips against his neck. "You want to go find a room?"

# Chapter 9

## *Arik*

She was wearing silver chains.

Her entire fucking dress was made up of silver chains that ran from her shoulders down to just below her ass.

When she moved, it offered glimpses of the pale flesh beneath, glimpses that made every inch of me hard and ready. If she hadn't suggested that we get a room, I wasn't sure I would've been able to control myself much longer.

A dark alcove would work.

A closet would work.

Anything that would let me get my hands on her, and my dick inside her.

She got us into a room faster than I would have been able to. She just smiled at the attendant in the back and accepted a keycard. No ID requested or anything.

I remembered my talk with Gavin from the past night.

They were friends.

And apparently that came with some serious club privileges.

This room was a step up from the ones I'd been in before. None of those had been anything to sneeze about, but this one was...palatial.

"Nice room," I said as I locked the door behind me. "We won't be spending much time appreciating what it has to offer, though."

Dena lifted an eyebrow, a puzzled expression on her face. "Oh?" She pushed her hair back, her tongue coming out to wet her lips. "Why is – mmm..."

The rest of her words were trapped under my lips. I caught her up against me and spun around, then she was trapped as well, her body under mine, pinned between me and the door. The need for her was almost overwhelming. I could feel my tenuous grasp on control slipping.

I rasped against her lips, "Fucking want you."

Hands braced on the door behind her head, I caught her plump lower lip between my teeth and tugged. It made her shudder so I did it again, then sucked it into my mouth.

The rasp of a zipper being lowered came a moment before I felt a small hand wrap around my cock. I growled, my eyes practically rolling back in my head as she dragged her hand down, then up.

Shit. If she didn't stop, I was going to embarrass myself and lose face as a Dom. I needed to get that control back.

Tearing my mouth away, I stared down at her. "I didn't say you could touch me."

"You didn't say I couldn't." She lifted her chin and stared back. "And I don't think I want to play by your rules tonight."

The way she threw it out there, like a challenge, had every dominant instinct I had rising to the fore, desperate to bring her to submission. But I remembered what she said.

She was only submissive sometimes.

She wasn't a sub.

Sometimes, she wouldn't want to play my way.

And none of this was a surprise.

She was too dominant in her own right. I'd seen that in her from the first moment I'd seen her.

And I still wanted her.

"Trying to take control already?" I whispered against her ear. I bit the fleshy lobe with enough force to make her gasp, then whimper.

"No," she said. "I'm just not going to let you have control tonight." She grinned. "Not all of it at least."

She dragged her hand up, then down, twisting her wrist as she neared the head of my cock, then stroking back down with excruciating slowness. Oh, fuck. I was driving into her hand without realizing it, ceding some of my control to seek relief from the burning in my balls.

I reached down and closed my hand over hers.

She stared at me, waiting to see what I was going to do, what I'd say.

I didn't really know how I felt about what was happening, about what she'd said, but I did know that I no way in hell was I walking away right now. I'd worry about the rest of it later.

Tightening my hand over hers, I began to pump into her fist.

"How do you get this dress off?" I wanted to come all over her.

She angled her chin to her shoulder without missing a stroke. "Hook and eye. There."

I released her hand and reached up, dealing with the fastening as she continued to move her fingers over my skin, continued to drive me closer and closer.

She let me go so the dress could fall, the chains making a soft clinking sound as they hit the ground, leaving her wonderfully naked from the waist up. Her panties were a pale ivory that almost matched her skin, the sheer fabric doing little to hide what was beneath. Her nipples were tight and hard, her small breasts perfectly perky.

"No bra," I muttered.

"No." She licked her lips and then smiled a temptress's smile. "I was hoping to find you. The chains on my skin, my nipples...I've been on edge all night."

I swore, reaching for her panties. "Stop. I want you naked."

She stopped long enough to rid herself of her underwear, then looked up at me.

"I want to come on you," I said. I didn't make it a question, but it wasn't a command either.

Her breath hitched, and then she nodded. "On me. Not inside me. Not yet."

She started to reach for my cock again, but I stopped

her with a single shake of my head. One hand braced on the door by her head, I stared into her eyes as I fisted my cock, moving slowly at first, wanting to savor the moment.

Her eyes slid down to watch, and she licked her lips, almost making me moan.

"I want your mouth on me when I do this," I said.

"Not without a condom. Not yet." She didn't look away.

"I know that." Gritting the words out, I demanded, "Just tell me you want it, too. Tell me you want to feel my cock inside you. Bare. Nothing between us."

Dena's eyes flitted to mine, her pupils wide, leaving only the thinnest circle of pale around it. "I do. Soon. If we...work out."

"No *if*," I said. "We're going...oh fuck." The last two words came out in a half-growl.

She'd slid two fingers into her mouth and then reached down to circle her left nipple, leaving it wet and gleaming. I watched her do the other one and my cock twitched in my hand.

I just might have gone to my knees for her in that moment. Then she slid those fingers down her midsection and I began to understand just how easily some men could submit. Submitting to her...that almost seemed inevitable.

When she pushed those two fingers inside her pussy, my cock jerked. Heat raced down my spine, into my stomach. My balls drew up and pleasure coursed through me as I came. Semen splashed on her belly and the back

193

of her hand, but she continued to stroke herself, staring at my hand as I fisted my cock, jerking out the rest of my climax.

When I was done, I all but tore off my shirt as I strode to the small bathroom, washing away the come before grabbing a washcloth to clean her up. When I stepped back into the bedroom, she was still leaning against the door, panting now, eyes glazed as she worked herself closer and closer to orgasm.

Without even thinking twice, I knelt down and grabbed her thighs, draping her knees over my shoulders to open her to me. She was so light that I barely registered her weight. Then again, it could've just been that I was far too enamored by what I had in front of me.

She was open now...exposed...beautiful. I licked her cunt, teasing the sensitive skin with my tongue. She gasped and writhed, but I held her hips tightly. After flicking my tongue across her clitoris, I caught it between my teeth and tugged. She keened, her head thudding back against the wall with a hollow sound.

"Come, Dena," I ordered, suddenly needing to see her come apart. "I want you to come now."

She did.

And before she even finished screaming out my name, I shifted us both, catching her behind the knees as I lowered her to the floor. I drove inside her even as I stretched over her. We both moaned at the sensation, and I started to pull back, wanting to take her harder and faster than I'd wanted anyone.

Before I started to move, however, it hit me.

194

No condom.

I stopped.

Frozen, my cock wrapped in the sweetest, tightest, wettest heat I could ever imagine, I stared down into her eyes. "Fuck, Dena..."

"Need you," she whimpered as she arched her hips and tried to work herself against me.

I grabbed her hip, fingers tightening until she stopped. "No. Not...Dena, don't. I forgot the condom."

"Hurry up, then, you son of a bitch."

I gave her a strange look as I went up on my knees, my cock throbbing painfully. "I thought you'd be mad."

"I am! I'm that close to coming again and you stopped." Her hips rolled restlessly as though she could still feel me inside her. Hell, I could still feel her wrapped around me.

Mother fucking...

Hands fumbling, I managed to take the condom from my pants pocket, tearing it open and dragging it into place before going back to her. It took less than two minutes, but I felt like it'd been an eternity since I'd been inside her.

She whimpered as I stretched back out over her, my throbbing cock brushing against her flat stomach. Both of us moaned as I worked my way back inside her clenching pussy. She was so tight, the pressure was almost painful.

"You're so close," I said with a grunt, sweat beading on my forehead with the effort of controlling myself.

"I *told* you." She arched her back, thrusting against me, her nails biting into my neck as she reached up and grabbed me. "*Need* you."

Working a hand between us, I found her clit. It was swollen, pulsing against my fingers.

I stroked it once, twice–

She came with a scream, her nails clawing at my skin.

Unable to hold back, I thrust into her again, burying myself deep. She cried out again, her voice cracking. She clung to me as I pummeled her, driving into her with all the strength I had in me, bruising her, hurting her, but she never asked me to stop, never used her safe word.

And I was pretty sure she kept coming even as I found my own release.

Perfect. She was fucking perfect.

And I was falling way too hard.

Way too fast.

It was midnight when I finally left the club.

Dena left nearly twenty minutes earlier, and judging by her somewhat reserved attitude, I think she'd picked up that something had changed between us.

"Something?" I almost punched a wall as I waited to hail a cab. There was no *something* to it. Everything had changed, even if neither of us said a word.

It was just now hitting me how much I wanted her,

196

and how much of it had to do with ways that weren't entirely sexual.

Sex was one thing, and even that hadn't been simple tonight. Fuck, I hadn't even remembered to use a condom until I was inside her. It didn't matter that I realized it right away. All it took was a few seconds for pregnancy, or worse. Granted, I knew I was clean, and Dena didn't seem like the kind who'd be involved in this lifestyle and not do regular testing. And someone with her obvious control issues would most likely be on the pill.

But it wasn't just about the consequences. It was the fact that she'd made me lose enough of myself that I'd forgotten.

And then there was how I'd gone down on her.

I had no problem performing oral sex on my partners, but the woman was the one to go down on *her* knees. Not me. I was always on top.

But Dena...I suspected she could put a man in that position easily enough.

I hadn't given her enough credit.

She hadn't even *tried* to put me on my knees.

I'd just gone there.

Maybe it was the fact that it *didn't* bother me that was making my stomach hurt.

Maybe it was everything.

Brooding, I spent the ride back to my place in silence. Dena had written her phone number down while I was in the bathroom, but when I'd come out, I'd already been in a mild state of panic, and I hadn't even looked at it.

I'd left it behind.

Now that my head was clearing, I realized I was being an asshole. Still panicking, but an asshole. So what if I didn't know how to handle this? I didn't know how to handle a lot of things, and I did them anyway. Hell, being a lawyer sort of mandated it.

That's what this was, another of those things I hadn't done before but needed to do. I had to figure out how to balance a relationship for the first time in my adult life.

"Fucking pussy," I muttered to myself.

The man sitting in the front slanted a look at me as he pulled alongside the curb in front of my building, but he didn't say anything. I swiped my card and left him a decent tip. He hadn't been the talkative type, and I hadn't wanted to talk, so it'd worked out well.

I was still kicking myself for forgetting her number, so much so that I was almost tempted to tell him to take me back to the club, but I was fooling myself. The room we'd used would have already been cleaned up, the phone number thrown away.

I'd have to wait until I saw her again.

And this time, I would do whatever was necessary to make sure I didn't leave until I knew for certain that I could contact her again.

# Chapter 10

## *Dena*

Staring into my tea, I replayed the events from the night before in my head. Over and over, trying to figure out just what I could have done to make Arik start acting weird when we'd said our good-byes. Half-way through, I made myself stop, because why in the hell did it have to be what *I* had done?

So I shifted to the circumstances.

Then I went back to being stupid and looking at what I could have done.

Something had gone wrong, that was for sure.

Even though for me, it had seemed like all sorts of things had been going right. I'd been completely and utterly satisfied...until things had turned weird.

It wasn't news to me that men and women often spoke different languages. Two of my best friends were madly in love, but it wasn't like their relationships had come easy to them. I remembered the circumstances both of them had gone through to get to where they were.

Arik and I were just...

"What are we?"

My whisper, so quiet, seemed awfully loud in my little nest. Staring out over the streets from my balcony, I wondered when I'd started to feel this alone. Yeah, I'd been alone for a while, but I'd never felt this way before.

I didn't like it.

The ringing of my phone caught me off-guard and I sighed as I reached for it. I almost ignored it when I saw who it was. The last person I wanted to talk to right now – well, next to Arik – was my boss.

I didn't want to talk to Arik until I knew if I wanted to ask for an explanation or tell him to kiss my ass, but I couldn't avoid talking to Bethany.

Bracing myself, I answered. "Dena Monroe."

Bethany didn't even bother with a greeting. "We've got a problem."

Translation – *I have a problem, and I'm about to make it yours.*

I made a face and wondered what sort of *problems* it would cause for my career if I just told Bethany that I quit. Right there. Just said the words and hung up the phone.

I'd have trouble finding another job as an ADA, that much was certain.

But it wasn't like this was turning out to be my dream job. I hadn't gotten to do anything hands on, and it wasn't like I was learning anything more than how to shove work off on other people.

"There's been some sort of mess over at Leayna

Mance's place." Bethany sounded bored.

Off in the background, I heard another voice, lower, deeper. A man. And I was pretty sure I knew who it was.

Bethany said, "A moment, Monroe."

There was a muffled, quick discussion, one that wrapped up with a sharp, *"This is how we're doing it, so just deal with it."*

I couldn't make out anything else and then Bethany was back on the line a moment later. "So here's what we're doing. I'm in the middle of something urgent and Pierce is tied up as well."

I wondered if I should read more into those words, but decided it wasn't worth the effort. "And you're calling me because...?"

"For fuck's sake, Dena. Don't act like you haven't been chomping at the bit to get involved. Here's your chance. Get over to the defendant's residence. You're going to oversee everything while the police come in and do a report. I'll text you Mance's new address. Don't fuck up."

"Why are the police–?"

But she'd hung up. Unfortunately, it hadn't been in time for me to not hear a man's guttural groan.

Disgusted, I shoved my cell phone into my pocket and braced my hands on the railing.

I'd wanted something to distract me. My less than competent boss hadn't exactly been what I'd hoped for, but it was something.

Besides, if I went over there, I could talk to the woman myself. Make sure there weren't any additional 'missing' reports.

I lingered long enough to finish my coffee, then I headed back inside. I hurried through a shower and dressed in what should pass for casual dress.

It was, after all, Sunday.

I couldn't be expected to be completely official, could I?

A security guard from the building rode up in the elevator with me, his expression a mask of cool, polite hostility. It was something that had to be taught to those who served the wealthy elite, I was sure of it. I'd been on the receiving end of it before. There was nothing off about the look, nothing that I could complain about, but I could guarantee he didn't like me.

There was something extra there, too. He *did* like the defendant. He liked a woman accused of murdering her husband better than me.

Perfect.

I almost sighed. I'd known Bethany was concerned about the character witnesses the defense was sure to call because most people liked Mrs. Mance, but I hadn't experienced it until now.

The elevator glided to a stop and the doors slid open. A low murmur of voices greeted my ears as the security guard stepped out with me.

"I can find my way. I'm sure you have other duties," I said, trying a smile.

"I'm to stay with you until you leave the building." He nodded politely. "I can wait at the door if there's a chance I'll get in your way, but I was told to stay on this floor until you're ready to leave."

I didn't bother to argue.

Instead, I just followed the commotion. "Are you friends with her?"

He didn't respond right away, but after a moment, he shook his head. "It's discouraged to have personal relationships with the residents, but I've spoken to her. There was..." He stopped, a mental debate taking place.

I stopped too, curious. I had yet to meet Leayna Mance, and I had a feeling that this would tell me as much about the woman as a conversation with her would.

Finally, he looked at me. "Two years ago, I was hit by a car. One of the other residents was drunk, and he came over the curb in his car. I couldn't get out of the way in time. I was out of work for two months. She heard about it, arranged for food delivery, and paid my rent for one of the months. We would have been evicted if she hadn't helped. We'd just had a baby."

He stopped again, but this time, he gestured toward the door in front of me. Processing what he'd told me, I moved past him and into the apartment.

My phone chimed, letting me know I had a message. I glanced down as I pulled out my phone, intending to turn it off. Bethany's name flashed across the screen, so I opened the message and read it.

*I hope to hell you're there. Defendant's house was tossed. Stay there until the cops and her lawyer are done. Take pictures if you can. She's going to use this as a ploy for sympathy. Call me ASAP when you're done.*

Irritated, I silenced my phone and shoved it into my pocket.

*If you want to know so badly, you should have crawled out from under Pierce and been here*, I thought, annoyed. I didn't get paid enough to get pulled out on a Sunday for something like this.

"Ma'am, can I help you?"

I looked up at the officer stationed next to the door, then flashed my DA's badge. "I'm with the DA's office."

"Bethany, glad you could–"

That voice.

I jerked up my head and found myself staring into a pair of all-too-familiar emerald eyes.

My voice came out a rasp, practically trapped in my throat. "What are you–?"

A pretty woman with chestnut hair appeared behind him. She had hollow cheeks and pretty green eyes. She barely glanced at me before turning to Arik. "Arik, can I...am I allowed to lie down?"

"Just a moment, Leayna, okay?" He laid a comforting hand on her shoulder.

I found myself staring at that, at the way he touched her. The protectiveness of the gesture.

As if sensing my gaze, his eyes came back to mine. "Ma'am, I'm not sure what you're doing here, but you need to leave. This is a crime scene," he said, his voice flat.

Hard.

Cold.

*Ma'am.*

He'd called me *ma'am*. Like he hadn't been deep inside me not even twelve hours ago.

Fine.

The bastard.

And then it hit me. His hand. His perfectly pressed suit. The manner in which he'd just spoken.

His eyes studied mine closely as pieces fell into place.

*Ma'am.*

*Yeah, fine. We'll go with that,* I thought dully. Maybe he had his reasons, but that didn't mean it wasn't going to hurt.

"Again, ma'am," Arik said, taking a step toward me. He spoke a little louder, enunciating the *ma'am*. "This is a crime scene. You can't be here."

I gave him my best bitch look, pulling on the steel I'd relied on for so many years. The steel that was part of what made me a good Dom.

"Oh, I'm aware of where we are, but I'm not going anywhere."

His eyes narrowed.

"I'm with the DA's office." I put out my hand as I prepared myself for the fallout of my next sentence. "Dena Monroe, assistant district attorney. Nice to meet you."

# Unlawful Attraction - Vol. 3

# Chapter 1

## *Arik*

"Arik!"

I hadn't been inside the door more than thirty seconds before Leayna flung herself at me. I gave her a quick, reassuring hug before easing back. She would've clung to me if I'd given her the chance, but the last thing I needed at the moment was for word to get back to the ADA that something inappropriate was going on between me and my client. Granted, there wasn't, but a rumor didn't need proof to cause damage.

Tucking a handkerchief into her hand, I squeezed her shoulder as I looked around her apartment. It had been an elegant living space just a few days ago. Now, it was trashed. I felt for the woman next to me. She'd already been through so much, with her husband's murder, the arrest and false allegations.

"Thank you for coming," she said, her voice hitching a little as she struggled to bring her emotions under control.

"You were right to call me." While there was always a possibility that a considerate cop would've notified me, if she hadn't called, I might not have heard about what happened until I read about it in the paper.

Looking up, I saw an officer come around the corner, hands encased in protective latex gloves. "Officer."

He looked over. "You with the DA's office?"

"No." Frowning, I glanced over at Leayna. She paled, her throat working.

"The DA?" she whispered.

"Yeah. I just got a call from the department. Apparently, they don't trust us to do our jobs." The officer scowled. "If you're not with the DA–"

I interrupted, "I'm Arik Porter, Ms. Mance's attorney."

The frown furrowing his brow cleared and he nodded, although he clearly wasn't happy. "Going to be lousy with lawyers, then. My chief called. The DA is sending somebody out too. High profile and all."

I mentally cussed a blue streak, but kept it all inside as I nodded. Aside from being unprofessional, I didn't want to let them know I'd been caught off guard. "Alright. Is it okay if we take a look around?"

"Be my guest," he said with a shrug. "Just don't touch anything." His mouth tightened. "I've been trying to get Ms. Mance to help us determine if anything's been stolen, but..."

Leayna shivered a little. "I'm trying."

The cop didn't roll his eyes, but I was pretty sure he

wanted to. I knew Leayna needed hand holding, but she'd been through a lot. Some compassion wasn't uncalled for. I took her arm and resisted the urge to glare at the cop. Defense attorneys weren't generally well-liked as a rule, so the last thing I needed to do was antagonize him.

"Come on, Ms. Mance. Why don't you and I take a look? We'll see what we can find." Leaving the cop behind, we moved deeper into the apartment. I kept talking to her and tried to ignore the way she leaned into me. "It will be okay, Leayna. Just take a deep breath and focus on here and now. Look around, remember where things were, what you need to check on."

She managed a weak smile before nodding to the double-glass doors off to the right. "That's my study in there. It's where my important things are. If someone was coming after me, that'd be the first place they'd go."

I followed her inside and immediately got an idea of what she meant. Pieces of art were everywhere. Everything from framed photographs to what looked like might have been a couple of one-of-a-kind paintings. I didn't know anything about real art, but there was one piece that I thought I could at least identify the artist. The face was all out of proportion, the nose on the side of the head. Frowning, I looked over at Leayna. "Is that a Picasso?"

She gave me a sheepish smile, as if I'd caught her doing something childish. "I love art. I even thought I'd be an artist before I met my husband."

"And it's...is it original?"

She nodded, looking at it fondly. "It belonged to my

father. He kept it in this climate-controlled, light-controlled room where nobody ever saw it." She shook her head and I saw something real shine through the flakey trophy wife I knew. "But that's not why art's created. It's supposed to be enjoyed."

I looked around, studying the flipped over chair, the desk with its drawers ripped out. Sculptures had been knocked over, and there were pieces of glass all over the floor, glittering in the light.

"They broke things," I said softly.

"I know. Some of it...not all of it was expensive, but it was mine." She swallowed and I could see tears shining in her eyes. "I collected all kinds of art. Blown glass and..." Her voice skipped. "At least they left the paintings alone."

I started to respond, but heard voices. Glancing back over my shoulder, I said, "I think the DA is here."

I left the study, wondering why somebody would break in, but not take priceless artwork. And they hadn't destroyed it either. It was almost as if they'd chosen to wreck things that meant a lot to Leayna, but nothing that was excessively costly.

A voice caught my ears.

Female, low.

My skin prickled. Bethany McDermott was the ADA on the case, but I thought she'd foist something like this off on an underling.

"I'm with the DA's office."

"Bethany, glad you could–" The words died in my throat as I rounded the corner.

The petite blonde standing there in a tan jacket and jeans was most definitely *not* Bethany.

*Dena.* Lust hit me hard and fast.

For one split second, her pale gray eyes brightened. "What are you—?"

"Arik?"

I locked my jaw at the sound of Leayna's voice. There were too many people here for me to say any of the things I wanted to say.

Leayna angled herself into me. "Can I...am I allowed to lie down?"

"Just a moment, Leayna, okay?" I squeezed her shoulder and looked back over at Dena.

Her eyes jumped back to mine and I was suddenly overly aware of the fact that my hand was on Leayna's shoulder. In that moment, I felt like I'd been caught with my pants down, and that irritated the hell out of me. She didn't have a claim on me. And why was she here, anyway? I was working here. It was rude of her to have burst in like this, unannounced.

"Ma'am, I'm not sure what you're doing here, but you need to leave. This is a crime scene."

*Ma'am?* I knew why I said it, and it was even partially justified. We'd met a handful of times and usually it had to do with me getting her naked as quick as possible. Now, I was working.

Even so, I felt like an ass as soon as the words came out of my mouth.

Dena's lashes lowered ever so briefly over her eyes, but I caught a flicker there. Her mouth tightened.

Oh, shit.

As much as I didn't want to, I steeled myself. "Again, ma'am. This is a crime scene. You can't be here."

Something seemed to click inside her. "Oh, I'm aware of where we are, but I'm not going anywhere."

My eyes narrowed. Was she kidding me? I must have seriously misjudged her.

Her smile was almost good enough to pass for real. She took a step forward, hand out. "I'm with the DA's office. Dena Monroe, assistant district attorney. Nice to meet you."

I stared at her, her words echoing in my head.

*Dena Monroe, assistant district attorney.*

Dena.

Fuck.

Dena was an ADA.

I'd been *fucking* an ADA. And apparently one close to the case.

Shit.

Her gaze swept past me and came to rest on Leayna. Automatically, I went back to the role I was supposed to be playing, and I placed myself between Dena and my client, but she didn't try to speak to the other woman. Instead, she turned toward the officers.

"Has anything been taken?"

"Hard to say." The cop who'd been acting like a dickhead earlier jabbed a thumb toward Leayna. "She's not exactly forthcoming."

"My client is understandably upset," I said.

Dena looked around the apartment, her mouth flat.

Cushions had been overturned and slashed, pictures knocked off the walls. Several large plants that had been placed near the large palladium window had been upended, leaving dirt on the plush carpet. Dirt that was being ground into the fibers with every step the cops took.

With a derisive smirk on her face, Dena swung her head to look at Dickhead. "One couldn't possibly imagine why she might be upset, Officer...Dietz, is it?"

The other uniform, a giant brute of a fellow who looked just barely out of the academy, covered a laugh behind a clearly fake cough. Dena turned toward him and I had to cover a vicious jolt of jealousy as she smiled at him. She offered her hand and started to fire questions at him.

Deciding it would be better to focus on Leayna – and not Dena and my dick – I looked over at the slump-shouldered form of my client. Resting a hand on her arm, I asked, "Have they finished checking your room?"

She shook her head as she folded her arms around her stomach.

I worked hard to keep my voice gentle. "Okay, let's take care of that. You can't lie down until they're done, but if we take care of your room, maybe you can rest for a bit."

"Wow."

Dena came in behind me and my skin immediately felt about two sizes too small. The sound of her voice, that was all it took. The subtle scent of her shampoo or perfume or whatever it was she used came with her and my cock started to swell. This was not good.

She picked a spot about five feet off to my right, her boots crunching over the shards of glass. "Hope whatever that was wasn't something important," she said quietly.

"It was all important to my client." I knew what Dena actually meant, but I was feeling like enough of an ass to pretend that I didn't.

She was quiet for a moment and then continued along what I assumed was her original train of thought. "Seems strange to trash an apartment as classy as this, but leave things like that Picasso untouched. If you're going to do it, why not go all in? Or at least take some stuff with you."

I looked over at her. "Leayna wasn't here when the place was tossed."

"I'm not saying she was." She sounded sincere, but her eyes were cool, distant even.

Like I was a stranger.

I didn't like it.

I took a step toward her without even really thinking about it.

She took a step back, keeping the distance between us the same. "Does she have any idea who might have done this?"

Keeping my face carefully blank, I thought back to the discussion I'd had with Leayna earlier this week. Her late husband had been involved in some rather shady activities, some of which were connected to organized crime. They'd threatened her, wanting her to plead guilty to having murdered her husband. Doing this to her house seemed like a good way to send her a message without quite crossing the line enough to warrant a thorough police investigation. Whoever these guys were, they were smart, and I couldn't completely rule out the possibility that they had someone from the police or even the DA's office in their pocket.

I'd have to reconsider how I went about getting protection for Leayna. And while I was doing that, I needed to play my cards close. I didn't think Dena would be involved in something like this, but I also wouldn't have pegged her for an ADA either, so I wasn't going to trust anyone.

"I'm considering a couple angles." I kept my answer as vague as possible.

Dena slid a look at me, clearly not happy.

That made two of us.

"We're pretty much done." The newbie cop appeared in the doorway and gave us both a nod, his gaze making it clear that he was talking to Dena and not me. "Ms. Mance finished up her list of damaged items. She seems much calmer now."

I'd been with Leayna while she'd given her statement, but making a list of everything that had been broken wasn't something she'd needed a lawyer for, so when

215

she'd asked me to check something for her, I'd been all too willing to go. I'd needed a moment to get my head together.

It hadn't worked.

"I had a feeling you'd have a gentler touch than your partner, Rubens," Dena said.

Rubens blushed and I had to bite back a smart comment. It wasn't the kid's fault I was in knots.

Dena started for the door.

"Well," she said, speaking to nobody in particular. "This has been fun."

I reached for her, but she sidestepped me.

"Mr. Porter, I'm sure I'll see you around."

"Dena—"

She stopped and gave me a blank look. "It's *Ms. Monroe*," she corrected me. "And if you'll excuse me, my boss wants a full report as soon as the cops were done."

I didn't even have a chance to try to stop her from leaving, because Leayna appeared in the doorway, her eyes wide and lost.

So while the woman I wanted disappeared, I was left with the widow facing the murder charge.

# Chapter 2

## *Dena*

The entire way back to my office, thoughts circled in my head, not giving me a moment's peace. But not thoughts about the case, not about my report to Bethany.

*How had this happened?*

*Had Arik known who I was all along?*

*Had he approached me just because of where I worked?*

It seemed like an awful lot of work, especially considering it hadn't been like we'd simply bumped into each other at a coffee shop or even at a regular club. Then again, some people would do anything to win.

Once back in the safety of my coffin-sized office, I locked the door. Sinking into my seat, I closed my eyes and buried my face in my hands.

What had I done?

"Don't think about it." I said the words out loud, like that would help. I took a deep breath. Not thinking about it was one way to handle it.

If I didn't think about it, then I didn't have to deal with the pain that lurked just inside my heart.

No, I reminded myself.

It wasn't inside my heart. All we'd had was sex. Sure, it would suck if it turned out he'd been using me, but only because of how stupid I'd feel for having been taken in.

And the fact that it would mean the best sex I'd ever had would never happen again.

That was all.

"Dammit." I stood and crossed my office. It took like two steps. Sinking down into my chair, I stared at the white board I'd affixed to the wall and made myself acknowledge the truth.

I *had* to think about it.

If I tried to ignore it and it came out that Arik had known, then, well, I was fucked. My career as a prosecutor would most likely be over before it even got started.

"It could end my career." My stomach twisted as I said it. It wasn't a certainty, I didn't think, especially since I hadn't shared anything with him, but it was possible. Depending on who found out, who said something, and how much trouble it caused. At the very least, it'd make anyone think twice about giving me anything more important to do than arguing traffic tickets.

Dropping my forehead into my palm, I closed my eyes for a moment and breathed, in and out, in and out. I did that for probably close to a minute, just to settle my stomach and my thoughts.

Once I felt a little clearer, I opened my eyes. I needed to be smart about this, think with my head. I flipped open my notepad and started to sketch a few things down. I would have to shred this, but I needed to put it all down, even if only for long enough to make everything concrete in my mind.

Without allowing any emotions to come into play, I jotted down a series of notes, numbering them as I went. Having started with the question that seemed to be the most important, I followed with how I needed to handle it. Once I was finished, I took a deep breath and then began to read back over what I'd written.

1. *Did he know I was working with the DA's office?*
2. *Find out*
3. *Figure out potential problems*
4. *Figure out potential outcomes*
5. *Figure out potential revenge*

I underlined revenge several times just to make myself feel better, although it wasn't like I'd actually do anything. I wasn't a vengeful person. Though if I just happened to talk to one of my good friends about what happened and she just *happened* to tell her somewhat overprotective boyfriend who *happened* to be the owner of Club Privé, and Arik suddenly found himself persona non grata...I wouldn't complain.

And, of course, if I found proof that he'd known who I was and had acted inappropriately, then I'd turn him in to the ethics committee. That, however, wasn't vengeance. That was a consequence of doing something unethical.

But I wouldn't worry about that until I'd done everything else on the list. Evidence first.

Staring at it for a long, hard moment, I committed it to memory and waited for my gut to settle.

It didn't.

But at least some of the chaos in my mind settled to a dull roar.

I could think.

Folding the paper into twos, then fours, I put it through the crisscross shredder. I definitely didn't need Bethany or Pierce finding out about Arik. The bin itself was locked, collected by an outside company for disposal weekly. Somebody would have to be particularly determined to get inside there and even more determined to re-create anything they got out of the bin.

I studied it for a few more minutes, uneasy.

But it wasn't over the list I made. I was uneasy over the man I'd left behind in the defendant's home.

Had he known?

I didn't know.

But I was going to find out.

I spent the next twenty minutes trying to work on my report before I gave up and decided to take a break. A coffee and bagel run should help. It usually did.

My boots made hollow sounds on the tiled floor, reminding me how empty the building was on a Sunday. If it hadn't been for the fact that I wanted to get everything typed up while it was still fresh in my mind – not to mention needing something to distract me from my personal problems – I wouldn't have been in at all. As I made my way down the hall, however, I saw that I wasn't actually alone. I bit back a dozen curses and wished desperately for a ladies' room to duck into.

There wasn't one.

Pierce Lawton, the other new ADA hire, glanced back at me. Judging by the look on his face, he seemed to be having as good a day as I was. Maybe Bethany had decided to kick him off her for a while, and sent him off to do actual lawyering. I could only imagine how difficult that would be for him.

He slowed his steps until I had no choice but to either slow down myself, or walk next to him. As he glanced over at me, I stared straight ahead, nodding in response to his greeting.

It sounded almost...*normal*.

But Pierce didn't do normal. He did stuck-up. He did arrogant. He did asshole. He didn't do *normal*.

"How did things go at the suspect's house?" he asked.

I wasn't surprised he knew Bethany had sent me, just that he cared. "I'm working on the report right now. Figured that way Bethany could read it as soon as she got in tomorrow. I just need a bagel and some coffee."

"That wasn't what I asked," he responded, smiling a

little. "Everything cool?"

I slid him a narrow look. "I'm hungry. I want to get some food. Some of us didn't get to...sleep in."

His face went a dull shade of red, but he manned up quick enough. "Look, Dena. I'm just wondering how everything went. This is my case too."

"Is that why you're here?" I asked.

His turquoise eyes narrowed. "I'm here because I needed to look over a few things for tomorrow."

He fell silent as the two of us made our way to the front doors.

Just before I stepped out, I glanced over at him. "You do know, she's got a reputation for being something of a shark." I paused, then added almost thoughtfully, "You could probably even call her a man-eater."

I strode through the doors before he could respond.

I'd probably regret my last comment, but my patience with all of this was wearing thin. I hadn't spent all these years working my ass off to play these high school games.

I finished the report in a caffeine-driven haze. The bagel had been half stale and lousy, but I'd eaten it anyway, needing the fuel.

Once I was done, I emailed a copy to Bethany,

Pierce, one to my own email account, and then I CC'd the DA. I also printed up three paper copies. I'd give her one personally tomorrow morning, keep one in my own files and then sealed the third in an envelope that I planned to mail to myself.

No way in hell would I let Bethany pull the same shit with me that she'd done with Officer Dunne's differing reports.

I'd been thinking it through, and I had a feeling she was behind those missing reports. There'd been a look in her eyes when I was talking to her. One I didn't trust at all, but I wasn't going to think about her right now. I wasn't going to think about Bethany, or Pierce...or Arik.

My stomach churned, but I slipped my sunglasses on and strode out into the brilliant sunlight of a New York afternoon. Instead of hopping on the subway to head back to Chelsea, however, I decided to do some window shopping. Anything to avoid hanging around my apartment with nothing to do but think.

I swung into a small shop that sold custom chocolates and picked up some ancho-chocolate chili treats and a bottle of water. With the water in my bag, I popped one of the spicy chocolates in my mouth and strolled down the sidewalk, not really seeing much of anything.

Could Arik have really done it? Could he really be that cold?

"So much for not thinking about him," I muttered.

The spice of the chocolate exploded on my tongue. Some part of my brain could appreciate it, but too much of me was thinking about Arik.

I honestly couldn't say if I thought it was out of character for him or not.

I didn't *know* him.

I knew how he tasted, and I knew how he felt inside me. I knew the thick dark red color of his hair and the way it felt between my fingers. The rich emerald of his eyes. I knew the feel of his hands on my skin...

No.

I didn't think he could.

But sex, for all its intimacy, wasn't really the same as *knowing* somebody. Not when there was nothing else to go with it. It wasn't like we'd gone on a couple of dates, and then had gone to bed together.

We'd met, danced, fucked.

Then we'd seen other people, and fucked again.

All told, we'd spent maybe six or eight hours together? Probably not even that, and some of that had been sleeping.

Very little had been spent talking about anything other than sex.

"I can't keep doing this." I popped another chocolate into my mouth as I stopped in front of a window displaying mannequins in underwear.

I'd go back to the club, I decided. Find a guy. Somebody who was a far cry from Arik. Maybe I'd try to find the guy I'd been with a few days before I'd met Arik. Or somebody completely different. I didn't know. But I'd do something.

I'd find a way to make Arik nothing but a hot,

pleasant memory.

*Yeah, right.*

It was a few hours before I managed to actually get to Club Privé. I had to go home and change, of course. I could've gotten in dressed the way I was, but I never went there unless I looked good.

Really good.

And I did.

My skin was itching, my heart pounding. Familiar symptoms. I recognized all the signs, and I wanted to tell my body to chill the hell out. I wasn't looking for *him,* and even if I saw him, I planned to turn around and walk the other way. There was no *way* I'd try to talk to Arik right now. I couldn't stand the idea of it.

That's what my brain said.

My body had an entirely different message.

Fortunately, my brain was in charge.

For the moment, anyway.

"Idiot," I muttered, ignoring the odd glance I got from the woman manning the door. "Sorry. Not you. Ignore me."

"Never, Ms. Monroe." She gave me a benign smile and nodded toward the door. "Have a good evening."

I gave her a smile as I headed inside. By the time I

reached the VIP level, my pulse had almost settled to normal. *Take a look around,* I told myself. *Make sure he isn't here.*

That was the first thing I needed to do. I didn't want to risk running into Arik.

It took almost ten minutes for me to feel comfortable in the knowledge that he wasn't here at the moment. Unless he'd gone back to one of the rooms already. I knew I could ask Gavin to find out for me, but that seemed...stalkerish.

No.

I wouldn't do that.

I'd just go find a guy, dance.

Something.

A quick look around told me that neither Gavin nor Carrie were up here either. I did see two of Gavin's top management personnel, which told me he was probably off for the night. Sundays tended to be slower here, so he and Carrie were probably enjoying a quiet night at home.

*Lucky,* I thought, oddly miserable. I didn't know what had gotten into me. It'd never bothered me before.

I got a drink and headed for the lower dance floor, determined to find a way to lose myself. I needed a release before going back to work tomorrow, or I was going to snap the first time Bethany did something bitchy.

Down in the crush of the bodies, sipping on an ice cold beer, bodies pressing in on me, I tried to let go.

I failed.

I was about ready to just give up when a tall form danced into place next to me. Swinging a look up at him,

I saw a face that was beautiful, carved, almost cold, but in an attractive sort of way. He brushed a hand across my shoulder questioningly.

I inclined my head and nodded. He moved in closer and spun me around, pressing my back to his chest.

He was hot. He wore a white T-shirt, but through it, I could feel his body heat and it warmed some of the cold places in me. That was good.

For a while, all we did was dance. He could move. Again, good.

After the first few dances, he pulled me in closer and let me feel the hard length of his cock against the small of my back. When I didn't pull away, he pressed his mouth to the curve of my neck, then moved up to speak into my ear.

"I've been watching you for a long time."

Angling my head up to meet his dark eyes, I said, "Is that a fact?"

"It is."

He splayed a hand over my belly, bared by the lace-edged top I'd paired with my mini skirt. His palm was hot against my skin, and when he swept his thumb upward, it grazed the lower curve of my left breast. I gasped in reaction.

"Maybe you'd like to check out one of the private rooms." He made it a statement rather than a question.

I swallowed, staring at the lights pulsing on the floor. His teeth raked my neck and a shiver went through me.

"Yeah, I would."

Twenty minutes later, red-faced and trembling, I stood by the wall while the man glared at me, pressing the back of his forearm against his bleeding nose.

"Whad da fuck 'ou do dat for?" he demanded, his voice a harsh, nasal twang.

I was pretty sure I'd broken his nose, but at the moment, I didn't feel bad for it.

"I told you," I snapped, my voice shaking. "If you want me on my knees, you ask. *No one* forces me."

"Are you a fuckin' sub or not?"

The door behind him opened and one of the bouncers stepped in, a menacing expression on his face. His eyes widened when he glanced at the man and then at me.

I'd inadvertently hit the room's panic button when I clambered away from him. I could have deactivated it, but I wanted the guy out. I was miserable and embarrassed. All I wanted was to be alone right now.

The man pointed a finger at me before looking at the bouncer. "If she tries to say I violated the rules, she's lying. She said the safe word, and then she busted my nose. I stopped when you said it, didn't I?"

"I didn't mean to hurt him," I said tiredly, directing my comments at the bouncer.

I was pretty sure his name was Bennie or something like that. He gave me a look that clearly said he didn't

228

believe me.

"I didn't," I insisted. Crossing my arms over my chest, I stared at him. "I jerked my elbow and hit his nose."

"I want her gone," the man interrupted.

"Not gonna happen," Bennie said. "We can either check the security footage together, or you can agree to go your separate ways."

I was suddenly glad that I'd come to Club Privé instead of someplace else. Gavin insisted on having cameras in the private rooms for situations like this – or worse. No one was watching the monitors, and only he or Carrie could access the files for playback, but knowing the cameras were there had always made me feel safer.

"I'll go," the man said, looking sulky.

Bennie nodded as the man grabbed his shirt and headed back out to the main floor. I wondered if he'd still try to find someone tonight or not. A guy like that, it was hard to tell.

"Ms. Monroe?"

I sighed and ran my hand through my hair. "I'd like to be alone, if that's all right. I'll pay for the room as long as I'm here."

Bennie nodded. "If you need anything, just let me know."

He walked out and I flopped down on the bed, staring up at the ceiling. I was still completely dressed. I hadn't even gotten around to taking my boots off. I hadn't even gotten around to being turned on enough to want to be undressed.

My almost-partner hadn't done anything, not exactly. Not when he'd tangled his hands in my hair and tried to push me to my knees, talking about how he wanted to see my lips wrapped around his cock.

It'd been all about him.

Not like Arik.

My breath hitched.

Slowly, I slid a hand down my stomach, under the waistband of my skirt, under the waistband of my panties. Fingers skimmed the thin curls covering my sensitive flesh.

I didn't need my fingers to tell me I was wet.

All I had to do was think of Arik, and my body was ready.

In, out...again. My pussy was wet, gripping my fingers as I began to slide them into me. Rolling onto my stomach, I began to ride my hand, imagining it was him. His cock, his hand, his mouth...all of him. In me. Beneath me. Around me.

The climax came on quick and hard. Too easy.

Just thinking about him could do more than some real men could manage with endless patience and eagerness.

"Please," I whispered into the smooth white sheets. "Don't let him be a fake."

# Chapter 3

*Arik*

The cops had left.

The security personnel from the building had left.

Dena was long gone.

Nobody was hovering around.

Now, I just needed to get Leayna to calm down and actually *listen*, although that seemed like wishful thinking.

After she swung by the table for probably the fifth time in three minutes, I got up and caught her arm, trying to stop her endless pacing. She stopped, staring at me with wide green eyes. She blinked up at me, her lower lip trembling a little.

I felt awful for her, and wished there was some way to make any of this easier, but there was nothing I could do, no matter how much my gut said she was innocent.

"We need to talk," I told her softly.

She gave me a nod, falling in step with me when I

led her back to the table, although each step was reluctant. She was only walking with me because I had my hand gripping her arm gently. If I let go, I had no doubt she'd bolt like a rabbit.

When we sat down, I took her hands and she gripped mine. "This has been a lousy day, huh?"

Leayna just stared at me. I tried a smile, hoping to see some sort of response from her. Nothing.

After a few more seconds, I squeezed her hands gently and said, "How about a drink? Would you like some tea?"

"I want a drink." Her mouth tightened into a hard, flat line. Leayna pulled her hands back and I watched as she stood. "But I damn well don't want tea. I've got scotch. Want any?"

Tempting. "Ah, no. Thanks, but no. I'm working, Leayna."

She shot me a look over her shoulder, her mouth turning down into a vulnerable sort of frown.

"Feel free to get some yourself, though," I said. "You've had a rough day."

As she started going through one of the cabinets, I moved to the hall, finding myself drawn back toward her study and the array of paintings, the smashed bits of glass. She trailed along behind me and I could hear liquid sloshing in her glass as she swirled the scotch. "Do you have an idea how much was destroyed in here?"

"No." Her voice was sad. "I know there's value, but the value to me wasn't the money. It was something…different. Something deeper."

I understood what she meant. And I couldn't help but think that whoever had done this had purposefully destroyed things that mattered to her.

"Is there any chance the person who broke in..." I hesitated. How did I ask it? Maybe straightforward was the best way to go. "Leayna, could the person who did this have been sent by the people who threatened you? Was this a way to hurt you?"

The laugh that escaped her was awful. Awful and broken, and it echoed in my ears like nails dragging down the chalkboard.

"There's nobody else left to hurt, is there?" Her shoulders shuddered. "He's gone because they killed him, so who else is left?"

"Who are *they*, Leayna?" I caught her hands and squeezed. She'd given me a general idea before, but no names. Every time I pressed for a name, she shut down.

This time was no different.

She pulled back and I let go, watching as she got up and began to pace. "I don't want to talk about this, Arik." Her hands were trembling. "Have you been able to see about getting me protection?"

I waited for her to turn and look at me. "I'm still trying to decide the best way to do that. If we go to the DA's office with this, they'll want information, Leayna."

She flinched. "Information on what?" Her voice cracked. "I don't *know* anything. He was a dirty son of a bitch, but I loved him anyway. I was so *stupid*."

Her face crumpled and she started to sob. Rising to my feet, I crossed over to her. She tried to move away, but I caught her around the shoulders and guided her back to the table.

"We're going to get through this," I said gently. "Okay? We're going to get you through this. But I need you to talk to me. I need you to tell me everything you can. I need to know who could have broken in here."

"I don't *know!*" Her voice rose to a sharp wail before breaking off into sobs.

I wouldn't get anywhere with her like this. Sighing, I patted her shoulder and let her cry it out. When it finally ended, I handed her a handkerchief and let her dry the tears. But when I started to move away, she lay a hand on my thigh.

It wasn't apprehension that filled me, exactly.

More like resignation.

"Thank you," Leayna said, her voice husky and raw.

"You're welcome." I took her hand and moved it away, but all she did was turn her body more fully to me, snuggling her head up on my shoulder.

"He never would have sat here and listened to me cry like this. I'm starting to realize how stupid I was to stay with him after I realized he never really loved me." She rubbed her cheek against my suit jacket.

Dammit.

"You'll find a man who does love you, Leayna." I patted her shoulder and eased away.

She lifted tear drenched eyes to me, beautiful despite the reddened eyes. The tip of her nose was pink, but she still managed to look lovely.

But when I looked at her, touched her, I felt nothing.

My reaction wasn't based on the fact that it was wrong to be drawn to her because she was my client. It was simply because I didn't want her.

I caught her hand before she could touch my face.

"You're feeling lost and you need somebody to turn to, I understand that. I can talk to you and offer advice, but I can't be anything else, Ms. Mance. It's not even wise to be a friend. I'm your lawyer, but that's it."

She jerked as if I'd slapped her, but I kept going.

"I'd like you to pack a few things. I'm taking you to a hotel."

Lower lip trembling, she tore away from me. "I don't want to go."

"You should follow my advice." As she started to pace again, I tucked my hands into my pockets so she couldn't reach for them again. "I can't make you go, Ms. Mance, but it's not safe here for you. They've already proven they can get in without leaving any sign."

She ended up going to the hotel, but she was still upset with me.

Once I had her settled, I headed for a bar a block away from my apartment. I wanted a drink, and I wanted some hard, fast sex.

Dena's face flitted through my mind, but she was out

of the question.

Had she known who I was?

It was hard to believe that Bethany was unaware of *anything* having to do with this case, and that manipulative she-devil would do anything, use anybody to get ahead. Even if it meant sending one of her underlings to fuck with me.

Or, more accurately, fuck me.

But Dena hadn't seemed liked that.

Not at all.

But maybe that was the whole point.

My gut twisted as I settled at the bar I usually went to when I wasn't in the mood for a club scene. I flagged down the bartender.

"Your usual?"

I nodded and a moment later, a glass of Glenlivet 18 Year was placed in front of me. As the rich taste slid down my throat, a woman settled on the stool next to me. I glanced over. After a second drink, I took another look.

She was pretty.

Long black hair swept into an elegant chignon, sleek red dress. Her dusky olive skin made me think she was Latina. She was beautiful, that was certain.

"Hi." She gave me a smile, her Cupid's bow mouth curving up invitingly.

I nodded at her.

She stroked a finger along the low neckline of her dress, purposefully drawing attention to her generous cleavage. "Would you like some company?"

"Sure. Want a drink?"

She touched her finger to the tip of my glass. "What's that you're drinking?"

I offered it to her and she took a slow sip. When she put the glass down, she smiled at me again.

"I love it. I'll take one."

I ordered another scotch, watching her dark eyes. She slid her tongue over her lips, slicked the same red as her dress. She was definitely here looking for a good time.

When she settled her hand on my thigh, her fingers just a few inches from my crotch, my cock twitched, but I knew it was just a normal male reaction to an attractive woman. It wasn't anything special. Not like when I thought about Dena.

That was all it took to make my cock harden.

My companion thought it was her, and that was fine with me.

She also thought it was her when we left a few minutes later. She invited me to her apartment, and I found myself thinking about the safety precautions Dena had taken the first time we'd been together. Carmen hadn't taken any such precautions, and it made me think a little less of her.

She was all over me in the cab, and it didn't stop when we reached her apartment. It wasn't in the best neighborhood, but it was far from the worst. I had a vague recollection of her saying that she worked as a pharmaceutical rep. Her apartment seemed nice, but I wasn't really paying attention to much of anything. Fortunately, judging by the way she was rubbing herself all over me, she wasn't interested in anything else either.

She peeled off the dress in record time, revealing a strapless bra that barely managed to contain everything, and a pair of panties that were little more than a strip of lace and silk that covered nothing. I barely had time to kick off my shoes and remove my shirt before she was on her knees and reaching for my belt.

When I pulled out a condom, Carmen pouted a little. I didn't doubt that she normally had men begging for that mouth, but I wasn't even tempted.

"Sorry," I said. "It's this or I leave."

Presented with that, she took the condom from me and yanked down my pants and underwear. With a glance up at me through her lashes, she tore open the wrapper and proceeded to roll the condom on with her mouth. It was an erotic sight and, finally, some real interest in her stirred.

It couldn't compare to the image in my head though. Someone petite, with very little curves. But a mouth that could get me off in seconds. Eyes that I couldn't forget.

I was a class-act bastard, I knew, thinking of another woman while I had this beautiful one in front of me, but I couldn't banish the thoughts of Dena, no matter what I did.

Carmen stood and reached for me, intending to draw me closer, but I didn't want that, didn't want to have to look her in the eyes and lie to her even more than I already was. I grabbed her hips and spun her around, pulling her ass back against my cock for a moment. She giggled a little as I bent her over the couch, then gasped as I nudged her ankles apart, not bothering to be gentle about it. She didn't seem to want gentle, and I definitely didn't want to be it.

Keeping one hand on the small of Carmen's back, I wrapped my hand around my cock and slid the head between her legs. I hooked a finger around the essentially non-existent crotch of her panties and pulled them aside. A moment later, I found her entrance and, without any finesse, pushed inside.

She was tight and hot, which is all I cared about. Blocking out the squeals she made as I began to thrust, I thought of Dena.

The throaty way she moaned, the way I had to drag each bit of submission from her. The way she curled against me after I made her come.

Perfection.

This...this was just release.

Still, I was enough of a gentleman to make sure Carmen got hers. When I felt my balls start to tighten, I slid my hand under her and found her clit. She was panting as she pushed back against me and I knew she was close.

"Come," I growled as I rubbed her clit.

"More," she begged. "More, baby. Please, more."

I gritted my teeth and tried not to think about how Dena would've reacted to a command to come. I moved my other hand to one of Carmen's breasts, pulling down the cup of her bra so I could get my fingers on her nipple. When I pinched it, her pussy clenched around me and I knew I'd found her sweet spot.

Less than a minute later, she was coming, her

muscles clamping tight around me. I squeezed my eyes closed and allowed myself to picture Dena bent over in front of me. Allowed myself to imagine that it was her gripping me.

The release was brief, and as soon as it was over, I pulled out. I was done.

I pulled off the condom and disposed of it down the toilet in the small bathroom off the hall, grabbing up my pants as I passed.

Carmen was stretching and smiling as I drew up my trousers. She'd adjusted her panties and bra, but made no attempt to cover herself.

I gave her a nod as I headed toward the door. Fortunately, it wasn't far, and I was able to get it closed before whatever she'd thrown at me hit it. She called me something in Spanish that I was sure wasn't complimentary, but I didn't bother to attempt to translate it. Whatever it was, I was sure she wasn't off base. I really was an asshole. This was just further proof.

# Chapter 4

*Dena*

"What is this?"

Bethany's eyes were as cold as her voice. She was clearly trying to pull out all the intimidation stops. I could've told her not to bother. I wasn't someone easily bullied on a good day. And this was definitely not a good day.

I had a brutal headache, like an icepick was slowly rotating into my skull right at the base of my neck.

Still, I'd rather deal with the icepick than my boss.

Sadly, I didn't have the luxury of choice. I had to put up with both, and the acknowledgement stretched my patience to the breaking point.

Glancing at the paper she held, I pursed my lips for a moment, and then looked back at her. "It appears to be the report you asked for." I somehow managed to keep my tone polite.

"This is bullshit," Bethany snapped. "It's whitewashed bullshit. You basically have nothing to report. What the *fuck*, Dena? Do you want to be a prosecutor or not?"

I made myself take a slow breath before I responded. It wouldn't do to lose my temper. I did, however, ask sweetly, "Would you like me to fabricate something?"

Her lids flickered, and I wondered if I'd gone too far.

When she didn't answer, I continued, my head pulsing. I figured I might as well say it all. "Shall I expand the report to include something along the lines of *the defendant's home was surrounded by numerous mafia types and I observed her whispering into the ear of her lawyer*?"

A dark flush was creeping its way up Bethany's neck.

"Perhaps I should include something about how I saw her passing money to the officers who'd shown up to take the report."

"Did you?" She bit off the words.

"No." I rubbed my forehead. "And you should know that I've filed several copies of this report, so if one happens to...go missing, we have backups."

"That was hardly necessary." Bethany's voice was stiff now, but she clutched her pen so tightly, it was a wonder it didn't snap in two. "It's not like I would *ask* you to falsify a report. I just wish you'd been more observant."

I took a slow breath. I'd already pushed things too far. I needed to dial back some, or I was going to be looking for a new job.

"I noted, to the number, how many paintings were in the house, how many items had been destroyed, and the value. I noted when Ms. Mance believed she'd left, and when she'd returned. I gathered as much information as I could from the cops without having an official report. I even made a few calls to get the value of the damage. I have no idea what else you want me to provide."

Her jaw was set, expression livid. For several seconds, she said nothing, and then she took the report, closed it up inside a folder and set it aside.

Flicking a hand at Pierce who'd been watching the exchange without a word, she said, "You'll be working with Pierce. We need to keep this from being introduced at trial. Unless we can prove that she did this herself to gain sympathy, it has nothing to do with her killing her husband."

I frowned. "What if someone is trying to threaten her?"

"Threaten her why?" Bethany rolled her eyes. "If it walks like a duck and talks like a duck."

I glanced at Pierce, but his face was impassive.

"It was a random B&E, Dena. That's all. Don't let the defense turn it into something it isn't."

"You don't know that it was random. The police have barely begun investigating," I protested.

"Yes, Dena, I do know." She turned back to her computer. "You two, get to work."

We'd been dismissed. Glancing over at Pierce, I bit back a sigh and turned to go.

I was almost at the door when she spoke again, "Dena, it was very...thorough of you to copy the DA on the report, but it was hardly necessary. I keep very good records."

I looked back at her and gave her a wide, empty smile. "It's habit, I'm afraid. We always copied all parties at the old firm. After all, we didn't want to take a chance of a report being...lost. More than once, having multiple back-ups saved my ass."

We'd spent nearly two hours working and not speaking outside what was necessary for the case, but there was enough to do that I didn't mind the silence.

We had a fairly expansive history to draw on, building a motion in which to have the break-in kept from being introduced at trial, but I knew any decent defense attorney would have an equally compelling argument to say the break-in was evidence supporting an alternate theory of the crime.

And Arik was far from just a "decent" lawyer.

Arik.

I hadn't told Bethany that I'd met him before.

I probably should have, but it wasn't like we actually had a personal relationship. Sex wasn't personal. Sex could be terribly intimate, but what we'd had hadn't been part of a relationship. It'd been an arrangement that fulfilled a basic need. It wasn't much different than...

*You're fooling yourself. It was personal. You're not*

*involved, but it* was *personal.*

That little voice would be the death of me.

"You know, you're not doing yourself any favors, jabbing at Bethany like that," Pierce said, his voice low.

Jerking my head up, I stared at him, but he wasn't looking at me.

"You said she was a man-eater and you're not wrong." He hesitated, and then kept going, "But you're not really right, either. She doesn't limit it to men. She's an eater. A shark, through and through, and you're probably looking really tasty to her right now." Finally, he lifted his head and met my eyes.

For the first time since I met him, he looked real. The slime and sleaze that he'd worn like a second skin was gone. Something in his eyes looked heavy. Like he felt almost the same way I did, that the career he'd been reaching for was slowly slipping out of his hands.

He reached out and touched my fingers with the tips of his. "You need to back off," he said softly.

Lowering my gaze, I stared at his hand. He wasn't hitting on me. The gesture felt more like he was trying to convey how important this was.

I started to pull back, but before I could, I felt an eerie crawling sensation on my skin. Lifting my head, I slid my eyes to the side and found Bethany looking in the window of the conference room. Staring at us.

Staring at the way Pierce was touching my hand.

He swore under his breath and jerked his hand back, but she'd already turned and walked away.

There was one thing I had to know. "Why in the hell

are you sleeping with her if you're so damned scared of her?"

Pierce stared at me, eyes wide. "Just leave it, Dena. Okay? Just leave it."

# Chapter 5

## *Dena*

When my alarm went off, I was already awake.

I had been for close to an hour.

Smacking at my annoying clock to get it to stop, I closed my eyes and wished for a few more minutes of sleep, but it wasn't going to happen. I'd never used a snooze button and didn't intend to start now.

Still...

I turned my head and stared at the soft blue numbers glowing dimly from the clock. Another minute ticked by before I actually sat up and swung my legs out of bed.

Yesterday had been one of the worst Mondays on record, and I doubted today would be much better. Pierce and I managed to get the brief that Bethany had wanted drafted, although I doubted it would work to keep the break-in from being presented at trial. We'd included everything we could, but I knew that anything Arik argued would convince a half-way competent judge.

Hell, even I was starting to think that we'd jumped the gun arresting and arraigning Leayna Mance, even if she had been found at the crime scene with her husband's blood on her clothes.

I hadn't shared any of my doubts, however. Pierce had hauled ass out of there as soon as we'd finished, and for the last hour or so we'd been working, he'd kept checking his phone as it buzzed, looking more and more harassed by the minute. Somebody had been texting him. I hadn't needed to ask who it was.

When Bethany had sent him the final text, he slammed the phone down with enough force that I was surprised it hadn't broken. He hadn't responded when I'd asked if he was okay.

I hadn't really needed to.

He definitely wasn't okay.

I was going to kick his pathetic ass.

And probably hers too.

Staring at Bethany for a long moment, I forced myself to take a deep breath. Then a few more for good measure. Pierce wouldn't look at me, and it was clear why. Son of a bitch couldn't stand the idea of facing me while Bethany laid this trumped up shit down at my feet.

After a few more seconds, my pulse slowed to a near-normal pace, and I looked over at him for a few

248

moments. His eyes flicked in my direction, but he never once actually looked away from the surface of Bethany's desk.

Fine. He could be a coward.

*I* wasn't one, though. I wasn't confrontational by nature, but I also wasn't going to be a doormat. Especially not for something like this.

Piling on scut work was one thing. I might not like an unfair playing field, but the whole missing police report, and now this...Bethany hadn't just crossed the line. She'd obliterated it.

"Would you care to repeat that?" I asked calmly.

"Which part?" Bethany gave me a close-lipped smile.

"All of it. I want to make sure I understood you correctly."

She gave me a suffering sort of sigh. "We both know you understood it all well enough, Dena. Look, you're very lucky that Pierce came to me instead of filing an official complaint–"

"Not really," I interrupted.

She tensed. "Excuse me?"

"You heard me. If he'd filed an official complaint, then I'd be able to file an official response. There's a process that allows everyone to have an official say. You're not giving me any sort of process."

Her eyes narrowed, and I watched as her shoulders stiffened minutely under the pale lavender of her silk blouse. "Dena, you need to be careful here. I'm trying to be lenient. But if you persist in this unprofessional behavior of yours, then you just may well find yourself gone before you get your first real case."

"*Unprofessional.*" I echoed her word choice, hardly able to believe the balls she had, after all she'd done, referring to me as unprofessional. "My behavior is *unprofessional* because I would like to be part of a process that allows for a response to false allegations? And yet your behavior..." I looked from her to Pierce and cocked an eyebrow. "The behavior between you and the subordinate – one who's been given a better office, as well as second chair on a headline case – who's now making a false allegation, isn't unprofessional?"

"Just what are you implying?" Her skin flushed.

"I'm not implying anything, just being tactful." I'd officially reached my limit. I took a step forward. "Go ahead and terminate my employment, Bethany. See where *that* gets you. Because I do know where to file official complaints. And I won't be as tactful then."

There was a weird, almost choking noise that came from Pierce, but when Bethany and I both glanced at him, his face was bland. He stared straight ahead, looking at neither of us.

After another tense moment, Bethany said, "I hardly think it's necessary to terminate your employment simply because you made an advance on a co-worker, and didn't react well when he rebuffed you."

Her voice was stilted, eyes fixed at a point somewhere just over my shoulder.

"Really." I didn't call her out on the bullshit lie she'd spun together. And that's what it was. All three of us knew it. I wasn't even sure Pierce had anything to do with it, other than the fact that he was too whipped to refute what Bethany was claiming.

"However," she continued. "I think it would be best for you to step down from the case for now. We don't need any additional tension on the team. You'll work with the paralegals." The smile on her face looked forced, almost plastic. "Is that a workable solution?"

I wanted to ask her if kissing my ass was a workable solution, but decided not to. I knew the difference between taking a stand and going too far. Most of the time anyway. To keep myself from doing anything stupid, I turned on my heel and strode to the door.

Before I could open it, however, she said my name.

I stopped, but didn't look back, not trusting myself.

"You need to understand something. I can be a powerful ally in this office. Perhaps you're a decent lawyer, but you need allies working in this field if you want to make something of yourself. Do you really want to start off your career by alienating people?"

I finally looked back at her. "My ambition is less important to me than my ethics, Ms. McDermott."

I left rather than waiting for a response. I forced myself to keep my pace even as I made my way down the hall. Once back in my office, I started writing up a report of everything that had transpired since I started working for Bethany.

I wasn't filing anything, but I needed a chronological log of the problems I'd had and it was best to get it all down while things were still fairly clear in my mind. I didn't want anything to go on record officially, so I saved all the data to my Google docs drive under my personal email. It would be there if I needed it.

It took over an hour.

It was a quiet hour, too. Nobody called me. Nobody knocked on the door. Nobody came by with a file of reports that needed to be addressed or demands that I look into something.

When I finally decided to take a break, I glanced down the hall toward Pierce's office. I should have just turned and walked away, but instead, I found myself walking toward it. The door wasn't completely closed, which wasn't strange, but it also wasn't welcoming either. I almost turned back, but instead, I walked sedately by, casually looking over my shoulder as I did so.

The lights were off so I almost didn't see him through the few open inches.

He was sitting at his desk, staring off into nothing. Hands folded on his desk. Not moving.

Through the door, I heard the phone ring. After a second ring, he turned his head and stared at it, like he wasn't sure what to do. It rang a third time before he finally moved to pick it up.

There was something terribly unsettling about the whole thing.

Shaking it off, I turned and continued on down the corridor.

I didn't have a destination in mind, but I needed to move, needed to think.

Needed to get away from Pierce and anything that

made me think of Bethany before I exploded.

# Chapter 6

*Dena*

I ended up taking an early lunch. Considering how many times I'd worked through lunch since I started at the DA's office, I doubted anyone would say anything, especially if I was back within an hour.

I didn't, however, tell Bethany that I was going. If I saw her again right now, I couldn't guarantee how I'd react.

I needed to talk to someone about all of this. With Krissy on LA time, she was probably right in the middle of getting her day started. If Carrie worked at the club last night, she'd just be getting up. Leslie already knew some of what was going on, so she was the logical choice.

I took the subway to Queens rather than a taxi, using the time to gather my thoughts. She had a nice practice going already, and I could tell I was interrupting, but she gave me a smile after her administrative assistant ushered me in. We always made time for each other.

I sat on the scoop chair by the window, staring outside and trying to brood through the mess in my head while she finished up something on her computer.

"Are you going to talk?" Leslie asked after a few minutes of silence.

"Yes." Then I paused, giving her a wry smile. "I'm not sure. I might yell."

Leslie laughed. "You don't yell often. It must be bad. Some asshole stand you up?"

I slid her a narrow look.

"Okay, then." She pursed her lips and then glanced around. "The walls are soundproofed. You remember how it was at Webster and Steinberg. No one in divorce cases wants to hear another couple screaming at each other."

I managed not to laugh. If I started, it would come out as something harsh and jagged, and I might not be able to stop. I was more on edge than I thought. Unable to sit still though, I got up and began to pace. "My boss is a piranha."

She cocked a brow. "We've all been called something like that at one point or another."

I shook my head. "Oh, trust me. She really *is* one. A piranha. A shark. A bitch of the highest order." I turned to face Leslie. "You want to hear what she did?"

Leslie raised an eyebrow.

I scowled. "She's fucking the other attorney who was hired the same time I was, gave him the good office, the best cases. As long as he's playing the good attorney anyway. And now..." I was too angry to even finish the

256

sentence.

"Now what?" Leslie prompted.

I turned and stared at her. "Pierce and I were working on a motion yesterday and I said something to him about her. He told me to stop pushing her. He touched my hand, and she walked by, saw it. Then, this morning..." I had to stop and take a deep breath to keep my voice even. "This morning, she tells me that Pierce has made an informal complaint against me. That I'd acted unprofessionally toward him. So now, I get the fascinating job of working with the paralegals."

Leslie's eyes widened.

"Yeah. Bad Dena. Time out for me." I stopped by the window and looked down on the busy streets, grinding my teeth together until my jaw ached.

Silent seconds ticked by.

"Well." Leslie's dry voice finally shattered the silence.

Turning to look at her, I waited.

She stared at me pointedly. "What are you going to do about it?"

"I..." Blowing out a breath, I pressed the tips of my fingers to my temples. I was starting to get a headache. "I don't know. I've written everything down that's happened, but..."

"But *what*?" Leslie asked. "What would you be telling me to do if I were in your shoes?"

Rolling my eyes, I said, "If we were talking about *you*, I'd be having to post bail right now, because you would've already torn her eyes out."

257

"True." She smirked a little. "But you're the calmer one. You think. You plan. What would you do if this was happening to me? What advice would you give if it was me? Before I bitch-slapped her."

I chuckled and it helped some of the anger drain away. "Okay." I sighed. "I'd be telling you to file a formal complaint."

"So do it."

"Against which one?" I spread my hands wide. "Her or him? He didn't tell her shit."

"But he stood there and let her say it. Go for them both." Leslie's smile was cold. "She's screwing with you, Dena. She's going after the career you've always wanted. You can't let her get away with it."

I looked back out the window, my thoughts spinning. I knew Pierce hadn't made any damn complaint. But he also hadn't stepped up to refute it either.

No way was I letting them take my career.

Yeah, I knew what I had to do.

I thanked Leslie and headed back to the office, stopping only to grab some take-out along the way.

I had work to do.

It took longer than I liked.

I'd filed formal complaints before. Only two, but neither one of them had been anything like this. It was the hardest I'd ever written, having to walk the line between professionalism and accuracy, giving details without sounding like I was complaining. Since I knew my accusations against Bethany were more serious, I decided to divide and conquer by filing a complaint against Pierce first, then using that to leverage his support in a complaint against Bethany.

When I was done, my brain felt like mush. I stared at the television for a while before deciding to take a long bath and then head to bed.

Tomorrow was going to suck more than a little and I needed to be fully rested to deal.

The first thing I did when I arrived at work was file my complaint.

The second thing I did was deal with the box that had been placed on my desk at some point yesterday, along with a note in unfamiliar handwriting.

As I looked at the contents, I felt like I was a law student again. The box had nothing but legal briefs that needed to be re-filed. Boring work even for a paralegal.

The only good thing about it was that I spent the entire day not having to see or hear from Bethany. The one time I saw Pierce, he practically ran to get away from me. I was tempted to go after him and give him a piece of my mind, but decided against it.

He'd get the idea soon enough, and talking to him now would only make matters worse. Besides, if he didn't have the spine to stand up against his boss when she made false allegations in his name, then he had no business working in the DA's office anyway.

The seconds on the clock moved by so slowly, I thought I'd lose my mind, but just when I thought I couldn't take any more, it was quitting time. I didn't even bother to finish what I was doing. I'd put in a hundred percent while I was here, no matter what shit they gave me, but I wasn't working a single minute of overtime like this.

Unable to stand the idea of another night at home watching zombies try to devour the world, I went by my place only to grab something to eat and change my clothes.

Skinny black jeans, a silk tank top and boots – nothing that would get me hassled on the subway, but still nice enough for Club Privé. I wasn't looking to hook up with anyone though. I just wanted to talk to Carrie and get a drink. Just enough of both to relax after a shit day.

If it had been Friday, I probably would've gotten drunk and talked Carrie into dancing half the night away, or maybe I would've just called Leslie for ice cream and a girls' night in. For now, a few drinks and a few dances would have to work.

Despite the fact that it was the middle of the week, the club was packed when I got there, the line extending down the street. Using the VIP entrance, I headed straight for the top level, looking for Carrie or Gavin. I didn't see either of them, but that wasn't surprising for a busy night. They were probably out making their rounds and if I stayed in place long enough, they'd get to me.

Somebody asked me to dance, but I just shook my

head.

One of the servers caught my eye and I nodded. A few minutes later, I had a drink in hand.

Settling in one of the elevated seats along one the upper railings, I studied the crowd, hoping to spot Carrie or Gavin. There was no way I'd unload on Gavin, but if I found him, he could point me toward her.

That was all I wanted.

My skin started to tingle, then heat and I raised my head, heart already racing.

No.

Hell no.

I knew what my body was telling me even as I tried to deny it.

No, please...

Slowly, I turned my head and saw him standing at the top of the stairs, his eyes locked on me.

"Shit," I muttered.

Deliberately looking away, I lifted my drink to my lips and drained it. Heat flooded me, and I let myself blame it on the alcohol. My head buzzed pleasantly, taking some of the edge off.

From the corner of my eye, I could see him moving my way, and I pondered my choices. I could head for the stairs to my left. If I was fast and lucky, I could be out the door and into a cab in no time.

Before I could take a step toward my escape, the server appeared between me and the stairs. I could've been rude, but she didn't deserve that. When she asked if I'd like another drink, I told her to get me some bourbon, a double. If I was going to stay, I'd need more alcohol.

She nodded and then walked away. As my gaze followed her, I caught a glimpse of Arik moving even closer. Spinning the opposite way, I slid off the stool and started toward the bar. There was no way I would just sit there and wait for him to decide to join me.

Asshole.

*Serious* asshole.

It had been bad enough that he'd asked for my number and then never used it, but then he'd treated me like a stranger instead of simply acknowledging that we knew each other.

*Asshole.*

I dropped into a vacant seat at the bar just as the bartender finished making my drink. The server gave me a look of mild surprise, but motioned for the bartender to pass it over. As she brought it to me, I signaled to her and she leaned in close enough for me to be heard over the music. "Is Carrie here tonight?"

She nodded.

"Anyway somebody can let her know I'm here?"

She gave me a smile and I breathed a little easier.

If Carrie was around, then she could be a buffer. I didn't want–

"Hello, Dena."

I tightened my hand around my glass of bourbon and angled my body toward Arik. "Hello." I took a sip and lowered the glass, trying to pretend that I didn't care. Sliding off the stool, I said deliberately, "Good-bye, Arik."

I didn't make it two feet before he caught up to me.

# Chapter 7

## *Arik*

*Good-bye, Arik.*

Staring at her back, my blood pulsing through my veins, I told myself to take a few minutes to think it through.

Hell no.

It only took a few strides to catch up with her. She'd settled back over at the railing, staring down over the dance floor with a look of patent boredom on her face. She was clearly trying hard to pretend she didn't care.

Or maybe that was just my wishful thinking.

When I touched her shoulder, she gave a long-suffering sigh before slanting a look up at me. "What?"

I bristled at her tone. "You sound like you're having a pleasant day."

"Not that it's any of your business." The pointed expression on her face might've scared a lesser man off.

Fortunately, I wasn't a lesser man.

"I think it's time the two of us had a little chat." I put

my mostly-empty drink down on the nearby railing, but when I tried to touch her cheek, she jerked a hand up, catching my wrist with a speed that I had to admit was fairly impressive.

"Hands off," she said bitingly.

"Okay." Lowering my hand to the railing on the other side of her, I leaned in and studied her face. "Is that a permanent thing, or are you just having a bitchy day?"

I doubled over as she drove an elbow into my stomach, then ducked under my arm and moved away. I was more caught off guard than in pain though, and my stunned disbelief only lasted a few seconds.

Grabbing her arm, I caught her and jerked her back before she could take off. "Okay, sweetheart. How about you explain just what the ever-loving fuck that was about?"

She tried to twist out of my grasp, but all it did was put her pelvis in close proximity to mine, reminding both of us of just what happened when the two of us were together. Her breath caught and I slid a hand up her back, tangling my fingers in her short hair.

"Keep moving like that, Dena. I'm enjoying it. It's been a little too long since I've been able to bury my dick inside you."

A second later, I tasted blood as she slammed the heel of her hand against my chin. I bit my tongue and pain flared.

"Alright, that's it." Spinning her around, I caught her wrists and twisted them behind her back. I lowered my mouth to her ear, desire and anger pulsing inside me.

"What's with the guerrilla tactics, Dena?"

"Let me go," she said, a warning note in her voice.

I'd never been one to hold a woman against her will, but I knew if I didn't push her, I'd lose her. Lowering my head, I whispered against her ear, "Make me."

She stiffened instead. When it became clear she wouldn't do anything, I swore and pulled back, giving her a few inches of space. She took that space and tried to walk away again.

"I don't think so." I stepped around her, cutting her off as I planted myself in her path. I glared down at her. "Just where in the hell do you think you're going?"

Her lips twisted into an unpleasant scowl. "I'm going anywhere that isn't here."

"Fine. I'll go with you. We need to talk."

"No." She shook her head. "We don't."

Closing the small distance between us, I stared down at her, but if I thought my height would be intimidating, I was underestimating her. She just tipped her head back and crossed her arms.

"Look, Mr. Porter–"

"Arik."

She arched her brows. "*Arik*? I'm sorry. I was under the impression you wanted me to address you as *Mr. Porter*, given our professional relationship."

It was only then I saw the depth of anger in her eyes.

Oh shit. I'd seriously fucked things up with her.

None of that should've mattered. We weren't in a relationship. We fucked. That was it. No commitments, no explanations.

267

Then why did I feel like I'd done something wrong?

"Dena, we need to talk," I said, softening my voice. "Especially about that."

"No." She reached up and patted my cheek. "We don't. See, *that* is really all there is. You have a good night."

She turned away. Again. I was really getting sick of her doing that. I caught her arm, but this time, when I whirled her back to face me, she came back swinging.

My head flew back from the impact of her fist against the side of my face, but I didn't let go.

"Did that make you feel any better?" I demanded as I gingerly touched my jaw. It was pounding and from the corner of my eye, I could see her flexing her fingers. If my face was any indication of how hard she'd hit me, her hand had to be hurting.

"Why, yes, actually." She gave me a slow smile that didn't reach her eyes. "I feel better than I have in several days. Thank you for asking." She jerked on her arm. "Now let me go."

I tightened my grip, aware that if I squeezed any harder, I'd bruise her. And not in a good way. "Not until you calm down and agree to talk to me."

"Not on your *life*," she snapped.

"Dammit, Dena!"

"Is there a problem here?"

Both of us looked up.

As Gavin emerged from the crowd that had gathered around us, I uncurled my fingers from her arm and let my hand drop to my side. He gave me a pointed glare before looking over at Dena.

She made a face at him. "No problem, Gavin."

"And that's why you hit one of my guests in the face?" he asked, sounding almost amused.

She curled her lip. "He asked for it."

"Did he now?"

Carrie was with us now and she looked between us before moving to Dena's side. She caught Dena's hand and lifted it. "Oh, honey."

Gavin's presence was enough to disperse the crowd, but I barely saw them go. I was looking at Dena's hand, my gut twisted in a bunch of slippery knots. Her knuckles were already swelling. Carrie waved at somebody, gripping Dena's hand tightly when she tried to pull away.

"The two of you want to tell me what's going on?" Gavin asked.

"Difference of opinion," Dena said.

"Failure to communicate."

We both spoke at the same time. Gavin's mouth flattened into a line. Aggravated, he shoved his hands into his pockets and watched Carrie press an ice pack to Dena's hand. Then his eyes slid to me.

Something told me that he wanted to make my face look like Dena's hand.

"You two are going to work this out," he finally said. "Otherwise, I'll have to revoke your guest pass, Porter. Permanently. And Dena, you'll be suspended for the next two months."

I stared at him, but Dena flinched as if he'd slapped her.

Carrie made a low sound of protest, but Gavin didn't even look at her. He was angrier than I realized.

"I was pushing too hard," I said. "I should have waited until she was calmer before I tried to talk to her. I'll leave. There's no reason to suspend her."

"There is. She violated the rules and she knows it." Gavin shrugged and held out his hand to Carrie. She hesitated, looking at him with narrowed eyes, but after a moment, she placed her hand in his. He looked back at us. "Take one of the private rooms and work whatever this is out."

As they both walked away, I turned my gaze to Dena.

She wasn't looking at me. In fact, she was trying very hard not to look at me.

After a few more seconds, I held out my hand. "Shall we?"

Dena lowered her gaze to my hand and scowled. She edged around, presenting me with a view of her narrow back as she started toward one of the private rooms. Falling into step behind her, I bit back a curse and wondered how she managed to do this to me.

I couldn't think around her.

Not at all.

She didn't look at me until she stopped in front of a door, and only then it was a glance. Still, it was enough for me to see the faint flush on her cheeks. I couldn't place the tension in her body right away, but once we stepped inside, I caught on easily enough.

The room was familiar.

In fact, it was the room I'd brought her to the first night we'd been here.

The lights were low. The bed was close by and I could instantly imagine backing her up against it, stripping her naked, tugging the slim-fitting jeans she wore down to her ankles, kissing the hollow at the base of her neck as I slid my hand inside her panties and found her wet.

I'd make her come for me before we did anything else, even before we talked. She was pissed off, angry and brittle. Hard. I didn't want her hard. I wanted her soft and wet and welcoming in my hands.

I'd make her come, then she'd cuddle up and sigh against me. I could hold her and then we could talk. Work this whole thing out.

But then she closed the door and dropped the key into a glass bowl on the low lying table near the couch. Instead of going to the bed, she settled down in an elegant sprawl on the couch and crossed one slim leg over the other.

"Well." Her lips were pursed in a mockery of a smile. "We were sent to our room, Mr. Porter. How long do you think we have to pretend to talk before we can go our separate ways?"

# Chapter 8

*Dena*

A muscle pulsed in his temple.

Or maybe it was a vein.

Either way, it was a clear sign he was pissed.

His jaw clenched tight and his eyes burned as he stalked toward me. Part of me wanted to draw back, but then he stilled a few feet away and I relaxed a little. I still wasn't entirely sure I should have come into this room with him. Actually, I was almost *positive* I shouldn't have come into this room with him.

But we were going to bump into each other. And he was right that we needed to talk. If not about whatever this was between us, then at least about...

"What were you doing at my client's house?" Arik demanded, the question coming out like an accusation.

I didn't remember moving. One minute I was on the couch, and the next, I was in his face, jabbing a finger into his chest. "What was *I* doing? I was doing my job. There. I answered your question." I raked him up and down, putting as much scorn into my look as I could. "Now you answer one of mine. Just how much of a coincidence was it that you showed up here right around the time I got hired at the DA's office."

Arik dipped his head, his mouth less than an inch away from mine. "I don't think I care for the accusation I'm hearing coming from you."

"Just doing the same thing you are, jackass," I snapped. "Doesn't feel very good, does it?"

I started to move away, wanting to get as far from him as possible.

Except I didn't get far.

Strong arms came around me and I bit back a gasp as he hauled me back against him. This time, I didn't dare struggle. I didn't even move. I'd felt his reaction to me out there. More, I'd been painfully aware of mine. If I pushed him too far now, we'd be all over each other in a blink and that wasn't what I wanted.

*Liar.*

It was a manic, delighted little voice that came from deep inside me. I wanted to throttle that voice, lock it in a trunk and throw in the Hudson, then toss the key into the sewers.

I hated it, but I couldn't actually deny it.

"What's the matter?" Arik whispered, his voice a husky purr in my ear. "Where's all that passionate fight now, Dena?"

"Let me go, Mr. Porter."

I fell back on formality, focused on the wall in front of me, hoping that maybe, just maybe, if I kept my wits intact, I could get out of this with my dignity not totally shredded. I never should have looked twice at him. I never should have looked *once* at him.

He could ruin my career.

It was already teetering thanks to Bethany. And this wouldn't be a claim I could deny.

A smooth, warm hand slid up my bare arm, higher, across my collarbone and then he placed his palm against my throat, curled his fingers. It was a terribly vulnerable position to be in, his hand around my neck. I could feel my pulse fluttering against his hand. Then he lowered his mouth and skimmed it along the curve where neck met shoulder and it took everything I had in me not to respond, not to tremble.

"Dena..." His voice was like honey. Like silk.

Fuck that.

It was pure sex.

"Let me go." I tried to demand it.

"Why?" he asked, his tone so terribly reasonable. "It seems to me you were happy here just a few days ago."

"That was before I found out you were defending a woman my office is trying for murder."

"Hmmm." His lips slid down my neck, then up.

That really shouldn't feel so good. I hated that it did.

"That is something to consider," he admitted. "But I didn't know you were an ADA, Dena. I didn't even know you were a lawyer."

His teeth caught my ear and I shuddered. For that long moment, I was so caught up in what he was doing to my body that I barely noticed his words. Heat exploded

275

through me as he tugged on my hip, and I had to fight a whimper as he moved forward, bringing my butt in full contact with his cock.

We were both clothed. That was the only reason he wasn't already inside me, and we both knew it. I wanted him inside me so badly that it nearly hurt. I wanted to feel his cock stretching me, invading me, bringing me to another earth-shattering climax. I wanted the release that only submission to him would bring.

When he slid a hand up my belly, my breath exploded out of me in a rush.

"Did you know?"

I had no idea what he was talking about. All I knew was the feel of his touch.

His fingers popped the button on my jeans as a part of my brain screamed at me to listen.

I caught his wrist, stopping him. I was pretty sure there was a reason he didn't need to be undressing me, and I'd figure it out in a minute.

"Know what?" I managed to ask, panting in an effort to restore the flow of oxygen to my brain.

"Did you know I was a defense attorney?" His voice sounded far too serious and stable considering the fact that his fingers were tracing a path up and down the inseam of my jeans.

How could he talk about anything even remotely logical?

But then my brain locked in on just *what* he was talking about and surprisingly, my brain cleared.

I pulled away from him and took a few shaky steps.

276

Turning toward him, I swallowed. My hands shook as I smoothed back my hair. Face burning and heart pounding, I looked around at anywhere but his face.

"If I'd known you were an attorney of *any* kind, I never would have come into one of these rooms with you, much less gotten naked with you." Pulling up the threads of my control, I managed a faint smirk. "Apparently, I need to start some sort of background check next time I get naked with a man."

Arik didn't even crack a smile.

I didn't really think it was funny either.

He came closer and reached up, shoving a hand into my hair and tangling it, tugging back until my head was cranked to a near painful angle. "My temper is already at a snapping point. Want to see me go over? Talk about getting naked with another man, Dena."

I shoved at him, disregarding the hand he had fisted in my hair.

He let go, but my scalp felt raw. "We don't have any sort of *understanding*, Mr. Porter," I said scathingly.

"We can change that."

The words caught me off guard. So much so that when he turned me around and brought me back against him, my back tucked to his chest, I didn't even think to move. It felt so good. His chest was warm and solid, heating me through and through.

"I have a hold on you now," he murmured against my ear. "I like this hold. You like it."

I did. But I shouldn't.

"You need to let me go," I said, my voice rough.

277

"Why?"

*Why...*

His question bounced around in my brain. There was a reason. I knew there was.

Finally, after far too long, I remembered.

I swallowed to loosen my tight throat before I spoke, "Because we can't be doing this. We're both working the same case – on opposite sides." My breath hitched as he rubbed his thumb across my belly through the material of my shirt.

The garment might as well have not even been there with the heat coursing through me. Struggling to think about anything that didn't involve him touching me, his hands on me, his body, I managed to drag my mind back to the present.

"We can't be doing this because it's unprofessional. I'm an ADA assigned to the prosecutor in the case. You're the defendant's lawyer. It's called conflict of interest. Surely they taught you about that in law school."

When he didn't let go, my frustration at the situation, at myself, spilled over, and it came out in a waspish bite. "Come on, unless you got your law degree from a crackerjack box or you bought it online, you know this is a problem."

"I assure you, my law degree didn't come from a box or online." He chuckled, not sounding at all offended by my words. "You've got nasty bite to you, don't you? Keep it up, and I'll be tempted to do something about it."

His palm flexed, pulling me more firmly against him, but he spoke at the same time, distracting me from the hard, heavy pressure of his cock against the small of my back.

"What are you doing on the case, Dena? I know Bethany. She's a shark. If she smells blood in the water, she goes after it. She doesn't share." His teeth caught my ear, tugged.

I felt my knees weaken. I had to get away from him before I did something really, really stupid. Like beg him to take me.

Twisting out of his arms, I put some distance between us before looking at him. "Bethany's my boss, and she's the ADA of record on the case." My mind struggled to remember all of the legal arguments as to why we shouldn't do this. "That's enough. Besides, I was at your client's apartment. Seems like I'm plenty involved."

He didn't seem bothered at all by what I said. "Yes, you were there, but it was the weekend. Bethany thinks too much of herself to work on the weekends if she can dump it off on somebody else."

A hundred possible replies popped into my mind. Part of me wanted to tell him the truth, that I'd been moved off the case so that there was nothing keeping us apart. But I knew that this was a bad idea all the way around. I'd eventually have to face off against him.

Unless I got fired first.

Arik's eyes narrowed. "What, specifically, are your duties on this case?"

Dammit.

"Bethany wasn't pleased with some bullshit I called

279

her on. I've been pulled from the case," I finally said, biting each word off. "I'm mostly working on research and filings with the paralegals."

"You called her on her bullshit?" He looked impressed. "What was it?"

I could tell by looking at him that he wouldn't let it go, even if he should. "You know damn well I can't tell you that." I shook my head. "See, this is why you and me and this..." Abruptly, I laughed. "There *is* no you and me. Who am I kidding?"

I was so done with this shit. I got up and started for the door.

I closed my hand around the doorknob, but his arm came over my shoulder and kept me from opening the door.

"No you and me?" His voice was low. "Are you sure about that?"

I shivered as he pressed his lips against the side of my neck.

"You don't really think you can ignore what we have between us, do you?" There was a pause, and then he added, "Do you even want to?"

I didn't bother to answer his question. Easing out from between him and the door, I turned to look at him. "I don't see why not. You asked for my number and then ignored me. I'm not one of those Subs who takes whatever a Dom dishes out. I don't sit by the phone waiting for anyone, Arik." My mouth curved into a brittle smile. "Now you tell me, how many of those nights did you spend alone? Any of them?"

"I never thought you were that kind of woman."

"That's not an answer." My chest tightened. I knew what I'd done. Or, at least, tried to do. I had no reason to doubt he hadn't done the same, no matter how much I wanted to think he hadn't.

"You want to hear that I fucked someone? Is that it?" His mouth twisted. "Fine. I did. But all I could think about was you. It was nothing more than a mindless fuck. No more than jerking off would've been."

It was a hell of a lot different than jerking off.

"Don't worry about it." I shrugged, trying not to let him see how much the thought of him with another woman hurt. "You're not the first man who offered a line of shit to get in a woman's pants. We both had fun, so no harm, no foul, right?"

His eyes darkened and I knew he was angry at how flippant I sounded.

Too bad. Hurt shifted into anger.

Rising up onto my toes, I put my hand on his chest and pressed my lips to his ear. "Besides, it's not like I've spent every night alone pining for you."

It wasn't even a lie. Stretching the truth, maybe. But not a lie.

In a blink, I found myself pinned to the wall, his mouth a breath from mine. "I'm not the sort of man you can toy with."

My breath hissed out of me in a shocked rush as he licked my lower lip, then sucked it into his mouth. When he let go, I had to fight not to whimper.

"Do you really want to keep pushing me?" he asked,

sliding a hand down my belly, his fingers pointing down so that I could feel the tips brushing over my crotch. He curled them in, and I gasped as he pressed them against me, forcing the seam of my jeans to rub into my sensitive flesh.

Swallowing, I stared at him.

He did it again, and then licked my lip, sucked it into his mouth. This time, before he let me go, he sank his teeth into the fleshy bit. He released it a little slower even as he increased the pressure of his fingers between my thighs. I couldn't swallow the moan, and my hands curled into fists as I tried not to move my hips against him.

"Tell me you met up with some guy. That you found some Sub here and let your inner Dom out. Did it help any? You sure don't feel like anybody has let you burn the edge off."

He popped the button on my jeans and dipped his hand inside. When he slid his fingers past the waistband of my panties, I closed my eyes, my head falling back as I sucked in air.

"You're so tight." His voice was rough. "I think you'd come if I just...did..."

He twisted his fingers and I felt my body tightening, ready, eager. But before I could reach it, he stopped.

"See how close you are? Tell me about the guy you were with, Dena. Did you let him get you naked? Did you suck his cock? Did he go down on you?"

I opened my eyes to mere slits and glared at him.

"You're an asshole," I said.

"That's not an answer." He pushed one knee between

my thighs and shoved upward. "Unless it is. Is that it?" Jealousy laced his words. "Did you take his cock there, Dena? Up that snug, sweet ass? Did you make your Sub fuck your ass?"

I leaned in, quick as a snake, and nipped his lower lip. He responded by fisting his hand in my hair and yanking my head back. We glared at each other for a long, tense moment, and then, slowly, he lowered me back to the floor.

"I didn't pick up a Sub." I ran my tongue along my swollen bottom lip. "I found a Dom...and I brought him into one of the rooms here."

Arik growled.

"No one Dominates you but me." His voice was fierce.

I dug my nails into the back of his neck. "I don't do one-way claims, Arik."

His eyes held mine for several seconds.

And then his mouth slammed down on mine.

The next few minutes were a struggle between us. He controlled the kiss, but I didn't want to yield. I was too angry. Angry for wanting him, for not being able to have him. Angry at him for fucking another woman and at myself for caring.

He fought to free me from my clothes and after a moment, I began to tear at his shirt, then his jeans. I wasn't even sure how we managed to get our clothes off, only that they seemed to be there one moment and gone the next.

When he stopped kissing me, I swore at him. He

chuckled and flipped me over, pulling me onto my hands and knees. I barely had a moment to adjust to the new position when he was there, pushing inside me with one near-brutal thrust.

He was big and hard, and I felt every ridge, every groove. I'd be feeling him inside me for days.

Suddenly, he stiffened. "Shit, Dena...I'm not...I didn't..."

He didn't have to finish the sentence. I reached back as he started to pull out, my fingers wrapping around his wrist. I looked over my shoulder at him.

"I'm on the pill. I'm clean. Are you?"

He groaned, a shudder running through him. "Yes."

I shivered at the want in his voice. Something inside felt a little broken, a little battered. Still watching his face, I opened my mouth, uncertain what I was going to say until the words came out.

"Either we have something going or we don't. If you don't want to see me for anything but this..." I gasped as he rolled his hips. "Then enjoy it. This is the last time."

"Dena," he rasped out my name as he withdrew and then slammed forward again.

Over and over, he drove into me, his fingers digging into my hips. Every inch of me was on fire, pleasure and pain coming together until I knew I wouldn't survive the explosion. There was no finesse in this, no S&M games. It was sheer domination and submission in its purest form. One person handing over control to the other with the sort of trust that rarely existed between two people.

When I came, I managed to stay upright only through

284

sheer will and the grip of Arik's hands on my hips. Then he followed, curling his body over mine, lips pressed to my shoulder. He stayed there for a minute, not putting his full weight on me, but enough that I felt...safe. Protected.

I tried to get to my feet as he straightened, but my legs were still quivering too much to hold me. A few seconds later, I no longer needed to worry about it because he picked me up and carried me over to the bed.

Closing my eyes, I waited to hear the door close. But it didn't. Instead, I felt the dip of the bed, and then the warmth of him as he wrapped his arm around me, tucking me against his chest as he pulled a blanket over us. I tried not to think about how perfectly my body fit with his.

"What's your phone number?" he asked, his voice drowsy. "I was careless last time and forgot the paper."

"Maybe it just wasn't that important to you," I countered. "Since you were so *careless*."

"Tell me."

His tone didn't leave much room for argument, and I didn't really have the strength to push back anymore.

I told him and he recited it back.

But I didn't ask him for his number.

Not yet. I wasn't sure if I was ready.

# Chapter 9

*Arik*

I'd lost track of time.

I knew it was late, and I knew both of us had slept off and on. And I knew Dena was still asleep now.

I also knew that if I was smart, I'd wake her up, because we both had a job to do in the morning and even if she was friends with the owner, I doubted they'd want us spending the whole night here. Besides, it wasn't like we could wear club clothes to work.

My stomach tightened at the thought of seeing Dena in a court room, arguing a case, while wearing those tight jeans and that shirt. I doubted a single straight man in the room would hear a word she said.

All I could care about, though, was that Dena felt amazing in my arms and I was more at peace now than I had been in a very long time. Since moving here for sure. I wasn't certain I'd ever felt this way even back in Chicago.

She made a grumbling sound under her breath, an odd noise that made me smile. I thought about maybe rolling her onto her back, spreading her thighs and licking a path down her belly to her pussy. I'd bring her close to the edge, and then bury myself inside to trigger her orgasm.

Dena closed her hand around my half-hard cock.

My breath hissed out from between my teeth as I arched up into her touch. She fisted me tight, dragging her hand up, then down. As I watched, she sat up and stared down at me, eyes heavy-lidded, hair mussed. Her bottom lip was slightly swollen and I wanted to bite it again.

"I was..." I paused, trying to gather my thoughts as she twisted her wrist just near the head and tightened her grip to just this side of painful. "Hmmmm...do that again."

She did and whatever I'd been thinking scattered. It took me a moment to regain it.

"I was thinking about waking you up."

"You missed your chance." Her voice was lower than normal, full of something deep and sexual, of something that was purely *her*.

I started to sit, but she pushed me down with a hand on my chest and threw her leg over my hips. I caught her waist, but didn't move her. I watched as she straddled me, waited to see what she was going to do next.

"I'm not in the mood for *master may I*," she said, staring at me, a defiant look in her pale eyes.

She slid against me, her cunt slick and hot.

"I..." I supported her weight as she lifted up. "I have no problem with that."

A moment later, she sank down on me, and I groaned. She was so tight, her body so small that I had to wonder how I managed to fit inside her. Then she began to move, leaning forward to give herself the leverage she wanted.

The view was mesmerizing.

There's nothing like having a woman straddle you, the way her breasts lift and move, feeling her pussy gripping your cock. And a woman like Dena...with her delicate features and pale skin, she looked like some sort of ethereal creature.

A faint half-smile curled her lips as she rode me, her breath catching when I arched up into her. Her fingers flexed on my chest, nails biting into my skin, sending the sweetest pricks of pain through me. She was going to leave a mark on me.

As if she hadn't already.

She panted my name and my eyes met hers. Our rhythm sped up and, all too soon, we took each other straight over the edge, ending the best damn ride of my life.

As she collapsed against my chest, I curled my arms around her and wondered if maybe I hadn't found the most perfect woman in the world.

We stood on the curb outside the club, the chilly October air waking me up more than anything else had. I'd already flagged her down a cab and it sat idling at the curb. A part of me didn't want to let her go.

As she climbed inside, I leaned down after her. She gave me a sober look and I whispered her number into her ear.

Instead of the smile I'd been hoping for, I got a blank face that told me she was already pulling away.

"I'll be impressed if you actually use it," she said.

*If.* She said *if* rather than *when.* I couldn't be offended, though, not after the way I'd acted. But, still, there was something I wanted to know.

"You didn't ask for mine."

That blank look didn't change. "I'm not going to. Not until I know you're not being an ass again."

She shrugged and looked away.

I kissed her cheek and then pulled back, resisting the urge to take her mouth...or climb in the back with her and go back to my place where I could take more than her mouth.

After they'd pulled off into the night, I turned and started to walk. It wasn't that far to my apartment, and I needed to think.

I never should have left her number behind to begin with, and I sure as hell wasn't going to neglect calling her this time. I ran through the number again just to make sure I still had it. I'd never been with a woman who made me feel what Dena did. I couldn't even describe it, but it was...something.

Something different.

Something amazing.

Something...real.

It was time, I decided. Time to stop chasing one woman after another, time to stop bouncing around, hoping I could find more than one Sub I clicked with. Time for something more than just sex.

Although, it was funny. If I'd been looking for a woman, I never would have chosen her. I wouldn't have thought I'd be happy with a switch, somebody who had their own dominant streak, who made me work for every inch. But that was one of the things I found myself drawn to, something I wanted in a partner. A person who automatically did everything I said to do without a word had once been appealing, but I now realized that desire had stopped when I'd stopped caring only about sex and started looking for something outside the bedroom.

I wanted Dena.

# Chapter 10

## *Dena*

Face down in the pillows, I tried to ignore the world a little longer.

It was raining, which wasn't strange for New York in October. I could hear the persistent drops pelting my window, and the dim light that had managed to filter in through the edges of the blinds was that thin watery gray that only came with an autumn rain.

It would've been the perfect day for sleeping in, then laying around and doing nothing but reading a book, maybe watching some TV before ordering in Chinese. It was too bad I hadn't been born independently wealthy. Then I could call Bethany and tell her to kiss my ass.

I could find a hundred other ways to help people.

But I didn't have that option.

When my phone chirped, signaling a text, I flopped over onto my back and stared up at the ceiling.

It wasn't quite six which made it an awful time for

anybody to be texting. It could be one of the girls, though. And if it was Krissy, that meant something was wrong.

Or she hadn't gone to bed yet and was drunk-dialing me. If that was the case, I was going to kick her ass the next time I saw her.

If it was someone else...

Sighing, I picked up my phone.

I didn't recognize the number and the first few words creeped me the hell out. I bolted upright, pulling my blankets more tightly around me.

Then I processed the name.

Arik.

He'd signed the dirty little text.

> *Are you naked? If not, you should be, because I've been thinking about you naked all night. —Arik*

My breath hitched a little. Shifting under the blankets, I considered the camisole and brief boy shorts I'd pulled on after my shower a few hours ago. Stretching a little, I took my time in composing a reply.

> *I only sleep naked if somebody is around to help me stay warm.*

The clock kicked over to six, and right on time, my alarm went off. I turned it off as Arik's reply came up.

> *I was thinking that maybe you and I could hook up soon, maybe take some time and go away somewhere. I've got a*

*cabin right on the edge of*
*Lake Michigan. We could*
*take a week up there, and*
*I can keep you warm all*
*night. Interested?*

There was a funny, painful little twist in the vicinity of my heart. I couldn't believe how much I wanted to immediately accept the offer. The thought of an entire week with only the two of us was enough to make me even wetter than I already was.

Still, I wasn't so certain what he proposed was smart. Actually, I was pretty damn certain that it was *stupid*. It didn't make me want it any less, didn't make me want *him* any less.

I needed to stop. He was a defense attorney and I worked for the prosecution. Maybe he didn't seem too concerned about it, but I had to be. I was still trying to build my career, and the ugly truth of it was that women always came out of anything looking worse than a guy did. Especially in a career like law. And especially for a prosecutor.

Refusing to let myself even consider what he was suggesting, I tapped out a brief answer.

*It wouldn't be smart,*
*Arik. You know that. None*
*of this is smart.*

I swung my legs over the side of the bed and waited for him to answer.

He did, and surprisingly, his answer was laid back.

*I find myself not*
*caring about smart when*
*it comes to you. We don't*

*have to do it now. After
this case is over, we can
talk about it then.*

Rolling my eyes, I blew out a breath. He made it seem like this case would end in the next few weeks, the next month or so. And that we would still want this then.

*It's a murder trial,
Arik. It could take months,
longer.*

A moment later, my phone rang, and I wasn't all that surprised to see it was Arik calling.

"It won't take months," he said matter-of-factly, not even bothering with a greeting. "It would be nice if you had a boss who cared about the truth, but all she cares about is winning. You strike me as a woman who does care, though. My client is innocent, Dena. I'm going to find a way to prove it, and if Bethany doesn't listen, I'll go over her head."

Which is exactly what I planned on doing if she tried to screw with things in the police report.

"I know Bethany's not going to listen to me or to you, but if you know that Leayna's innocent, I know you won't stop trying. Maybe if you find something..."

My gut twisted. Pressing my hand to my forehead, I whispered, "Arik, stop. I've got a job to do."

"Yeah. Part of that job is searching out the truth." His voice softened. "Bethany doesn't get that, but you do."

Quiet fell, an awkward, uncomfortable lack of sound, and I pushed up from the bed, moving over to the window to stare outside at the slowly falling rain. I was about ready to tell him that I needed to go when he broke the silence.

"I'm sorry," he murmured. "I didn't mean to turn this into something about the case. I've spent most the night thinking about you...about us."

"There isn't an us," I said automatically.

"You and I both know that's a lie." His tone changed, now gruff, low and heated. He sounded the way he did when he was inside me. "There is an us. There's something between us, and you know it." A moment of silence, and then he continued, "I want there to be even *more* between us." He paused again, then asked softly, "Do you want that?"

I closed my eyes, tried to ignore everything that his words made me feel. "Arik..."

"Don't think about our jobs, the case, any of that. We can figure that out, Dena. Just answer the question. Do you want it or not?"

I wanted it so badly that I hurt. And I was tired of denying it.

"Yes."

"Then we'll figure this out," he said. The tension in his voice told me just how much that single word meant to him. "Go to work. I'll talk to you later." A beat of silence. "And I'll think about you all day."

The call ended even while I was still shivering from that last sentence. It was strange, how freeing it had been to admit that. I let that feeling soak into me as I showered and got ready for work.

Yes, I wanted to find out what was going on between

Arik and me. I wanted to see where it was going, and what might come of it. He'd been right to tell me to focus on that and not the job before I answered. My dream job that was turning into my nightmare, a fact I had to accept now as my steps slowed to a halt outside the all-too familiar building.

Staring up at the imposing structure, I could feel the bagel I'd eaten turning to a stone in my belly, the coffee becoming acid.

I was going to end up with an ulcer.

"Six months," I told myself. I'd have an ulcer within six months if things didn't change.

I thought about all the times I tried to talk to Bethany about things I'd noticed about this case, about the report Dunne had filed, and how she'd just brushed it off.

What would happen if Arik found evidence of Leayna's innocence? What would happen then? Would Bethany have a way of making it disappear just so she didn't have to admit that she'd indicted the wrong person?

A burning sensation settled mid-center of my chest and I had to force myself to take the first stair. After that, it got easier. As I ascended, I gave myself a mental pep talk. The one good thing about this mess with Pierce was that I wouldn't have to deal with the two of them as much. The paralegals were easier to get along with. Maybe I could do some more digging into Leayna with my time too. If Arik was that convinced of her innocence, there had to be something to prove it, right?

Walking down the hallway, though, it took only one minute to have my mood go from cautiously optimistic to straight down into the bowels of hell. I couldn't even call what I was feeling now pessimistic.

I was feeling downright nauseated and it took everything I had not to throw up as Bethany continued to speak.

Pierce was cleaning out his desk, not looking at me, although the back of his neck was red. Under his designer suit, his broad shoulders were rigid and he moved in jerky motions. I wouldn't have been surprised to see him erupt at any second.

Bethany continued to talk in cool, concise tones as I stared at Pierce, unable to believe what I was hearing, unable to believe he was putting up with this shit.

Finally, Bethany stopped speaking and lifted an eyebrow, a pleased expression on her face. "You've been awfully quiet, Dena. Don't you have anything to say?"

I opened my mouth, then closed it. I wasn't sure it was smart to say what was going through my head at the moment. I needed time to think things through. She started to smirk. Slowly, I angled my gaze back to her.

"Yes, Bethany. As a matter of fact, there is something I'd like to say."

Pierce tensed, his hands tightening on the files he held. Bethany's features froze.

I ignored her, focusing completely on the man who had yet to speak a single word in his defense. "Are you really going to let her do this, Pierce?"

I stared at him hard, and his cheeks flushed. Finally, he shot a look up at me, and I couldn't have imagined that glint of temper in his eyes. Anger burned there, but it wasn't directed at me.

Bethany cut in, "Perhaps if you hadn't done something stupid, and filed a report–"

"I'm done with playing, Bethany." The cold, sharp bite of my voice surprised even me. "We all know I didn't make a move on Pierce, and that I haven't acted unprofessionally with him. There was no way I'd let that go on my record, so *yes*, I filed a counter-complaint. If you think I should have let it go, then you haven't been paying attention to the kind of person I am."

She started to tap her foot, a small foot shod in pink Prada. *A predator in Prada.* Arik had called that right.

"You might be able to throw your weight around with him." I jerked my chin toward Pierce. He'd stopped gathering up his personal belongings and stood there, rigid and unblinking. "But that won't work with me."

Her eyes were cold, assessing. Deciding to ignore her, I gave her my back and focused on Pierce.

"You did good work when we were putting those briefs together, Pierce. I've seen some of the others you've drafted for her. I think you're probably a good lawyer. She's got no right doing this to you." I shook my head. "Is she *really* that good in bed?"

A weird choking noise escaped him, and I wondered if he was trying not to laugh.

Bethany took a step toward me. "That's quite enough."

"Well, you've already complained that I'm unprofessional." Giving her a saccharine smile, I offered, "You want to write me up on that, go ahead, but you

300

might want to consider that I'll make sure any inquiries specifically state why I made that statement."

Pierce was no longer the only one in the room with a flushed, angry face. Bethany's shoulders were rigid, her mouth pinched into a tight, small line as she closed the distance between us.

I tensed, wondering if she would finally snap and slap me. Part of me even wished that she would, that I'd have something I could really use against her.

Surprisingly, she just studied me. After a moment, she spoke, but only to address Pierce. "Please finish getting your things together. You need to be out of here within the hour. I don't know how long the investigation will take. Hopefully, you'll be back to work once it's complete."

The smile she gave him made me want to roll my eyes, but I refrained. Pierce looked away, not looking very impressed.

She reached out and laid a hand on his arm. "I'll put in my recommendation. I think you'll just get a warning on your record. More than likely, you'll be back to work within the next couple of weeks."

"Gee, thanks." The words were thick, bitter with irony. He didn't shake off her hand, however.

She pursed her lips and added softly, "That is assuming Dena doesn't decide to press charges. They will talk to her about her claims."

"I'm betting on it." I gave her a hard look. "I'm looking forward to giving them my thoughts on how this all unfolded. From beginning to end."

Her smile wobbled, then fell away entirely.

She made no other attempts to bait either of us over the next three minutes. That's how long it took Pierce to vacate his office. Bethany followed him to the door and closed it behind him. When she turned to look at me, I could tell she was going to say something, but I was ready for her.

She saw the phone I'd pulled out of my pocket and blinked.

The outrage on her face smoothed away like it had never existed. Her eyes cleared, her mouth curved into a perfunctory smile.

"Please don't tell me you feel the need to record everything you and I say. We're coworkers." She took a step toward me, as if she was trying to regain her footing. "Actually, I'm your supervisor. You're supposed to be able to trust me with things."

"Yeah. That'd be nice." I glanced at my phone again, tapped the screen. It was on my email account, not that she knew. Just the possibility that I was keeping a visual record of her behavior had sucked the malicious wind out of her sails.

It wasn't the ideal way to handle this, but I wouldn't let her screw with my career any more than she already had. And since I wasn't actually recording, no one would be able to claim any sort of breach of privilege.

She flicked another look at the phone, and then walked past me. There was an expression of acute dislike on her features, but she kept her face turned away enough that if my phone had been recording, she couldn't have been seen. "As you can imagine, Pierce's suspension came at an inopportune time. We're trying to expedite the trial on Leayna Mance, and now I've lost my co-chair. You'll be taking his place."

Her words hit me like a punch in the chest. I gripped the phone tighter as I sucked in a breath.

I couldn't have heard her right.

"Second chair?" I said softly. A few weeks ago, I would have been delighted. Now...shit.

"Yes." Her blue eyes for hard as she stared at me. "Welcome to the big times, Dena. You're going to trial."

# Unlawful Attraction - Vol. 4

# Chapter 1

## *Dena*

*Welcome to the big times*, Bethany had said.

The big times could kiss my ass.

When my phone vibrated, signaling the arrival of yet *another* text, I closed my eyes. It wasn't quite noon on a lazy, rainy Sunday and if life had been perfect, I could've maybe responded to one of those texts, asked him to come over. Maybe we could have taken the next step to see if whatever this was between us could be more.

But life wasn't perfect.

Not even when I'd gotten the one thing I thought I wanted.

The autumn rain that had always seemed so comforting was now driving me crazy. I rubbed my hands over my arms. For some reason, I felt trapped inside my apartment. No matter how much I liked to go out, I'd never been the sort of person who got stir-crazy being in one place too long. At the moment, however, I was

305

almost claustrophobic.

Staring out my window at the leaden gray skies, I made myself ignore my phone. Again. But every text, every call I didn't respond to, or that I let go to voicemail, made it that much harder to ignore the next one.

The sight of his name flashing on the screen was like a punch to the gut.

Not that Arik had said anything or done anything to upset me. On the contrary, his texts ranged from teasing to tempting to sly, and despite my miserable outlook on everything at the moment, each one managed to make me smile.

The phone calls that rolled over to voice mail? The same. He left me smiling...right up until the third call. That one had been laced with a bit of an edge. Nothing rude or even close to hurtful, but I knew I was pushing him further and further away with each passing moment.

Not that I could blame him for being annoyed at me. Here I was dodging his calls, and just a few days ago, I'd been giving him grief because he'd asked for my number but hadn't called back. I hadn't even considered that he might've lost it. Now, he was doing what I'd wanted him to do, and I was leaving him hanging without a word of explanation.

I owed him that.

Except I didn't know what to say.

Things had changed?

Things had *really* changed.

And that was simplifying it to the $N$th degree.

Wandering back over to my desk, I looked at the case

files Bethany had insisted I take home. She'd given me a snide *you need to get up to speed,* and it'd taken all my self-control not to point out that if she hadn't kept me in the dark all this time, I wouldn't have needed to get caught up.

But there hadn't been a point to saying any of it. She would've found a way to make it my fault and possibly take me back off the case. Dodge, blame, make excuses. It was her MO. Basically do everything except take responsibility for her own actions. She just wanted the win, no matter how she got there.

How in the hell she ended up a prosecutor, I wondered. She should have been an ambulance chaser. Not even a respectable defense attorney like Arik would stoop to the lengths I suspected Bethany had gone to ensure a victory. She was on par with those sleazy dickwads who used every trick in the book to get their own way.

Finally, I settled down on the couch with one of the files and my fourth cup of coffee. I already had notepads and pencils there from earlier. I'd gone through a couple things before needing to get up and stretch my legs. Now, it was time to focus on the report from the medical examiner.

Within just a few minutes of starting the report, I felt myself starting to get a headache. Considering this was supposed to be an open and shut case, the report from the ME was going to have the jury wondering what the hell was going on.

It sure as hell had me wondering.

I wasn't a medical examiner, and I didn't have a lot of experience reading these types of reports, but from where I sat, it cast plenty of doubt on Leayna Mance as the murderer.

Except I was supposed to help Bethany put Leayna behind bars.

If I'd seen this report earlier, I barely would've considered Leayna a suspect at all. Basically, just someone who needed to be talked to and then crossed off the list before we could get down to finding the real killer.

A killer who no one else seemed to be looking for.

I knew nothing I said would be listened to though, especially considering that a witness I wanted to talk to wasn't exactly around to interview about an alternate theory of the crime.

He was sort of, well, dead.

I'd called Dunne to see if he could help me track the guy down. It hadn't been too hard, as it turned out, because the guy had just been fished out of the river.

In pieces.

A couple of detectives were pissed about it, too, since it turned out he'd been a police informant. Dunne was supposed to let me know if it that investigation connected to my case at all. I wasn't holding my breath. Considering the cops had found fifty thousand in cash in the guy's apartment, finding that murderer wouldn't be pleasant.

I could already imagine what Bethany would say if I went to her with any of this. She'd probably theorize that

Leayna Mance had paid the guy to kill Mr. Mance, even if I brought up the fact that the guy had been a possible witness to the late Mr. Mance having cheated on his wife. A tenacious prosecutor wasn't necessarily a bad thing, but one who got a theory in their head and never considered any other possibilities might go too far to protect what they thought of as the truth.

Bethany was definitely the latter.

It'd take a literal smoking gun to sway her opinion, and even then I wasn't sure she'd accept anything less than an actual recording of the crime, complete with authentication certification that the recording wasn't a fake. Maybe not even then...

My phone rang again, interrupting my thoughts. I glanced down at it, almost ready to answer it just so I could have one less thing to worry about. This wasn't really the sort of thing I wanted to discuss over the phone, but I couldn't keep avoiding him. And obsessing about it wasn't doing me any good either.

But it wasn't Arik.

*Unknown number* flashed across the screen. I would've preferred to ignore it, but considering all of the weird shit going on in this case, I didn't want to miss anything important. It could've been Officer Dunne calling from a payphone. There might be a handful of those still left in the city I supposed.

I answered, keeping my voice flat. "Dena Monroe."

On the other end of the line, I heard open-air, but no response.

I noted the time and gave my name again. "This is

Dena Monroe. Can I help you?"

The call ended.

Even as a divorce lawyer, I'd had my fair share of this sort of thing. Yeah, my personal number was unlisted, but it didn't take much to track down a number these days.

It also could've been a wrong number. That did happen.

Still, an uneasy feeling tripped its way down my spine, and I set my phone down on the desk. I didn't have any proof, but my gut told me that the call was about this case, that things were definitely not as cut-and-dry as Bethany wanted to make them appear.

Outside, the rain continued to batter my window, and it didn't stop until around mid-afternoon. The cessation of the white noise didn't really help me focus though. A little while later, the sun teased me with a few rays of sunshine, and that was the only sign I needed to get out of the apartment for a while.

As soon as I stepped outside, I saw that I wasn't the only one who'd been going stir crazy. The streets were already bustling, and my destination, the little Indian place on the corner, was packed by the time I got there. The hostess recognized me, giving me a quick smile and pointing to a single table in the corner. Tucking myself into the minuscule space, I had barely sat down when my phone buzzed.

It was Arik.

Again.

I didn't like it, but it was the perfect time to respond.

I had an excuse not to answer in any way other than a text. It might've been cowardly of me, but I was okay with that at the moment.

Decision made, I started drafting my text. I was still working on it when the server came by with my usual tea. "Do you want your usual, Dena?"

"Yes." I gave her a distracted smile, my attention on the man I was texting.

As she left, I looked back down at the message, wondering if this was the right thing. He'd told me, made me believe we could have something. Then this mess happened with the case.

Was it over before we even had a chance to figure things out?

I read it again.

> *Hi, Arik. Sorry I haven't been able to answer your calls. I'm eating right now. Things with the case have gotten a bit complicated, keeping me busy.*
>
> *We need to talk, but I won't be able to until later this week.*
>
> *I deliberated a moment and then added,*
> *Thinking of you.*

I sent it, then put the phone in my purse, telling myself that I needed to put this out of my head so I could focus on work. We would talk later, once I'd had some time to get my priorities sorted out and had a plan in place.

Monday was about as far away from Friday as it could be. It dawned sunny and bright, the sun's light trying to scorch my corneas, teasing the headache that had been nagging me on and off most of the weekend.

I didn't want to be here at all, but there wasn't anything to be done for it. I had to go to work.

I hadn't heard from Arik since a text he'd sent Sunday evening saying that he'd get back to me when he had a time he could talk.

He needed to hurry the hell up.

On the other hand, I needed time to think through what I wanted to say, because I still had absolutely no idea. No idea what to do or say. No idea of what I even really wanted.

Distracted by my thoughts, I didn't even notice the commotion going on outside my office door until I almost ran into one of the maintenance guys on my way in. One who seemed to be carrying things *out* of my office.

What the hell?

"What is this?" I demanded.

He glanced over his shoulder at me. "Cleaning this old place out." He paused, squinting at me. "Are you Ms. Monroe?"

"Yes." Planting one hand on my hip, I stared at him and tried to look intimidating. It was hard to look tough though when you stood five foot nothing, and had a skinny vanilla latte with a double shot of espresso in your hand, but I did my best. "You want to tell me why you're cleaning it out? It happens to be my office."

A part of me hoped that Bethany had just decided to fire me. If she had...I hated the thrill of happiness that went through me. I should've been devastated that I lost the job I'd wanted my whole life.

Before I could get too excited though, the guy spoke again.

"You got a new office." He pointed down the hall and rattled off a number. "Down there."

My heart sank as I realized the office was right next to Pierce. It'd be bigger, but I really didn't want to be any closer to the man than I had to be.

"Okay." I waved a hand at him. "Sorry about getting snippy. I was just surprised. Thank you."

"Don't thank me. Thank your boss." He turned and ambled off, pushing a cart laden with boxes.

I stepped into my office and then looked back down the hall. "I'll finish up in here, if it's okay with you. Most of it's my personal stuff."

He glanced at me and shrugged as if to say it didn't matter to him one way or the other. I ducked inside the tiny space I'd been using as an office and looked around. It looked like pretty much everything, save for the corkboard and a few other little odds and ends, had already been moved.

Blowing out a breath, I reached for the door behind me.

A hand shot out, and I didn't have time to panic or even think.

Two seconds later, the door was shut and Arik Porter stood in front of me.

"Miss Monroe, I believe you wanted to talk." His voice was calm, even professional.

"What're you doing?" I demanded, gaping at him. "This is—"

That was all I managed to get out before his mouth slammed down over mine.

A hundred indignant questions and statements faded away, replaced by an insatiable, irrational sort of need clawing through me. Arik's thigh pushed between mine, and the flirty, flippy skirt that I'd worn today was no barrier. He kept moving until his knee was pressed directly against me.

He tore his mouth away, nipping at my bottom lip. "Do you know how long it's been since I had you wrapped around my dick, Dena?"

Things inside me twisted.

"I can tell you...far too long."

Shit.

He wasn't kidding. It'd been too long.

I took a deep breath, trying to clear my head. It did no good though, because with it, came the scent of him. Soap and spice and whatever it was that was him.

Fuck.

When he pressed his lips to my neck, I swallowed a whimper, and then he kissed me again.

Greedy, I sucked his tongue into my mouth, and when his body drew tight in response, a primitive sort of victory welled up inside me. I loved that I could do this to this man. This dominant, powerful man.

Arik ran his hands through my hair.

We needed to stop, I thought hazily. This was crazy.

I couldn't bring the words to my lips yet. I wanted him so much.

Cool air caressed my chest, and I realized he'd let go of my hair at some point to start unbuttoning my blouse. If he touched his hands or mouth to my breasts, I'd be gone. There'd be no stopping.

"Stop," I finally managed to say. "Arik, stop...we're not doing this here."

He reached down between us and cupped me, one finger rubbing against my panties. I was already aching and wet for him.

"Are you sure?" he asked, a hot, sweet teasing note in his voice.

I bit my lower lip to muffle my moan as his fingers pressed against me. He backed me up against the door and leaned into me, his body hard in all the right places.

In the sane, rational part of my mind that wasn't already completely undone by him, a voice whispered, *"You're in your office. You're supposed to be meeting with Bethany soon. You can't do this."*

Bethany.

Office.

Dammit all to hell.

I caught his wrist and dragged his hand away. "No, Arik."

They were the hardest two words I'd ever had to say.

Against my lips, he murmured, "No?"

Feeling the edges of my control fracturing, I forced my hands between us and shoved at his chest. "No."

315

He took a step back, his expression wild for a single moment before he brought himself back under control.

Voice shaking, I gestured toward the hall. "Bethany McDermott might think it's just fine to screw around on the job, but I don't. I'm not doing this here."

Arik held up his hands to show that he was backing off. "You're right. I'm sorry." He scraped his fingertips down his jaw, scratching at the stubble already darkening his chin. "I...Dena, you make me lose my mind a little. I'm sorry."

He meant it, I could tell.

"If we're working, we can't do this. We can't work if we do this sort of thing." *We might not work anyway.* The thought flitted through my head. Looking away, I pushed a shaky hand through my hair to smooth it down. Taking a deep breath, I forced my gaze back to his. I had to tell him. I'd waited too long. "Listen, Arik, about the case–" The shrill sound of the phone on my desk interrupted me. Feeling drained already, I moved toward it and picked it up. "Dena Monroe."

"We're meeting in fifteen. You've got a decent office now, so use it. Get your ass together." Bethany's voice, flat and emotionless, barked out of the receiver. I had no chance to respond before she hung up. Still, as I lowered the phone into the cradle, I snapped a sarcastic little salute.

"The queen has spoken." Arik said, his voice dry. I looked back just in time to see him run a hand through his hair, settling it into place. He adjusted his tie and the lapels of his jacket. Just like that, he looked like he had just stepped off the cover of GQ Lawyerly.

Me, on the other hand? I needed to swing by the ladies' room and make judicious use of one of the stalls, otherwise I'd get to walk around with damp panties for the rest of the day. I was sure Arik would've loved that, but it wasn't something I planned on sharing. Of course, I also needed to touch up my lipstick since smudge-proof wasn't really much protection when it came to Arik's kisses. Then I had to brace myself to deal with Bethany.

Fifteen minutes wouldn't be nearly enough time for that, but I had a feeling it was all I'd get. What I wasn't going to be able to do was tell him the one thing he needed to know.

Shit.

I paused with my hand on the door. "I'll go first." I glanced up at him. "When can we talk?"

"I was thinking about tonight. I'd like to take you out for dinner."

I closed my eyes. Dinner. It sounded like a date, wonderful, really. But it also sounded like a terrible idea at the same time, and if I was smart I would've been thinking up ways to explain that to him. There were a thousand reasons why going out tonight would be a bad idea, and yet I couldn't think of a single one that would make sense without a much longer discussion.

I opened the door and stepped out. A part of me breathed a sigh of relief when I was able to slip into the bathroom before Arik emerged. I took as little time as possible, hoping it was enough time for Arik to have left, but he was still in the hall when I stepped out.

I suppressed a scowl as he came over to me. I wanted to demand that he leave, but he gave me a polite smile and started talking.

"Ms. Monroe, I'd like to thank you for the advice on the divorce attorney," Arik said, head bent toward mine. His voice was brisk, business-like. "I'll take those recommendations to my friend. I'm sure she'll appreciate it as well."

"Ah, yes." I swallowed. "Of course. No...no trouble at all." I felt like I was rambling. Did I need to say anything else?

He stopped walking and I did the same, looking up at him. He held out a hand. Befuddled, I reached out and he shook my hand once, twice. Just a nice, professional handshake, nothing strange here.

It was one of the most surreal things I'd ever experienced.

"Dena...oh, and I see you two have already found each other. Excellent."

At the sound of Bethany's voice, my blood chilled. My smile froze on my face.

Shit. Shit. Shit.

She drew closer as I let go of Arik's hand. Her eyes slid all over him and a stab of jealousy went through me. I would've hated anyone looking at him like that. It being Bethany was so much worse.

"Feeling out the opposition already, Miss Monroe?" She jerked a hand toward my office. "I was just heading your way. Let's go to your new office, shall we?"

She turned, the indication that I should trail along

318

behind her like a disobedient child very clear.

Then I realized she hadn't only been speaking to me.

She'd been speaking to Arik, too.

Was he here...?

Oh. Oh, *shit*. This was what I got for dodging his phone calls all weekend.

"You're here for a meeting, aren't you?" I asked, my voice low as I started to follow Bethany.

He glanced my way, then nodded, his expression puzzled.

I really should have just blurted it out earlier, but it was too late now. It was time to face the music.

# Chapter 2

*Arik*

Dena made me into a complete moron. I still couldn't believe I had almost pushed her up against the wall and sank my dick inside her, right there in the middle of the cubicle that had been her office.

I completely lost my mind around her. That's all there was to it.

And I loved it. I couldn't deny it.

Everything about her, from the way she submitted to the way she fought, the way she responded as a Dominant in her own right, how she gave as well as she took. All of it challenged me.

But I was going to have to be a lot more careful. She was right. What I'd almost done had been beyond stupid, beyond irresponsible. It wouldn't have only ruined me if we'd been caught, it could've destroyed Dena's career. It didn't matter what Bethany did. If she'd caught Dena and me together, she'd have made sure Dena paid for it.

Slanting a look over at Dena, I opened my mouth to

say something. I didn't even know what I'd been planning to say, because whatever it was died as I caught sight of her pale, strained face.

Her mouth was drawn into a tight line, and I wondered if maybe she hadn't been feeling well over the weekend. She'd avoided my calls, or at least it seemed that way, despite her text where she insisted she'd been busy. Granted, I wouldn't have put it past Bethany to dump a shitload of work on her ADAs at the last minute just so she could go out on the town. It wasn't like Bethany was exactly known for her work ethic. That was practically common knowledge at this point.

I wanted to pull Dena aside, ask her if she was okay, but there was no time for it. And no place.

Bethany led us to a door and pulled out a key, but instead of unlocking it, she turned the key over to Dena. "It's yours, after all. You should be the first one to go in."

"Well, besides the maintenance people who moved me in, of course." Dena's tone was perfectly level, but Bethany and I both heard the bite.

Bethany's sapphire eyes flashed, but when she saw me looking, she just laughed. "Like we'd make *you* do all that heavy lifting, Dena. You could break a nail...or your back, as tiny as you are. We wouldn't want that, would we?"

I wiggled my jaw, recalling the strength Dena had in her small frame. Somehow I didn't think hefting a few boxes would do her any harm.

Dena unlocked the door and stepped inside, flicking on the lights. From where I stood, I could tell that it was just the typical office any ADA would get, but as I watched, Dena's shoulders rose, then fell on a breath that seemed more than a little unsteady. She stepped to the side quickly, allowing Bethany and me to enter. I waited for Bethany and she lingered, her gaze drifting over me. I resisted the urge to curl my lip.

I didn't mind a woman finding me attractive, but there was something about how Bethany looked at me that made me think of one of those female insects who ate the males after mating.

Moving toward the desk and the two miserable chairs in front of it, I looked around. "Where's your other ADA? Lawton, right?"

Bethany had probably sent him out to get donuts already.

She gave me a sharp smile, as though she'd caught that last thought. "I haven't had a chance to eat anything today." She gave Dena a dazzling smile. "I'm sure Arik is also hungry. Why don't you run to the deli on the corner and grab something for us? You can get it this time, can't you? I'll get it next time."

"No need." I gave them both a pleasant smile as I sat. "I ordered a dozen bagels and coffee for four on my way in. It's being delivered. We've got maybe five minutes. I'm sure the delivery person will be able to find us, right?"

Bethany's eyes went frosty for a split second before she smiled at me. That smile didn't reach her eyes. It rarely did. "How kind of you, Arik. Although we won't need the fourth coffee. I didn't get around to notifying anybody outside my office, but Pierce Lawton has been temporarily reassigned. He'll be back in a few days, but Dena has been made second chair."

Dena.

It hit me almost like a physical blow.

I turned my head and stared at her.

*The case had gotten complicated.* Wasn't that what she said in her text?

Complicated?

That was a hell of an understatement.

"Dena might like that fourth coffee, though," Bethany said, chattering on like any one of us actually gave a fuck about an extra coffee. "She seems to have something of a caffeine addiction, I'm afraid."

"It's either coffee or the blood of my enemies, Bethany." Dena gave a tight smile without looking my way. "Coffee seems the safest option."

I was still looking at her. Only when I sensed Bethany staring at me did I look away, forcing myself to meet Bethany's gaze.

"I assure you," Bethany said, smiling prettily. "She looks young and inexperienced, but I've been watching her. She's got a sharp mind. She'll do fine."

"I've no doubt." I was surprised how even I managed to keep my voice.

Second chair.

She'd known. All fucking weekend.

I could tell by the way she wouldn't look at me that this hadn't come as a surprise.

She'd known when we'd been in her office, dammit.

Not even ten minutes ago, and she hadn't said anything.

How could this be happening?

A million things raged inside me, but my game face was exceptional, as always. I managed a nonchalant air as I put my briefcase on my lap and opened it.

"We need to get down to brass tacks, don't we? I want to talk about the break-in, among other things."

"The break-in has nothing to do with anything." Bethany waved a dismissive hand. "Mrs. Mance lives in a nice neighborhood. I heard she had some pretty expensive pieces of art. Somebody probably wanted to make some money."

"Your average thug wouldn't know a Picasso from a postage stamp, Bethany." I slapped a list of the destroyed pieces on the desk. She'd settled down behind it despite the fact that it was supposed to be Dena's office. "All the damaged pieces seem to be accounted for. Nothing was stolen. Just...destroyed."

"It's still not related to this case."

"We don't know that," Dena said from off to my side.

I resisted the urge to look at her.

"We do." Bethany gave her a cold look that made my hands curl into fists. "There is *no* evidence connecting the two events. No reason for anyone to ransack Ms. Mance's house. Unless, of course, she was trying for sympathy. Or maybe an insurance scam."

"She has no reason to do that," I said through gritted teeth. I wasn't sure which was pissing me off more, Bethany's treatment of Dena or her attitude toward

Leayna.

"Money's always a motive. If her late husband had been planning on divorcing her..."

"She doesn't have any money issues," Dena neatly interrupted as she pulled a file out of a box and put a report down on the desk in front of Bethany. "I had a source look into it."

I saw a real flicker of surprise on Bethany's face. "You were able to follow up on quite a bit this weekend."

Maybe Dena really had been busy.

Dena started to say something else, but Bethany cut her off, dismissing her as she focused on me. "We have a solid case against Mrs. Mance, Arik. She'd be wise to just plead out."

I took a second to make sure my voice was calm. "My client is innocent."

There was a knock at the door.

Dena answered while Bethany glared at me. The cute college coed who bustled in, handing out coffee and depositing the box of bagels ended up hurrying out as quickly as possible. I hoped the twenty-dollar tip would make up for the tension in the air.

Dena seemed unaffected, but I knew better. She stood at the window, staring outside as she slowly stirred cream and sugar into her coffee.

Absently, I noted the cup on the desk. Skinny vanilla latte. Next time, I told myself.

*Next time...* What in the hell? Why was I thinking about the next time? Or coffee? Or anything other than the fact that she'd hidden something pretty damn important from me?

And why was I thinking about any of this when I had a case to focus on? A client whose life was on the line.

"Mrs. Mance really should make a deal," Bethany said, her voice even. "None of this is going away."

With that, she stood up, selected a bagel and took a coffee. As she started to walk out, I focused on Dena.

No way in hell would I just let this go. If I walked out of this office, I had no way of knowing when I'd get to talk to her again.

"I'll need your ADA for a little while this morning. I'm sure you're...busy, Bethany, but my client needs to get a few things from her house, and I'm sure you'll want somebody from the DA's office there." Rising, I looked back at her. "To make sure everything's done by the book, of course."

Bethany paused, studying me. Then she shrugged. "Just make sure you don't keep her long. She's needed here."

Shifting my gaze to Dena, I picked up my briefcase.

"Let's go."

I wasn't waiting to have that talk.

And I sure as hell wasn't making that a request.

# Chapter 3

*Dena*

What I wanted to do was tell Arik that I'd meet him at Leayna's, but it didn't make sense for us to take separate cabs, especially since the first one had been so hard to get.

When we stopped a block short of the Mance address, I looked around. Not that parking was easy anywhere in the city, but I didn't think we were going to be walking from here.

The luxury high-rise in front of us hadn't yet opened for general viewing, but real estate agents and businesses were making grabs for prime spots.

But that didn't explain why we'd parked here.

"What are we doing?" I asked as we rolled to a stop.

"Talking."

I didn't bother to play dumb and point out that he'd said we were going to his client's house. I'd known it was bullshit from the second the words left his mouth. It was strange how well I seemed to know him already.

"This place isn't open to the public. How are we...?"

The words stopped as a man came rushing up to the cab door, opening it with a wide smile. "Mr. Porter, it's great to see you, sir. Coming by to see how the construction's going? I hear the penthouse will be ready soon."

"Before Thanksgiving," Arik said easily as he shook hands with the other man. "My father said he ran into a few snags with some permits. He's still learning the differences between building codes in Chicago and New York."

His father?

What the hell?

"If this one does well, do you think your family will continue expanding here?"

His family?

Arik nodded without looking at me. "That's the plan."

"Well, sir, we really appreciate the jobs around here." The man opened the front door. "You and your friend take your time. The building inspector's not due for another few hours."

Arik thanked him and stepped inside, seemingly waiting for me to ask. I didn't because I'd already connected enough dots to construct a decent picture. Defense attorneys made damn good money – or they could.

But it sounded like Arik was already loaded. Family money, even if he hadn't gone into the family business.

Part of me wondered why that was, but I didn't ask. We had enough to deal with without adding family into the mix. Maybe, eventually...I shook my head. No use even attempting to think that far ahead.

Neither of us said a word as we rode up to the top floor, then walked down a dimly lit hall. It was clear that even though things looked completed, there was still a bit more that needed to be done.

It was all black, white and chrome, completely masculine. As Arik locked the door behind us, I looked at the modern fixtures and then over at him. "This place doesn't suit you."

"No." He paced over toward me, crossing his arms over his chest, his emerald green eyes narrowed. "I'm not here to discuss my future accommodations, though. Why didn't you tell me?"

I didn't have to ask what he was talking about. "I was going to," I said. Averting my face, I blew out a breath. "As soon as I figured out how."

"It would have been easy. All you had to do was answer one of my calls, or one of my texts, instead of blowing me off." Biting anger underscored his voice, but I couldn't really blame him. "Look at me."

When I didn't, he shot a hand into my hair.

He. Did. Not.

I jerked against his hold, glaring at him. "Let go."

"And not just blowing me off, but doing it to figure out how to put an innocent woman in jail."

He still hadn't let go of my hair and my scalp was starting to tingle from the pressure, but not in a good way.

331

"*I* spent the weekend getting caught up on a case that had been assigned to me by my direct superior." Rising up on my toes, I shoved my face into his. "And if you don't let go of my hair *right* now, this discussion is through and this so-called *relationship* is through."

Something flickered through his eyes and slowly he let go. Tension radiated off of him, and for the first time since I'd met him, I was thoroughly aware of just how much larger he was than me. More than a foot taller, broad shoulders, muscled torso...

"I'm sorry," he said, his voice strangely gentle. "I just–"

"I found out on Thursday morning," I cut him off. "Bethany has been fucking with me almost from the get-go, and then she throws Pierce under the bus, claiming he made some bullshit unofficial complaint about how I acted unprofessionally and made an advance on him. None of it happened, of course, and we all knew it. He stood there and let her say it, knowing it was all crap." Now that I'd started, it all came pouring out. "I filed a formal complaint against him and told her I'd be happy to explain in detail everything that's happened since I started. He ended up getting suspended while they investigate him. So that meant I became second chair."

Arik was the one looking away now.

My lips trembled. I could feel the tears threatening, and it pissed me off. I didn't want to cry. I never wanted to cry. I wanted to yell at him. I was angry and hurt. And too much had happened in the past couple months for me to be able to handle it.

Turning away, I sniffed and reached up to press my fingertips under my eyes as I tried to hold the tears at bay.

"Dena…" Arik's voice was hoarse.

I heard him coming up behind me. I started to shake my head, tried to step away from him, but I was too slow.

He was already wrapping one arm around my hips, his palm pressing to my belly while the other came up and covered my throat. The gesture should've been threatening, oppressive, but for me, feeling the strength of him was comforting. Safe.

"Don't do that," he whispered against the top of my head. "I'm...fuck, baby, I'm sorry. This is messing with my head. I told you that I couldn't think straight around you."

"You're an asshole," I snapped. Then I sniffled, taking the sting out of my statement. "I told you getting involved was a bad idea."

He pressed his lips to my hair, his thumb making circles over my pulse. I told myself I needed to pull away, end this.

That was what I needed to do.

So why was I letting him turn me around and tip my face up?

Why was I letting him kiss me?

Why was I letting him push his hands into my hair? He unerringly sought out the areas of my scalp that ached a bit and massaged, his touch tender rather than rough.

I moaned into his mouth. When his teeth gently scored my lower lip, I whimpered, and without letting myself think about the stupidity of what we were doing, I

333

placed my hands on his chest and slowly slid them up, shoving his jacket back.

He shrugged out of it, and while I fumbled with his tie, he pulled up my skirt. My hips jerked as he ripped off my panties and I gasped into his mouth. I fumbled with his shirt, desperate to feel him. He tore at his belt, and then he boosted me up, his need fueling my own.

I gasped as he thrust inside me, holding me up in the middle of that cold, sterile room that didn't suit him at all. I wrapped my legs around his waist as his cock stretched and burned. I wasn't ready, and it hurt, but when he would have waited, I rocked against him, urging him on.

His eyes burned into mine, desperation in the depths. "We shouldn't do this," he said, his voice harsh. I could feel his body trembling. "I do the stupidest things with you, Dena."

"Me, too." I tugged his face closer, kissing him, exploring his mouth with mine.

We said nothing else. In the middle of that room, with him holding me, I rode him. It was slow, almost torturous, as I used my inner muscles to squeeze him. His hands gripped my ass and I wound my arm around his neck, the two of us moving together in a way that I could never be with anyone else.

He felt huge inside me, my weight driving me down on his cock until I was so full of him that I didn't know where he ended and I began. The sensations were almost too much and every muscle in my body trembled, but I held on.

The room began to whirl around us, then my vision

focused and I realized it wasn't the room moving, but us. Arik took two strides, putting my back to the wall before he caught my knees, and began to hammer into me. Each driving thrust pulled a moan from me, and before I knew it, he had pounded me straight into orgasm.

He came a moment later, his groan smothered against my throat even as he pulsed inside me, the feeling enough to trigger a second, smaller climax.

We stayed like that for a couple silent minutes. I could feel an internal clock ticking in my head as his weight continued to spread my thighs. Muscles strained and I started to feel all of the aches that came from being thoroughly fucked.

A deep sigh escaped him, then slowly, he eased me to the ground. I sucked in a breath as he pulled out, my pussy throbbing with the sudden loss.

As he tugged his trousers up, I stepped around him. A black silk scrap lay on the floor. Face flushed, I picked it up and moved over to the kitchen area. I hoped the water was on. I was wet, his semen leaking down my thighs. Thankfully, the water was indeed on, and I quickly wiped myself, using the destroyed remains of my panties.

When I turned, Arik was staring outside.

Good. I wasn't ready to look at him. Or myself. I flushed with shame.

So much for respecting my office and not having sex on the job. I was such a hypocrite.

Throat tight, I smoothed my hands down my skirt and looked toward the door. I took one shaking step, then another. My purse and briefcase waited there, on the floor. I didn't even remember putting them down.

"Dena. We need to talk," Arik said. He sounded tired now.

He couldn't be any more tired than me.

"No," I said softly. "I've said everything I needed to say. I'm just trying to do my job, you know." Now I glanced back at him, myriad emotions churning inside. "All I ever wanted to do was be a prosecutor. This was supposed to be my dream job and it's become a nightmare. Everything went to shit with Bethany. So, yeah, I took a few days to come to grips with how things changed last week. I needed time, Arik. That's who I am. You're pissed off about it. Fine."

"That's...dammit, Dena!" He started toward me.

I held up my hands. "Don't. I'm not ready to talk about this now. I have a job to do, and it doesn't involve getting fucked on the taxpayer's dime. Dammit!" My voice broke. "I'm no better than she is."

"That's not...Dena!"

Grabbing my bag and briefcase, I hurried through the door and practically ran for the elevator. He was right behind me, but as I darted inside the elevator, I looked at him. "Don't, Arik. I can't do this right now. I mean it."

He stopped, but I could see how much it cost him to do nothing. The pain on his face nearly destroyed my resolve, but what I'd done was still too clear in my mind.

I let the doors close.

# Chapter 4

*Dena*

I ate lunch while I was out.

Well, it was sort of lunch. I didn't think that a giant pile of French fries and a milkshake *really* counted as food, but I needed comfort in the worst way, and I wasn't in the mood to talk to anyone. Even my friends.

I'd done the stupidest thing imaginable. No, I hadn't realized Arik was a defense attorney right off the bat, but once I *had* known, I should have ended things, period. Completely and totally.

But I hadn't.

I could do it now, but I didn't want to.

I let myself brood over that for a short while as I splurged on my sugary, salty, junk food lunch, and then I made one more stop before heading back to my office.

I had to get new underwear.

There were flowers on the table by the door when I arrived back in my new office. Knowing it was probably rude, but past the point of caring, I took them to the nearest trash can and threw them out. I was allergic anyway. I left the vase sitting on a long table just outside my office. I had no idea who the flowers came from, but I left a note inside my office. *No flowers, please. Allergies.*

Not even five minutes passed before the phone rang.

Massaging my temples, I closed my eyes as I answered, "Dena Monroe."

There was a brief pause, then Bethany's voice, far more friendly and warm than I'd ever heard from her, came over the line. "Good afternoon, Dena. I was just wondering how you're settling into your new office."

The tone threw me off balance for a moment, but I was too used to her personality to be lured in by a couple of kind words. Besides, I was a lawyer. People changed their faces in this business as often as they changed their underwear. Probably more in some cases.

I flushed at the thought of underwear and forced aside the memories that quickly followed.

Tapping my pen against the blotter on my desk, I opened my eyes and stared at the mostly empty calendar. "It's fine, thank you. Is there something you need?"

"No – well, yes. I was wondering if you'd like to join me for lunch. We could go over what you learned at Mrs. Mance's apartment."

"I picked up lunch on the way back, but I can tell you what I learned. Nothing. He was just there to pick up a few personal effects for Mrs. Mance, just like he said." I lied without batting an eyelash. "We didn't talk much."

*That* wasn't a lie.

The connection between us buzzed, followed by a high-pitched noise that was like an icepick in my already aching head.

"Was there anything else, Bethany?" I asked, determined now to get off the phone. I needed to take something for this damn headache and get to work. Maybe then I wouldn't think so much about everything that happened today. Or the past several days.

"No," she responded, her voice cooler now, as short and sharp as I'd come to expect from her.

Maybe I hadn't been as appreciative of her olive branch as I was supposed to have been.

Oh, well. Of all the things I'd fucked up recently, that was near the bottom of my list.

"Okay, then." I hung up without another word and grabbed my purse. I dry-swallowed a couple of over-the-counter painkillers and focused on the files on my desk.

Work.

I'd just focus on work.

Hours later, I threw my pen down and shoved back from the desk.

I didn't know how many phone calls I'd made, but it hadn't made a difference. I hadn't been able to find any motive for murder. No affairs, no money issues...at least

341

nothing on her side. The victim, however, he'd been far from squeaky clean. I didn't have anything substantial, but there was definitely more to his story than anyone had said.

Then there were the forensics.

Leayna couldn't have killed her husband. There was no way.

The crime scene reports showed that no blood or fibers or anything had been found in the sinks, bathroom drains, or anywhere else in their home. She would have had to wrap herself completely up, including her face, and dispose of whatever she'd worn during the attack.

All before the cops arrived.

Before Arik had gotten there.

I tried calling the cops to ask if they'd done a search of the dumpsters and trash cans within a mile or so of her home, but they said they'd been instructed that such a procedure wasn't necessary.

When I'd asked why, they'd told me to talk to my boss.

"I'm second chair on this case. That means following up on this very line is my job, Detective," I'd said, pacing the room as I continued to talk into my Bluetooth.

"You're basically an errand girl," the detective on the other end had said, clearly disinterested. "Lawton was the errand boy, now you're the errand girl. Why don't you take it easy and wait for your boss to tell you to fetch some donuts or something? Leave the detective work to the professionals."

He hung up then.

I'd debated over it long and hard, and had finally decided that while it would be fulfilling to talk to Detective Dumbass' superior, it wouldn't have been the *wise* thing.

I'd been here only a short while, and had already filed one complaint. It had been justified, yes, but word got around. I didn't want to become known as the woman who was constantly making problems. Even if there were actual issues. The more I made of each problem, the worse they'd become.

There were real problems with this case, but since Bethany refused to pay attention, and it seemed that the cops weren't all that interested, I'd have to continue to see what I could dig up.

The good little lawyer in me reminded me that I needed to update my superior.

The good little lawyer needed to shut the hell up and leave me alone, but I didn't see that happening any time soon.

So, grudgingly, I packed everything up, save for the few notes I'd kept in my notebook. I did most everything digitally, but sometimes I just focused better if I wrote things out.

The notes I held were the bits and pieces of the case that didn't add up.

I'd hoped that if I wrote them down, I could find some magical way to make them make sense, or some string that would connect them that I just hadn't seen yet. That miracle hadn't yet occurred.

The holes were obvious, too, so I was going to show

everything to Bethany, and then head on out.

That was the plan, anyway.

When I stepped out into the hallway, an almost ghostly silence greeted me. It was nearly seven, but I hadn't noticed it until that moment when I flicked a look at my phone and saw the time glowing up at me. The lights had been dimmed in the lower corridors, and I sighed as I hurried toward the stairs. Bethany wasn't buried down here in the tombs liked the rest of us plebes, so I had to walk through several equally darkened hallways to reach her.

I knew they did it to conserve energy, but I didn't really like walking down dimly-lit corridors of mostly empty buildings. Especially cavernous ones that made every step echo.

I spent far too much time watching zombie shit, I thought as I made my way down the corridor to Bethany's office. She might not even be here. It was way past the time somebody as important as *Bethany McDermott* would work. Especially when she had such a capable ADA to help her.

Smirking, I shook my head.

And then a sound caught my ears.

Oh, for crying out loud.

Those low grunts, the moaning.

She was like a fucking cat in heat.

Immediately, though, I flushed in self-reprisal. Had I really been any better? So I hadn't done it in my office. Did that really make a difference?

I paused outside her office, glancing toward the

window automatically.

She hadn't even completely closed the blinds. It was like she almost *wanted* to be caught.

I guessed that meant Pierce hadn't stayed that mad at her, because there they were, Bethany bent face down over her desk, while he stood behind her...

Wait.

That wasn't Pierce.

The man bent down and fisted a hand in her hair, yanking roughly as he pulled her up high enough for me to see more of her breasts than I wanted to.

She whimpered, her face screwed up as a passionate moan escaped her. By contrast, the guy slamming into her looked detached. Almost disinterested. Then he straightened, and I found myself staring at his face.

He had a cold face, sharply cut with long, hollow cheeks, and a mouth that might be considered sexy. But he was...cold.

To say the least.

Shivering, I backed away, moving far more silently than I had earlier.

I didn't know why, but I didn't want them to know I was there. And it had nothing to do with Bethany and everything to do with that man.

For the first time in my life, a man truly scared the shit out of me.

# Chapter 5

## *Dena*

I made two stops on the way home.

After the day I'd had, I needed two things: sushi and sake.

I placed the order for sushi from my mobile before getting on the subway, and after I picked it up, I hit the liquor store and got a bottle of sake. Unsurprisingly, the guy behind the counter carded me, then hit on me when he saw I was twenty-six.

I was going to have to show some serious willpower not to overindulge and show up to work hungover tomorrow.

Juggling my food, liquor, and briefcase as I rode the elevator up, I barely heard the buzz of my phone.

My heart leaped. Stupid of me, but every time it had done that today, I thought it might be Arik. Yes, I told him I needed time and I did, but that didn't mean I wasn't thinking about him. Constantly.

Once inside, I emptied my arms as quickly as

possible, and then grabbed my phone, but it had already stopped ringing.

The call log showed a missed call alright, but it had been from Bethany. Boss Bitch had called nearly an hour after I'd seen her fucking some guy – or rather some guy fucking *her* over the desk in her office. I had to push the catty thoughts out of my head, though. I'd lost the right to get all snide and condescending on that one when I'd let Arik fuck me on the clock.

Did the location really matter?

Not so much in my mind.

The phone buzzed a moment later, signaling an incoming text.

As her name came up, I sighed, then forced myself to read the message.

> Came by your office, needed to discuss a few pertinent details about the case with you. You weren't there. Did you leave already?

I fought the urge to hurl the phone. I hated how much she screwed with my temper. I was usually a level-headed person, but Bethany brought out the worst in me.

I didn't even want to think about what Arik brought out in me.

Before I could say something stupid, I grabbed a piece of paper and scrawled down all the mean things I wanted to say, and then I shot her back a quick, professional response.

> I left about an hour ago. I didn't think you'd still be there. Sorry. Can it wait until tomorrow or should I call?

There. Nothing like the *bite me, bitch* that I wanted

to say.

It can wait, of course. See you in the morning.

After reading the text, I turned off my phone, something that might end up causing problems if anything important happened during the night, but I was the second chair, not the ADA actually trying the case. That's why they paid her more.

Once that was done, I got my sushi and my sake and flopped down on the couch.

A few minutes for myself, I thought. I just wanted a few minutes for myself.

Silken, warm water lapped against my skin.

Arik's strong arms wrapped around me.

His lips slid down my neck, and I sighed in pleasure as the jets from the tub had the water frothing all around us.

"This case doesn't make sense," I told him.

"Don't talk about the case." Arik caught my ear between his teeth and bit down. "Take a few minutes for yourself."

For myself? I looked down at the bubbling water, at the tanned arm that held me tight against a hard body. "Isn't that what this is?"

He chuckled. "This is part of it. But even now, you're thinking about the case. About everything that isn't right. Think about the things that *are* right."

"And what's that?" I demanded, my voice sharp.

He slid his hands up my belly to cup my breasts. I moaned, writhing against him.

"You're with me now." He palmed my breasts and pinched my nipples. They tightened and he ran his tongue along the rim of my ear.

"I–" Shaking my head, I looked up at him. Water rushed over the sides of the tub and I couldn't see him.

I didn't know where we were.

"I'm not sure if it's right or not. We needed to talk to—"

Arik kissed me, his tongue stabbing deep into my mouth. The hands that had been stroking my breasts moved. One going to my hair, and the other to my hip, gripping me and pulling me in tight against his cock.

The water...

It was gone.

So was the bathtub and the bathroom.

We were in one of the rooms at Club Privé, and when I tore my mouth from Arik's to look around, I saw Carrie and Gavin sitting at a small, round table in the corner.

"What are you doing here?" I demanded.

"Making sure you don't break the rules again," my best friend said, tipping the glass toward me. She nodded over to the side. "Those two are all about breaking the rules, but you're not, Dena. You're a good girl."

"I am not." I glared at her, trying to make sense of the conversation even as I tried to figure out who she was talking about. One quick look told me. It was Bethany and the guy she'd been with. His face – it nagged me. Harsh, handsome and cold. "Who *is* he?"

"Trouble." Arik kissed the middle of my breastbone, easing my arched back over his arm. "You know who he is, or you wouldn't see him here. He's trouble. Stay away from him."

"It's not like I was going to ask him to join us," I snapped.

"Good. I don't share." Arik went to his knees in front of me, pressing his mouth to the midline of my torso before starting down my stomach.

"Why are those two in my club, darling?" Gavin asked, gesturing to Bethany and her companion.

Two of the security guards pulled them away from each other, then dragged them away, still naked.

Carrie answered Gavin's question, "Ask Dena. She's the reason we're all here."

"I'm...no." Shaking my head, I tried to get my bearings, but couldn't.

Not with Arik's lips brushing against the sensitive skin between my thighs.

Carrie and Gavin watched, almost curiously. "He has good technique," Carrie said softly.

I moaned, hardly able to think about them now as Arik flicked my clitoris with his tongue, then dipped it inside me.

"He's being stupid. Both of them are. And don't

comment on his technique. Mine is all that matters."

Gavin's voice was even fainter.

When I looked back up, both of them were gone, and Arik and I were in my bedroom. I was sprawled on my bed while Arik pressed his mouth against my cunt.

"I'm going to lick you clean," he said gruffly. "Then I'm going to make you wet and we can start all over again."

He slid two fingers inside me, and I cried out, arching my hips up to meet the next thrust, but all he did was lower his mouth, wrapping his lips around my throbbing clit.

"Please," I whimpered. Ready to beg, ready to plead. To promise anything if he'd just give me the release I needed.

"Please what?" Arik looked up, his mouth glistening, wet. As I watched, he licked his lips. "I'll let you pretend to be in charge for a little while, baby. What do you want?"

"I want you to fuck me. I want you to want me."

He crawled up my body, keeping his pressed close to mine. His cock slid against me, but before he gave me what I needed, he stopped, hovering just a breath away as he kissed me. His cock twitched against my hip. "I want you, baby, can't you feel it?"

"You want sex." My eyes fell away from his, and my heart started to ache. "I want..."

I didn't know what I wanted.

Did I?

His hands cupped my face. "I know what you want,

my Dena."

He drove inside me then, hard and fast.

"This." He ground his hips against mine, and I whimpered as his cock pulsed inside me. "This..."

But it wasn't.

I cried out against his lips, uncertain how to tell him that I needed more. That I needed something else.

Gripping his shoulders, I arched up under him as he slammed into me again and again. "Tell me that this is it, Dena...tell me this is what you want..."

He growled the words against my mouth as a climax came rushing up on me.

"Tell me..."

A phone rang, shattering the dream and waking me up.

A dream.

Shit.

Sweat slicked my skin, and everything in me was tensed with the need to come.

And it had been a dream.

The phone rang again, cutting through my still-muddled thoughts. It was my landline and I couldn't figure out why.

Sitting up, I looked around groggily and realized I'd

fallen asleep on the sofa, the remains of my sushi sitting on the coffee-table next to the bottle of sake. Dimly, I took a second to be thankful that I wasn't hungover. Then, I grabbed the phone halfway through the third ring, not even thinking to see who was calling.

"Yeah?"

There was a pause, followed by, "Dena?"

I blinked. "Carrie?"

"Ah, yeah. You sound...are you alone?"

"Sadly, yes." The second I said it, I wished I could yank the words back. I ran my hand over my face, trying to wipe away the lingering sleep.

Carrie's chuckle drifted across the line. "Well, I guess that explains that."

"What does it explain?" Weary, aching, and desperate for the climax she interrupted, I stood and gathered up the trash one-handed while clutching the phone with the other hand. She wasn't making any sense and I just wanted her to explain so I could...

"Arik."

I almost dropped the phone and the trash.

"Huh?"

Was this still part of my dream?

"He's here and he looks about as happy as you sound."

For a moment, I thought she meant that Arik had come to her and Gavin's place, but then my brain caught up and I realized she meant that Arik was at the club.

"And you're telling me this why?"

"Because I thought the two of you had made up after

Gavin sent you to a room the other night, but now he's here looking like he'd happily rip someone's head off if they look at him cross-eyed. What happened?"

Closing my eyes, I blew out a breath. At least there was a simple way to make her understand. "He's the defense attorney, Carrie."

There was a pause. "He's *a* defense attorney?" she asked delicately.

"Yes. He's also the defense attorney for the defendant whose case I'm assisting on. And I just got moved to second chair." Swallowing, I continued, "Neither of us knew until...the point is, we didn't know. Then we did, but I wasn't going to be co-council. Then Pierce was suspended and now I'm second chair and it's a mess."

Carrie was silent for a moment, and I assumed she was processing the whole mess. "Yeah." Her voice was faint. "Yeah, I guess it is." There was another pause. "Well, I guess that's why you don't have your cell turned on. Trying to avoid him?"

"My boss." Grimacing, I shoved my hair back and squinted at the clock. It was just after ten. I'd slept maybe an hour. "Look, Carrie, I need to go. I'm exhausted, and I don't want to talk about any of this yet."

"Okay." She hesitated before adding, "You will have to talk about it, though, you know. Soon. You're treading in dangerous waters."

I sighed. "I know."

I hung up and then went through my familiar routine of making sure everything was closed up before I headed to my bedroom. I just wanted to sleep and not think about anything.

I was still lying in bed, staring up at the ceiling nearly an hour later, no rest in sight.

My entire body throbbed, my pussy ached, almost like I could feel him moving inside me, keeping me hovering on the brink without providing any actual relief.

It was too much.

I slid my hands up and down my thighs, closing my eyes. Even that light touch was enough to drive me closer to some edge I could feel deep inside me.

*I want you...*

The echo of his voice from my dreams wrapped around me. The memory of his hands ghosted over me.

My nipples tightened, rubbing against the thin silk of the camisole I wore. Shifting restlessly, I whimpered when that small movement had my panties moving against my cunt.

Need overwhelmed everything else.

Sliding a hand down my belly, I pushed the tips of my fingers just past the edge of my panties. I let my imagination take over, produce the fantasy I needed.

He hooked his fingers around the lace sidebands of my panties and dragged them down my legs.

As I pushed my fingers inside my wet passage, it was his tongue flicking against me, then entering me.

*I'm going to lick you clean...*

I moaned as my fingers slid in and out, as the palm of my hand rubbed against my swollen clit.

*Tell me you want me...*

I did want him.

But there was more. He'd been pushing for something.

I thrust harder, faster, grinding the heel of my hand against my clit.

Now that I was awake, I couldn't deny that there was more to the dream than mere sexual frustration.

And I knew what it was.

I'd avoided it for years, but here, with the worst guy imaginable, I'd gone and fallen for Arik Porter.

The worst man imaginable.

The perfect man.

Bracing my heels against the mattress, I pushed up against my hand and twisted my fingers. A wail ripped out of me, one that had Arik's name echoing off the walls.

As I came back down, I closed my eyes.

I didn't fight the wave of sleep that came over me.

I didn't want to.

Tomorrow would be soon enough to think, soon enough to deal.

# Chapter 6

*Arik*

Silence wrapped around me as I lay in my bed.

Alone.

I'd given up trying to work at midnight, although realistically, I hadn't gotten anything accomplished most of the evening.

Most of the damn day, really.

Work, productivity, thought...all of it had gone down the drain the moment Bethany had dropped the bomb on me about Dena being moved to second chair.

*I told you getting involved was a bad idea.*

Dena's voice had been shaking when she said it and even now I could still see the way she'd been struggling against emotion. Pain and anger, and I'd been responsible for most of it.

She'd said it was a bad idea, but I hadn't paid attention, and the second things got dicey, I'd blamed her.

I'd done the one thing a Dom should never do.

I'd put my own wants ahead of her. And I did want her, more than I'd ever wanted anyone before. Even if we hadn't talked about a real relationship, it was always the Dominant's job to take care of their Sub, and I hadn't done that. I'd gotten angry and blamed her simply because it had screwed up what *I* wanted.

Maybe she should've told me as soon as she'd been made second chair, but that didn't excuse my behavior. She was a strong woman, and even though she'd made it clear that she could be a Dominant in her own right, if I wanted the privileges that came with dominating her, I had to accept the responsibilities too.

And I'd fucked up.

It wasn't her fault she ended up with this case. She was a newbie ADA, assigned to a worthless ADA. Although, honestly, for all of Bethany's many faults, it wasn't really her fault Dena and I were on opposite sides of the table. I had no doubt Dena was a great lawyer, which meant she deserved second chair.

Just because I'd spent the weekend thinking about her, instead of digging further into this case, didn't mean I could blame either Dena or Bethany. It'd been hard for me to concentrate, and I could only imagine how difficult it had been for Dena, wondering how to tell me what happened while still trying to catch up. And she'd even managed to find information that actually shot down the motives she was supposed to be supporting.

Bitter humor twisted inside and I recalled what I'd learned from inside sources. They said the prosecution was trying to build a case claiming that Leayna killed her husband because he planned to divorce her and she would lose everything in the process. Except there were no records of him ever having visited or even spoken to a divorce lawyer. I could pick apart their motive without a problem, especially since Dena had made it clear that they didn't have any support for those claims.

I sighed and flung an arm over my eyes, trying to block out everything, including the case...and especially the look Dena had given me before she walked out of the penthouse.

I wasn't going to think about her.

I wasn't going to think about her at all.

Mentally, I focused and began to count down.

Twenty.

Time to let go of all the tension of the day. Deep breath in, out, let it all drift away.

Nineteen.

Loosen the muscles, tighten them, then loosen. From the nape of the neck all the way down.

Eighteen.

Deep breath in, out. Flex the muscles of the lower legs, then release.

Seventeen.

My phone rang.

I jerked upright and grabbed it, hoping against hope that it was Dena.

Staring at the display, at the unknown number showing there, I swore.

So much for not thinking about her.

All the tension I'd managed to wrap under some

semblance of control now seemed to be coming back with a vengeance. Swearing, I kicked free of my sheet and punched my fist into the mattress.

This was just a bunch of bullshit, really.

Nothing more.

Ten minutes later, I stood in the shower with a glass of scotch on the shelf beside me, letting myself be wrapped in billows of steam.

If I couldn't talk myself out of thinking about her, I'd do the next best thing. Under normal circumstances, I would've called her, demanding she come over where I'd fuck her out of my mind, but I was starting to think that my usual *normal* might not be possible with her.

And I wasn't sure I wanted it anyway.

Water slid over me, a gentle caress against my skin.

It wasn't even close to as good as having Dena sliding over me, but as I wrapped my hand around my rigid cock, it was pretty clear that my dick didn't care. I was thick, swollen and aching, and what I needed to do was come.

Up, down. Repeat.

Hissing out a breath, I imagined her coming to me through the steam, going to her knees and taking me in her mouth. I stroked my thumb over the head of my penis, imagined it was her tongue. Remembered the heat of her mouth. The suction and pressure.

Inside my head, a hot, X-rated little fantasy played out. Pale in comparison to the real thing, it was enough to keep me going, to make my balls tighten and my body tense.

In the shower, I shifted so that I had my back to the spray, leaning against the wall while I fucked my fist. Water pounded down around me and I panted, teeth peeled back and bared a grimace.

The release that came was just that and only that.

A release.

When I dried off and half-stumbled back to the bed, I had to fight the urge to sigh. It hadn't done much more than take the edge off.

What I needed was Dena.

# Chapter 7

## *Dena*

Dreams of Arik chased me all night long.

Waking up feeling like I'd fallen through the looking glass and still hadn't quite found my way out of Wonderland, I gulped down two full cups of coffee even before getting into the shower. I'd grab a third on my way to work.

I wasn't up to verbal sparring today, but I was pretty sure there'd be plenty of it on the plate, so I needed my caffeine.

The dreams...

Even after Carrie had interrupted the first one, more had waited for me.

The second one had been like an acid-laced trip through hell. Not that I'd ever done acid, but a friend had used the description once, and it seemed fitting. It had been all about me and Arik sitting in one of the 'viewing' rooms at Club Privé, while Bethany and her new toy of the week went over reams of paperwork. Naked. There had also been several heads sitting around the room. Just heads. Human heads. Without bodies.

I was positive that paperwork and human heads were important, that they meant something, but damned if I could figure out what.

*"If you'd listen to me about how my client was innocent, none of this would be happening."* Arik had told me several times in the dream.

"None of *what*?" I muttered out loud now, hours later. "Naked filing?"

Disturbed by all of it, I tried to push the images and voices all out of my head as I showered, but I was only partially successful. By the time I was ready to head out the door, I was so edgy, I actually decided to skip the latte I usually grabbed on the way into the office. If I needed it later, I'd grab one at lunch.

I'd dressed a little more sedately than normal, a concession to my headache and sleepless night. The black pantsuit and vivid pink cami would also be good enough for the club if I lost the jacket, so if I needed to blow off some steam after work, I'd be ready to go. I wasn't going to toss and turn all night like I had last night. Better to dance myself into exhaustion.

Habit had me going straight to my old office. I stopped a few feet away when I remembered, then turned around and trudged back down the hall to where I'd been relocated.

I was halfway there when I collided with Pierce.

Literally.

Crashing into him, I hissed as hot coffee splashed on

my hand, and more of it splashed on him.

"Dammit, Dena! Bad enough you're fucking with my career," he snapped, glaring at me. "Do you really need to throw second degree burns on top of it?"

The apology I'd been formulating died on my lips.

"*I'm* fucking with *your* career?" Aware that people were staring at us, I kept my voice low. "I'm not the one who started it, Pierce. All you had to do was speak up."

"And you could have just ignored it and let it go. Nothing would have happened." His eyes darted around, his handsome face an ugly shade of red.

"Wrong." I reigned in my temper. No matter how I felt about him screwing Bethany, she was the one in the position of power. "When you ignore a bully for shit like that, they just do more. They want to see what else they can get away with. How far they can push you." Reaching into the side pocket of my purse, I pulled out a couple of tissues. "Here. For your jacket."

He ignored the offer, continuing to blot at the liquid with an already drenched napkin.

I started to shake my head and step around him, but stopped part-way around. "You know, she's not worth it. She's already trying out her desk with some other guy. Maybe I'm crazy, but I don't think you're a half-bad guy under all of it, Pierce. You could do better. You deserve better."

Before he could say anything else, I headed to my office and shut the door, locking myself in.

The first three times I called Bethany, I was snapped at, hung up on, and put on hold for twenty minutes – in that order.

Finally, tired of waiting, I gathered up my notes and the bullet point list I'd made of the reasons why Leayna Mance wasn't the killer. All of which I was almost positive Arik would be presenting in court. We needed to either find ways to refute all of these points, or we needed to find a better suspect. The real suspect.

I just needed to get Bethany to see that.

As soon as I reached Bethany's office, however, I knew things wouldn't be going my way. Her receptionist, Barbara, cut her eyes to the door, then shook her head. Based on the expression on her face, she wasn't merely telling me to sit and wait until Bethany was done with whatever she was doing.

Through the partially open door, I could hear Bethany talking. As there wasn't anybody responding to her curt questions, I had to assume she was on the phone.

I settled myself in one of the chairs and gave Barbara a little smile. In her fifties, she once told me she was counting down the months to retirement. I was pretty sure she only had eight months left. I couldn't imagine having to work eight months directly under Bethany. At least now I could escape to my office most of the time.

There was a heavy smashing sound and Barbara and I shared a grimace before Bethany appeared in the doorway. Her glare flew past me to lock on her receptionist. "Find out who in the *fuck* is handling the docket this afternoon. I want a name. They're going to be very sorry they fucked with me." She drew in another breath and then stopped, her gaze drifting back toward me. "Did we have something scheduled?" she asked, her voice icy.

"No." I managed a polite smile. "I can always set up a time for later, but I had a few things about the Mance case that I needed to discuss with you, and I wasn't having much luck calling you earlier."

"This was why I wanted Lawton on the case," she said, turning on her heel and stalking into her office. "He seems perfectly capable of working independently."

Since she hadn't closed the door, I assumed that meant I was to follow.

"As it seems he's back from his suspension, perhaps you'd prefer him to resume being second chair." I kept my voice neutral.

"No," she snapped. "The back and forth is slowing things down, and it won't look good when we finally get to move to court. Speaking of which..." She took up position behind the desk and spread her hands wide on the surface before giving me a hard look. "You had something to discuss. Let's hear it."

Placing my file down on the desk, I flipped it open.

"Nothing about this case adds up," I said bluntly. She wouldn't like it, but at least she wouldn't throw me out before I had my say. "Mrs. Mance is being painted as a woman scorned, murdering her husband for planning to divorce her, and leaving her with nothing. Except no one can find any record of him even speaking with a divorce lawyer."

"All he had to do was say it, and it set her off." Bethany crossed her arms over her chest.

"But there's no proof," I continued. "And according to their pre-nup, if he filed for divorce for anything other than infidelity, he had to pay her half."

"Just because we haven't found proof of an affair doesn't mean it didn't happen."

I took a slow breath. "We have no motive, and none of the forensics supports her being the killer."

"She was in the building," Bethany snapped. "She had his blood on her."

"But not as much as she would have if she'd killed him. The medical examiner said that the killer would've been covered from head-to-toe. The pictures of Ms. Mance after the fact show blood on her shirt and her hands, nowhere else."

"Dammit, Dena! Are you a prosecutor or her bleeding heart defense attorney?"

"I'm a lawyer, same as you. And things don't add up. We might be prosecuting the wrong person."

Bethany snorted, the sound thick with scorn. "Oh, honey. You need to grow up." She gestured toward the file as if she didn't even want to touch it. "Put that away. This is about getting a conviction."

I squared my shoulders and asked the question I

hadn't wanted to ask. "And if an innocent person goes to jail?"

An unladylike noise came from her throat. "Don't be so naïve, Dena. Nobody's innocent."

# Chapter 8

## *Dena*

*Nobody's innocent.*

There was nothing Bethany could have said that would've pissed me off quite as much as those two simple words.

It wasn't just the opposite of people who thought everyone was innocent. Thinking that nobody was innocent, in Bethany's mind, seemed to be a free pass to charge anyone with any crime, whether they did it or not, simply because they must be guilty of something.

I knew that, more and more, the belief of innocent until proven guilty was being put through the ringer, especially by the media. It annoyed me, but it wasn't the same.

Bethany made a mockery of everything I'd chosen to believe in, everything I wanted to believe in. She preferred to ignore all the evidence pointing to the possibility that her suspect might be innocent. She just wanted to put someone away, get a win. Justice didn't matter to her.

I still believed in justice, and I'd do what I needed to make sure that it was served.

Even if that meant going over Bethany's head with any evidence I found.

At least it seemed like I'd have plenty of time to work. Pierce was going out of his way to avoid me. Since he wasn't working on anything connected to the Mance case now, it was easy to stay away from him without actually looking like I was avoiding him. And, of course, Bethany was tied up in court. If the courthouse grapevine was anywhere near accurate, she'd nailed somebody's ass to a wall on the stand just the other day.

Between now and Monday morning, I probably didn't have to worry much about Bethany appearing at my shoulder or calling me. Her current case would probably be going to closing arguments tomorrow and handed off to the jury over the weekend.

Come Monday, though, Bethany would be on my ass again. More importantly, she'd be looking for a way to lock Leayna Mance up for a murder I was becoming more and more certain she hadn't committed.

*If she's innocent, you just need to find a way to prove it,* I told myself. Regardless of what Bethany said, there was more to my job as a prosecutor then putting people in prison. Everybody lost when an innocent person was found guilty.

I kept that in mind as I stayed closeted away from the world, feeling more and more isolated as Thursday wore on. Except for a text from Carrie, I didn't speak to anybody outside a few people to request evidence.

Well, and the barista on the corner.

I really wouldn't have minded a call, say from somebody like Arik.

But the phone stayed stubbornly silent.

*"You're looking in the wrong place."*

*Arik slid his hands up my torso. His mouth grazed mine before he caught my wrists and guided them behind my back. "You should have told me about getting second chair. You didn't. Now I'm going to punish you."*

*The shiver that slid through me was delicious. I shouldn't have felt so excited. I was still mad at him, wasn't I? And I had a right to be. Didn't I?*

*Making myself look at him, I said, "I was going to tell you. I just needed time to think about what it meant."*

*"You could have thought about it and told me. We could've talked about it. If we're going to have a relationship, we don't hide things. We talk." He tugged me closer, tucking me up against him so that his cock was pressed against my ass. "So...do we have a relationship?"*

*"Yes." I whimpered as I said it, loving the way it twisted something inside me. Something stroked me*

375

between my thighs, dragging a moan from my lips. "Are you...how are you going to punish me, Arik?"

He laughed, the sound low and husky.

"You know you deserve to be punished, don't you?"

Face flushed and hot, I nodded. "Yes."

"Good."

He stroked a hand down my hair and stepped away. I strained to see him and that was when I realized I was tied to a chair. My office chair. And I was naked.

He passed in front of me, tapping a crop against his thigh. I licked my lips and Arik wagged a finger at me. "Don't go getting impatient, Dena. This is the reward. Not the punishment. You only get the reward if you solve the puzzle."

"What puzzle?"

He gestured toward my desk.

"That's the punishment. You have to solve the puzzle."

Confused, I shook my head. "That's not how this works. Arik, untie me."

"No. You have to solve the puzzle. Look again."

I looked and this time, I saw something else. The courthouse. In miniature. Like a dollhouse.

I tried to stand up and realized I could.

I was dressed again, and Arik was gone. I wasn't worried about that though. I was focused on the puzzle. Moving forward, I stared down into the courthouse. The roof was gone and I could see a miniature me standing outside Bethany's office. She was in there, with that guy.

"Solve the puzzle."

376

*I jumped at the sound of Arik's voice.*

*He was behind me and I almost yelped.*

*He grinned at me, his teeth flashing white. "Jumpy, Dena. You should get more sleep. You wouldn't be so nervous. Who is he, Dena?" He pointed at Bethany and her...friend.*

*"I don't know!"*

*"That's the puzzle." Arik went back to staring at the miniature of the man I'd seen with Bethany. "Solve it and you can have your reward."*

*The miniature man and Bethany weren't having sex now. The man was going through the papers on Bethany's desk and Bethany...I swallowed when I realized she was on the floor with a bright red dot in the middle of her forehead.*

*"What happens if I don't solve it, Arik?" I didn't look at him as I asked the question.*

*He hugged me against him. "You have to, Dena."*

I jerked awake, my temples throbbing. That hadn't been the best dream I'd ever had. If anything, it just made things worse. Then I looked down at my desk and sighed as I remembered why I'd closed my eyes for just a minute.

"This doesn't make sense."

Rubbing my temples, I went over the figures again.

I didn't know why I was even bothering, because I'd already done the calculations a good four times, and had come up with the same result.

It wasn't my math that was wrong.

As much as I hated finances, over the past few years, I'd become depressingly good at eyeballing things and seeing where the discrepancies were, where the lies hid. Too many of my former clients had spouses who tried hiding money to avoid claiming the assets. Then there'd been the ones who tried hiding an affair or some sort of crime.

If there was one thing I'd learned from years as a divorce lawyer, it was that numbers talked.

And these numbers were telling one hell of a story.

Mr. Mance had spent more money than he'd made, and his corporation had been in trouble. He'd tried to get loans over the past year, probably trying to shore things up, but he'd been turned down.

"Banks know a bad bet." Blowing out a hard breath, I leaned back and studied the sheets filled with my scrawling notes.

The data for the business had all looked pretty much the same for three years running, right up until six months into this past year. Then, things had turned around. A sudden influx of money. I would've assumed a loan, but there was no sign anybody legit had paid anything out. However, he'd suddenly been able to do exactly what needed to be done, shored up some of the areas that were bleeding money, cut some of them off entirely. He'd managed to salvage his company.

I just had no idea how he'd done it.

"Where did he get the money?" I ran my finger down the column more slowly.

Shit.

There it was.

Fifty thousand.

In cash.

My heart thudded loudly in the silence.

Coincidence.

Had to be.

But...

I ran my hands over my face. The police had searched the apartment of my dead police informant slash possible witness.

And they'd found a bag of fifty thousand dollars in cash.

Officer Dunne had told me that the rumor around the station was that the guy had been involved in organized crime. I'd originally thought that the man had been Mance's lover, though that hadn't been an angle I would've brought up to Bethany unless I had proof. Now, however, I was thinking that might not have been true. Or, at least not the whole truth.

Organized crime. Large amounts of cash found. Equal deposits of cash. Secret meetings at strip clubs.

What the hell had Mance gotten himself into?

# Chapter 9

## *Arik*

I'd had worse weeks.

Really, aside from one personal matter, things hadn't completely sucked. It was just that the one *personal matter* had colored everything else I'd done.

"Personal matter," I muttered, climbing out of my car and tossing my keys to the valet outside the building. I paid a small fortune just to keep a car in the city, but I was too used to having my own transportation. The few times I'd tried car services and taxis, it'd been all I could do not to backseat drive.

"Sir?"

I looked over and saw the valet's puzzled expression and realized I'd been grumbling out loud. "Sorry. Just talking to myself."

"Of course." He nodded as if that was perfectly normal.

Then again, I could've told him that I was talking to

an elephant in a pink tutu, and he wouldn't have blinked. When you had money, you were allowed more than a few eccentricities. People excused all sorts of shit when dollar signs got involved.

Which was why I didn't really let anyone know that I had money. I liked people taking me at face value, for who they thought I was or wasn't, just based on how I acted.

Like with Dena. I'd acted like an asshole, and now she was making it pretty damn clear that she wasn't impressed.

What in the hell had I been thinking?

As I headed into the high rise, I debated on whether or not to call her. She'd said she needed space, time to figure things out. I'd given her that. A few days, at least. But if she didn't have an idea about whether or not she was going to forgive me by now, then I'd like to know when she thought she might be ready to talk to me.

Besides, I should apologize, right? I'd been a tool.

In front of the elevator bay, I glared at the numbers as if they were responsible for how things were going between Dena and me. I might have continued to do that if somebody hadn't delicately cleared her throat. Jerking myself out of the brooding haze, I looked up just in time to see a thin blonde dressed in yoga gear lean over and punch a button.

She gave me a cautious look, one of those speculative looks that I might've acted on a couple of months ago.

Instead of initiating a conversation or even smiling, I

382

just nodded and punched in my own floor. We rose in silence, and she got off first. When I reached my floor, however, instead of going to my apartment, I headed out to the rooftop to think.

Somebody was up there smoking. That went against the tenant's rental agreement, but as long as they kept the smoke on that side of the building where the wind could grab it, I didn't care. Hands braced on the railing, I stared out over the sprawling Manhattan skyline.

Part of me was homesick. Not for Chicago, exactly, but for the friends and family I had there. I might've grown up with money, but my family had never really seen themselves as rich. We worked hard for our money, got our hands dirty alongside our employees. There'd been no hard feelings when I'd gone into law instead of business. I'd been grateful for it, just as I'd always been grateful that my parents hadn't cared if my friends were rich, poor or in-between. Some had moved away after high school, some after college, but there'd always been someone I could call to go out and have a drink with when I needed one.

And I sure as hell needed one right now. Both a listening ear, and a drink.

This whole case was rubbing me the wrong way and not just because of Dena. *That* was pissing me off, but that wasn't the main thing nagging at me.

The case...I didn't like anything about it.

I'd talked to the cops who'd handled the investigation and any number of steps had been missed. The autopsy had pointed at somebody other than Leayna, but no one had made much noise about that. She was tall, but still not tall enough to have created the right angle for the wounds. And then there had been her clothes. She hadn't had enough blood on her face or her clothes. I knew Bethany would argue that Leayna had changed into something else before calling me and the cops, but there wasn't any forensics to support that either.

I pointed all of this out just a day ago when I managed to get a judge to talk to me about the case. He'd nodded and smiled, and then told me to present my findings in court. When I said I planned to file for a dismissal, he flat-out told me that he wouldn't rule for that. In his mind, if a grand jury had seen fit to indict, then there should be a trial.

So, unless there was a plea deal – or the real killer came forward – we were going to court. Possibly as early as next week, although I'd already put things in motion to stop that from happening. Bethany seemed determined to get through this as quickly as possible, and that made me that much more determined to slow it down, let other evidence have time to come to light.

Thunder rumbled overhead, and I lifted my gaze, staring up at the clouds gathering overhead. A fat raindrop fell, hitting me right between the eyes. Somewhere off to the east, lightning cracked down and the smell of ozone tinged the air.

"Can't even get a brood-on going with this case," I scowled. Even Mother Nature was against me.

Shoving away from the railing, I turned. I paused, though, when I saw the guy with the cigarette still there.

Leaning against the railing, his gaze was fixed in my direction.

I had the weirdest feeling he'd been staring at me.

And that wasn't creepy at all.

His face was too far away for me to make out details, but as rain began to beat down on the rooftop, he didn't move. The cherry-red tip of his cigarette went out, but he stayed there, half-hidden in the shadows, and I knew I was right. He was watching me.

Shit.

Starting toward the door, I kept my steps slow and even, my body balanced so I could fight if necessary. I'd never been mugged, and I had no intention to experience it any time soon.

But he never moved.

Once I was inside, I debated on calling building security, but if the guy had just been staring off into space or even watching me because he was trying to figure out if he knew me, I didn't want him to get in trouble. Besides, I was determined not to be *that* tenant who acted like everything was all about them.

I shook my head as I headed for the stairwell, ready to get inside my apartment now. Take a hot shower, have a scotch. Call Dena.

I almost reconsidered that last thought, but I really didn't want to.

I needed to talk to her. I couldn't think clearly when it came to her, and I was just realizing that when things weren't right between us, it was even worse. I needed to call her and make things right, then focus on the case so I could get through it.

Once that was done, I could focus on Dena. I'd figure out a way to make things work, even if she was with the DA's office. There were ways. I just had to find them.

Mind made up, I swung around the landing for the third and last flight of stairs. In the natural pause between my steps, I heard a faint squeak. The same squeak I'd heard when I opened the rooftop door a few minutes ago.

Shit.

I didn't know why that guy had been looking at me, but I didn't want to be alone in a stairwell with him.

I wasn't an idiot.

I pulled out my keys and hurried down the last few stairs. I hadn't been in New York long enough to have any former clients or family members of former clients pissed at me. And I seriously doubted anyone from Chicago would've followed me. Most of my stuff had been white-collar crimes.

Then I remembered the threats Leayna had gotten.

Shit.

I pushed inside, thinking only about getting the door closed behind me.

If I'd taken a moment, I might have noticed a few things.

Like the fact that all of the lights were off even though I always left the entryway light on.

I might have noticed that the alarm wasn't beeping its annoying little reminder to disarm it.

I might have noticed the shadow in the corner *before*

he spoke.

"It would seem my associate was both right and wrong."

At the sound of the voice, I tensed, but didn't run. I reached over and turned on the lights.

A man sat in a chair, a gun pointed square at my chest.

I didn't try to fight the panic that automatically came when I saw the gun. It was a human response. All I needed to do was hide it. Voice calm, I said, "I didn't realize I had an after-hours meeting scheduled tonight."

"You're a cool one." He jabbed the revolver at me, grinning wide enough to show a gold-capped tooth on the bottom. "Drop the phone."

I glanced down at it, almost negligently and shrugged before tossing it down.

He didn't say anything about the keys, and I wondered if he'd noticed them. I held them cupped loosely in my hand which meant it was possible he hadn't seen them, although how he thought I'd gotten in, I didn't know. Not really my problem if he didn't notice them. I was more interested in what was going to happen next.

He held the gun like a man who knew how to use it, and I suspected he was a man who didn't *care* if he had to use it or not. I didn't think he planned on killing me tonight, but I also didn't think he would care if his plans were changed. It wouldn't matter to him if I lived or died. That much was clear.

"Have a seat," he said, a faint smile curving his lips. "We should talk."

There was a faint accent to his words, very faint. It was like he'd grown up speaking another language, but had long since switched to English. I couldn't quite place it though.

"If we're talking, mind if I get a drink?" I asked as I took a step forward. "I was planning on doing that as soon as I got home anyway."

"Sit. I'll get." The words grew shorter, more tense and the accent was a bit more pronounced. "I'll have drink, too."

*Slavic*, I thought. Maybe…

*Fuck.* Everything came together all at once.

Leayna's husband had connections to the mafia, the *Russian* mafia. And now I had an accented man with a gun in my living room. Probably a hitman.

Deciding it wasn't wise to argue with him, I settled in a seat, still gripping my keys, and watched as he circled around the room toward the wet bar I'd set up in the corner. It was fully stocked already. He studied everything with a faint smile before cocking his head at me. I never once got the impression he was distracted. He was making a show of letting me think he was distracted by the bar service. I wasn't that stupid, though. I'd wait to make my move.

"At least you have good vodka," he said.

"Well, you never know when you'll have your friendly local Russian mafia hitman stop by for a drink." I shrugged as I said it, although I was hoping those wouldn't be the last words I said.

He flashed me a wide smile. "Yes. I am the friendly

one. If they had sent Olaf, he would have already just beaten the information out of you and cut your throat. I prefer...less messy tactics. We are more civilized these days."

"So you don't plan on cutting my throat?" I wasn't buying it.

"Only if I have to." He picked up a bottle and studied it. "You like this one?"

He'd picked up the Macallan.

"Yes."

He opened it, sniffed. "Not bad. I shall try this instead of vodka. We'll share a drink, talk."

Wonderful.

As he splashed the expensive scotch into two highballs, I carefully lowered the keys so they were in the seat next to my thigh, out of sight. I wasn't considering using them as a weapon, not unless they were a last resort. I wanted to keep them with me because the key fob for the panic alarm was on it. He'd disarmed my system. Not just disarmed it, but deactivated it entirely. I could see the control panel was open, wires sticking out. But hopefully the panic button on the key fob would still work.

Once I pushed it, cops would be here in maybe ten minutes.

If it worked.

If it didn't...well, I would just have to see what Mr. Civilized wanted, and maybe just how good I was at extricating myself from sticky situations.

"You look like a man thinking serious thoughts."

I blinked everything back into focus as he came around the wet bar, holding both of the glasses in one hand. He paused by the chair where he'd been sitting, and after a deliberate look at me, put the gun down on the arm of the chair so he could relieve himself of one of the scotches. I didn't do anything. He was too far away, and I wasn't about to delude myself into thinking I could get to him quicker than he could pick up that gun and kill me. Or maybe shoot out my kneecaps so he could still question me.

"You are a cool one," he murmured again as he picked up the gun before coming over to offer me my drink.

I accepted the scotch with a steady hand and tossed back half of it. Apparently, he had an iron liver because he'd filled the highball well over halfway. I drained half of it in that first swallow.

He chuckled as he backed away and then settled back down in the chair across from me. "Now, we can talk."

"Like civilized men."

"Exactly." He took his scotch and lifted it in my direction in a salute.

I saluted him in similar fashion, and held still as he took a slow, savoring sip.

"It is good," he said approvingly. "I cannot do business with a man who doesn't have decent taste in alcohol." He took another sip and then put the glass down. "We need to discuss your client."

"I can't discuss my clients."

He grinned. "Client confidentiality. You will use that

when I have this pointed at you?"

Dropping my gaze to the gun, I swallowed. I'd never thought I might have to consider client confidentiality over my own life, but I'd taken an oath.

"It is a good thing they sent me instead of Olaf," he murmured.

I looked away from the gun to meet his eyes. He was nodding to himself as if he'd reached some deep, meaningful conclusion.

"He would have decided to beat you on principle the first time you showed any sign of having a spine. Me, I appreciate a man with courage. But it might end up getting you killed, Mr. Porter."

Yeah, that's about what I expected.

He leaned forward and pinned me with cold, hard eyes. His accent thickened. "Don't discuss the case. I do not give a flying fuck. Here is what we need to discuss. Your client needs to plead out. We already told her this and she was ready to do it. You must have talked her out of it. Change her mind again. She will plead out, plead guilty to murder, manslaughter, whatever the fuck. She pleads out."

I stared at him, working at keeping the blank expression that usually came so easily to me.

"Do you understand what I'm telling you?"

That was easy enough to answer. "I understand what you're saying."

His lids flickered. I had a feeling he wasn't fooled by my response into thinking I was agreeing to do what he said.

"Her husband had something that belonged to my employer. And because the son of a bitch decided to play hardball, he's dead. We told him what would happen. He didn't believe us. Now she gets to suffer the consequences."

My mind had been piecing everything together and with this, the rest came together. "Are you telling me that Leayna has been caught up in this solely because her husband was an asshole?"

"She married the asshole. She stayed with him." He shrugged, looking unperturbed. Scraping his short nails down the stubble on his cheek, he said, "You know, I have a good relationship with the boss. I could...well, *perhaps* I could suggest he leave her alone if she'll give him what her husband tried to cheat him out of. He tried to find it already, but it wasn't there."

The final piece. "The break-in."

His eyes gleamed. "She is lucky she wasn't there. Olaf had been given permission to do whatever was needed."

Olaf could get fucked.

"Would you like to know what my boss is looking for?" he asked softly, leaning forward.

# Chapter 10

## *Dena*

*Solve the puzzle.*

My mind kept going back to those words Arik had spoken during my little nap. *Solve the puzzle.* Personally, I would've preferred to linger on that crop and all of the wonderful things I was sure my imagination would've come up with, but first things first.

The puzzle of Bethany and her desktop lover.

It wasn't surprising that she'd already found somebody to take Pierce's place. Although, it was highly possible that Pierce had never really had a place. Not that he'd known that. There'd been real surprise in his eyes when I'd mentioned the other guy. No denying that.

*Solve the puzzle,* Arik's voice whispered again.

Not his voice, really. My subconscious.

"The puzzle of *what?*"

I knew it had something to do with Bethany and the guy, but what about them? Or was it more him than them?

"The guy," I mumbled, answering my own question.

The swaying of the subway came to a stop. Automatically, I looked up to make sure I hadn't missed my exit. That was when I realized a couple of people were watching me. The second I looked up, though, they busied themselves with something else, anything else, even if it was just to study their own fingernails.

Apparently, I'd been musing my problems out loud. Looking out my window, I rolled my eyes and ignored the other people. It was the New York subway, for crying out loud. All sorts of people talked to themselves on the subway. Granted, not too many of them were dressed in a chic little suit and carrying a briefcase that cost a few hundred dollars, but seriously. If you couldn't be eccentric on the New York City subway, where could you be eccentric?

As the train started to pull ahead, I took note of where we were. One stop from where I needed to get off. Gathering my things, I stood up and moved closer to the exit.

Once through the doors and onto the platform, I went through the tangle of people, and started for the surface, my mind already back on Bethany and her man. More specifically, on him. I'd seen him somewhere before. Where did I know him from?

The jangling of my phone interrupted my reverie, and I came to a halt in front of a big, plate glass window as I stopped to tug my phone free. Eyes on the TV on the other side of the window, I answered the phone without looking to see who was calling. It was Carrie's new ringtone.

I didn't get it out in time to keep Carrie's call from rolling over to voicemail. Sighing, I pulled up my call log and hit her number, eyes still on the daily news that the electronics chain had blasting across the screen.

I rolled my eyes at some of the headlines, fought a pang at one of them. Typical day in the Big Apple. A cop was in trouble in this precinct, while in another, one had taken down some career criminal who never should have been released from prison to begin with.

There was another terrorist threat, and the mayor was assuring New Yorkers and our numerous visitors to continue life as always. We'd mourn, we'd get pissed and we'd carry on.

Carrie came on the line just as a prominent NYPD lieutenant's face came on the screen. The text down at the bottom of the screen read:

> Second alleged NYPD snitch found murdered, dismembered in dumpster in Harlem precinct.

"Hey, stranger," Carrie said. "You never write. You never call..."

"You too good to talk to voice mail now that you're engaged to a seriously hot and rich man?" I asked distractedly, my head cocked as I stared at the TV. Every single thought in my head seemed to stutter to a stop.

*Solve the puzzle.*

The words seemed to echo in my head now, growing louder and louder and louder.

"And when was the last time we talked?" she demanded.

"Over the weekend. I texted two days ago." Moving closer, I squinted my eyes, although that wouldn't make it any easier to hear what was going on. The sound was probably muted. The captions were rolling, but they were patchy. Better than nothing. Reading them, I managed to catch up enough to have an idea of what was going on.

"Yeah, yeah. So what?" Carrie didn't sound impressed. "Hey, we haven't talked, seriously, in forever. If you're not doing anything, why don't you come down to the club?"

"Can't." My eyes raced back and forth over the captions. Shifting the weight of my briefcase and purse, mind whirling, I tried to keep up with Carrie and with what I was reading. This was it. *This* was the puzzle. "I'm too distracted. The case, Carrie. Something big just came up."

She said something, but I didn't really process it. Everything inside me seemed to be on edge, processing what I'd just figured out.

The puzzle.

I was pretty sure I was getting close to figuring out the puzzle.

I didn't realize I'd spoken out loud until Carrie asked, "What puzzle? Dena, are you okay?"

"No. Yeah." I shook my head, trying to clear it. "Have you seen today's news?"

"Same old crazy shit for New York."

"Yeah." I shifted my weight from one foot to the

other. "The guy they think was a snitch. He's dead. There was another one, too. Two snitches, dead. I wonder if he was connected to the mafia."

Carrie groaned. "The mafia. Hell, Dena. You know how trite that is? The mafia and New York. People still think they might run afoul of the mafia if they simply come to New York. I've lived here all my life, and I've never so much as met a single Mafioso type."

"That's because the Italian mafia isn't what it used to be. People just think it is. This..." I blew out a breath, barely hearing what I was saying. "The Russian mafia, the Mexican cartels? Those are the big problems now."

Arik's voice vibrated inside my head again, and now, as if they were in front of me, I could see Bethany and her guy again. Then she faded out, like a washed out, old photograph and all I could see was him.

The guy.

He was in stark, clear color. Those harsh, cut cheekbones, high, arched eyebrows and dark eyes. Eyes that were almost black. He was handsome, in a cold, brutal way.

Cold.

Brutal.

Yeah, that summed it up.

I'd thought that the first time I'd seen him, and suddenly realized that it hadn't been with Bethany a few days ago.

"Oh, *shit*," I whispered as it slammed into me.

I knew his face alright. His face, yes. But not him.

I'd never seen him in person before that night, but I'd

known that face all the same.

"Okay," Carrie said, her voice holding a note of finality. "That's it. You're going to tell me what's going on."

"I can't." Clearing my throat, I turned away from the news cast. A sense of foreboding washed over me, and I had to fight to keep from sending furtive glances all over the place.

"You damn well better," she retorted. "You're starting to freak me out."

"I'm fine." I'm pretty sure I even sounded like I believed it. Which was good. I didn't need carry or Gavin to come rushing out looking for me. Not now that I finally figured it out. Not now that I finally solved the damn puzzle.

The last thing I needed to do was put my friends in the same danger I was pretty sure I was putting myself in if I kept digging into Leayna Mance's case.

"I just figured out something pretty important to my case, Carrie. I can't talk about it, though. And I kind of need to go. It's important."

*Talk about the understatement of the year.*

She huffed out a sigh. "Fine. I wish I didn't understand that *I can't* so well, but a lawyer's oath doesn't change, no matter what type of law we practice. Call me when you can. And whatever it is, kick its ass, okay?"

"Yeah." I managed a weak smile as I disconnected and stood there, staring at absolutely nothing.

What in the hell was I supposed to do now?

My skin was crawling as I stood out there on the

street. It had nothing to do with the stories I'd seen on the news, though, and all to do with the things that I'd finally managed to put together.

My potential witness, the police informant. He'd been Russian. And he'd been connected to Leayna Mance's husband.

Oh shit.

The Russian mafia.

Arik had been so convinced his client was innocent. *So* convinced that there was something else going on. He was right, dammit.

I'd had more than a few reservations of my own, all of it because things just didn't add up and Bethany had refused to listen to me. That had rubbed me wrong, although now even that made a twisted sort of sense.

Swallowing hard, I made myself take one step, then another. It wasn't likely that I had people following me, not really. But if I did, it would be best if I acted normal, right?

That guy in Bethany's office. He was connected to the mafia. Connected in the worst possible way. He was also wanted. Not just by the NYPD, but by the FBI and probably several other law enforcement agencies. Wanted on the national, and possibly the international, level.

He was a known hit man for the Russian mafia.

And my *boss*, an assistant district attorney for Manhattan, had been fucking him.

Shit.

# Unlawful Attraction - Vol. 5

# Chapter 1

*Dena*

"Talk about sleeping with the enemy."

After five minutes of being completely shocked into silence, I finally managed to come up with something to say.

My boss – the Manhattan assistant district attorney who was supposed to be training me, teaching me the ropes, making sure I didn't screw up or get in trouble – was sleeping with a man suspected of being a hitman from the Russian mafia. This wasn't just a rumor either. Or something I merely suspected. I'd actually seen Bethany McDermott bent over her desk, the strange man I just identified pounding into her from behind.

A chill raced down my spine, and despite the warmth that came with the press of bodies around me, I felt cold.

I could have bundled up in front of a fire and still been cold.

It didn't help that my clothes were damp. I'd started

401

walking almost automatically after hanging up on Carrie, ending up half-soaked before I even realized it. I managed to take refuge in the nearest coffee shop, along with what felt like half of New York City, but even the smell of coffee hadn't been able to get my mind off of what I'd seen.

But the rain had stopped a few minutes ago, and now I was walking along the street, taking my time as I made my way home.

I had to...

I stopped in the middle of the sidewalk – a cardinal sin in New York City.

Somebody crashed into me, knocking me out of my daze, and I offered a distracted apology as I moved over to the side and stared out into the crowd. I couldn't keep from looking around me, my eyes bouncing from one face to the next. I didn't know what I was looking for, or maybe hoping to find, but there was something.

I was looking for something.

Somebody.

An attack maybe. I felt like I was caught in a spotlight, that somebody was going to swoop down and pull a gun on me, shoot me for what I'd seen.

I knew something now, didn't I? Did that make me a risk? Someone who needed to be eliminated? Was that how it worked?

"You're being paranoid," I muttered.

But even as that thought faded from my mind, I realized something crucial. I couldn't go back to the office on Monday. What was I going to do? Confront

Bethany? No way in hell. But then who could I talk to? I didn't know anybody at the DA's office I trusted well enough for something this potentially deadly. For all I knew, there were half a dozen dirty ADA's.

To be honest, outside of Carrie, Krissy, and Leslie, the list of people I'd trust with this information was decidedly short. And I wasn't going to put any of my friends in danger. They might claim to be able to take care of themselves, and maybe they could, but I sure as hell wasn't going to put that to the test. Maybe Gavin or DeVon, if he'd been on this side of the country. But maybe not even them. They were Alpha Male with a capital *A*. They would've called the cops and not let me out of their sight.

A face flickered through my mind and I went rigid.

Arik.

I could go to Arik.

That would probably be the stupidest thing to do, but the moment the thought crossed my mind, the muscles in my shoulders started to relax, and I managed to take my first easy breath since I'd seen Bethany in her compromising position. My nerves were stretched so taut that I felt like even the slightest touch would break me. Talking to Arik might help. Even if he was too new in the city to have a lot of contacts, maybe he'd have at least a general idea of where to start.

"Grasping at straws." Shaking my head at myself, I moved to the edge of the curb and held up a hand, waiting for a cab.

I probably *was* grasping at straws, but one thing was

certain – between Arik and a stranger at the DA's office, Arik was the safest option. Talking to him might be a bit unethical, but it wasn't like I was planning on discussing the case. And I knew, with him, I didn't have to worry about him telling the wrong person, resulting in me getting acquainted with the business end of something sharp and shiny.

I tried calling his number, but no one answered. I wasn't sure if that meant he was busy or if he was just ignoring me. Either one was a possibility, I supposed. I left a brief voicemail, asking him to call me back, but not giving any details. This wasn't the sort of thing I wanted a recording of.

Him not answering, however, meant I'd have to find him and hope he'd agree to talk to me. I didn't know exactly where the two of us stood at the moment, but I was fairly confident it wasn't bad enough that he'd turn me away without hearing what I had to say.

I didn't know the exact address of the place where Arik had taken me earlier this week, and I didn't even know if he was living there or somewhere else while it was being finished, but it was a place to start. My only other options were to go to his office and hope he'd worked late, or find out if there was any way Officer Dunne could get the information. Most defense attorneys, even ones who'd been born and raised in New York, didn't have their home addresses available to the public.

I was going to take my chances with the first option before I did anything else. I was second chair on a case that Arik was trying. Showing up at his office would probably be a bad idea. The less people who knew that the two of us were acquainted outside of the courtroom, the better. But, if I had to, I'd go there.

I needed to talk to someone, and he was my best option.

Even if I wasn't entirely sure how I felt about him at the moment.

An idea occurred to me as I was waiting for a cab to finally notice my out-stretched hand, and I felt dumb for having not thought of it first. I'd been so focused on seeing him, I hadn't considered calling first. At least that way, I'd know where he was.

When I couldn't reach him on his cell, I tapped my screen to call his office. A woman answered on the second ring. "Sheldon, Simon and Sharpe. How can I help you?"

"Good evening." I worked to make my voice as business-like as possible. "I'm with the DA's office and I need to speak to Mr. Arik Porter."

"He's not here right now," the woman replied. "Can I take a message?"

"No," I said quickly. Then, before I could stop myself, I asked, "Is he at home?"

There was a momentary pause, then the woman's voice got decidedly cooler. "I'm sorry. I can't give out personal information."

"Of course," I said. "I'll call back tomorrow."

When I ended the call, I closed my eyes for a moment. That had been stupid, asking if he was at home. For all that woman knew, I was some psycho former client. Just because I said I was from the DA's office didn't mean I actually was.

I opened my eyes and told myself that it didn't matter. I'd at least narrowed down the possibilities of where he was. I supposed it was possible that he'd gone out, but I wouldn't bother trying to figure any of that out until I found out if he was home or not.

A cab finally pulled up to the curb and I got inside. I was going to go broke on cab fare the way things were going lately. I gave the address and settled back into the seat. At this time in the evening, it would take a while to get there.

As we inched forward, my phone started to ring. I wasn't able to get it out of my purse before it stopped ringing, but I looked at the screen anyway. I hoped it was Arik, that he'd somehow sensed how much I needed to talk to him and had gotten back to me right away. It was silly, I knew, because we weren't like that, and even if we were, things like that were romanticized. Arik and I were logical people. We thought things through.

I frowned when the words *unknown caller* popped up on my screen. Whoever it was, it looked like they'd left a voicemail at least. I glanced up and saw that we'd only gone a couple blocks. At this rate, I might've been able to walk there faster.

I called the voicemail, thankful that I had a fairly taciturn cab driver. There was a long buzz of dead air before I heard...something. My frown deepened as I strained to listen.

There was a series of muttering voices, mumbles

more than anything else. I was about ready to lower the phone and delete it when something sharp and ear-piercing came through the receiver.

A scream that cut off abruptly when the call ended.

I almost dropped my phone.

"What was the street number again, miss?"

Jerking my head up, I looked at the cab driver. Shaken, but fighting not to show it, I told him. Then I clamped my mouth shut before I could ask him to hurry the hell up. Suddenly, I needed to see Arik, and it wasn't because I was worried about me anymore.

# Chapter 2

## *Arik*

My cell phone rang for the second time in a space of ten minutes. Not that I could answer it this time any more than the last. With it being face-down, I couldn't even see if it was the same person calling.

It lay on the plush, steel gray carpet of my entry way, some fifteen feet away from me...and from my friendly neighborhood hitman. He flicked a look at it before shifting his attention back to me and smiling.

I had to give him credit. If he'd been a man I had to defend, it would've been a piece of cake to coach him. He was actually quite polite, charming even. He'd be the kind of man who'd be cool-headed on the stand when questioned about a murder, but not make the jury think he was being cold.

Then he could go out and put a bullet in someone's head without blinking an eye.

A good thing in a defendant. Not such a good thing

when the man had a gun pointed in my direction.

"The second time. You are quite popular. Are you expecting to speak with someone tonight?" His accent was Russian. Maybe one of the surrounding countries. I couldn't quite distinguish it, especially since it was fairly faint. He'd been in this country for a while.

Lifting one shoulder, I said, "I'm a lawyer. I'm always expecting calls. Alleged criminals don't always keep usual work hours."

It was both the honest truth and the best non-answer I could come up with. I also thought it couldn't hurt to throw a little humor into the mix.

He looked amused, so I supposed that was a good thing. A happy hit-man was less likely to kill me, right?

When the phone went silent, he gestured at me with his gun. "You are not drinking your scotch. Were you not so thirsty after all?" He raised an eyebrow. He'd finished his first glass already.

I'd forgotten about it, to be honest. Looking down at the glass, I lifted it to my lips and sipped, letting it glide down my throat like fiery velvet. Being drunk wasn't a good idea, but something to take the edge off wasn't necessarily a bad idea. "I'm afraid I'm off my routine. Your unexpected visit caught me off guard."

"Again, I like your style, Mr. Porter." He nodded slowly as he took a sip of his drink as well, sighing lustily in appreciation.

Nice to know he enjoyed the scotch. The shit cost more than a thousand dollars a bottle. Not that I couldn't afford it, but I didn't really want to waste that kind of money on someone who was probably considering where in my body was the best place to put a bullet.

The Russian mafia, sitting in my penthouse, and drinking my Macallan. If someone back in Chicago had told me that this was where I'd end up, I never would've believed him.

He swirled the dark amber liquid in the glass as he studied me over the rim of the cut crystal. "You know, a man like you could be useful to us...if you can convince your client to plead out. You don't get nervous. You don't get..." He waved a hand in the air. "Panicky. I had a man once, he screamed like a little girl when I pulled a gun on him. Fucking pathetic. Annoyed the shit out of me. Pissed his pants before I shot him."

"Glad I'm not...annoying the shit out of you." Had I hit that key fob? Was it working? Would the cops get here?

He grinned at me, showing me brilliant teeth in a sharp smile. "I hear sarcasm in your voice, Mr. Porter. Sharp, smart – you have balls." He leaned back a bit but there was nothing relaxed about that pose. "Would you like to be useful to us, Mr. Porter? To me? To my boss? I could make calls."

"No." I replied without even blinking an eye.

I didn't even have to think about it. Aside from the fact that there was no way I wanted this bastard coming back here, there was no way in hell I was going to work for the mob. I'd just as soon he put a bullet in my head right now.

I kept my tone as polite as possible. "Let me be clear,

411

Mr...well...sir, I'd like to be very clear. Hell, no. I don't want any misunderstandings."

To my surprise, he laughed. I didn't really see the humor in it, but who was I to tell him he couldn't find this amusing.

A bead of sweat rolled down the back of my neck and I swallowed again, the tension in my neck so heavy now, I thought it might crack if I even turned my head. The alcohol wasn't really doing a whole lot to relax me. Or, if it was, I wouldn't want to know how strung out I'd be without it.

"You want to be clear, hmm. No misunderstandings? Smart man." He nodded. "You do not wish to get...involved in certain elements. I understand this. I am not surprised. You are smart. It is..." He paused, his brow crumpling as though he was searching for the word. Then he smiled. "Okay. It is okay. There are other people we use, better probably. They are predictable. You are not. You are smart, and smart is always good. But predictable is better. I know a lost cause when I see one."

He came out of his seat then, that gun loosely held at his side.

I didn't let myself look at it, as much as I wanted to. No. I didn't *want* to. It was that my gaze felt *drawn* to the weapon. But I didn't think that was a good idea.

He took another step toward me, and I tried to decide which was going to be my best bet, grab for the gun or try to get out of the way.

The landline rang.

It surprised me enough to distract me from the gun,

412

and this time, I couldn't stop myself from looking at the object that held my interest. From looking at the phone, sitting innocuously on my counter, waiting for me to pick it up and answer.

The damn thing hardly ever rang. I had the cellphone, and used it more often than not. But sometimes, cell phones didn't work. Storms had knocked cellular service out more than once, even in the city, and I'd learned early on to have a more reliable way to stay connected with the world.

However, the worst thing I could have done was *react* to it.

In the months I'd been in New York, that landline had rang maybe five times.

Why in the hell was it ringing now?

The hitman noticed my attention, and his brows arched. With a smile curling his lips, he walked over, cutting a wide circle that kept me in his line of sight as he moved to the phone. He held my eyes as he picked it up, a different kind of amusement in his gaze. In the other hand, he lifted the weapon, pointing it at me.

"Hello, Mr. Porter's residence. Can I help you?"

In the faint pause that followed, I could make out nothing about who was on the other side. He was too far away and the caller spoke too quietly. A part of me wasn't sure I wanted to know, because if it was someone I cared about, I didn't know how I'd react.

Though who would...?

Shit. Dena.

If that was her...

My stomach clenched.

"No, I'm sorry," he said, head cocked. "I'm a friend. I'm afraid Mr. Porter is indisposed for the next few minutes. May I take a message? He will be back presently."

The man sounded like a damn diplomat's personal assistant. He barely had an accent at all.

Amusement glinted in his eyes as he looked over at me. "Oh, hello, Mrs. Pott – oh, *Miss* Pott, I apologize. May I say, you have a very...no, forgive me. That is inappropriate. I just feel as though I know you because Mr. Porter speaks of you so often."

Jaw clenched, I fought not to come off the chair and go after him. The only thing that stopped me was the fact that I wasn't bullet proof, or faster than a fucking bullet. My assistant at the firm seemed competent. She was certainly eager to prove herself to me. I just hoped she was smart enough to not give out any important personal information to the schmuck on the phone.

Although chances were, the hitman knew more than I wanted him to anyway. I wouldn't have exactly counted Ella Pott as someone I cared about, but she wasn't someone I wanted to see hurt. I needed to get out of here.

"In answer to your question, I'm a friend of Arik's. Yes, we go way back. I'm just in the area for the evening – dropped in to ask for a favor and a..." He swirled the scotch around in a glass and smiled. "Drink. He had to step out to take a call. Business related. Shall I take a message?"

A few moments later, he hung up. He'd delicately

tried to push for more information from her.

He'd failed.

I'd be giving Ms. Pott a bonus.

Assuming, of course, that I lived.

"She is very professional." He returned to his seat, the weapon lifted and pointed dead at my forehead once more. "You should give her a bonus."

I didn't like how his thoughts echoed mine so closely, but I managed a casual shrug. "I should. Good help isn't always easy to come by."

When he grinned at me, I decided that I wanted to see him choking on that shit-eating grin. Hitmen really shouldn't be so easily amused, especially not when they're contemplating how to kill you.

"She says that a woman called for you." He really seemed to be enjoying himself now. "Said she was from the DA's office and needed to speak to you. I wonder who that could have been."

Dena.

I forced myself to keep very still, not wanting to give him the slightest hint that I cared.

"It's getting late," I said.

"It is," he agreed. "Let's get back to business then." He leaned forward, the gun dangling negligently between his knees.

Yet again, I wasn't disarmed by his supposed lack of caution. His eyes were far too alert for him to *not* be paying attention to everything. I assumed that he wouldn't still be alive if he wasn't good at his job. I felt pretty certain that most hit-men who were distracted rarely lived long.

Case in point, his eyes shot to the door almost a second before the knock came.

"You are a busy man for somebody who didn't seem to be aware he had plans this evening, Mr. Porter," he muttered, looking vaguely disgusted for the first time that evening. As he rose again, he looked over at me. "Were you expecting company?"

I shook my head. Keeping my voice low, I said, "Ignore it. They probably have the wrong apartment. Whoever it is will go away."

I hoped so anyway. I could only think of one person who knew about this place. I hadn't finished moving in until a couple days ago.

He ran his tongue across his teeth as he flicked his eyes between the door and me.

The knock came again.

Slowly, he walked over and looked into the hallway. "It's a woman. She is pretty." He glanced at me. "I know her, Mr. Porter."

Shit.

He walked partway back toward me and spoke in a low voice. "It is the assistant DA. Perhaps she is the one who called your Miss Pott. I have seen you with her."

The smile told me that he didn't just mean in the courtroom.

"You…well, you have an interesting relationship with her, do you not? And Bethany McDermott? She doesn't like her at all."

"Fuck Bethany McDermott," I said before I could

stop myself.

His lips rolled in like he was suppressing a laugh.

The knock hadn't come again.

Blowing out a slow breath, I hoped that meant Dena had left. I needed her to be safe. More than my own life, I wanted her to be safe.

But just as I started to relax, her voice rang out.

"Arik? Are you in there? I need to talk to you."

"She'll go away," I said again, making it more firm this time, as if that would make a difference. *Go away, Dena... please*

But he was already walking to the door. "I don't think I want her to."

My body tensed and I half-rose, already prepared to shout out a warning. But he had his gun lifted, pointed to the door. If he squeezed the trigger...I had good security, but I didn't know how well the door would hold up to a bullet.

Slowly, I lowered myself back into the seat, and when he opened the door, I saw her.

My heart seemed to freeze inside my chest.

This couldn't be happening.

# Chapter 3

*Dena*

I almost turned to leave after he didn't answer the second knock. But I didn't have any place else to go other than home. Leslie would have no problem with me staying with her for a couple days, but it wasn't like she lived in some heavily guarded building with bulky security guards. I knew Club Privé was open, and that all I'd have to do is go there and tell Carrie and Gavin that I was worried, but I didn't want to put this on them. Gavin was the type who'd want to take charge, and that would make him a target.

I didn't want to put them in danger.

But, apparently, I had no problem putting Arik in danger.

I might've been a horrible person for it, but instead of turning away, I called out. "Arik? Are you in there? I need to talk to you."

Several more seconds passed without an answer, and

I started to turn away, certain that he'd chosen to ignore me, but then the doorknob turned. The memory of our last encounter was all that kept me from taking an immediate step toward him.

Except it wasn't Arik standing there.

I recognized those eyes right away, and I supposed that was one of the things that saved me. That, and the fact that I hadn't taken that step toward the door. A few moments ago, I'd been standing right there, but now, with a distance of a few feet between me and him, I had a precious split second for my brain and body to react.

My brain screamed *shit*, but my gut took over. Later, I'd have to thank my dad for insisting I take some seriously grueling self-defense courses once he realized I was serious about going into criminal law.

I was far from tall or muscular, but I knew how to use what I did have. What I had was the knowledge that my legs were the most powerful muscles in my body, and when he went to reach for me, I moved *toward* him instead of away as he probably expected.

It also helped that he was partially behind the door, because that was where I kicked. I kicked straight at it, snapping out with my knee the way I'd learned. I hadn't gone to class in years, but I'd studied throughout middle and high school, and muscle memory was a beautiful thing. The door drove back into him and he grunted. With a gliding little half-hop, I kicked forward again, driving him back farther, and battering him with the door a second time.

That was when somebody else joined the fight,

ramming the stranger into the wall.

Something clattered on the floor and, instinctively, I kicked at it before I even realized it was a gun. It slid away as I squeezed myself in through the tight space allowed by the two struggling bodies.

Arik drove a fist into the man's face hard enough to make me wince.

He spewed out something ugly in a harsh, deep language – Russian, I thought. Of course it was Russian. I knew who he was now, and he sure as hell wasn't murmuring sweet nothings in French.

While my mind kept up the strange babbling, another part of me stepped up and took over. I didn't feel like *me* as I bent down and grabbed the gun, and I sure as *hell* didn't feel like me as I gripped it and checked the safety. It had been on. How weird was that?

But it didn't matter the reasoning. What mattered was that, even though I'd never owned a gun or intended to own one, a couple years ago, I'd taken a gun safety course and done some target practicing.

When the hitman managed to flip his way on top of Arik, I stepped closer and pressed the nose of the gun to the back of his head.

My voice was as cold as I'd ever heard it. "Safety's off now."

He froze.

A split second later, a weird, whining noise escaped his throat, and he rolled off to the side, curled in on himself and clutching at his crotch. People rarely acknowledged that, in a life-or-death situation, even a man will knee another man in the balls.

Arik sat up, panting. His nose was bleeding, his bottom lip split. He looked at me as he staggered upright, the concern on his face focused all on me. When he took a step toward me, hand outstretched as if to take the gun, I backed up.

"I think I can handle the fucking gun. Why don't you tie him up or something?"

Arik's eyes widened slightly, but I didn't really care about his surprise at the moment. I wanted to make sure the man on the ground didn't sense a moment of hesitation.

"The...little girl...thinks she can...handle a gun." The hitman wheezed out a laugh.

"Fuck off," I snapped. I'd always prided myself on my level-headedness, but that part of my self-control had snapped at some point in the last few hours.

The hitman rolled onto one knee and I shifted, making sure the gun was still aimed at him.

"Give me the gun. I'll go. My...business here is done."

"I'm curious about that." Off to the side, Arik was rummaging around in nearby drawers.

I couldn't figure out what was taking him so long. He had to have something here he could use. The man was a Dom for fuck's sake!

Then it hit me. All of Arik's bondage things were in his bedroom or playroom, not out here. And he apparently didn't want to leave the room. It almost made me laugh.

The hitman shifted again, bringing my thoughts back to the present. I knew I was dangerously close to going into shock. I needed to focus on something, anything, to keep my head on straight.

"While we're waiting, why don't you tell me about those plans, and maybe about your relationship with my boss?"

His eyelids flickered and he tensed. For a moment, I thought he was going to come after me, then his mouth opened slightly as he started to say something.

Whatever those words were, however, died when Arik smashed something heavy down on his head. I figured out what it was a moment later when the potent fumes of whiskey flooded the air. The hitman slumped forward, his eyes rolling toward the back of his skull.

Over the unconscious body, Arik looked up at me. His emerald gaze burned, his chest heaved. "Unconscious is just as good as tied up, right?" He swiped at the blood on his face and took a half step toward me.

I swallowed and looked away. "We need to call the…"

"Police!"

"Mr. Porter, we received–"

"Ma'am, drop the gun, hands up!"

"Oh, for crying out loud."

Lifting one hand into the air, I knelt down and put the gun on the now-blood splattered carpet. Idly, I wondered how much it would cost to clean it, or if Arik would just have it replaced. Pity. The place was so new.

Arik spoke up as he edged toward me. "Officers,

you're holding a weapon on the wrong person. This is ADA Dena Monroe…"

As he started to explain, I closed my eyes and tried to deal with the spinning in my head.

This was going to prove to be one long, long night.

One of the officers approached me as I stood in the kitchen drinking water a few minutes later.

"I'm sorry about…" He gestured toward the door.

Shaking my head, I said, "You're doing your job. Security alert, unknown person holding a weapon…you did what you're trained to do."

He nodded. "Appreciate the understanding, Miss Monroe. Mr. Porter explained everything to us, but I'll need to take your statement as well."

I really didn't want to go over anything, but I knew procedure. "Of course."

We were only halfway through my explanation of what had happened – with the careful but legal exclusion of the fact that I'd seen the hitman fucking my boss earlier this week – when there was another knock on the somewhat askew door. Between me kicking it and Arik's unexpected guest shoving back, even its excellent construction hadn't been able to hold up. It was a good thing Arik's family owned the building. Otherwise, that would've been a bitch to try to explain.

The new addition didn't bother to introduce himself or be invited inside.

"I'll be running the investigation from here on out," he announced.

I stood to the side and listened as he walked around, introducing himself to the officers, to Arik. Based on the way he was carrying himself, Lieutenant Beale considered his presence to be quite important.

I already didn't like him.

When he paused by the suspect, a faint smirk curved his lips and he shook his head.

"Always knew that arrogance would trip you up sooner or later."

The now semi-coherent hitman sneered, but didn't say anything.

Lieutenant Beale came toward me at last. "Ms. Monroe, I take it?"

I glanced down at his hand and debated shaking it. Then I reminded myself that I was an ADA and there was no reason to be rude. I'd probably have to work with this man at some point and he hadn't really done anything that deserved my dislike. His grasp was firm, precise, like he'd practiced the perfect handshake.

"I take it you're in the middle of giving your statement?" The smile that came with the question was close-lipped and didn't reach his eyes.

"Yes." I pushed a hand through my hair, and tried not to sigh. "I take it I need to start all over?"

"It would simplify things."

I looked at the water I was still drinking. Taking a sip, I said, "I'm still a little shocky. I need the fluids, Lieutenant. Give me a minute and I'll start this all over again."

"I hate to be an inconvenience." The corner of his mouth hitched up in a smile more infuriating than the last. "But it's useful, as you are probably aware, to get solid facts. The sooner we can get this done, the sooner you can go home."

Asshole. I took another sip of my water, half out of spite, and when I lowered the glass, my hand shook badly enough that I spilled the liquid across my hand and arm.

The officer I'd originally been talking to handed me a paper towel.

"Thanks." I gave him a grateful look and then looked at the lieutenant.

"Miss Monroe," Lieutenant Beale said my name, as if reminding me that he was still here. And that I was wasting his time.

That thin veneer of control I'd managed to get back in the last few minutes cracked. "I'm so sorry, Lieutenant, if I'm being an inconvenience. Please excuse me." Sarcasm dripped off of every word. "I mean, it's not like I've never had a gun pointed at me, or had to point a gun at someone else. I'm sure every native New Yorker or ADA has been in this situation numerous times. I'll try to get my shit together."

Lieutenant Beale's eyes narrowed even as color crept up his neck and cheeks. "Why don't you do that?" He yanked his phone out of his pocket. "I'm going to call

1PP to give them an update." He stalked away.

"Excuse Lieutenant Beale," the officer next to me said. "He's only on the force to meet the asshole quota, Ms. Monroe." He gave me a grin. "That or the dick quota. Actually, I think he meets both."

I smiled to show him I appreciated the support. Then my eyes met Arik's and I saw that he didn't think any of this was funny either.

It took forever for Lieutenant Beale to finish taking my statement, and an equally long time for him to finish with Arik. I was pretty sure he was dragging it out intentionally. By the time it was all said and done, I wanted to collapse. Actually, I pretty much *did*. Sitting on Arik's couch, my legs curled up beneath me, my eyes had drooped closed, and the next thing I knew, Arik was rubbing my shoulder.

"Dena."

Jerking upright, I automatically swung for the person touching me.

He caught my wrist, his grip firm, but not rough. He gave me a wry smile as his thumb brushed across my racing pulse-point. "I've got to tell you, Councilor. That's one hell of a right hook you've got."

Staring at him, aware of the fact that more than a few

of the officers were watching with varying degrees of interest, I jerked on my wrist.

"Sorry," I muttered, embarrassment making my voice sharp. Blood rushed to my face as I stood up and took a few unsteady steps off to the side. "I'm a little…jumpy."

"Understandable." One of the cops moved between us and gave me a professional smile. He wasn't the one I'd given my statement to, but he seemed just as nice. "We were just telling Mr. Porter that he'd have to pack up for a few days. I doubt there's much evidence to collect, but the techs will have to go through. And…"

His eyes slid to the hitman.

His name. I knew his name, but I couldn't think of it.

Shock, I told myself. Shock, exhaustion. Both.

As the officer caught my eyes, I nodded. I understood what he'd been saying. If the Russian mafia knew where Arik was, then it wasn't safe for him to come back here for a few days.

A shiver raced down my spine, and I had to wonder if it was safe at my place.

"I've got somewhere to go," Arik said, distracting the officers as I turned away. They spoke for a few more minutes as I wandered over to the large, floor to ceiling windows that ran the length of the living room. My body tightened as I remembered what happened the last time I'd been here.

I wanted to tell him to come home with me, that I didn't want to be alone. That I wanted him to be with me.

But it was probably a bad idea to say that in front of

an audience. Especially an audience who I might see again for work.

It didn't take long for everybody to clear out once the cops made it clear we wouldn't be left alone inside the apartment. Reluctantly, I bit my tongue and didn't say anything to Arik as we walked out. From the hallway, I watched as the officers placed bright yellow crime scene tape over the door.

We rode down to the lobby in two silent parties, Beale and half the uniforms with the now-upright cuffed suspect going first. His eyes glittered at me before the elevator door closed, blocking him from sight. By the time we reached the lobby, he was already being hustled out to an unmarked, flanked by two black and whites, their lights flashing in the pouring rain, but I could still feel his eyes on me.

"Make sure you let us know of your whereabouts, Mr. Porter," one of the officers said to Arik.

"My office will be able to contact me if you need me." His voice was polite, but purposely vague.

I knew he wouldn't be telling anybody anything. Judging by the expression on the young cop's face, he knew it too, but he didn't press. As glad as I'd been to see them arrive, I couldn't deny the relief at seeing them go.

When we were alone in the lobby, Arik finally turned to me.

I opened my mouth to tell him he could come stay with me, even though part of me was still angry, still hurt. We'd figure that part out later. Right now, I just couldn't deal with being alone.

He put his finger over my lips, effectively stopping the flow of words before they even started. A faint smile cracked his lips and he quirked an eyebrow. "Remind me to never get on the wrong side of a door with you."

I started to answer, but all that came out was a shaky sigh.

In the next minute, I was caught up in his arms. His lips brushed my temple as he whispered, "I don't think I've ever been that scared before."

"Don't go to a hotel," I said quietly, all but desperate now. My arms were around his waist, and I knew I should be embarrassed at the way I was clinging to him, but I couldn't manage to feel any of that at the moment. "Come home with me."

"Don't go home," he said in return. "Come with me."

I pulled back, staring up at him. He brushed my hair back from my face. "He knows who you are, Dena. He recognized you."

That very thought made my heart pound and I sucked in oxygen, although it didn't seem to reach my lungs. Or maybe the blood wasn't reaching my brain. Either way, I felt lightheaded and queasy.

"He...he what?"

"He knows who you are." Gently, Arik cupped my cheek, his thumb rubbing back and forth over my bottom lip. "Come with me. I want you to be safe."

"And go where? To a hotel? Is *that* safe?" I asked, only half-joking. Every bad movie I'd ever seen with shoot-ups in hotel hallways started to flash through my mind. Even less comforting was that most of them dealt

430

with people trying to hide from the mob.

"We're not going to a hotel. We're going someplace I *know* is safe." He dropped his hand so that both of his arms were around me again.

I stared up at him, my brain struggling to keep up with all of the reasons why this wasn't a good idea. Even if I had been the one who'd originally suggested it. "We shouldn't. The case…everything. This is stupid."

"Do you care?" he asked, eyes intense as they cut into me.

"Do you?" I countered.

"You have an annoying habit of answering questions with questions." Arik bent his head, pressed his lips to mine in a firm but chaste, kiss. "But no. I don't care. Right now, the only thing I care about is having you some place safe." His voice lowered to that tone I'd already come to recognize. "Once I have you safe, I plan on getting you naked and under me."

"That…" Some of the knots inside me started to relax, and I blew out a breath. Fuck it. I'd played by the rules my whole life and I needed this. Needed him. "That sounds like a good plan. Even if it is stupid. And no, I don't think I care if it's stupid."

"Neither do I."

He curled an arm around my waist and we started for the door. "For the record, if you'd insisted on going back to your place, I would have been parked in a car out front the rest of the night. Just so you know."

"Stalker, much?" I managed a half-teasing smile.

"If that's what it takes to keep you safe," he said.

431

I curled into him as he led me out into the rain, the warmth of his words protecting me from the chill of the night.

# Chapter 4

*Dena*

The towering, imposing structure jutted overhead as we climbed out of the car. It was made of old stone, the kind you didn't see very often any more. This was the furthest thing from Arik's place in the city that I'd seen. If the circumstances had been different, I would've been more impressed and less feeling like this entire thing was becoming more surreal by the moment. The fact that it was nearly one in the morning after the hardest day I'd ever had wasn't helping matters much.

"What did you do, bring me to Frankenstein's lair?" I asked, shoving my damp hair back. I'd been too distracted to get a trim recently and my hair was longer than I usually liked it.

A man was already at the curb, holding out an umbrella, but I wasn't much in the mood to have somebody at my elbow, so I waved him off as I climbed out of the car. Rain now plastered my hair to my skull as I looked over at Arik.

He was also staring up at the house, and a faint smile curled his lips. "Welcome to my home away from home, Dena."

This was definitely not what I'd been expecting. We'd taken his car since he hadn't trusted a cab driver not to share information with anyone who paid enough, but he hadn't told me where he was taking me. There'd been twists and turns that I wasn't sure were necessary, but were rather his way of guaranteeing that we weren't being followed.

"Marcum," Arik said, nodding at the man with the umbrella as we began walking toward the house.

It sounded much classier than Jeeves, although not as cool as Alfred. If he'd been an Alfred, then I could have teased Arik about taking me to the bat cave. It hit me in that moment just how exhausted I must be, standing in the grand foyer of this insane house, making internal Batman jokes while the man I was...whatever with quietly chatted with a couple of others – and he had blood on his suit.

Blood. From fighting with Mr. Russian Mafia Hitman. Some of it was the other guy's...but some of it was Arik's.

A shudder wracked me and it had little to do with how cold I was. I turned away from him, pressing the tips of my fingers to my lips before the low noise building in my throat could escape. Just outside the heavy oak doors and the thick frosted glass, the rain pounded down even harder and I was actually tempted to step out into it, wondering if maybe that would wash away the shock of the night.

Would I be able to go back to my place in Chelsea tomorrow? Or any time soon? Had Bethany been tipped off? Did she know I'd been at Arik's when her 'friend' had paid him a visit? Could somebody be watching me even now, having somehow tracked us down?

I just didn't know.

Something hit me then. The call I'd gotten in the cab. Had it really been some random thing? Or had that scream on the other end, the one that had ended the call, had that been someone I knew? I thought, when I'd gotten it, that it had been Arik. Then when I'd gotten to the apartment, I all but forgot about it. Now, however, I couldn't help but wonder if it had been Bethany.

Thinking of her was like a splash of cold water in my face, and I reached for my phone, needing for the police to know. I wasn't going to call that asshole lieutenant though. I was going to call someone I trusted.

Despite the late hour, Officer Dunne answered. I gave him the quick, short version, as well as the name of the lieutenant. He promised to look into it, and reminded me to be careful.

I'd just hung up when Arik came over. "Dena, I'm so sorry. You're standing out here soaked after everything that's happened."

As his voice trailed off, I turned to look at him. "Don't apologize. I needed to make a call anyway." I paused, and then added, "I'll tell you later."

I had to tell him about it, about Bethany, and her

connection to the man in his apartment. But not now, even if he asked.

He looked like he wanted to say more, but instead, he just nodded and held out a hand. "We'll sleep in my old room."

"Your old room?" I asked.

As he led me deeper inside the house, I tried to see everything, if only for the distraction. The house was...posh. Opulent, over the top and *posh*. I couldn't think of a better way to describe it. I'd known Arik came from money, and that his father had invested in property in the city. I just hadn't realized they had a house like this nearby.

"So is this where you spent long, boring old summers while your parents were out yachting or something?"

A quick grin flashed across his face. "No. I had a place like that, but it was in upper Michigan. Not quite as far from Chicago as New York." The smile faded as we mounted the stairs. "This place...well, it belonged to a relative. It's ours now."

As we climbed the stairs, he placed a hand on my lower spine. I lost track of the halls, the turns, the twists. After what seemed like an endless journey, we were in a massive, elegantly decorated room, and I turned, facing Arik once more. "So you have this...and that place in the city?"

"Sort of." He tucked his hands into his pockets, looking around. "This isn't mine. It's my dad's, more or less. But it's safe, and that's all that matters for now."

He rubbed a hand back and forth over his damp hair,

droplets flying everywhere. "This place...well, nobody's lived here other than the household staff for years. I think Dad and I stayed here maybe three times in twice as many years."

"And we're here now because...?"

"I already told you." Flat, simple words. "It's safe."

He turned away and moved to the window. I followed him, staring outside and wondering what it was he saw. Despite everything going on around us, I knew that something wasn't right. There was an ache of sadness in the air, and I knew it had something to do with this place.

"What happened here?"

"That," Arik said in a heavy voice. "Would depend on who you ask. But I don't want to talk about that tonight."

He turned back to me and reached out, drawing me to him.

The warmth of his body bled into my cold one, making me shiver. He felt so good, so steady and strong. Through his damp clothes, the heat of him was like a furnace and I was drawn to it. I wanted to rest my head on his chest, but stopped, staring at the blood on his shirtfront.

I braced a hand a few inches below the stains, wondering how much of it was his, thinking about how close the both of us had come to getting seriously hurt. How close we'd come to dying.

Arik restlessly rubbed his hands up and down my hips. "I can't tell you how scared I was when I realized it was you at the door, Dena. And when he made it clear he knew who you were..." His fingers flexed even as his eyes darkened.

He dipped his head, pressed his lips to mine. He didn't deepen the kiss, just stood there, as if he needed the reassurance of my presence as much as I needed his. I slid my hands up and cupped his face, feeling the abrasive scratch of five o'clock shadow against my hands. My entire body throbbed at the thought of how that would feel against the insides of my thighs.

I broke the kiss, but kept my forehead pressed against his. "I've been trying to tell myself that I'm not ready to talk to you yet, that I need to think things through more." I closed my eyes. "I want to be mad at you, but I can't."

"I can't either," he admitted.

I opened my eyes, meeting his emerald ones. I lowered my hands, and stared at the splatters of blood on his clothes. Suddenly desperate to be rid of all reminders of the evening, I pushed at his suit jacket.

"There's blood on you." My voice was shaking. Normally, that would have pissed me off, but I didn't care at the moment.

Once I had his jacket on the floor, I reached for his tie. My fingers fumbled for a moment, then his hands covered mine, stilling the restless movement. Then he was easily taking care of the knot while I started on the buttons of his no longer pristine white shirt.

He left me to it, his hands returning to my hips once he'd finished with the tie, but once I reached for the buckle of his belt, he stopped me.

"Now you," he said, his voice gruff.

It was my turn to stand there, unmoving as he stripped off my shirt and bra. He paused a moment as I shivered, then dipped his head and closed his lips around a nipple that had gone tight with cold and need. The exquisite contrast between my chilled flesh and his hot mouth had me moaning.

He did nothing but that. One deep, drawing tug of my nipple between his lips and then he went back to stripping me bare.

Once I was completely naked, he picked me up and carried me across the room.

Not to the bed, though.

There was a fireplace, and after he'd laid me down on a thick rug, covered me with a nearby blanket, then turned to the cold hearth. Within a few moments, he had a blaze going.

"You're good at that." My voice shook. I don't know if it was cold, nerves, or need...or all of them above.

He stretched out next to me and tossed the blanket aside. "Stop talking."

He didn't give me a chance to argue, covering my mouth with his. I moaned as his tongue slid into my mouth. A moment later, he moved over me, his skin hot against mine. He'd stripped his trousers away without me even noticing, and it was all bare flesh to bare flesh. I didn't even know how he managed to generate so much heat after the rain, but I didn't really care.

I wanted more of him – a lot more.

Bringing my knees up, I rubbed against him, felt the length of his cock pulsing against me. Arik caught my wrists and drew them over my head, staring down at me with hungry eyes.

"I don't want to play tonight," I warned him. "I need this – need you – too much."

"I'm not playing." His voice had that low, authoritative note to it that made my insides squirm. Then he drove inside me with one single thrust. I cried out from the suddenness of it.

He didn't give me any time to adjust either, simply withdrawing and then surging forward again, deep and hard and fast. Bracing my heels on the floor, I lifted up to meet him. I wanted it to ride that line of almost-pain. I wanted something that would obliterate everything else. Shatter everything that wasn't him and me.

Arik kissed me then, a bruising, carnal kiss that filled all the dark and cold places, eased every unspoken fear. His cock filled me, the kiss, savage as it was, soothed me. It was almost too much for me to handle, but I clung to it. Clung to every sensation.

He was here. I was here.

We were together and that was what mattered.

He tore his mouth away and lifted his head, staring at me with eyes glittering with something dark and somehow...full.

"Don't ever scare me like that again," he said, his voice harsh, commanding.

I nodded, nearly whimpering as I ground against him.

He kissed me again, just as hard, just as deep. Just as fierce and hungry.

"Say it, Dena. Say it," he rasped against my lips.

"I won't scare you like that again." Then, before he could break the kiss, I bit his lower lip, hard. His hips jerked against me, driving deeper. He made a sound like a growl.

"Now you," I said, the words breathless.

He understood. His body covered mine fully as he murmured against my mouth. "I won't scare you like that again."

His strokes slowed, gentled, and he let go of my wrists to push up onto his knees. I was warmer now, but I still missed the warmth of him. His large hands cupped my breasts, thumbs circling my nipples while he rolled his hips lazily against the cradle of mine. His cock, thick and hard, pulsed inside me, and I could feel the climax building.

He slid his hands over my legs, then his hands between my thighs to where we joined. "I've missed this," he murmured, stroking my sensitive skin. "Having you with me, feeling you wrapped around my dick. I've missed that smart mouth, those beautiful eyes."

I wanted to say something to him, tell him I'd missed him too. But the feel of him pumping inside me, the way he watched me, and the way he spoke – he shattered me in ways nobody else ever had, ever could.

"Arik..."

I came then, a slow, sweet climax so at odds with the vicious need that had fueled this.

441

As though he'd just been waiting for it, Arik bent over me again, and thrust hard, once...twice...three times before he joined me, his entire body shuddering with the force of his orgasm.

I wrapped my arms around him and held tight, wanting to keep his body curled around me. For those few moments, all the insanity of the day faded.

This was all that mattered.

We – whatever we were – were all that mattered.

# Chapter 5

## *Arik*

It ought to have been downright criminal to be awake at this hour, especially considering I hadn't even managed to get to sleep until after two. But the silvery moonlight coming in through the window fell on the antique clock hanging on the wall, clearly showed me the ungodly time of four fifty-two.

I might have had a little over two hours of sleep, and I was now wide awake. There was absolutely no chance in hell I'd be getting back to sleep either. My brain was already working overtime.

The soft, warm body next to me stirred, and I turned my head, staring at the shadowed outline of Dena's face. I had one quick glimpse of her before she shifted and wiggled deeper into the covers. A low, unhappy sound escaped her, telling me that while she was still sleeping, her rest was far from *restful*.

That bothered me more than I thought it would.

If I stayed there, I was going to wake her.

I blew out a breath. There was no point in both of us being tired, exhausted messes when we finally managed to have our talk.

Climbing out of bed, I rummaged through the dresser in the dark. Although I rarely came here, I'd always kept clothing on hand. With only a little difficulty, I managed to find a pair of jeans and an old T-shirt. After I pulled them on, I moved to the window and stared out into the early morning. I'd grown up in the city and it still amazed me sometimes how different things looked in the dark when there weren't any city lights around.

I'd had a relatively easy life. A happy one, even. There had been one dark period, a mar in my teens, and that was what had driven me to law.

That dark period was also tied to this house, and coming back here was never...easy.

But that one incident hadn't permanently scarred or warped me, turned me into a closed-off loner. It hadn't even really made me hate this place, even with the darkness. Things had always been fairly easy for me too. I was smart, successful, and never looking for anything even close to romantically complicated.

The emotions I was dealing with now, however, were the kind I'd never had to deal with before, at least not on this level.

Rage, fear, doubt...guilt wanted to come in and play too. Not to mention all the self-recriminations for everything that happened, but I wasn't going to start beating myself up over what I couldn't change. I couldn't afford to, because if I let anything trip me up, next time I might not come out on top.

Next time Dena and I might not survive.

Dena…that single thought pushed me into an ugly spiral, and I dropped into a chair, staring at nothing while I relived each and every moment from the night before. I didn't know how long I spent trapped in my own thoughts, or how I might have stayed there, if Dena hadn't stirred, a soft, shaky sigh coming from the bed.

Pulling myself out of the reverie, I looked over at her just as she started to stretch.

Fuck, she was hot.

When she rolled onto her belly and turned her head toward me, one hand sliding down the empty space where I had been sleeping next to her, I rose from the chair. I wasn't about to let her get the wrong idea.

She was pushing herself up onto her elbows as I settled down on the edge of the bed. I caught her hand in mine and lifted it to my lips. Some of that white blonde hair fell into her eyes as a sleepy, sexy smile curved her mouth.

It was in that moment, as I felt all the fear inside me melt away, replaced by a gut-wrenching warmth and need, that I let myself finally admit the truth. I had gone and fallen for her.

I could have lost her. Just the thought made me feel sick. Turning her palm upward, I pressed a kiss to the center and whispered her name.

I crawled across the bed toward her and caught her up against me, holding her. Her back to my front, I buried my face in her hair and just held on tight, needing that vital, physical reminder that we were both here, that she hadn't been hurt. That I hadn't lost her.

That it wasn't too late to figure out what was going on with us. After all we'd been through, I couldn't lose her just because I'd been an ass.

Rubbing my cheek against hers, I said softly, "We need to talk."

"I know." She craned her head around and pressed a quick, soft kiss to my lips. "That's why I came over last night in the first place."

For a second, I didn't get what she meant, and then I laughed, pressing my face into her hair as I understood. Dammit. At least she wasn't still pissed at me. That meant what I had could wait.

"I'm talking personal stuff. I get the feeling you aren't, are you?"

"No." She wiggled around and stared at me, her face solemn in the dim light. "Personal stuff? Did last night finally convince you that this really *is* a bad idea?"

Her voice was light, teasing. But there was an edge to her words. My heart twisted in a way I'd never felt before.

"No." Leaning over, I pressed my lips to hers. "No."

A shaky sigh escaped her lips, but I couldn't tell what it meant.

"Then you must want to have a...relationship talk."

"You're a sharp woman, Dena Monroe. That's really sexy." I grinned.

She bit my lower lip. Heat tightened in me, but before I could do much about it, she pulled away, taking

446

most of the covers with her as she slid off the bed. As she moved over to the window, I drew one knee up and braced an elbow on it, watching her.

Fuck, I could spend all day just watching her.

"I'm going to go first," she said softly. "You're right, you know. We do need to talk, but there's...shit. Things are a fucking shit-storm, and personal things will have to wait. Especially after last night."

When she turned to look at me, the expression in her eyes made the tension inside me expand. Instantly, I pushed everything else aside and focused on whatever it was she needed to tell me.

"What's going on?"

Dena tipped her head back. "What's going on?" she murmured, echoing my question. "Where do I start?"

She rolled her head back and forth, then reached up to rub at her neck. The blankets she had gripped in one fist sagged, allowing a glimpse of one small, firm breast. I had to force my eyes back up to her face. I knew whatever she had to say was important, but I was only human.

"I'm about to do something that's toeing the line on some ethical boundaries, Arik. We're not going to talk about the case, so we're not quite at that crossing point, but what I'm about to tell you..."

She lapsed into silence then, and when she didn't say anything else for a couple of minutes, I cleared my throat and she lifted an eyebrow.

"Maybe you could sit down with me while you talk," I suggested. Sliding my gaze down, then back up, I

447

added, "You did kind of steal all of my covers."

"You're dressed," she said easily.

But then she shrugged and came back to me, so I was content. I tugged her down to straddle me and she wrapped the blankets around us both, curling one arm around my neck. She didn't lean into me, though. She kept a few inches between us and her eyes stayed on mine.

"I knew the guy in your apartment," she said, worrying her lower lip with her teeth. "I saw him and I knew him. The cops, they told you who he was, right?"

"Yeah," I said. I was really hoping that the reason she knew him was because he was a wanted criminal and that was sort of her department. I brushed her hair back from her face. "I might be from Chicago, but I've never had to deal with the mafia before."

"You don't understand, Arik. It wasn't the first time I've seen him."

Now she leaned in, pressing her forehead to mine. Her voice, her eyes, everything about her was intense, and I had a sudden flash of how she would look in court. Damn, if she put that much passion into her cases – and I knew she did – she'd be a formidable foe.

Then she was speaking again. "It took me days to place him, but last night, I figured it out."

Again, she stopped.

I knew the expression on her face. It was the one somebody wore when they were piecing together a puzzle, and it looked like hers had a lot of pieces. Resting one hand on her thigh, I stroked up and down, and told myself I was doing a damn good job of not letting her see that I wanted to ask clarifying questions.

She'd *seen* him?

What the fuck, and where the fuck?

Had he threatened her?

Would he have hurt her?

The thought made something vicious, something I'd never felt before, rise up inside me.

Caught up in my own thoughts, when Dena started to talk again, it took me a minute to process anything she said.

"…late, almost everybody was gone…"

Giving myself a mental shake, I focused on her words. Her skin was soft under my hands, but her eyes were distant.

"When was it?" I asked when she paused.

"Just a couple of days ago. Wednesday, maybe?" She rubbed at her temples like she was getting a headache and I didn't blame her. "I was ready to just go home, call it quits." She sighed. "I've been thinking more and more about just quitting."

The expression on her face was near desperate, and I hated it. Hated all of the reasons why she was wearing it.

"I've always wanted to be a prosecutor. Taking some of the monsters off the streets, keeping them off so they can't hurt the innocent." She laughed then and it was an ugly, bitter sound. "But nobody's innocent. Not if you ask Bethany."

"Bethany can get fucked," I said, irritated. I didn't want to talk about Dena's bitch of a boss.

449

"She does. A lot." Dena looked at me, her eyes turbulent. "Sometimes by mafia hitman."

I stared at her, thinking I had to have misheard her.

"Okay, can you..." I stopped and cleared my throat. "Dena, I think you need to explain that. In detail."

"Are you asking for positions or facts or what?"

"Dena..."

"I saw them, Arik. Bethany was with *that* guy. I went by her office to talk to her – maybe to quit, I don't know – but she was fucking that guy. Or rather, she was being fucked by him. A distinction, I know..."

"The hitman," I said slowly. I had to make sure I was understanding this right. "You're telling me that Bethany McDermott, a Manhattan assistant district attorney, was fucking the guy who pulled a gun on me in my apartment. *That* guy?"

She nodded, clearly distressed.

Easing her off my lap, I got up and started to pace.

Fuck.

What the hell was Bethany thinking?

"That was why I came to the apartment," she said. "To tell you all of this because I have absolutely no clue what to do."

I turned to look at her, but she was staring at the wall. I knew she wasn't seeing it, though. She wasn't seeing anything at that moment, unless it was Bethany and the giant shit-storm her boss had caught her in – not to mention the danger.

"My boss is sleeping with the *mafia*, Arik." She made an amused sound. "And to think I was worried about the ethics of sleeping with a defense attorney."

# Chapter 6

*Dena*

"What exactly do you think you're going to find?" Arik asked.

I stood in the middle of my office, arms folded around my middle as I looked around. Shooting him a look over my shoulder, I shook my head. "I don't know."

Coming down here had been a spur of the moment idea, but now that I was here, I had no idea what to do. At least it was Saturday afternoon, which meant the place was essentially deserted. There were a few lingering paralegals and ADAs working on cases, but not enough that Arik and I really needed to worry.

I knew what I needed. Proof that Bethany had ties to the Russian mafia. Something other than the fact that I'd seen her having sex with one of their known hitmen, but beyond that? If I was going to be believed, there would need to be corroboration.

Except I wasn't sure where to start or what even to

look for. I also wasn't sure who I could trust.

I sniffed, my nose starting to tingle in a familiar way. Out of habit, I glanced over to see if somebody had brought in more damn flowers, but the table by the door was empty. I rubbed at my nose, annoyed, but turned my thoughts back to the problem at hand.

I had half a mind to call one of the senior partners from my old firm. Granted, it was full of divorce lawyers, but they had connections. One of them was bound to know somebody I could trust, but first I had to find evidence.

Fuck it. There was a reason I hadn't gone into police work.

As if sensing my dilemma, Arik came up behind me and rested his hand on my shoulder. His mouth opened to say something, but before he could manage, a sneeze caught me off guard. Embarrassed, I moved away and went to the desk to dig through my purse. I didn't even have a chance to find tissues before I sneezed a second, then a third time.

"Bless you." He almost sounded amused.

As I turned to rummage for a tissue, Arik chuckled behind me. "Don't tell me you went and developed an allergy to me."

I might have laughed, except my eyes landed on a small vase of flowers sitting discreetly by the window.

"Oh, for crying out loud."

I went over to grab the flowers, but another sneezing fit hit. My right hand hit the vase and it fell, glancing off the corner of the desk and shattering. Water sprayed, and if I hadn't been busy sneezing my head off, I would have started cussing my random flower bringer to hell and back.

As it was, since I *was* busy sneezing, I wasn't the one to see it.

Arik was.

I only heard a door open, close...then his hand squeezed my shoulder. Something about that gesture communicated tension rather than comfort, and as my sneezing eased, I shot him a look. He had one finger pressed to his lips. His face was serious, but when he spoke, his tone was light.

"Well, I guess I'll save a fortune on flowers, won't I?"

His eyes slid down. Once, twice.

Mystified, I didn't say anything, but rather glanced down and saw his hand. He held it out, palm up. There was something inside it. Was that...?

Oh *shit*.

Again, Arik pressed his finger to his lips. Casually, he said, "I dumped the flowers in the trash across the hall. Why don't we step outside, let you breathe some fresh air?"

My entire body was tense, and I was full of questions, but I had to assume the device – the bug – Arik had in his hand was still transmitting to something, somewhere. He dumped the bug into the trash in my office, along with the remains of the vase, and led me into the hallway, his hand on my back.

Once we were out in the hall, I started to walk faster,

455

needing to be away. Arik followed. I didn't have a conscious destination in mind, but a few minutes later, I stood in front of Bethany's office.

Logically, there was no reason why I'd stopped there. It wasn't like she was here. The one thing I did know was that if Bethany was in bed with the mob – insinuation definitely intended – they wouldn't need to bug her office, so if there was any place in the whole building that wouldn't be compromised, it would be here.

I tried to open her door, but of course, it was locked.

As I started to turn away, though, Arik crowded up against me, his voice casual as he said, "I don't think she's going to be in, but it can't hurt to…"

He spoke in a voice louder than necessary for our proximity, and I shot a look up at him. He stood too close for such a public place, and I went to step away, but he caught my arm.

That was when I saw he was busy with his right hand. His body blocked most of his actions, and he tugged me in to hide what he was doing.

"Son of a bitch," I whispered, shocked and furious at the same time. What the hell was he thinking?

Apparently, he was thinking that he knew what he was doing. In under five seconds, he had the door open.

"What do you know, the boss must be in." He gave me a brilliant smile and turned his head as he caught my arm and pulled me into Bethany's empty office.

"You crazy son of a bitch," I said to his back as he locked the door behind him.

He looked at me, a cagey grin on his face. It was so

far removed from anything else I'd ever seen from him that it caught me off-guard.

"Two questions — one, how did you learn how to jimmy locks? Two, are you planning on defending us both when we get caught?" I demanded.

"I have absolutely no idea what you are talking about, Ms. Monroe." Arik looked at me, his face the picture of innocence.

For a brief moment, I caught a glimpse of what he must've looked like as a child, getting caught with his hand in the cookie jar. I felt safe in assuming that he'd gotten away with a lot, and not just because he came from a rich family.

His grin softened. "The door was open. We came inside, hoping Bethany might be in, and now we're sitting down, patiently waiting since we assumed she wouldn't leave her door unlocked."

Whatever he'd used to pick the lock had disappeared back wherever it came from in the first place.

Growling, I turned to storm back out into the hall, but then stopped, remembering the reason I'd come here in the first place.

"We are so fucked," I whispered, lifting my face to the ceiling.

Sooner or later, Bethany was going to go down, and because I was one of her ADAs, I would be guilty by association. My career would be over.

"We're going to be fine." His voice was surprisingly gentle. "Bethany is messing with people's lives, Dena. She's not just screwing with the justice system – and that

457

pisses me off probably as much as it does you – but she's putting people's lives at risk."

I turned toward him and he came to me then, lifting a hand to cradle my cheek. I couldn't stop myself from leaning into the touch.

"Are you willing to take some chances and stop her?"

"Hey, I came to your place yesterday, didn't I? And I didn't freak out with the breaking and entering. Not too much, anyway." With a rueful grin, I stepped away and stared at my boss' office. "So…where do we start? I don't think we're going to find a neatly organized calendar itemized with things like…*screwing the hitman on Wednesday…destroying an innocent woman's life on Thursday…*"

Not even fifteen minutes had passed when a noise came from the hallway.

Panicked, I shot a look to Arik and he grabbed my arm, hauling me to the chairs. "Remember," he said, his voice low as he slowly unlocked the door. "The door was open. And it was for you, so you're not lying. That's all you need to focus on. You came looking for Bethany. Just keep your head and we'll get through this. I promise."

The door swung open, hot and cold chills dancing all over me and I squeezed my eyes, battling back the most intense wave of nausea I'd felt since my first day in court. When I looked at the door, prepared to see Bethany, all the adrenaline drained out in a wave that left me feeling even sicker.

It wasn't her.

"Pierce." I stared at the man in the doorway with a mix of shock and relief. Next to me, I felt Arik relax as well.

Head cocked slightly, the other man studied us silently for a moment before stepping into the room. I opened my mouth to say something, but Arik laid a hand on my arm and gave it a gentle squeeze.

Pierce turned toward the door but instead of shutting it, he nodded and curiosity overrode everything else I was feeling. An older, slightly stooped gentlemen walked in. The man gave both Arik and me a long hard study as Pierce closed the door.

What the hell was going on here?

"The coffee shop across the street would have worked just as well if you needed air," the old man said.

His eyes, sharp and dark, glinted against smooth brown skin. If it wasn't for the pure white hair on his head, and the slight stoop to his shoulders, he could have passed for a much younger man. He came toward me, moving slowly and flicked a glance at Arik.

Without even needing to look at each other, we both stood. I didn't know about him, but I wasn't feeling comfortable dealing with what was going on from a sitting position.

"You." The older man pointed at me. "You have been a pain in the ass from day one, Ms. Monroe."

I blinked, unsure if it was an insult or if I should take it as an unintended compliment.

From the corner of my eye, I saw Pierce opening a glass-fronted cabinet, but I didn't turn to look at him.

"Just how have I been a pain...?" The rest of the question died as Pierce came back to join us.

"We need to leave," he said to the older man. "She's left her apartment. I'm not sure if she's going to come in today or not, but she's made some calls."

Before I could speculate on whatever the hell this meant, the older man gestured to a door. "We really should talk, Ms. Monroe. I assure you, you'll be interested in what I have to tell you, and I believe you'll want to hear it too. But this isn't the ideal place."

"Are you suggesting a coffee shop?" Arik asked, his voice biting.

"If you wish."

Sitting on a bench in Central Park, I sipped at my coffee while Pierce took his turn talking. The other man looked like he was more caught up in the antics of the kids playing by the Balto statue, but I wasn't fooled.

His name was Washington Rule. He was with the state attorney general's office and apparently, they'd been investigating Bethany for a while now. And Pierce was their inside man. When they'd caught wind of the job opening, they'd pulled some strings to get Pierce in as well.

Washington had also told me he had a feeling his

office wasn't the only one looking into her, and if I was as smart as he thought, I'd listen to him, because he would go to bat for me when things went down. Not *if* but *when*. I didn't want to be implicated in her fuck-ups – his words exactly. And he was right about that.

Once Pierce stopped talking, I looked at him. It might've been a bit juvenile, but I had to know. "Is it standard practice to sleep with people you're investigating?"

He smirked at me, lifting his coffee to his lips, but he didn't answer. Apparently, his smug attitude wasn't just a cover. He looked over at Washington, one eyebrow cocked as if to ask, *Shall I answer or do you want this one?*

Washington sighed deeply, leaning forward slightly and pressing the tips of steepled hands to his lips.

"Ms. Monroe. Let me say that we've tried any number of times to get close to Ms. McDermott, and she always manages to keep her cards close to her chest, so to speak. We've tried dozens of times, and she always manages to keep one step ahead of us. So when we had the opportunity to put somebody in her office, and she started to...well..." Washington slid his gaze toward Pierce. "It wasn't exactly what we would have wanted, but I can't say it caught any of us off guard, either. As I said, we've been watching her for some time."

The lawyer in me had to ask. "And what are you going to do when she brings up their relationship in court?"

"It won't be brought up." Pierce shrugged and looked

away, whether it was embarrassment or just boredom, I didn't know. "Chances are, Bethany won't ever go to court."

I stiffened, immediately understanding what he meant. "Are you telling me that she's jerking people around, abusing her office and you're going to make a deal with her?"

Washington's eyes narrowed, but it was more speculative than aggressive. "That's the way the system works, Miss Monroe. You use the smaller fish to get to the bigger ones. With the evidence we have on her now, she's not going to risk this going to court, because she's not going to risk her acquaintances thinking she's going to balk on the stand. As soon as she's arrested, they'll be worrying she might become a liability. Once we lay all our cards on the table, she'll be begging for protective custody in the most secure facility we have. And that's assuming we can bring charges before any other agency can. Believe me when I say that her liaisons with Mr. Lawton are nothing you need to concern yourself with."

Rising, I moved over to the edge of the path, staring at the playing children who had so captured Washington's interest a few moments earlier. Arms crossed over my middle, I blew out a breath. Arik had been quiet through all of this, but I'd gotten the impression it was because he was letting me take the lead since it was my boss we were discussing. He was definitely interested in what we were saying.

"Why are you telling me all of this?" I asked finally. "It seems to me that your investigation is going fine the way it is. Why come to me?"

There was a terse moment of silence, followed by a single name.

"Leayna Mance."

Surprised, I looked back at Washington.

"What about her?" That came from Arik. He'd been mostly silent through all of this, but now, as he rose from the bench, I turned to look at him. His jaw was tight and his eyes hard.

Washington looked at me rather than Arik even as he answered the question, "The death of Mr. Mance and the arrest of his wife piqued our interest as we'd been aware of him as something of a player in the Russian mob."

"So you decided to use the case as a way to see where Bethany's loyalties lay?"

"You are quite intelligent, Miss Monroe. I'm sure you would've figured the entire thing out, given a bit more time." He rose and came toward me. "I've had a man going in and out of her office for months, listening, doing odd jobs for her."

It hit me then. "Planting bugs?" I asked.

Washington nodded. "Yes. The flowers were part of the investigation."

"You bugged her office." Arik sounded as pissed as I felt.

"I did." Washington lifted his chin. "I also had my man warn her, as best he could."

Shit. I suddenly realized who the other inside man had been. Someone who Bethany could order around, but also not see if she didn't need something.

"The janitor. He's the one planting the bugs. He moved everything into my new office." I frowned. "You call that trying to warn me? Could he have been more cryptic?"

"We do what we can." Washington shrugged. "I also had him make some minor adjustments on your phone line, ones that conflicted with the adjustments her people had already made. Since you made most of your calls on your cellphone, she didn't get suspicious when she wasn't getting much from your office line."

As much as I loathed the idea that the state attorney's office had been listening to my calls, I also understood that having Bethany listening would've been much worse. "Thank you."

"I don't want thanks." Washington's voice was hard, but not harsh. "I want you to do your job. You seem to care about justice, truth, making sure the right person pays for the crime."

"I do," I said, wondering where he was going with this.

"Good." His expression hardened. "Because I have work for you to do."

# Chapter 7

## *Dena*

Nerves jittered inside me as I waited in the outer office for Eugene Hurst.

The DA.

Bethany's boss. And, technically, my boss too.

Washington had assured me that Mr. Hurst was a good, solid district attorney, and he was the person I needed to speak with. I had a stack of evidence, both what I'd figured out and what Washington and Pierce had collected, and I needed Mr. Hurst to see it before Leayna Mance went to court this afternoon.

When I'd asked Washington why he hadn't just taken things to Mr. Hurst himself, he'd told me that his office was trying to keep things quiet. He knew if he made an appointment to see the DA, word would get back to Bethany and she would know that someone was on to her. If I went, however, it would just look like a newbie ADA trying to kiss up to the boss.

I was just worried that Mr. Hurst wouldn't believe

me. I'd been assured that Washington's sources would be in touch with Mr. Hurst shortly to confirm everything I was saying, but I was the one who needed to convince the DA that one of his office's attorneys was operating with some pretty shady personnel and it was imperative that he intervene.

We could've gone to the judge in Leayna's trial to try to get Bethany's motions thrown out, or even delayed, but Washington had informed us that things ran deeper than just Bethany. He had evidence to support that even the judge was involved with the mafia.

So we needed a power player.

Not too many had more power than Hurst when it came to legal hardball. His trial record was among the most impressive in the country, and he'd never been afraid to take on anyone, regardless of who they were. We needed him to handle Leayna's case, as well as making sure Bethany didn't suspect anything. We also needed someone to support Arik's protection request for Leayna.

My stomach had been a mess all weekend, and not even the call from Officer Dunne yesterday saying that the mysterious call I'd received on Friday had been a hoax – some teenagers had been paid a hundred bucks to prank me – had been able to make me feel any less anxious. And it wasn't because I suspected it'd been some of Bethany's friends behind the call. I didn't really care about that.

No, the reason for my nausea and insomnia was simple.

Too much depended on me.

The door opened and a tall, thin man appeared. He looked at me, his lips pursed thoughtfully. After a moment, he beckoned to me and I rose, clutching my bag tightly.

My phone rang and I didn't have to look at it to know who it was.

Bethany.

I hadn't called in sick or given her any sort of indication that I wasn't coming in today. Pierce wasn't there either, and I doubted he'd given her reasons either.

Chances were she was getting pissed, but better pissed than suspicious. And I was pretty sure that a pissed Bethany was someone who made mistakes. Mistakes that could only help at this point.

I'd have to answer her soon, but I wanted to introduce myself first. When the phone buzzed again on my way to the doorway, I grimaced.

"No rest for the weary, Ms. Monroe."

I managed a strained smile. "I thought that was the wicked."

He gave me an amused look. "Well, sometimes the wicked get more rest than they let on, the bastards."

I was pretty sure I was going to like this guy.

He stepped aside and let me enter before shutting the door behind me.

When my phone buzzed again, I gave him an apologetic look. "It's my supervisor. I need to let her know I'm running behind. A quick text, if it's okay."

"Of course, of course. Coffee?"

467

While the Manhattan DA actually got me coffee, I sent a text that was all lies and sunshine.

*Problem on my train in the subway. Be there soon as possible.*

I had just sent it off when Mr. Hurst put the coffee down at my elbow.

I'd just lifted the coffee to my lips when Bethany responded. I blanched at her foul reply and almost managed to choke and scald myself at the same time. I barely kept from swearing, but I couldn't stop myself from dropping the phone. Mr. Hurst picked it up, and I could tell by his gaze that he'd read the text, although he said nothing, simply put my phone face-down on the table where he'd placed my coffee.

Then he sat down – not behind the monolithic desk – but in the chair next to mine.

"So just what is it that has you…caught up on the subway, Ms. Monroe?"

His tone was no nonsense, but not judgmental. I felt a stab of hope. Maybe he truly was the real deal.

Lowering my coffee, I started to reach for the bag that held all the evidence I'd been asked to give him, but then I paused and turned toward him. "Do you believe that everybody is guilty? That nobody is innocent, and if you have the bad luck to end up in the wrong place at the wrong time, then you just have to pay the piper?"

He didn't look taken aback by the question. On the contrary, he settled more comfortably in his chair and studied me. One finger tapped his lips while his gaze held mine.

I felt like he was dissecting me, the way he watched me, like he was trying to figure out what made me tick. I didn't let myself look away, though. I had the feeling the next few minutes would make or break things. Not only my career, but also the freedom and lives of everyone connected to this thing. I couldn't let them down.

"If that was how I felt, then I wouldn't – or at least I shouldn't – be sitting here in this office. Wouldn't you agree, Ms. Monroe?"

Blowing out a hard, shaking breath, I smiled a real smile. One of the bands constricting my chest fell away. There was still a lot to do, but I felt better about my chances of convincing him.

"I do agree, sir." I reached into the bag at my feet. The phone on the table rang, but I ignored it.

"Is that your supervisor again?" Mr. Hurst asked.

"Yes." I didn't look at the phone, or at him.

"Is there a reason you're dodging her?"

Focusing on the files and the disc in my hands, I nodded slowly. "Yes, sir. I'm afraid there is." Now, I did look at him. "My supervisor, she tends to think that way. She wants a win, regardless of a defendant's guilt or innocence. It's not about the truth, or justice. That's not the kind of law I want to practice."

He nodded and gestured toward his desk. I put the files down and took a deep breath. He was going to listen, which meant the rest was up to me.

I started with what I'd done myself.

Over the next hour, as my phone rang repeatedly, and the texts began to come almost on the end of each other,

Eugene Hurst and I went over the evidence I'd compiled regarding Leayna Mance. Then we went over the data on her husband, the late Mr. Mance and just how deeply in debt he'd been. When I reached the data showing when he'd come out of debt, Mr. Hurst rose to refill our coffees and I paused to rest my voice.

"I take it you presented all of this to Ms. McDermott."

"Yes."

He came back to me and sat down, holding out the coffee. I accepted, but didn't drink. I was already jittery from nerves, plus the caffeine I'd previously consumed.

"What did your boss say when you presented her with all of this?"

"It depended on the information." I tried not to frown. I couldn't let any of this be personal. It had to be all about the facts. "But it pretty much added up to the same thing. I was told to concentrate my efforts elsewhere, or look deeper because there had to be something else that fit our case better." I hesitated for a moment, then gave a specific example. "There was a break-in at Ms. Mance's penthouse, and when I had nothing to report, Ms. McDermott gave me the impression that I should have made something up."

At that, his graying brows shot up. "And you're certain you didn't misunderstand her?"

"Quite sure, sir."

He shook his head as he looked down at everything I'd spread across his desk. "This is to go before a judge today, correct?"

"Yes, sir." My phone went off again and I resisted the urge to throw it against the wall.

His eyes flicked to it and I had the odd feeling *he* wanted to do the same thing. He reached over and picked up his phone.

I listened as he called his administrative assistant in, and over the next five minutes, I sat, an enthralled audience of one as the two of them successfully managed to pull Leayna's case from the docket.

"Reason, sir?" his assistant asked, her eyes competent and focused. She never once looked at me, her attention focused solely on him.

I didn't mind. It was clear it wasn't a slight to me, but rather just her doing her job.

"A last minute change in council." He wasn't looking at her. His eyes skimmed one of the files in front of him. "I'm taking over the case personally, and as I haven't had a chance to review all the evidence, I'll be unable to be there this afternoon." He paused and then looked up at her. "If Judge Engler has a problem with that, have her contact me directly."

"Yes, sir."

He turned to another page, putting the one he'd been reading facedown. "That should be all for now, Ms. Holcomb."

"Yes, sir." She turned to go.

"Oh, if by chance Ms. McDermott calls, I'm indisposed." The look he gave her over the edge of his glasses was hard, the sort of look that had gotten him his reputation as one of the toughest DA's in the country. "I'll be able to talk to her soon, but not today."

Once we were alone, he blew out a breath and looked at me, a wry expression on his face. "I expect I'll be talking to Bethany McDermott a great deal more than I wish in the days to come."

Unfortunately, I was pretty sure he was right.

"Now that we have that taken care of," he said as he sat down again. "I think it's time to look over the rest of what you have." He glanced at the clock. "I'll have Ms. Holcomb call in lunch. Do you like Indian food?"

By the time lunch arrived, I was pretty sure I wasn't going to work today.

Right after lunch, Mr. Hurst excused himself, and when he came back into the office, he had a look of aggrieved frustration in his eyes that made me almost feel sorry for him.

He'd had a dirty ADA in his house, and he hadn't known. Now he had to clean house, and try to explain how he'd missed it. I had a bad feeling that it wasn't going to stop with Bethany either. If Washington's intel was accurate, a lot of people were going to spend a lot of time in jail.

Sometime around three, Mr. Hurst escorted a couple of men in suits into the room, and I had my first encounter with the FBI who were investigating Bethany. Washington had been right about that.

The two FBI agents subjected me to a rather grueling series of questions about where I'd come up with my information. I supposed they believed they were intimidating me, but considering everything I'd been through over the last few days, I just found it aggravating.

When I explained my source was confidential, they threatened to arrest me. Before I could say a word, Mr. Hurst intervened and handed them their asses. They didn't like me any better after that, but at least they didn't try to threaten me again.

The day was proving to be insightful, frustrating, aggravating, enlightening...and damn long.

At the end of the day, however, Mr. Hurst did give me the news that made all of it worthwhile.

Bethany had been detained just as she tried to leave her office that afternoon. She'd also attempted to have a janitor shred a rather substantial number of documents that had somehow found their way into the hands of the New York City Police Department.

I wasn't a huge fan of Washington or Pierce, considering how that investigation had been run, but I was glad their source had given the information to the local cops rather than the Feds. Granted, it was probably to ensure that it stayed in-house, but after the way the FBI agents had acted toward me, I wasn't feeling particularly friendly toward them.

As Mr. Hurst walked with me to the elevators, he said, "You worked pretty damn hard to help out somebody on the opposite side of the law."

I stopped and looked at him. "It was never about Leayna Mance being accused of murder or me versus her. It was about justice, about making sure an innocent person wasn't sentenced for a crime they didn't commit."

"I like your attitude, Dena." For the first time in several hours, he smiled. "I hope this hasn't soured you on working for this office. I'll be needing to fill some positions soon, I suspect. You're not quite ready to go solo, but I need people like you around here."

He held out his hand.

Slowly, I reached out and took it. "Thank you, sir."

He nodded at me.

As I turned to leave, I saw a cluster of men in suits waiting for the elevators as well. The FBI, come to play. I sighed, then almost tripped over my feet, as my eyes landed on one of them.

"Son of..." I dropped my bag, my fingers suddenly nerveless.

The man I'd seen came up and knelt in front of me. He gave me an easy grin, smiling as he began to gather up the things I'd spilled.

The last time I'd seen him, he'd been bleeding, but those eyes had still been laughing. Laughing as he'd been taken from Arik's apartment in handcuffs.

Adrenaline flooded through me, and I grabbed the first thing that came to hand – my phone. Like I'd be able to do anything with that.

"You look like you've seen a ghost," he said, his voice softer than it had been, but the accent still there.

"Ms. Monroe, are you well?"

"Mikel, come on," one of the agents behind him said, his voice hard and flat.

He ignored the man, leaning in. "You broke my nose, Dena. I almost broke my cover over that, you know," he said, whispering directly into my ear. "Good work, by the way."

Broke his cover?

What the hell was going on here? Why were the Feds not dragging him away from me?

Dazed, I watched as he straightened, and when he did, I saw the badge.

Hanging around his neck was a lanyard with the words *FBI* in large, unmistakable font. His picture and the name *Mikel Bobrov.*

But that…that wasn't the name I'd seen with his picture before.

Were they fucking kidding me? Rubbing a hand across my eyes, I shook my head. After all the shit those two agents had given me, they'd never even once thought to tell me that Arik and I hadn't actually been in danger the other day. Or that they had a fucking inside man high enough in the mob to be considered one of the top assassins on the payroll.

I was going to be so fucking glad when this shit was all over.

I'd wanted to get through the rest of the day without any surprises, but as I walked down the steps and saw the man waiting for me, I thought maybe I could change my mind about that.

Arik had his hands in his pockets, and a smile on his face, which told me that at least he wasn't delivering bad news. I wanted to smile in return, but the entire day – hell, the entire month – had worn on me, and I found I had a hard time smiling or even standing there. I wanted to drop down on the ground and just sit. Sit and stare and not think about anything.

Well, that wasn't entirely true, I amended as I made my way down the steps. If I was going to be honest, what I really wanted was to curl up with Arik, have him naked against me. On top of me. Behind me.

My breath hitched a little as my heart gave an unsteady thump. Maybe what I *really* wanted was something I hadn't had in a long time, but this wasn't really the time and place to tell him that. Especially since I really didn't know how he felt.

"You look like you've had a rougher day than I have," Arik said softly as I took another step toward him.

All around us, the city continued to buzz and rush, but with him standing there, I felt like I could be still for a little while. I felt like I could just...*be*.

"Yeah." With a slow nod, I said, "That sounds about right."

He brushed his fingers across my cheek, a light touch, but enough to confirm my previous revelation for

476

me.

"What are you thinking about?" he asked, his voice doing that warm caress thing that made me shiver.

I tried not to lean into him, but it was where my body wanted to be. Where I wanted to be. I couldn't tell him that though. Not here, not like this. "I really want to be outside of my head for a while. But..." My voice trailed off.

He finished my thought. "We need to talk."

"Yeah." I forced myself to look away. Talk seemed like such a small word to describe what we needed to do.

"Come on." He took my hand as he raised his other one to hail a cab. Apparently, he hadn't driven in today. We were silent for a minute before he spoke again, "They've dropped the charges."

Whipping my head around, I looked up at him. "Leayna's free?"

"Yeah." He crooked a grin at me, and then lifted his face to the sky, sighing deeply. "She's already packed a few bags, contacted some personal security, and she'll be hightailing it out of the city first thing tomorrow. She's going to stay with some friends out of town, and has promised to contact me as soon as she arrives so if anything happens to her between now and then, I'll know. I don't think it'll be a problem though. I think pretty much all of her new security detail are ex-Marines or Rangers or Seals or something like that."

"Good for her." I meant it. Her freedom wasn't just a reminder that the justice system, however flawed, could still work. I felt glad for her personally. She'd been

477

through a lot and deserved a fresh start.

"Good for us, too."

I looked over at Arik, startled by his statement.

He opened the back door of the cab and stepped aside to let me get in first. After he'd slid in next to me and closed the door, he gave the cabbie an address, then turned back to me.

"Now that we don't have her case between us, we can finally have a real conversation." His gaze was intense, making me want to squirm. "No more interruptions. No excuses. One way or another, we're going to figure this out."

Shit.

# Chapter 8

*Arik*

The Waldorf Astoria wasn't exactly the place I would have chosen to take Dena, but we couldn't go to my place in the city – it was still off limits. I wasn't sure if her place was safe yet either, and the club just seemed like a bad idea. We could've gone all the way back to the house, but I wasn't sure I could last that long of a drive without addressing what was unsettled between us. Besides, I had a feeling neutral ground was the way to go.

But I wasn't about to take her to the Holiday Inn.

Judging by the expression in her eyes, she seemed to appreciate the surroundings, even if she didn't say it. As we rode the elevator up to the room, she slid me a look, a nervous little smile on her lips.

I didn't let myself lean over and kiss her.

I wanted to.

It was going to be hard enough to keep my hands off her once we got inside a room that had a bed *right there*, so the last thing I needed to do was start down the road to temptation. And even a chaste kiss with her, an innocent touch, was a temptation. Hell, just looking at her, thinking about her, made me want to...shit. I needed to get my thoughts away from that direction immediately.

With my hands securely in my pockets, I said softly, "I was surprised to hear from the DA's office so quickly."

"Eugene Hurst apparently doesn't waste time."

She stared at the doors, her fingers toying with a charm hanging from her necklace. The necklace itself was a slim silver collar, while the charm was long, thin and black, elegant and simple. I wondered if it was some sort of good luck charm, something with sentimental value. A flash of jealousy went through me at the thought that maybe someone had given it to her. A male someone.

Fuck.

I wanted to see her wearing nothing but that necklace while I wore nothing but her, wrapped around my cock.

Focus.

"I take it he believed you."

She blew out a breath, but before she had a chance to answer, the elevator stopped and the doors silently glided open. I gestured for her to exit and followed her into the hallway. In silence, we moved to our room and I unlocked it, stepping aside so she could enter. After closing the door behind us, I moved through the room, checking it out to ensure it was as secure as I'd hoped it'd be.

Once I'd finished, I turned to find her at the window. She stood with her arms wrapped around her middle, head tipped to the side so that her hair hid her face. I hadn't realized how much longer it'd gotten since I'd first seen her.

The need to gather that hair in my hand, bare her neck, brush my lips across the elegant slope hit me hard. I wanted to kiss her skin, lick my way down, down, down...

Fuck.

I wanted her against me through the night, wrapped in my arms. I wanted to wake up with her in the morning.

I sighed and raked my hands through my hair. "You were right when you said this would be complicated."

She angled her head, smiling a little as our gazes met. "I'm right about a lot of things."

The calm confidence in her voice was just one more thing that got to me. I was shocked at how much I enjoyed seeing her like that, enjoyed knowing how strong she was...and how it felt when someone that strong submitted.

Still, there were things we needed to discuss.

"Has all this soured things for you at the DA's office?"

Dena took a slow, steadying breath and turned to face me fully, leaning back so that her hips were braced against the windowsill. With the city as a backdrop, she studied me, and I waited, knowing she'd answer when she was ready.

"I thought it might," she said after a minute. "But Bethany wasn't a real lawyer. I can't let her be the filter through which I base my choices. Besides, I spent more than half my life wanting to be a lawyer, wanting to put

481

the bad guys away so they couldn't hurt people. What would it say about me if I let the first real bad guy I came across be the one to take that dream away?"

I crossed over to her.

Her eyes swept toward mine, and her breath caught as I brushed her hair back. Her lips parted, her tongue sliding out to dampen her lips.

Shit. I had no idea how I was going to have this conversation if she kept doing things like that.

"What made you want to be a lawyer?" I asked suddenly. "A prosecutor?"

She bit her lower lip and her gaze slid away. But not before I'd seen the shadow on her face, in her eyes.

"When I was four, the girl who used to baby-sit me disappeared suddenly. It wasn't until I was twelve that I found out what had happened. Jenny was married to this guy who used to beat her. One day, he went too far. Killed her."

Fuck.

"He got off on a technicality though," she continued. "Went away for a couple years. Then he came back and married the older sister of one of my classmates. He killed her six months later. Beat her to death, the same as Jenny. Manslaughter. Six to ten."

Pushing a hand into her hair, I tangled my fingers in the soft strands. "I'm so sorry."

"What about you?" she asked. "What got you into this?"

I gave her a sad smile. "Actually, my story's not too different from yours. Just from the other side."

She looked up at me, puzzled.

I didn't like telling this story, but she'd told me hers.

"The house I took you to, it was my uncle's. When I was a kid, he was arrested. His wife was found dead in a hotel, and the cops arrested him. It couldn't have been him, though. He was with us when she died. No one believed us. Said we were his family, of course we'd lie."

Sighing, I dipped my head and pressed my forehead to hers, rubbing my thumb against the soft underside of her chin. She didn't say anything, but I didn't need her to. All I needed was her to be there.

I continued, "The trial, all of it...it was too much. He killed himself, put a bullet in his brain the day before they read the verdict. I don't think he would have been found guilty, but he was tired. Tired of the guilt, the speculation. Tired of missing her and wondering who had really killed her."

Dena reached up and put her hand on my face. "Did anybody ever find out what happened?"

"Not officially." Rubbing my cheek against her palm, I thought back to the side investigation I'd done on my own, years later. "But she'd been involved with somebody. A cop. And when she died, she was pregnant."

"Oh, baby." Dena's expression softened and she pressed a kiss to my lips. "I guess we both went into this for our own reasons."

"Yeah." Looking out the window to the city she'd been staring at, I said softly, "You don't get to pick and choose your cases, Dena. A prosecutor for the city of

Manhattan can't."

Something flickered in her eyes, and I knew she was thinking that I was ending things, that it was too much.

Hell, no.

Stroking a finger across the soft curve of her lower lip, I tugged her closer, and told her what I needed to tell her before I chickened out.

"I can. I've talked to the senior partners, and I told them I don't want to take any cases that'll be in Manhattan."

"Arik–"

I kissed her hard and fast, pushing my tongue past her lips. I had to have that one taste, now. Just in case.

She was panting when I pulled back until only a few inches separated our mouths.

"I want this to work," I told her roughly, silently begging her to agree. "We have something. You know it. I know it. I want it to work, but if we're constantly dancing around things because of our jobs, we won't have a chance. Since you don't have any control over the jobs you'll be assigned, then I'll control the clients I'll accept."

Dena closed her eyes and curled her arms around my neck, but she didn't say anything.

Nerves started to pulse inside me. Shit. I was usually a patient person, but I didn't think I could make it much longer.

"You know, you could give me an idea what you're thinking."

"Be quiet a minute," she said, her voice husky.

I was hoping that was a good thing. She hadn't pulled away, and she still didn't as I held her, skimming my hand up and down her spine. I focused on that, on the feel of her, hoping to distract myself.

I tried. I really did. But I couldn't give her that minute. I had to know.

"Dammit, Dena. I just moved here. I'm trying to make senior partner, and I'm making demands on the top guys. You're worth it, but it would be nice to know if I'm doing this for a reason or wasting my..."

Dena's mouth slid against mine. As the chaos in my head tumbled to a halt, she stroked her tongue across my lower lip, scraped her teeth over it. Then she pulled back enough to speak.

"I'm not entirely sure how you ended up in my life, Arik, but I'm damn grateful."

Her words slid over me, through me, settled deep inside me. The relief was enough to make my knees weak.

Gripping her waist even tighter, I pulled her flush against me. I had to hear her say it. "Then we're going to make this happen?"

"Seems to me that we already are." Her mouth pressed to mine, then widened into a smile. When she spoke, her breath was hot against my skin. "You know, we're in this beautiful hotel. It seems that we should take advantage of it."

I liked the sound of that.

"Yeah. We should."

# Chapter 9

## *Dena*

The feel of his hands on me was every bit as erotic as it had been that first night. The impact of his eyes just as cutting, just as deep.

Now, standing in front of the window, with him behind me, we stared at our wavy reflections, my breath hitching as he freed one button, then another and another.

The city spilled out before us in a glittery array of lights just beyond the darkness of Central Park. I'd always loved the city at night, and tonight was no different.

Except it wasn't just the city we were looking at.

He stripped my shirt away, then caught my wrists. "Put your hands on the window."

I did, the glass cool against my palms, while the heat of Arik – the heat of *need* pulsed everywhere else – inside me, around me, behind me as he leaned down and pressed a kiss to the nape of my neck.

The catch on my bra gave, and I started to lower my hands so he could remove it. I wanted to feel his hands on me so badly that my skin nearly ached.

"Don't move," he said.

I froze, my body humming with anticipation.

The straps on my shoulders loosened. Man, multi-way bras...such a blessing, and I hadn't even considered this one.

I felt bereft when he stopped touching me to neatly fold the bra and put it off to the side. He seemed to take his time before he put his hands back on me again. My nipples throbbed and pulsed, hard little points. The need to have him touching me there was almost too much. When he put his hands on my waist, I arched my spine, instinctively readying myself to push my breasts into his hands.

But when he did touch me, it was to reach for the zipper of my skirt, dragging it down with excruciating slowness. Damn him.

"The bad thing about being here instead of at my place or the club, I have to improvise. No cuffs, no crop." His fingers tripped up my spine, a teasing sensation that left me shivering. "I don't want you moving, so you'll have to restrain yourself. You can't move until I tell you."

Flexing my hands against the windows, I dropped my head. "And what if I do?"

Arik brought his hand down on my ass with a sharp crack. "I just might not fuck you."

Keening low in my throat, I bit my inner cheek. I didn't think he'd actually do it. Or rather, not do it. His need was as obvious as my own. But I could never tell with him. He might choose to spend the rest of the night teasing me.

"That got your attention, didn't it?"

"Bastard." Squeezing my eyes closed, I reached deep inside for all the control I could muster. Fortunately, I had a decent amount.

He spanked me again, the heat spreading across my skin. "Call me names and maybe I won't fuck you anyway. Maybe I'll just get myself off, leave you...wanting."

Groaning, I tucked my head against the crook of my arm. "Arik, please..."

"Say you're sorry. Maybe I'll forgive you, Dena." Despite his words, his tone was gently teasing.

"I'm sorry," I said immediately.

"Want to make it up to me?" His voice dropped.

"Yes." What I actually wanted was to feel him inside me, and these hot, crazy games were almost more than I could handle tonight.

He skimmed a finger along the crevice of my ass. "Just how far are you willing to go to make it up to me, Dena?"

Anything. Just as long as he'd fuck me. "Whatever you want."

When he stopped touching me, my knees started to quake but that was nothing compared to what happened when he buried his hand in my hair, pulling me away from the mirror, forcing my body upright.

"I'm going to tell you something, Dena...I lied. I'm not entirely unprepared."

He kept me like that, one hand in my hair while the

489

other reached down between us.

When I felt the lube-slicked finger probing between the cheeks of my ass, the air I had in my lungs came out in a rush.

Oh, fuck.

He bit my ear, and then said, "I'm going to fuck your ass, good and hard. You're going to moan. You're going to scream. You're going to come. And later, if you're a good girl, I'll clean you up and fuck you again."

I gasped as he pushed two fingers inside me at once. My legs shook as pain and pleasure coursed through me. My clit throbbed even as he worked his fingers deeper.

There was a hard edge to Arik's hunger tonight, a deep, insatiable sort of need, and it washed over me, battering at me like waves against the beach. When he spread his fingers inside me and then twisted, I whimpered, arching a little as I fought to accommodate the penetration that would prepare me for an even deeper one. Usually, I would've wanted him to start with one, then work his way up to two, but another part of me wanted it like this.

The ache spread, my clitoris pulsing and I lowered my hand, needing to relieve the tension.

Arik bit my shoulder, hard enough to draw my attention momentarily. "Don't," he warned.

I whimpered. "Arik, please…"

He spanked me this time, hard, and without his steadying hand at my hip, I twisted on the fingers that invaded me.

"Be still and don't move, or I won't fuck this sweet

ass, Dena."

I didn't prefer anal sex, but there were times when I wanted the intensity of it. Right now, I needed him inside me, and I didn't particularly care where.

Curling my hands into fists, I braced myself on the window, and told myself not to move again. I even managed to keep that promise, right up until he removed his fingers and started to work his dick into me instead.

Despite his preparations, it wasn't easy. My ass burned as he kept up the slow, steady pressure, forcing himself inside. I rose up on my toes this time, twisting my spine although I don't know if I was trying to take him deeper or if I was trying to escape.

Arik went still. "Do you want me to stop?"

I shook my head, my breathing harsh. "No. Please, please...please don't, Arik."

He smoothed one hand over the slight curve of my hip. "Convince me. Tell me what you want me to do, Dena."

"I want you to fuck me, Arik." Heat sizzled and burned through me even as some part of me wondered at how easily he drew submission from me. "I want to feel your cock in my ass."

He put his mouth against my ear. "Are you going to be still for me?"

Whimpering, I whispered, "I'm going to try."

Inside me, he pulsed and I was excruciatingly aware of every inch of him, both what was inside, and what was still to come.

"You better try very hard, baby."

Then he began to move again, slow, pushing his cock into me in increments that seemed to take forever. My entire body was quivering, shaking. It was pure torture. Then, just when I thought he was almost ready to stop the torment, he would withdraw, and I had to bite my lip to keep from screaming.

But this was what I wanted. Why I wanted him. I knew I could give myself to him and he'd not only take it, he'd give me what I needed. He'd protect me.

When he was finally completely seated inside me, a harsh, shuddering moan escaped my throat, and I would have sagged if he hadn't steadied me with an arm around my waist. He rolled his hips, withdrawing just enough to have me tensing up, and then he filled me again.

"I love taking you like this," he said against my ear. "You grab at my dick and you squeeze it so tight...it's like you can't decide if you love it or not. Tell me, Dena. Do you love it?"

"Yes." Forgetting yet again that he didn't want me moving, I reached up and caught the back of his neck. "I love it...I love you, Arik."

He went rigid and I froze. I hadn't meant to say it like that, but it was the truth. A moment later, he pulled out of me altogether, and I sucked in a breath. One that carried pain, shock and disappointment.

He spun me around to face him, one hand coming up to cup my chin.

"What?" he demanded.

"I..." Blinking, a little dazed, I stared at him. I didn't understand what was happening.

He kissed me roughly, his teeth sinking into my lower lip. "What did you say?"

Oh, that.

"I..." Breath coming raggedly now, I met his eyes as he looked at me.

Shit. I'd never said those words to a guy. I'd never met anyone who I'd wanted to say those words to before. I'd come close, but what I'd felt on those few occasions was nothing like what I felt for him.

I might've been terrified, but I wasn't a coward.

"I said I love you."

"Dena..."

He kissed me again, and this time, it was soft and sweet.

My head was spinning when he picked me up, and then it seemed like the whole world was as he carried me into the bathroom.

"What..." The question was smothered under another kiss, and when he broke away, he was setting me on my feet, the tile cold under my soles.

The bathroom was gorgeous, large enough that half my living room could have fit in here and the sunken tub made me want to climb inside it and lounge around for maybe a week.

"What are we doing in here?" I asked, completely confused.

"I'm going to shower. You are too."

His voice had an odd note to it. Feeling a little off balance, I stared up at him. "Um...why?"

He backed me up to the clear glass wall that

separated the shower from the rest of the bathroom.

"Because," he said, kissing me again. Another soft, slow kiss, one that smoldered rather than exploded. "I'm going to make love to you. In that bed. Where I can see your face, and then you're going to say those words to me again. I'm going to have that soft, sweet pussy wrapped around me when you say it. That means...we have to shower."

"Oh." I couldn't manage anything else.

Dazed now, I let him guide me into the shower, let him nudge me under the water. It criss-crossed out from all corners, pounding at my body and hitting muscles that were so tense, I'd forgotten just *how* tense they were. How this whole thing had stretched me thin and tight.

Arik had shown me any number of faces: the sharp lawyer, the wicked lover, the playful lock-pick, the sinful, sexy seducer.

But now he was showing me another side, a side that seemed almost...unsettled, by what I said. But he hadn't run away, hadn't told me that he didn't feel the same way. Instead, he washed me, dried me, and I was little more than putty when he scooped me up into his arms and carried me out of the bathroom. He'd dried me in the stall, murmuring in my ear that he didn't want me getting cold.

I couldn't even fathom being cold, not now. With the downy softness of the mattress under me and the hard, hot length of him above me, the only thing I could *really* fathom was him.

He pressed kiss after kiss to my mouth, my neck, my

breasts.

Every time I tried to draw him down to me, he'd come, but only for a moment, only until a series of teasing kisses had my hands limp and lax against his shoulder, and I forgot how to do anything more complicated than breathing and moaning.

Then he caught my hands and pinned them above my head. His eyes locked with mine as he settled between my legs.

"Tell me again, Dena," he said against my lips as he thrust inside me.

I cried out, arching up against him. My climax was so close, it was almost painful. I stared up at him, my hips rising to meet his. It was as though nothing else existed.

Just him. Just me. Just us.

"Tell me," he ordered.

I couldn't deny him. "I love you."

He caught me in his arms and rolled, shifting our positions. I moaned as it drove him deeper, higher inside me. Hands braced on his chest, I let my head fall back as I rolled my hips against his. Fuck, that felt good.

"Arik…"

"Look at me." His hands tightened on my hips, and the command in his voice managed to cut through the fog in my head.

Forcing my lashes up, I met his eyes. He looked up at me, the vivid emerald color of his gaze searing me.

"I love you, Dena."

The climax slammed into me, hitting me with almost as much force as his words.

Almost.

But not quite.

"Say it again."

# Chapter 10

## *Dena*

"You look beautiful."

Looking into the mirror, I saw Arik standing in the doorway and grinned at him. "You better close the door. Seriously, Arik. Gavin was teasing Carrie about how he wasn't going to wait until the ceremony before he saw her today, and she's panicking because she thinks he meant it."

It was the middle of June, and in just over an hour, Carrie would be marrying Gavin.

I had a feeling Gavin's teasing had been meant as a distraction so she wouldn't panic about all the small, inconsequential details. Except, now she was panicking over her soon-to-be-husband jinxing their wedding by catching a look of her in her wedding dress before the ceremony.

Krissy was going to beat the shit out of him. Sometimes men were just clueless.

Arik slid inside and shut the door behind him. He

came to me and bent down, just barely grazing my lips with a kiss before straightening up and looking around. His eyes landed on Krissy and DeVon. He smiled at me.

"Seems like I'm not the only one who couldn't wait to see his woman."

There was a bit of sadness to that smile, and we both knew why. It was the same reason why DeVon was in here, and it wasn't simply because he couldn't bear to be away from her.

He wasn't exactly hovering over her – Krissy would never allow that – but he was staying close. My heart ached more than a little for them both.

"How is she?" Arik moved in closer and pitched his voice low so no one else could hear.

Looking up at him, I shrugged and managed a smile. "I couldn't say. I've never been where she is. She seems to be holding it together pretty well. Losing the baby…"

I swallowed and turned back to the mirror, staring hard at my reflection. If I thought too hard about it, I'd get teary and if I cried today, I'd rather it be over happy things. Happy.

"You know," Arik said as he put his hand on my shoulder. "I've been thinking."

"Today is *not* a day for thinking." Slanting a look up at him, I made a face before leaning forward to study my reflection. I was still wearing my robe, but my make-up and hair were done. Those were the two big things. The dress was the easy thing, for me at least. Carrie had gone with a simple, strapless style that flattered all of us.

Carrie's dress, however, wasn't simple. She had a

designer confection that would take several people to help her get into.

If I ever got married, I think I wanted to do a beach wedding. Something where I could wear a simple little white dress and no shoes. Well, considering the height difference, maybe shoes wouldn't be a bad idea, at least for the ceremony...

"Regardless, I *have* been thinking—"

The door swung open and a harried looking guy in a bad suit came in. His eyes narrowed when he saw Arik and DeVon.

"You two. *Out.* We want some shots of the bridal party getting ready and you two can't be in here for those."

Arik open his mouth to say something, but I leaned in, caught his hand. "This is what Carrie wants. Please, baby."

He blew out a breath, then nodded. Before he turned, he added, "We still need to talk."

"It can wait." Rolling my eyes at his back, I focused on the mirror once more. Pictures of the bridal party getting ready. "What is the deal with that anyway?" I muttered. "We sit around powdering our noses?"

A few feet away, Krissy laughed and the sound made my heart lighten. "Sure. Powder our noses, give each other manicures, maybe have a pillow fight."

I shot her a look and she rolled her eyes. "I think this is something they like doing, coming in hoping we're half-naked."

"Oh, please."

499

It took Arik nearly an hour to fight his way back inside. And fight was pretty close to the right word.

There was a woman at the door, one of Carrie's relatives. She'd planted her statuesque frame there, and was practically doing background checks before she let anybody in once the photographers left.

Even they tried to come back in, but Carrie sent them away, saying she'd rather hold off on the rest of the pictures until she actually *looked* like a bride.

I'd had to laugh at that.

Now, though…well, she looked like a bride and I found myself getting a little sniffly. At least this time, it was for a good reason.

Carrie didn't seem to be getting overly emotional just yet, and she proved it by shouting out, "Aunt Ida, it's Dena's date you're arguing with. He can come back if he wants. I don't think it's considered bad luck for *him* to see me. I doubt he's got Gavin hiding in his suit." Then she muttered under her breath, "Though I wouldn't put it past the bastard to try."

Krissy, Leslie and I shared a grin.

Carrie rolled her eyes at us in the mirror and went back to sitting like a statue as the hairdresser did last minute fixes on her already perfect hair.

"It's a good thing we go out there in the next few

minutes," Leslie said, rolling her eyes. "That woman might try to flat-iron and twist her hair out of existence if we stayed back here much longer."

"That's why I advocate short hair," I responded to her, but my attention was on Arik as he cut around flowers and everything else in the room.

He came to a stop in front of me, halting maybe five feet away. "I know it's supposed to be the bride's day, but I think the most beautiful woman is standing in front of me."

"I heard that!" Carrie called out, branding an eyelash curler.

"Technically, Carrie, all of you are standing in front of me," Arik replied without taking his eyes off of me.

"Don't be a lawyer today." Carrie made a harrumphing sound under her breath, but I heard the smile.

"Her mother will be rushing us out soon," I told him, gesturing to the dry-erase board that had the schedule written out on it.

Carrie's mom was like a drill sergeant. I was slightly in awe...and a little scared. I was pretty sure Gavin felt the same way.

"That's fine." He held out a hand. "Five minutes."

"What's the hurry?" As he folded his fingers around mine, I let him guide me to the corner, but when he would have kissed me, I turned away. "I don't believe in kiss-proof lipstick, pal."

"You're cruel. Cruel, evil and malicious," he said with a sigh.

"Guilty as charged." Reaching up, I traced my fingers over his lips. "I'll make it up to you...later. I promise."

"Good." He closed his hand over my wrist and squeezed gently. "Listen...I need to do this now. I kept telling myself I'd wait, but I was talking to DeVon, and seeing Krissy...I can't quit thinking about it."

My stomach lurched.

What was he...?

Arik shoved his hands in his pockets. "I know we haven't even been together a year. I know that. But after everything that's happened and after how Krissy and DeVon lost the baby...I just...look, I don't want to wait forever to start living my life with you."

Mystified, I stared at him. "Arik, we're already—"

"No." He closed the distance between us and stooped down until we were eye to eye. Thanks to my heels, that wasn't as much distance as usual. "We're dating, yes. I sleep at your place on the weekends, or you stay at mine. But sometimes, especially when we're with a busy case, we can go almost a week without seeing each other. It's too long. I want a life with you. A real one."

He nodded toward the women standing beyond us, at Krissy and Carrie and how they stood together laughing. "I want what they have. Something permanent—something real. Maybe later on, a family, if that's what you want, too. I just...I want more than the semi-casual thing we're doing. I want forever, Dena."

Feeling a little weak in the knees, I struggled to breathe as he leaned in and took my hand, lifting it to his lips.

"I want you to move in with me."

His words tumbled over and over in my head as he kissed the back of my hand. He wanted us to live together. I'd never lived with anyone but a college roommate. I'd never lived with a man.

"What do you think?" Arik asked.

I said the first thing that came to mind.

"No."

Arik tensed.

"What?"

The word was flat, and I hurried to clarify.

"I don't mean *no*. Not exactly." Frowning and feeling stupid, I rubbed my forehead. "It's just, I don't really feel like I'm home when I'm at your place. It's gorgeous, and huge, and expensive, but the only thing there I like is you. I don't want to give up my place, even if it is smaller."

His eyes met mine and I saw the hope in them. Hope that I wasn't actually turning him down.

"I want you to move in with me."

Arik stared at me for a moment and then he started to smile.

"Why, Ms. Monroe, you drive a hard bargain. Anybody ever tell you that you like to throw your weight around a bit too much?"

"Well..." I lifted a shoulder. "I just know what I want."

A wolfish grin lit his face. "I've always admired that in a woman." He caught me against him and before I could remember to tell him *not* to, he kissed me, hard, fast and deep. I was panting when he stopped, and ready to beg for more.

"I think I can agree to those terms...as long as I still get to be in charge in the bedroom."

"I can agree to those terms." I arched my eyebrow. "Most of the time."

He tugged me close again, but he didn't have a chance to do anything else.

The door opened and Mrs. Summers stood there, beaming at us. "It's time!" Her soft, southern drawl was warm and sweet – and brooked no argument.

Arik offered me his arm. "Allow me to escort you, Miss Monroe."

"I'd be honored, Mr. Porter." I wrapped my arm around his.

As we started out of the room, he bent his head close to my ear and murmured, "After this, I think we should go back to your – our place – tonight. Make it official. I'll make love to you in every room. What do you think?"

What did I think?

Hmmm...where would I start?

My face was flushed as we walked by the beaming mother of the bride.

"I like the sound of that."

## The End

# All Box Sets From MS Parker:

Unlawful Attraction Box Set
Chasing Perfection Box Set
Blindfold Box Set
Club Prive Box Set
The Pleasure Series Box Set
Exotic Desires Box Set
Pure Lust Box Set
Casual Encounter Box Set
Sinful Desires Box Set
Twisted Affair Box Set
Serving HIM Box Set

# Acknowledgement

First, I would like to thank all of my readers. Without you, my books would not exist. I truly appreciate each and every one of you.

A big "thanks" goes out to all the Facebook fans, street team, beta readers, and advanced reviewers. You are a HUGE part of the success of the series.

I have to thank my PA, Shannon Hunt. Without you my life would be a complete and utter mess. Also a big "thank you" goes out to my editor Lynette and my wonderful cover designer, Sinisa. You make my ideas and writing look so good.

# About The Author

M. S. Parker is a USA Today Bestselling author and the author of the Erotic Romance series, Club Privè and Chasing Perfection.

Living in Las Vegas, she enjoys sitting by the pool with her laptop writing on her next spicy romance.

Growing up all she wanted to be was a dancer, actor or author. So far only the latter has come true but M. S. Parker hasn't retired her dancing shoes just yet. She is still waiting for the call for her to appear on Dancing With The Stars.

When M. S. isn't writing, she can usually be found reading– oops, scratch that! She is always writing.